THE GUARDIANS *of* GA'HOOLE

"*Madam, may I be of service? You seem most distressed.*"

*It was a gentleman speaking, no doubt about that,
Madame Plonk thought.*

GUARDIANS
of GA'HOOLE

BOOK TWELVE

The Golden Tree

BY KATHRYN LASKY

SCHOLASTIC INC.

New York Toronto London Auckland
Sydney Mexico City New Delhi Hong Kong

No part of this publication may be reproduced, stored in a retrieval system, or transmitted in any form or by any means, electronic, mechanical, photocopying, recording, or otherwise, without written permission of the publisher. For information regarding permission, write to Scholastic Inc., Attention: Permissions Department, 557 Broadway, New York, NY 10012.

ISBN 978-0-439-88806-6

Text copyright © 2007 by Kathryn Lasky

Illustrations copyright © 2007 by Scholastic Inc. All rights reserved. Published by Scholastic Inc. SCHOLASTIC and associated logos are trademarks and/or registered trademarks of Scholastic Inc.

Artwork by Richard Cowdrey
Design by Steve Scott

12 11 10   11 12 13 14 15/0

Printed in the U.S.A.   40

First printing, March 2007

Northern Kingdoms

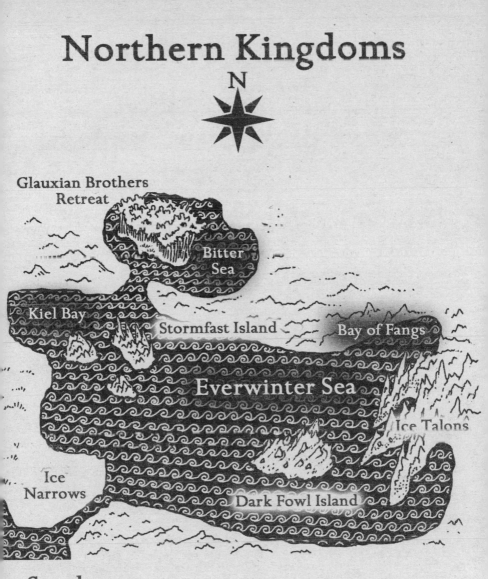

Glauxian Brothers
Retreat

Bitter
Sea

Kiel Bay

Stormfast Island

Bay of Fangs

Everwinter Sea

Ice Talons

Ice
Narrows

Dark Fowl Island

Southern
Kingdoms

Contents

Prologue

"Look at me, look at me!" the Great Gray hooted. His primaries sparkled silver in the moonlight as he carved a steep turn, then folded his wings and plunged toward a cresting wave. He swooped up, barely escaping the grip of the sea as the spume trailed behind him like a comet's tail. Twilight looked to the rest of the Band. "And they say seagulls do it better!"

Gylfie turned to Soren, and Digger sighed then churred softly. "We all know what's coming, don't we?"

"Indeed!" Soren and Digger both said at once. Then Twilight began:

I don't just do it better
I don't even get wetter
I'm prettier — hey, beautiful!
I'm a gorgeous owl and not a gull!
Waves crash, grass grows
I can whup anything before it knows.

The winds were capricious at this time of year and the owls of the Band entertained themselves by sliding in and out of their folds, rising and plummeting on the rogue drafts that buffeted the Island of Hoole.

There was nothing that owls liked doing more than playing with air, with wind, and none did it better than the Band. Despite the season, almost winter and the beginning of what the owls of the Great Ga'Hoole Tree called the time of the white rain, the great tree still retained the nearly golden glow of summer. It had remained this way ever since Coryn, the new young king, had retrieved the Ember of Hoole several moon cycles ago from the volcano in Beyond the Beyond.

Soren glanced toward the tree nervously. Its strange defiance of the seasons did not disturb him as much as knowing that his dear nephew, Coryn, was in his hollow, brooding. It was understandable that the responsibilities of kingship weighed heavily on the young owl, but Soren knew that it was the ember itself that added immeasurably to Coryn's anxieties.

Inside his rather modest hollow in the tree, the young king peered into the glow of the ember, the Ember of Hoole. Orange with a lick of blue at its center ringed with green, it was no simple coal, and he did not see simple things in it. Coryn was a flame reader, but reading the flames of a fire was different from understanding the shifting intensities of this ember. The images it yielded, like those of the flames, came without being beckoned, but they were more powerful than flame visions, often warped and not to be completely trusted. What the young Barn Owl was seeing now made his heart race and his gizzard quake. Peering into its flickering blue center he glimpsed a spot of white that grew rounder and larger. Like a moon, *he thought.* Like . . . a seam slants across the white sphere. . . . Like . . . like a scar. . . . Like my scar. No, not mine. NYRA's!

CHAPTER ONE

A Golden Glow

Coryn, you look as if you've just seen a scroom." It was midday and most owls at the great tree were fast asleep. Soren, Coryn's uncle and chief counselor, had just entered the hollow.

"If only she was just that — a scroom." Coryn looked up from the ember in its teardrop-shaped iron cask that Bubo the blacksmith had made.

So it's Nyra again! Soren thought. There had been no sign of Nyra or any of the Pure Ones since Coryn had retrieved the ember and defeated the Pure Ones in the Beyond. Nyra had escaped. Most owls believed that she was as good as dead, her troops virtually destroyed, and the ember safe in the talons of Coryn, a youthful but canny leader. The balance of power had at last changed. But Coryn was still haunted by her, and he imagined always would be, whether she was dead or alive. Of late he had become even more obsessed. Soren studied his dear nephew as the young owl peered into the glow of the ember. His heart went out to him and he felt a sorrowful twinge in his gizzard. The scar that slashed Coryn's face — a wound inflicted by his own mother — seemed to twitch in a private agony. He felt compelled to address Coryn directly now about this obsession. Perhaps getting it out in the open would be a good thing.

"Coryn, first of all, there is no evidence that she still is alive. And second, even if she is, with her forces all but annihilated she can be of little danger."

Coryn jerked his head around, unlocking his gaze from the glow. "But Uncle, Nyra is no mere evil owl, and if . . ."

"And if," Soren broke in testily. "I know, Coryn. I read the legends, too. If she is a hagsfiend . . ."

"No, Uncle. Perhaps not a full-blown hagsfiend but a relic from that ancient time who, through some twist of fate or nachtmagen, was reborn into this one. And if this is true . . ." He hesitated. "Well, you know what I said when we finished reading the first legend of Grank the Collier."

Yes, Soren knew. Coryn had concluded that if his mother had the taint of a hagsfiend's blood then his own blood must be cursed as well. It was idiotic, but no matter how often Soren reassured him, Coryn could not be convinced. Luckily, none of the rest of the Band nor Otulissa knew of Coryn's fears. The last thing Coryn wanted revealed was that he might be the offspring of a hagsfiend.

"So you saw something in the glow of the ember, I assume?" Soren asked.

Coryn looked up and blinked with a sudden curiosity. "Why are you here with me and not in your own hollow with Pelli and your little chicks? It's daytime. You should be sleeping."

"I'm not sure."

"A dream?" Coryn asked.

"Maybe." Soren shut his eyes for several seconds as if seeking patience or perhaps the right words. "You know how it is. . . . You have firesight and I have starsight."

"But starsight is when you dream about things that sometimes then happen. I don't understand what you are saying. You dreamed about me finding images in the ember? The images of my mother? Then you might well know why I am disturbed."

"Yes. I dreamed. But I don't quite understand the dreams myself." Soren sighed. He had been asleep in the cozy hollow that he shared with his mate, Pelli, and their three little chicks, Sebastiana, or "Basha" for short, Blythe, and Bell, when suddenly he realized that he was not in his own dream but another's — or perhaps sharing

Coryn's waking visions as he glimpsed them in the ember. It had rather unnerved Soren, because in the legends they had read that Kreeth, the infamous hagsfiend of ancient times, had an ability to do just this: to enter other creatures' dreams. Soren, however, was certain that it was starsight that he had experienced. Starsight was a peculiar and very rare phenomenon in which the stars in some mysterious way illuminated an owl's dream. Most creatures thought that during the day, when nocturnal animals slept, stars vanished, but for some they did not. The stars became little holes in the fabric of their dreams and through these holes they saw things that often came true.

And he had seen Coryn's vision, though it was not a dream of a terrible moon that turned into a scarred face, or of flames and fear and terrible loss. It was like fragments of a vision within a vision, a dream within a dream. But did this mean that Nyra still lived? Would she come to kill her only son? Soren did not want to betray the slightest hint of fear or worry. This was a magnificent time for the great tree and for the young king. "As I said," Soren began to speak with renewed firmness in his voice, "you have no evidence that she's still alive. Nor do you have any that she is a hagsfiend. She's just a miserable, evil owl. No more. No less."

"Maybe a little bit more," Coryn said softly.

"What do you mean?"

"Soren, when we were reading those legends, especially the parts about the hagsfiends — particularly Kreeth, when she was angered by Lutta — it reminded me ..."

"Reminded you of what?" Soren asked quietly. The glow of the ember cast deep red shadows that leaped through the air of the hollow in a wild and antic dance.

"It reminded me of my mother. When I was very young and she would get angry with me her face seemed to grow even bigger. There was a darkness like shadows beneath the white feathers of her face and her wings darkened near the edges, too, and seemed to hang like rags, torn and crowish. You know how crows' wings are ragged? At the time I thought it was my imagination, but while we were reading the legends and the descriptions of hagsfiends I kept thinking, 'This is familiar, I know this from somewhere.' The blood, the violence I learned of in those legends reminded me of a time in my own life: the Tupsi that required me to kill someone dear and close to me. And with my mother, as with Kreeth, it was not so much hate but the absence of any truly owlish feeling. She was so haggish."

Soren remained silent for a while. Perhaps the young king was right, but it would do him no good to brood endlessly about his origins and his inheritance. *Blood hardly*

5

defines one's character. We are made by our actions, not our blood, Soren thought. And Coryn was an owl of extraordinary courage, insight, wisdom and, most important, compassion. He of all owls had triumphed over the meanness of his life, the brutality of his upbringing. If he had haggish blood in his veins, he still had the noblest of gizzards.

Outside a bitter wind blew and, although it was midday, it might as well have been night for the sky roiled with dark storm clouds. It was odd that even though it was now the season of the white rain, the milkberries that normally turned white had a new luminous glow more reminiscent of summer and the time of the golden rain. Perhaps most curious of all, however, was that although many of the leaves of the great tree had fallen as always at this time of year, they had left behind a shimmering shadow of themselves. And some had not fallen at all, and still retained a golden splendor. The owls of the tree marveled at this peculiar phenomenon, exclaiming that it was like an endless summer. But Soren found this gilded beauty mildly disturbing. The shimmering nimbus of light that shone from where a leaf had fallen reminded him of scrooms, the unsettled spirits of dead owls that lurked until all their unfinished business on Earth was concluded.

The young king and his uncle Soren were silent, enveloped in the soft glow that streamed from the ember's teardrop-shaped cask. For several minutes, the two owls stood with their faces tipped toward the light of the ember, each alone in his thoughts. Most likely those thoughts were similar. Although they had read about the power of the ember in the legends, they knew it was not merely legendary. Its magic, with all of its good and its bad possibilities, was very real. With the ember came great blessings as well as grave dangers. When the ember had been retrieved after a thousand years, they both suspected that a small gash had been torn in the very fabric of the owl universe, an opening through which nachtmagen could seep.

Nyra was the very embodiment of evil, but there had always been evil. Coryn wondered if, with this small rip in the world of the owls, Nyra could gain a talon-hold through nachtmagen. And if she *did* have even a taint of hagsfiend blood, would this nachtmagen give her the powers of a creature such as Kreeth, the arch hagsfiend of the ancient world? In the legends, Kreeth — with her weird incantations and experiments — had created some truly horrendous monstrosities. Could Nyra perhaps be a descendant of one of her last and more successful experiments? Worse, even, than a simple hagsfiend?

That was precisely what worried Coryn. For what did that make him? This secret fear festered in him, haunted him, and caused him endless agony.

Soren's reading of the legends, however, had given him other concerns and other truths. In his gizzard, he knew that the most important lesson of the legends was to embrace reason and not magic, good or bad. He understood Coryn's obsession with his heritage, but he also knew that Coryn was intrinsically good. To rely on magic, or to become obsessed with the ember could only distract Coryn from the responsibilities of his role as king. To be a true Guardian of the great tree had always been considered every bit as noble as being its king. But it was up to the king to instill this sense of nobility — and to lead. In the oath of the Guardians of the Great Ga'Hoole Tree, there was nothing about magic. And the notion of nobility through royal birth was rejected. The words of the oath that Soren had taken so many years before coursed through his mind and set his gizzard aquiver: *I am the eyes in the night, the silence within the wind. I am the talons through the fire, the shield that guards the innocent. I shall seek to wear no crown, nor win any glory....*

That was the oath of the Guardians of the Great Ga'Hoole Tree on the Island of Hoole in the middle of the Sea of Hoolemere.

CHAPTER TWO

A Journey Is Planned

The ember's glow bloomed like an enormous bloodred flower, casting vermilion shadows over the white-feathered faces of the two Barn Owls.

"Coryn," Soren began to speak slowly. "I have been thinking. In the last few days many owls have come to the great tree. They are even calling it the 'Golden Tree' not just because of its golden glow but because a new era has begun since our defeat of the Pure Ones. Word of our library has spread. Owls are on the wing — and are less fearful. They want to know about our chaws. They are especially interested in our weather and navigation chaws." Soren paused and blinked. "What do you say, lad? Shall we have a go of it?" And to himself he thought, *Nothing like a little expedition with the Band to dissolve the gollymopes.*

"What do you mean . . . 'have a go'?" Coryn blinked at Soren. His uncle, although still a handsome owl, had uncountable nicks and marks of battles and from his life as a collier. His beak had long lost its pale tawny glimmer and was now tarnished from his years of plunging into forest fires to retrieve coals. His talons, too, had darkened and grown knobby with fire calluses. The white feathers of his legs were patchy and ash-colored. He looked like a hardened, seasoned owl and yet vigor and gentleness still flowed from him.

"I mean travel, dear lad. Get the lay of the land. See what, exactly, these owls want to learn from us. Besides, it's been so long since any of us have had a good flight — just for fun. Do you know that there is much talk that grog trees, which have been so rare in recent times, are now coming back? There's even rumor of gadfeathers, by Glaux. How lovely to gather with one's old friends in the branches of a grog tree and listen to the sweet tunes of a gadfeather. Ahh, to see old friends again!"

"Mist!" Coryn exclaimed excitedly.

"You call her Mist, but Gylfie and I shall always think of her as Hortense. She must be getting on now, but I long to go to Ambala and seek her out." Soren detected a new sparkle in his nephew's eyes. *Yes, this is it. I must get him out and on the wing. This obsession with his haggish mother is danger-ous. Too self-absorbed, an unwholesome indulgence for a king, especially one as intelligent and bold as Coryn.* "How about it?"

"Yes . . ." Coryn said slowly.

"You are worried that kings shouldn't just have fun?" Soren blinked at his nephew.

"Well, I don't want to be thought of as..." He hesitated.

"A sporting king?"

"I suppose so, yes."

"But," Soren said eagerly now, "even a king must be curious about how the hard-won peace lies on the land. These are exciting times."

"It is a good plan, Uncle!" Coryn spoke now with genuine enthusiasm. "But we should meet with the Band to discuss it first, don't you think?"

"Yes, of course," Soren agreed. "We'll speak with them immediately and the parliament must be consulted on the morrow. First Black."

"And Otulissa, will she come as well?" Coryn asked. Otulissa, although considered by many a prickly sort with a confidence bordering on arrogance, was a favorite of Coryn's. Otulissa was the first Guardian of Ga'Hoole that Coryn had met. Through some scroomish vision, an odd phenomenon in itself for an owl who was so dedicated to rational thought, Otulissa had been inspired to go to the Beyond. It was there she encountered Coryn and seemed instantly to sense his destiny and that she was part of it. It was Otulissa, the prodigiously talented and knowledge-able Spotted Owl, who first taught Coryn to dive for coals. She claimed no credit, however, for Coryn had a remark-able genius for colliering and in no time had learned to pluck the most challenging of coals from the volcanoes' spume — the bonk ones that many colliers never learned to retrieve.

"I doubt if Otulissa, with her additional responsibili-ties, will be able to accompany us," Soren said. "But I shall certainly ask her."

Otulissa, an esteemed teacher of the tree, had recently been appointed chief ryb, as her expertise extended over so many of the disciplines — from the literature of the legends to the sciences, including weather interpretation and metals. She hardly had a moment to spare. Nonetheless Soren would go to the hollow where she resided with her old nest-maid snake, Audrey, to ask if she would travel with them. But first he would meet with Gylfie, Twilight, and Digger. And, of course, he would have to explain to Pelli. No doubt Basha, Blythe, and Bell would beg Soren to wait until they had fledged their flight feathers so they might go, too. But they were at least a moon cycle away from fledging, and this was not a trip for young'uns.

Soren was just about to leave the hollow, immensely

pleased with himself for coming up with this idea, when Coryn suddenly said, "Uncle?"

"Yes?"

"What about the ember?"

"The ember? What about it?" Soren asked, slightly bewildered.

"Will it be safe here?"

"I can't imagine a safer place than here in the great tree. We certainly don't want to carry it around with us." He paused and looked steadily at the ember. In a low voice he said, "We do not want to become slaves to the ember. If the legends taught us anything, it was that."

"You are right, Uncle. We are free owls!"

CHAPTER THREE

What About the Ember?

Coryn looked across at the members of the parliament perched on the bow-shaped birch limb. In his head he was searching for the right words to announce this trip. Soren was right. It would be curious to see how peace lay across the owl kingdoms now that the threat of the Pure Ones was gone — or at least greatly diminished. He was interested in not only what he and the Band might learn, but what they might possibly share with the rest of the owl kingdoms now that this menace was gone and every ounce of energy did not have to be devoted to fighting and war. This reminded Coryn of the owls who had arrived at the tree recently and told them of a meeting in Ambala. Coryn coughed slightly and began.

"As most of you know, a small delegation from Ambala arrived three nights ago. They told us of a loose confederation of owls from the Shadow Forest, Silverveil, and, I believe, Tyto that came to meet there. It seems these owls are most interested in weather interpretation, as well as search-and-rescue techniques, and we felt . . ."

Coryn had hardly finished the explanation of the trip he and the Band had planned when there was a great rustling of feathers in the parliament chamber and a half dozen voices began murmuring, "The ember. What about the ember?"

The discussion dragged on with frequent interjections of "What about the ember?"

They're obsessed! thought Soren. And he believed if he had to hear those four words one more time, he would shree as only a Barn Owl could shree.

For perhaps the third time Soren made his argument that there was no safer place for the ember than right here in the tree. It was then suggested that Bubo make another cask for the ember.

"What's wrong with the one ye got?" Bubo, burly Great Horned Owl and chief blacksmith of the tree, growled.

"Is it strong enough, Bubo?" Elyan, a handsome Great Gray Owl and member of the navigation chaw, spoke up.

"Of course, it's strong enough. Fired with the best bonk coals around. Them coals are straight out of Dunmore. Caught on the fly they were, by Ruby over there."

Five volcanoes comprised what the wolves of the Beyond called the Sacred Ring, and the one named Hrath'ghar was the volcano from which Coryn had retrieved the ember. Ruby, a powerful Short-eared Owl known for her extraordinary powers of flight and her near legendary colliering skills, had caught four fantastic bonk coals on a trip back to the Beyond shortly after Coryn had arrived at the tree. "I don't know what more you could ask for!" Bubo fumed. His exceedingly bushy ear tufts twitched, and his eyes showed a touch of rancor. Although most Great Horneds had rather somber plumage composed of dusty browns and dark grays, Bubo's feathers were shot through with deep rusty reds and bronzes. It was almost as if they had taken on the hues of those bonk fires he nurtured. His coloring fit his temperament. Quick to flare, Bubo did not suffer fools gladly. He seemed on the brink now of doing just that as he looked at Elyan, for he suspected that a fool perched across from him.

"Surely the container is not the only security problem." Gemma, a Whiskered Screech, spoke up now.

"What other problems are there?" Bubo asked, feeling that there might be more than one fool in the parliament hollow.

Gemma straightened up and looked down her beak. "As my esteemed late kins-owl, Ezylryb . . ."

Ezylryb? She's comparing herself to Ezylryb! Soren thought.

"...always said, 'Vigilance is its own reward.'" Both Bubo and Soren looked confused. Soren, for one, could not remember Ezylryb ever saying such a thing. "It is my feeling that we not only need a much stronger container but that the coal must be under constant surveillance. A guard must be set up, a dedicated guard, chosen from the most trustworthy Guardians. An elite guard, the — how shall I put it?— Guardians of the Guardians? I am sure Ezylryb ..."

Otulissa blinked her eyes and twisted her head toward Soren.

"With all due respect, Gemma, you're no Ezylryb." The words were not Otulissa's but Bubo's. There was a sharp inhalation of breaths. The owls of the parliament blinked rapidly.

"I'm not sure what you mean by that," Gemma replied huffily.

"I mean *you* are *no* Ezylryb. He wouldn't put up with any of this nonsense about Guardians of Guardians, and some of us being more trustworthy than others —"

"I am sure that all of us here have only one thought in mind: the safety and well-being of the ember," Gemma interrupted. "Ezylryb valued vigilance. I mean, it's not a job that you would want to hand over to nest-maids."

"What!" Soren almost barked. He swiveled his head around. "I've never heard anything so absurd! What in the name of Glaux is not trustworthy about our nest-maid snakes, pray tell? We trust them with our very lives when we are sick or wounded. And you suggest we should not trust them with the ember? I'd wager they are as vigilant as they are skillful in the medical arts. And let us not forget their finely tuned sensibilities. If anything would go awry with the ember, or an ill-intentioned owl approached, it would be the nest-maids to first sound the alarm."

A wizened elderly Northern Saw-whet raised a shaky talon to speak.

"Fleemus has the perch!" Digger shouted. "Let the good owl speak."

Fleemus, the doctor and healer of the great tree, lifted an arthritic wing. "When I first arrived at this great tree many years ago, there was much of which to be fearful. There were the Pure Ones, as well as those thugs from St. Aggie's — with whom Soren and Gylfie were all too well-acquainted. When I began my practice here in the tree, only matron and her small contingent of nurse owls were trained as field medics for battle. Since that time, however, we have an entire new guild of nest-maid snakes whose sole focus is the medical arts. If you can't trust a nest-maid snake, you can't trust anyone." He paused. Then in a small creaky voice, he added, "I think all this talk about security is nonsense, nothing more than a pile of racdrops." He muttered something in a strange language.

"What was that?" Gemma asked. "What did you just say?"

"Krakish, from the Northern Kingdoms from which both your old kins-owl Ezylryb and I came. Indeed, it was the language of the famous sagas of the Northern Kingdoms, *The History of the Wars of the Ice Claws* by Lyze of Kiel."

"And what does this Lyze of Kiel have to say?" Gemma lifted her beak in a most haughty manner.

"Fyrndronken nyghot ig fyrnsfris."

"And for those of us not fluent in Krakish?" Gemma pressed. A sneer tinged her words.

"We have nothing to fear except fear itself," Fleemus replied. There was a murmuring among the owls. Soren and Gylfie were watching Gemma carefully. They sensed what was about to happen.

"And who is this so-called historian? 'Lyze of Kiel' you called him?" She could barely contain the contempt in her voice, and had Soren and Gylfie not known what the answer to her question was, their gizzards would have twitched in sympathy for old Fleemus.

"Why, Gemma," Fleemus said with a wicked sparkle suddenly infusing his rheumy old eyes. "Lyze of Kiel? You don't know him? Why, he's your old kins-owl, Ezylryb. He wrote these histories after the Ice Talon Wars ended, and before he came to the great tree. He spent years with Octavia at the Glauxian Brothers retreat on their island in the Bitter Sea, writing under the pen name Lyze of Kiel. Invert the letters and they spell Ezyl. And, as we all know, Ezyl, our dear departed ryb, came from the Bay of Kiel in the Everwinter Sea."

"Apparently not all of us," someone whispered as Gemma wilfed to half her size.

Soren winked at Gylfie and both the owls silently saluted the dear old healer who, many years after Ezylryb, had come from that same Glauxian retreat. Otulissa now turned to Gemma. "The books are in the library and are part of my standard curriculum for the young'uns, if you'd care to read them."

Several owls, perhaps a dozen, began to squabble again. The words "ember security," "tree vigilance," and "island protection" threaded through the air. Soren exchanged a quick glance with Coryn. The parliament seemed evenly divided. There were Fleemus and the Band in addition to Otulissa; Soren's sister, Eglantine; Ruby; Martin—in short, the renowned and remarkable Chaw of Chaws, a group that had no equal in terms of fighting skills, felt that the ember needed no special guard. The rest of the parliament thought otherwise. These ten owls seemed stunned by this new obsession with security and fear concerning the ember. Soren in particular wondered if it had been a mistake that they had not read the ancient legends aloud to the entire parliament. But Otulissa had given three extensive lectures on them and the "complicated goodness," as she had called it, of the ember. *Perhaps*, Soren thought, *she should have called it complicated "dangers" rather than "goodness."* But she had certainly warned of the pitfalls of overreliance on the ember's magic.

"Here! here!" Coryn flapped his wings and swooped off his perch. He flew up to Gemma and Elyan, who were the most obstreperous of all the owls, and glared at them. The hollow fell silent. "I shall not have you all talking at once. Dissent is welcome in this hollow, but I am hearing insults as well. You are talking about protecting something, the ember that many of you feel will somehow become vulnerable if I leave the great tree on this flight. I do not want you to feel uncomfortable in my absence. So, if it will make you feel better, yes, protect it. But there is no one owl or creature in this tree who is more trustworthy than another. The notion of an inner group of Guardians — Guardians of Guardians — is contrary to all that we value. If there is to be a watch — and I prefer to call it a watch, not a guard — it must have a representative from every chaw and each guild of the nest-maid snakes — those of the harp, the weavers, the lace-makers, the new medical and nursing guild, and so on."

"And how shall this . . . this . . . watch be chosen?" Gemma asked.

Coryn blinked. "The ember is in my hollow. I have spent more time in its presence than any other living creature. I think that it is only appropriate that I appoint those who will be perching in my hollow." Soren was proud of Coryn's quick and firm response. Coryn paused. "Now listen to me, owls, and listen hard." He blinked. There was a new sternness in his voice that went beyond the firmness they had just heard. Was it threatening? Some of the owls wilfed a bit. "When I first came here, I said to you that I had survived the ordeal of my upbringing with Nyra because I believed in the legends, the truths of courage and loyalty and of goodness and mercy. Those, indeed, were the truths of the popular legends that you all listened to as young'uns. The even older legends of which you have heard Otulissa speak held other truths. And one of them was that we must not become slaves of the ember. Fear enslaves. Remember that. And I command that the ancient legends, the ones that Ezylryb directed me to read with Soren, now be placed in the library and read by all of you. If you read these legends, you will learn respect and not fear. With knowledge comes freedom — freedom to think, freedom to reason. The ember and its magic have nothing to do with thinking and that is perhaps why it can be so dangerous."

No one said another word as the owls flew out of the hollow.

CHAPTER FOUR

The Band Takes Flight

The Band had gathered in Coryn's hollow to discuss the "security of the ember."

"No! It's out of the question. I don't want to be on some council for guarding this thing." Otulissa tossed her head at the ember, which did seem to spit a few sparks in reponse to her disparaging tone. "I have too much to do. You know that new bunch in training for colliering is a feisty group. Great Glaux, Fritha is always just winging off, chasing embers that she has no business going after. She has no sense of playing her ground position, which is essentially what we rely on the Pygmy Owls for. And then, of course, there are my chores in the library. No, I will not 'ember-sit' or whatever you call it."

"Well, I'd appoint Eglantine, but she's my aunt and I'm afraid that wouldn't appear, well . . . quite proper," Coryn replied.

"What about Audrey? You could do without her for a bit, couldn't you, Otulissa?" Soren asked.

"Audrey? Well, I suppose so. Audrey might even enjoy it. She might consider it an honor — bless her simple heart."

"Not so with Octavia," Gylfie said.

"Oh, Great Glaux," Otulissa churred. "Octavia would think the whole thing totally yoicks."

"Madame Plonk?" Digger offered.

"Now that's an interesting idea. It might appeal to Madame Plonk." Madame Plonk was the great singer of the tree, quite vain about many things, and the group thought it might be just her thing to serve on this ember watch.

It did not take Coryn long to come up with his suggested list for the watch. Ultimately, it was composed of twenty owls, some members of parliament like Gemma, Elyan, and Yeena, a Barn Owl, a half dozen nest-maid snakes, and the rest pulled from the various chaws. It was a well-balanced group in everyone's estimation. There were no hurt feelings, and no one, aside from Otulissa, refused to serve.

And so at First Black, the young king and the Band rose in the night on a snappish wind that swirled down from the north, and headed out across the Sea of Hoolemere on a course toward Ambala. The shadows of the five owls were printed against the almost full-shine moon with Coryn flying in the lead position, flanked on one side by Soren and on the other by Twilight. Gylfie flew just behind Twilight's starboard wing, her favorite position as navigator, for she was sucked along effortlessly by the powerful Great Gray's forward thrust and could concentrate on the stars rather than flying. Digger brought up the rear.

"Two points south by southeast of the bottom star, port talon of the Golden Talons," Gylfie called out.

Soren felt his gizzard sing. How long ago it had been since he and Gylfie had flown as young'uns in those early navigation practices with Strix Struma? One of her favorite exercises was for them to trace with their wing tips the outline of the Golden Talons constellation, which shone in the winter sky at its brightest just this time of year. It seemed like a lifetime ago. Now here was Gylfie, the head of the navigation chaw and regarded as one of the most brilliant celestial navigators in the kingdoms of owls.

But in owl years they weren't that old. Yes, older than they were back then, but still strong and fit. Soren knew they must show the rest of the owl world their wonderful king and bring with them the skills and knowledge that they had learned at the great tree. Coryn was right. Knowledge was freedom and no one could be enslaved if they dared to really think. If good things came out of this flight through the owl kingdoms they would be to dispel the myth of the ember and to help owls believe in themselves and their own power of thought. They would learn what could be accomplished through the disciplines that had been so highly developed at the great tree: colliering, navigating by the stars, and the science of interpreting weather. Soren had a name for all of this knowledge and it had nothing to do with magic. He called it the "glories of common sense."

A seagull flew up to them. "Hey, Twilight!"

"Sammy!" Twilight exclaimed. "Haven't seen you in an age."

"Gotta great wet poop joke for you," the seagull said.

"Oh, dear! Should I close my ear slits?" Gylfie asked.

"Oh, sure!" Twilight flicked his head toward the little Elf Owl. "We know how delicate you are! Who told that joke to that snooty great blue heron back in Silverveil and nearly got a fish thrown in her face?" Twilight turned his head to the seagull. "So what's the joke, Sammy?"

"What's the difference between a wet pooper and a pellet yarper?"

The Band looked at one another and exchanged glances. "I don't know. I give up," Twilight said.

The seagull had already started to laugh at his own

joke and could hardly finish it. "It's a matter of splatter!" the seagull screamed. He was now completely convulsed with laughter and ricocheted off the edge of a thermal draft into a cold trough and was gone.

"Glaux, he barely made it to the punch line!" Gylfie exclaimed.

They were all laughing now. *Lucky Otulissa isn't here*, Soren thought. She did not like what she termed "elimination humor." She always became very upset when they were out on weather-interpretation chaws and encountered seagulls, who were the coarsest of birds. But this rough humor was just what Coryn needed. He needed to get away — away from the tree, away from the squabbling parliament, and yes, away from the ember. Maybe in the good company of the Band he would relax, join in their easy, joyful camaraderie, and those terrible thoughts that haunted him would pass. If they had never read the legends, Soren had wondered lately, would Coryn have become so fixated on his past? Perhaps even more interesting, Soren wondered if Coryn had ever had any carefree days when he was being raised by Nyra. Did he ever have a friend as a young'un? Coryn had once mentioned an owl — a Sooty named Phillip. But he never wanted to talk about Phillip. It seemed to make him extremely sad. The Pure Ones were known to discriminate against any owl who was not a *Tyto alba*. Sooties — although a kind of Barn Owl — occupied the lowest perch in the world of the Pure Ones. So this Phillip's life was bound to have been a hard one.

Soren's life had not been an easy one, either, after his fall from the family hollow in the forest of Tyto. But it would have been unspeakably worse if he had not met up with Gylfie, Twilight, and Digger. The Band had become his family when he had none. They had become one another's reasons for living, flying on through obstacle after obstacle to reach the tree so long ago. In truth, Soren had learned as much from Digger, Gylfie, and Twilight as from any book. And he must not forget Ezylryb. Just as there was a Chaw of Chaws — the Band, plus Otulissa, Martin, Ruby, and Eglantine — there was also a ryb of rybs: Ezylryb.

CHAPTER FIVE
Tell It! Tell It!

A contrary wind had risen, and holding the course for Ambala was tiring after their crossing of the Hoolemere Sea. Dawn was approaching and so the five owls decided to head for Silverveil, one of the most delightful forests in all the owl kingdoms, with its lush meadows sprinkled with wildflowers in the summer and its forests of old and stately trees. Silverveil was the place where Coryn had first begun to understand what the color green really was. His entire childhood until the time he had escaped from Nyra and the Pure Ones had been spent in the barren, rocky scrub landscape of the canyonlands, which were bereft of anything resembling a tree, let alone green leaves or spruce or pine needles.

Within the forest of Silverveil, there was a pocket of green splendor called Blythewold that was as pretty as any place on Earth. Soren and Pelli had named one of their daughters Blythe after this place. And it was here that Coryn had lived for a long time before summoning his courage to leave for the Beyond. It was a place replete with memories — some good, some bad. It was a scroomish place where he had been haunted by the spirit of his father, Kludd, but also where he had heard for the first time some of the better-known legends of Ga'Hoole. He had eavesdropped on parents telling these stories at goodlight time to their hatchlings before they went to sleep. While in the forest, Coryn had lived hidden in the stump of a tree in a day-for-night world because too often he had been mistaken for his terrible mother.

"Winter is finally upon us, I think," Soren said as they lighted down on a wildly waving branch of a large fir tree. Soren was partial to fir trees. They formed part of his first memories. Like Coryn's, some of these memories were good and some were bad. But it was the good ones that he tried to concentrate on. Those times in the old family hollow of the fir tree in the forest of Tyto where he had first heard his father tell the stories of Ga'Hoole. Little did he know then that the great tree was a real place. And how vividly he remembered what his father had said to his brother, Kludd, when Kludd had asked him if the legends were true. "A legend, Kludd," his father had replied, "is a story that you begin to feel in your gizzard, which over time becomes true in your heart." But would his father ever have believed that there really was an island called Hoole, where the Great Ga'Hoole Tree did, indeed, grow? Could he ever have imagined that Soren would become a Guardian and that his own grandson, Coryn, son of Kludd, would become king? And would he have believed that Kludd had pushed Soren from the nest, attempting to murder him as part of his own rites of initiation into the brutal gang of owls called the Pure Ones? Soren shook the past from his mind.

It had begun to snow. "If I know fir trees, there will be a nice roomy hollow, dry and sweet-smelling," Soren looked up, "oh, I'd say about a third of the way from the top on the lee side of the trunk."

And there was. The five owls crowded in. "I'm starved!" Twilight announced. "This place is hopping with rabbits."

"Mmmmm!" Digger, Gylfie, and Soren all smacked their beaks in anticipation. Gylfie turned to Coryn. "Not up for a rabbit?" she asked.

"Well, rabbits are fine. Just don't go after one that has a white mark on its forehead."

"Why?" Twilight blinked.

"It's a long story," Coryn said.

"This is a morning for long stories," Soren said as he watched the thickening swirls of snow outside the hollow.

"Not on an empty gizzard, it isn't!" Twilight boomed. "Let's get hunting."

"I'll go with you," Coryn said.

"Good idea. I wouldn't want to grab the wrong rabbit."

Twilight and Coryn had been tracking a large gray rabbit when Coryn suddenly picked up soft mewling noises. "Grosnik!" he hissed.

"Oh, for the love of Glaux! Are you sure, Coryn?"

"I heard the babies," Coryn whispered. Barn Owls were known for their extraordinary hearing abilities, which allowed them to detect the subtlest of sounds.

"And no parent?" Twilight asked.

"No. Look — there's the den down there under that tree stump. I would have definitely picked up the parent's heartbeat if there was one in there."

Among owls it was strictly forbidden to eat baby animals or to kill a parent if there was only one parent, thus leaving the babies orphaned. Of course, this was not always known to the hunter and many small animals had been orphaned when owls had unwittingly preyed upon their parents. But the circumstances here were clear. These babies, at least four, Coryn thought, would have been orphaned.

Twilight sighed. "It's funny, once you get your gizzard set on something, you can almost taste it before your first bite and you want nothing else. Vole seems so boring to me right now."

"Well, as you said, there are lots of rabbits around here."

"Yeah, they can't all have babies, or white marks on their forehead . . . I hope!"

"No, believe me," Coryn said, "there was only one rabbit like that."

"What was its name?"

"He had no name."

"No name? What made that rabbit so special?"

"He just was. Don't worry about it. It all happened long ago, in the Shadow Forest. Not here. I'm just always really careful when I go out rabbit hunting to check to see if my prey has that mark. He called himself a mystic. You know, he could see things that other creatures couldn't — sort of like Soren has starsight and I can read the flames of a fire. Well, this rabbit could read things in spiderwebs."

"You gotta be kidding!" Twilight exclaimed.

"No, not at all." Coryn paused. "My visions are mostly about the present but the rabbit had bits and pieces of the past, the present, and the future. You see . . ." Coryn was about to explain what the rabbit actually saw. "There's one now!"

"Him? The one with the mark?"

"No!"

A large fluffy white rabbit darted under the bank of a creek. Amid the swirling snow, he appeared like a solid sphere hurtling across the frozen bed of the creek. Twilight was on him in a flash. Coryn admired the speed with which the Great Gray killed. No matter what the wind direction was, it never offset his kill angle and he always managed to plunge his talons directly into the brain of the animal so that it was an instant, nearly painless death.

"That is one beautiful rabbit!" Digger exclaimed as Twilight and Coryn returned to the hollow. It was customary among owls that whoever made the kill got the first choice of meat, or "firsts" as it was often called. Undoubtedly, Twilight would go for a haunch, for that was usually the meatiest on a rabbit. Soren, however, looked at the rabbit and said, "Hold on a second, Twilight. Before you get your firsts, don't you think we should skin this rabbit properly? This is a beautiful pelt. Trader Mags came by last moon cycle with a pelt like this torn from a robe."

"One of the Others' robes?" Digger asked.

"Yes, of course. And she sold it to Madame Plonk for Glaux knows what. The piece was moth-eaten and not nearly as glistening white as this pelt," Soren said.

"Are you suggesting that we try to best Trader Mags at her own game?" Gylfie asked.

"I'm just saying that the new sewing guild the nest-maid snakes formed might be happy to get something like this. Or maybe we should just keep it for ourselves. Divide it up. Everyone could have a piece for their hollow."

"Oh, for Glaux's sake, if you're going to skin it, skin it. I'm famished," Twilight roared.

"Let's skin it," Coryn said.

And so they did. As they sat enjoying the rabbit, which was unusually plump for this time of year, Soren suddenly said, "Do any of you remember that time — oh, we were much younger than young Coryn here — when we snuck out of the tree?"

"We snuck out at least a hundred times," Gylfie said. "Which time?"

"You snuck out?" Coryn blinked.

"Of course we did," Digger replied.

"Did you get into trouble?" Coryn asked.

"Sometimes," Soren said.

"Was it worth it?"

"Always!" the Band roared in unison.

"Well, what time was this one?" Coryn turned to Soren.

Soren wiped the blood from his beak. "Well, it was right after a visit from Trader Mags and we had this idea — we were always fascinated about the Others —"

"Who isn't?" Coryn asked.

"Anyhow," Soren continued. "We had this idea that we would go find a new castle, or church, or — I don't know — one of those stone hollows that the Others built, but one that Trader Mags hadn't scavenged yet for all the goodies. We were going to get rich. I guess that was the main idea. Going to start our own business. I mean, we were young. We thought it would be fun going around selling things or swapping them."

"Otulissa said that the idea was stupid and that noble owls weren't meant for business," Gylfie said. "Remember? That was why she wouldn't come with us. She said it was vulgar."

"That is soooo Otulissa!" Digger said.

"It probably *was* common, but it would have been fun," Gylfie said.

"Well, did you go?" Coryn asked.

"Oh, we did!" Soren said. "We flew first to Tyto thinking that if there were any undiscovered Others' ruins they

37

might be there. But we didn't find any. Then ... I don't know whose idea it was to head to the Shadow Forest ..."

"Mine!" Twilight chimed in. "I had dimly remembered something from my very youngest days. You realize, Coryn, that I was orphaned very young. Never knew my parents."

I should have been so lucky, Coryn thought.

"Had to teach myself everything. Orphan School of Tough Learning is what I call it. For me, the great tree was more of a finishing school than anything else."

"If that's not a pile of racdrops, I don't know what is!" Digger blinked.

"Give it a blow, Twilight. Finishing school, my talon." Gylfie stomped her tiny talons on the floor of the hollow.

"Anyway," Soren continued, "we decided to go to the Shadow Forest. And we did find a ruin. There were no jewels, no great tapestries like the ones Trader Mags salvages scraps from, no paintings. There was something much more precious."

"What was that?"

"Bess," Gylfie said quietly.

"Bess?" Coryn asked.

"Yes, Bess — the daughter of Grimble!" There were tears now in both Soren's and Gyfie's eyes.

"And who is Grimble?" Coryn asked.

"Was," Gylfie corrected, and wiped away a tear with her wing tip. "You see, Coryn, Grimble taught us to fly. It was because of Grimble that Soren and I were able to escape St. Aggie's."

Soren continued. "Grimble was killed when the Ablah General discovered him helping us to escape. There was a terrific fight. Grimble kept yelling, 'Fly! Fly! Now's your chance!' I looked back and saw him bleeding on the ground, a wing half torn off."

"And did he die?" Coryn asked.

"Oh, he died all right. But his bones brought Bess and us together."

"His bones!" Coryn blinked. "Is this a scroom story?"

"In a way," Gylfie said softly. "But it was because we had snuck out to look for precious things that we found Bess in that ruin. It was several moon cycles after her father had finally died. She would have rescued him if she could have. But she couldn't, so she did the next best thing and brought his bones to this secret place."

"Secret place!" Coryn was nearly jumping out of his feathers. "Tell me the story, please." *A child desperate to rescue a parent! How different from me. Would I ever dare rescue my mum, or . . . ? Would I dare seek out my da's bones?*

A shadow seemed to steal across Soren's gizzard, send-ing a deep chill through his hollow bones. "I can remem-ber her words almost exactly." Soren sighed.

"Tell it! Tell it!"

"Yes, you tell it, Soren," Gylfie said. Soren was the best storyteller of all. It was Soren's telling of the legends when he and Gylfie had been thrown into the moon-blaze chamber in St. Aggie's that had saved them from being moon blinked. There was a passion in his telling of stories that made the words take on new and deeper meanings. But it wasn't simply a story he would be telling Coryn. Soren would be telling him of a secret place that only a very few owls in the great tree knew about, only the Band, Otulissa, Ezylryb, and Strix Struma, and, yes, two nest-maid snakes — Octavia and Mrs. Plithiver. They called it the Palace of Mists.

CHAPTER SIX

Bess of the Chimes

W e had taken off during the milkberry harvest fes-
tival — always a good time to sneak out," Soren
began. "You know how all those older owls get tipsy on
the milkberry wine and berry mead. And then there is
all the dancing and singing that can go on for three days
or more. We knew that we wouldn't be missed. No one
paid much attention to young owls at these times, especially back then. We had hardly been at the tree a year,
maybe thirteen moon cycles at the most, when we got
this notion of getting rich. Beating old Trader Mags at her
own game, as Gylfie said. Otulissa would have nothing to
do with it. It was raining that night as well she argued. So,
why be out when there was so much frolic going on in the
great hollow of the tree?"

"Yes, but the winds were terrific," Twilight said. "Rain
or no rain, the winds were with us from behind. So we
flew fast."

"As I recall," Digger offered, "we made Cape Glaux by daybreak."

"But where would you even start looking for a ruin — an undiscovered one?" Coryn asked.

Soren blinked and began to speak in his thoughtful way. "Good question. We were smart enough not to go to Silverveil. We knew Trader Mags had discovered all the ruins there. But the one place that had never really been explored was part of the Shadow Forest. It's so dense with trees that there was not much space for the Others to build their stone hollows. We were young and impulsive, and although we had once been attacked by crows, we promised ourselves that we would be more vigilant this time. So we decided to go out and hunt during the morning hours but always together and then at night to go off separately to cover as much of the forest as possible in search of a ruin."

Coryn listened with rapt attention. What an adventure! A treasure hunt instead of a battle. Jewels instead of blood. And most of all, friendship. Daring young owls sneaking off from the great tree together on a quest.

"By the end of the second day, we had found nothing and we knew time was getting short. We would have to get back to the tree. But that night we went out once more separately and Gylfie . . ." Soren paused. "Well, Gylfie, you should tell this part."

Gylfie ran her beak through her primaries before she began her part of the story. "There is a place in the Shadow Forest where, if you fly high enough and are observant, you will notice the forest seems to dip down into a bowl. If you look closer, you will see the silvery ropes of a waterfall cascading from a great height into the bowl. I saw the falls sending up great plumes of swirling mist. I spiraled down and flew closer. Veils of mist were suspended in the air. The entire valley seemed to be neither quite of land or sky but hanging between the two. I began to see shapes in the mist as one sees shapes in the clouds. But then I slowly realized that these were not mere illusions or figments of my imagination. What I was seeing was real and made of stone. I flew back to the place we were to meet up if we found anything.

"When we all flew there together, the mist was so thick you couldn't see a thing. It was like a curtain hanging across the valley," Gylfie continued. "The rest of the Band thought I had experienced some sort of gizzard dream. There wasn't a stone visible. But suddenly, a sharp rogue wind tore through the curtain of mist like a knife. Four beautiful stone spires pierced the night. And that's when Soren heard the chimes."

"Chimes!" Coryn exclaimed. It all sounded so mysterious, so beautiful. "What was it?"

"I thought it was battle gear clanking in the night," Twilight said.

"Only you, Twilight, would think that!" Digger sighed.

"But was it chimes? A bell tolling?" Coryn asked.

"In a sense," Soren spoke softly.

Coryn felt a shiver pass through him. *This* was *going to be a scroom story*, he thought.

"We had fetched up just beneath one of the stone towers in a silverdrop pine. It took me about three seconds to identify the sound. It was a Boreal Owl! You know how the call of those owls often sounds like chimes in the night? Well, Boreals believe that if a Boreal dies in a bell tower beneath the clapper of a bell, then its scroom will go straight to glaumora. Or at least that was the tale that our friend Grimble told us."

"You mean," said Coryn, now aghast, "that it was a dying owl making this beautiful chiming noise?"

"It was not a dying owl but the sound was very mournful." Gylfie sighed. Her wings seemed to quiver at the memory of it all.

"And desperate," added Soren. "We decided we should go to her."

"Her? It was a female?" Coryn asked.

"We were pretty sure it was a female. So," Soren

continued, "we took off and flew toward the spire from which the sounds were coming. As we drew nearer, the sounds became louder — as Gylfie said the most mournful yet beautiful sounds any of us had ever heard.

"A strange sight greeted us as we lighted down on the windowsill of the bell tower," Soren continued. "There was a large bell that hung in the tower and from within it came the chimelike sounds mixed with the wing beats of an owl. On the stone floor were the bleached bones of another owl, one long dead."

Coryn felt as if the line between past and present were blurring. It was as if he were actually living within the story; it was as real to him as it was to the Band. Soren's storytelling voice slid through the dim light of the hollow as smoothly as the liquid ribbon of a river flows toward the sea. Coryn felt its current.

"We were perched on the window ledge of the bell tower," Soren said. "Now, we had all experienced scroomish, peculiar things in our days. Things that stilled our gizzards and sent quivers through our bones, but this was one of the strangest situations ever. From the bell we heard a beautiful song, a song that seemed to be made of silver. I cannot sing it but the words were so lovely."

"What were the words?" Coryn pressed.

"I hope I can remember. Say them with me." Soren looked at Gylfie, Twilight, and Digger. The four owls began to recite the song.

> *I am the chimes in the night,*
> *the sound within the wind.*
> *I am the tolling of glaumora*
> *for the souls of long-lost kin.*
> *I shall sing you to the stars,*
> *where your scroom shall finally rest*
> *'neath the great bell of the sky*
> *in a tower of cloudy crests. . . .*

"When the song in the bell finished," Gylfie said, "a beautiful owl flew from the bell and lighted down."

"I'll never forget that first glimpse of her." Soren shut his eyes. "She was the color of tree bark with lighter brown and creamy streaks. Her face was grayish-white with flares of small white feathers radiating out from her eyes. Her wings had five rows of white spots. And on top of her head there was a starry spray of small white feathered dots. The thought burst in my head and Gylfie's, too. She looked exactly like her father, Grimble!"

"Grimble, the owl who helped you escape St. Aggie's?" Coryn whispered excitedly.

"The very one!" Soren replied. "She was not young. I didn't need to ask her her name. I knew immediately she was Bess, Grimble's favorite daughter. She was astonished that we knew who she was. Then she looked down at the bones at her feet. 'And those are the bones of Grimble,' I said. I knew this in my gizzard as surely as I had ever known anything in my life."

Gylfie continued the story. "We told Bess how we had come to know her father at St. Aggie's and how he had saved our lives by teaching us how to fly and how we also knew that Bess was his favorite daughter." Gylfie paused before going on with the story. "Bess could hardly believe this, for she thought her father had abandoned them all. So we explained how he didn't want to stay with the St. Aggie's owls but they threatened to kill her and her mum and the rest of her brothers and sisters if he did not remain."

"Bess blinked," Soren said. His own eyes misted with the memory. "And two big tears rolled from her bright yellow eyes. 'That explains it,' she said. 'We thought he had vanished. That we were nothing to him.'"

Soren shut his eyes tight now and began to speak forcefully, as if he were trying to remember something very exactly. "But we told her that her father had courage in a place that bred cowards. That he had a nobility as great as any Guardian of Ga'Hoole's. And when we asked her how his bones had come to be in this place, she told us that the eagles Streak and Zan had brought them to the family. But that she had brought them to this place for she believed in the old tales her father had told."

Digger now spoke. "The rest of her family had warned her that she would have to go as far as Silverveil to find a bell tower. But she had found this place. And she liked it because it was so hidden in the valley, and the roar of the waterfalls was like a kind of music to her. She said that in many ways it made her think that this was what glaumora must be like and that is why she sang every day to her father. She said that she hoped he was in glaumora and that his business on Earth was finished so that he would not haunt the Earth and the lower air as a scroom."

"But," Soren said, "even though her father had long gone to glaumora, it was almost as if Bess was a scroom, as if *her* business was not finished."

Coryn felt a chill pass through his gizzard. Was his own mother, Nyra, still alive, or was she a scroom? And if she was a scroom, what business had she left unfinished?

CHAPTER SEVEN

The Palace of Mists

"But what was this place where Bess mourned?" Coryn asked. "A castle? Was there gold and silver and the kinds of things that Trader Mags looks for?"

"There was certainly some of that but there was something much more valuable," Soren answered.

"What?" Coryn asked.

"Books and maps." Digger's eyes began to sparkle. "Not just one library but many. Bess said these stone hollows were a university, a place of learning. But she called it a palace. The Palace of Mists."

Digger, like many Burrowing Owls, was a great appreciator of built spaces. As his species name suggested, he was expert in excavating underground tunnels and hollows and creating nests where other birds might not dream of living. He admired the way the stones of the university had been hewn to fit together perfectly and how the entire structure was tucked neatly behind the scrim of mist from the waterfall.

"The Palace of Mists." Coryn repeated the words dreamily.

"Yes, and just imagine, Coryn!" Excitement stirred Digger's normally even, slow speech. "The face of the waterfall formed the rear wall of this palace. And there were four spires, each a bell tower but not one of the four bells had a clapper."

"I bet Bubo could have made one," Coryn said.

"Bess didn't want one," Soren replied. "We were the first owls who ever came there, and she said she liked her secret place and that she needed no clapper to sing her da to glaumora. I'll never forget her words. She said, 'I am the chimes. I am the clapper.' And I do believe had there been no bell she would have become that as well. She is an extraordinary owl, one of vast intelligence."

"Is?" Coryn blurted out. "She still lives?"

"Oh, most definitely." Soren paused and lowered his voice. "You must understand, Coryn, Bess is the best-kept secret in the owl kingdom. When we left Bess that first time, we vowed to tell only three other owls: Otulissa, Ezylryb, and Strix Struma."

"And it was hard enough getting her to agree to that! Believe me!" Twilight said. "But tell Coryn about the stone Others."

Coryn was speechless, his eyes wide.

"Ah, yes, the stone Others," Soren replied. "Bess asked us if we would like a tour of the university. So we followed her in a spiraling flight down from the bell tower, winding in and out of the pillars of a garden where there were stone pictures."

"Stone pictures?" Coryn asked.

"Yeah, you've seen some of those scraps of paintings of Others that Mags brings around, haven't you?" Twilight asked.

"Sure."

"Well, this was sort of the same thing but cut in stone," Twilight replied. "Some were of animals, and there was even a strange-looking bird. And some of the stone figures were of the Others, but they might be missing a head, or a head might be missing a body."

"What in the world?" Coryn gasped. "Were they once alive?"

"Oh, no. It was part of the Others' art, like the paintings."

"But that wasn't the most interesting thing at all," Gylfie said.

"Sounds pretty interesting to me," Coryn replied.

"There were these maps," Soren said. "Maps like we'd never seen before."

"What do you mean?" Coryn asked. A pale lavender light began to suffuse the hollow. Lavender was the prelude of twilight and soon it would be First Black. They had told and listened to stories of Bess through an entire day. Coryn almost wished to stay the sun and fend off the night — a most un-owlish response. Owls lived for darkness, for the black pierced by a sliver of moon, or perhaps the silver disc of a full-shine floating eerily just above a horizon. But now he wanted not the darkness, not the silver, not the joys of flight through a long night, but to remain in the hollow of this fir tree reliving this fantastic tale of discovery, grief, mystery, and riches that were neither jewels nor gold.

"These maps," Soren continued, "were not ones of the owl kingdoms. There was no Sea of Hoolemere, no Everwinter Sea. No Northern Kingdoms. No Southern Kingdoms. So I asked Bess, 'Where are the kingdoms of owls?'"

"And what did she say?" Coryn tipped forward.

"She said they were maps of elsewhere and beyond," Soren said softly.

"It was even beyond our Beyond! We called it The Elsewhere," Digger whispered. The white feathers that streaked across the Burrowing Owl's brow seemed to intensify Digger's penetrating gaze. It was as if he were imagining this place.

Coryn was astonished. He was trying to take it all in.

"You mean there is a place that is not here? Not in this owl world? It's like . . ." Coryn looked out of the fir tree hollow and tipped his head toward the sky.

"Yes," Gylfie said. "And even the stars look different there — the constellations are different. One rarely sees the Golden Talons or the Little or the Big Raccoon. It's just a different world. It's The Elsewhere."

"Have you ever been there?" He looked first at Soren and then to each of the other Band members. They all shook their heads.

"But Bess knows the way there even though the stars are different," Gylfie said. She shook her head in wonder. "Bess is so very smart."

"That is why we call her 'the Knower,'" Soren said.

By the time Soren had finished the story of Bess and the Palace of Mists, it was night. The wind had shifted, so they set out on a course for Ambala. But they did not make much progress, for they were tired and shortly after midnight the wind shifted once again and became a fierce headwind with driving rain replacing the swirls of snow.

"No use fighting this," Twilight called out to the rest. If Twilight said it was too much — beating into this wind — the rest of the Band were quick to agree, for the Great Gray was the largest of them all and possessed the most wing power. They found an ancient cedar with a good-size hollow. The rain made the pungent scent of the tree even sharper.

"I can't say cedar is my fragrance of choice," Gylfie sniffed, but within two seconds she had fallen asleep.

All of the owls were soon asleep except for Coryn. For him sleep seemed beyond reason. "The Knower," Coryn repeated softly. He began to think deeply about Bess, the Knower.

His mind whirled with notions about Bess and this place dedicated entirely to learning, with many libraries. The Band had said they had never seen such maps and star charts. Coryn knew that the Others were thought to have been very advanced, but not so advanced as these stories of the Palace of Mists seemed to suggest. From the stonework to the star charts it seemed beyond belief, almost magical. Coryn's eyes began to droop. His last thought was, *Magic, or nachtmagen?*

Then Coryn began dreaming of stone gardens with the fragments of the Others and stone animals, and the strange-looking stone bird that Soren had described. In his sleep he saw a head. It was the head of the strange bird. But no, not just any strange bird — Kreeth!

He woke up immediately. "Why would I ever dream of Kreeth?" he whispered to himself. Kreeth, the infamous hagsfiend of the legends, was long dead. Surely if the strange stone bird looked like Kreeth, the Band would have said something. Although they had not known about the hagsfiends of the legends when they had first gone to the Palace of Mists, they would have remembered now. *This is totally irrational!* Coryn thought to himself.

Kreeth was a hagsfiend through and through, but she called herself by all sorts of other names — a philosopher, an experimenter, a scientist. It wasn't, however, science she practiced. It was nachtmagen. Although he had begun to suspect that beneath the plumage of a Barn Owl his mother might be a hagsfiend herself, a grotesque thought occurred to him again — that Nyra might be even worse than haggish. She might be some descendant of a remnant of Kreeth's experiments with nachtmagen. It was all too frightening to imagine. Coryn blinked. But imagine he must. He was a king, a leader. He must lead! And to lead was to imagine boldly.

He looked at the Band sleeping soundly around him. Outside the sun was high in the sky. He must go. He must risk being mobbed by crows. He must find out the truth about his mother. Hagsfiends were thought to have become extinct sometime long after King Hoole had retrieved the ember. And yet shadows of hagsfiends much less potent still lingered. And was that not what made the ember so puzzling? For with all its many blessings, there was always the lurking fear that, with the good magen, nachtmagen could return and real hagsfiends could slip back through what Otulissa called the ether veil of the owl universe. The ether was a windless layer of air in the upper regions of the sky that enveloped the entire universe of owls. The ancients believed that infinitesimally small tears in this layer could permit the intrusion of alien matter such as nachtmagen, the magic of hagsfiends. The ember could seal up these tears as well as open them. And if the ember came into the possession of a bad owl, or graymalkin as they were sometimes called, the ether could be ripped to shreds.

Coryn was fairly sure that no such thing had happened to the ether veil — yet. According to the legends, Kreeth had died. But were all her kind extinct? Like the Others? Perhaps not, if Nyra lived. Coryn knew what he had to do. He had to go to the Shadow Forest. However he did not need to see Bess. The Knower would not know what he needed to know. There was, however, a rabbit who might. And he needed to find that rabbit. He quietly stepped to the rim of the hollow. He looked back at the Band. *They're just going to have to understand*, he thought, and spreading his wings, he took off.

CHAPTER EIGHT

Otulissa Perplexed

"Can you feel it, Mrs. Plithiver?" Octavia asked. The elderly nest-maid snake was coiled on an upper limb of the Great Ga'Hoole Tree.

"Yes, they're flying in unison. I can feel the wing beats."

And indeed a surge of vibrations rolled up through the tree. The slender branch upon which they had arranged themselves was almost like a tuning fork, at least for nest-maid snakes. These snakes had extremely refined sensibilities and despite their blindness, they could pick up on the subtlest atmospheric pressure changes, sounds, wind shifts, even the feelings and moods of those around them. Octavia, a snake of ample girth with a very fat head, found it most comfortable to twine herself in a spiral around the branch. Lying flat on it was out of the question; she was simply too chubby to find it comfortable. Mrs. P., however, was suspended from the branch in an artistic configuration halfway between a question mark and an exclamation point. This peculiar geometry was perhaps a reflection of her mental state. *What is happening here?* These four words were spiraling through the length of Mrs. P.'s cylindrical body, and she thought they should be likewise screaming in every mind, gizzard, or whatever of every owl in the tree. Unfortunately, such was not the case.

"Why aren't you down there weaving your way through the harp?" Octavia inquired of Mrs. P.

"Don't be ridiculous. You wouldn't catch me jumping octaves or making music for this stupid ceremony. What do they call themselves — Guardians of the Guardians? All this folderol about guarding the ember! Silly rituals and all."

Octavia gave a funny little pneumatic snort in response to Mrs. P.'s outburst. This was her way of laughing. Mrs. Plithiver was a member of the harp guild directed by Madame Plonk. For centuries, the harp guild had been considered the most prestigious of all the nest-maid snake guilds of the great tree. Half the snakes played the lower strings and half played the upper ones. But there were a precious few, the most talented of the snakes, who were confined to neither. These snakes were called sliptweens, and their job was to jump octaves, which contained all eight tones of the scale. It was an energetic leap they had to make. It took skill, muscle, and timing. In her thinner days Octavia had been a sliptween. However, she had all but retired from the harp. Mrs. P. was now considered one of the finest sliptweens in the history of the tree.

"So how did you get out of playing the harp for this whatever-they-call-it ceremony?"

"I told them I sprung a tendon on that cantata the other night."

"I'm surprised that Otulissa didn't think up some way to excuse herself," Octavia said.

"She should have. I can feel her rage all the way up here."

"I know," Octavia replied.

The two snakes became very still and shut their slitted eyes. From at least forty feet above the Great Hollow, they could feel the waves of anger, frustration, of sheer embarrassment that rose from the Spotted Owl's plumage like thermal drafts on a hot summer day. Such were the sensibilities of a nest-maid snake.

Rough air, to put it mildly, Mrs. P. thought.

On the balcony of the Great Hollow, Otulissa perched, blinking in disbelief. Her gizzard was in a nauseating, dizzying turmoil. Her heart was aggrieved as she watched the tawdry spectacle below. An "Honor Guard"— the term itself made her almost yarp — was flying around the ember, which had been removed from Coryn's hollow and put in the center of the Great Hollow. The old box was encased now in a newer, larger, fancier one that had been designed by Gemma and reluctantly forged by Bubo. It was the Whiskered Screech, Gemma, and the Great Gray, Elyan, who were at the front of the procession of owls that flew in circles around the elaborately "en-hollowed" ember. "En-hollowed"— yet another newly coined term that nearly made a pellet swim up Otulissa's gullet. She swallowed hard and tried not to belch. But perhaps the most revolting word of all right now was "ele-vation." For this was the Elevation ceremony of Gemma, Elyan, and a Barn Owl called Yeena. They were to be ele-vated to the highest of the high honor guards, an order called the Guardians of Guardians, not of the great tree, but of the Ember of Hoole. Madame Plonk's voice soared in a newly composed celebratory song called "Chant of the Ember."

Oh, dearest Ember of great Hoole,
guard our tree most great.
Warm our gizzards, make us wise,
lead us in your holy ways.
Give us comfort, let tumult cease,
bless each owl so safe we'll keep.
We sing to you, your glowing splendor

Radiant with magen's grace,
So we ask that peace be with us,
and in you our trust do place.

Madame Plonk was in full voice. The song was quite beautiful, except for the words, Otulissa thought. And what a bunch of racdrops they were! Look at Madame Plonk, strutting about in the air. One would have thought her a peacock. Yet it wasn't even her own feathers she was showing off. It was the frinking cloak she'd gotten from Trader Mags. It was purple — royal purple as she liked to remind everyone — and it was trimmed in ermine. "Ermine is to eat, not to wear," Otulissa muttered. Another owl, a Barred, swung her head around and blinked furiously at her.

"What did you say?" the owl called Quinta hissed.

"I said" — Otulissa said furiously — "Strumina Von Fleet would stare."

"Huh? I thought you said something about eating ermine."

"No, not at all," Otulissa lied. "Strumina Von Fleet, you might not know her. An ancient sage from the Northern Kingdoms, known as much for her unparalleled elegance as for her brilliant mind. A relative of mine, actually. Thirteenth cousin once removed."

"Sssh!" someone else hissed. "It's almost time for the Ultimate Elevation."

Ultimate Elevation, my butt feathers! Otulissa thought, but she did not say a word this time. One could not be too careful these days.

Something strange had befallen the tree. It had really begun before the Band left but she had not taken notice of it then. The tree seemed to have entered a phase of eternal golden glory. But no one at that time had likened it to the glow of the ember itself. If anything, they spoke of it as a lingering tinge of color from the summer. But now owls compared it to the glow of the ember. It was, they said, as if the radiance of the ember had infused the very fabric of the tree. New nest-maid guilds had been started. One was a choir, the Choir of the Ember, that sang only songs composed for praise of the ember. Another group of nest-maids combined with a smaller group of owls wrote these hymns of praise. Owls who had once spent their days practicing their fighting skills with battle claws and ice swords were now painting and composing poetry. And young'uns were learning at astonishingly accelerated rates. Hatchlings rescued from forest fires were learning how to read almost before their flight feathers had fledged. Fritha, a Pygmy Owl, was well into a study of higher magnetics, reading texts that had stumped Otulissa when she was much older.

All this should have warmed Otulissa's gizzard. But she had felt a creeping dread. Because along with all this knowledge too many of the owls of the tree seemed to be growing more and more obsessed with the ember. The knowledge was not illuminating but seemed shadowed in a strange way — shadowed by the glow of the ember, if such a thing could be. This in itself was somewhat of a puzzle, a conundrum for Otulissa. For like all owls she valued the dark, the shadows. Darkness, the night, shades, and shadows had always been illuminating for owls. They did not fear the times when the moon dwenked to nothingness. They reveled in the long winter nights when the days shortened to mere hours. But now she was begining to think of shadows as dangerous things. She herself had begun to read deeply into philosophical texts about the meaning of light and the absence of light, of darkness in the world of owls.

From her perch in the hollow, she glanced about and caught sight of Eglantine peering with an intensely worried look at her best friend, Primrose, who had been asked for this ceremony to fly with a thimbleful of ashes shed by the ember. The little Pygmy Owl was doing a very good job of it as she turned and banked in a tight circle around the "en-hollowed" ember, casting its ashes in what Otulissa had heard was called the "flight path of Elevation." She had no idea what that meant. Every day there seemed to be a new ritual to be named, to be enacted, to be followed in service to the Ember of Hoole. *What does it all mean?* Otulissa thought. *Why have shadows become dangerous? Why is the world of owls being turned inside out?* She remembered how Soren and Gylfie had told her about the horrors of St. Aggie's, where owls were forced to sleep during the night and work during the day. St. Aggie's had been an inside-out world. Was that what was happening here at the tree? Her gizzard lurched fiercely.

Otulissa suddenly decided that this kind of contemplation and theorizing was impractical. She needed to think back and try to pinpoint when the changes had started. Even before the Band left she realized now that many of the owls had become very concerned about the well-being of the ember. Then, within nights of their leaving, Gemma had introduced the idea of moving the ember to a "safer" place where the watch that Coryn had appointed could better guard it. This suggestion did not seem all that unreasonable at the time. Coryn's hollow was small. Only so many owls could keep an eye on it. It was Elyan who had come up with the notion, despite

Coryn's orders that any guard should be representative of all the creatures of the tree, that, within the watch, there must be an "inner guard," an honor guard. Otulissa, Bubo, Eglantine, and Ruby had voted against this. Fleemus had abstained. But still the measure passed. Then all of a sudden they decided an honor guard wasn't good enough. There had to be an even higher level that had certain military powers, but not an army exactly: a militia that they called the Guardians of the Guardians of the Ember, or the GGE. The creation of the GGE had not been voted upon by parliament. It had just happened. No one was sure how, and now there was this Elevation! Elyan, Gemma, and Yeena, members of the militia through some complicated procedure, had been "Elevated." Otulissa, in reviewing the course of events, realized it had begun to accelerate with a visit from Trader Mags.

The magpie trader had discovered some new ruins of the Others and had arrived with a load of her cheap and tawdry gewgaws, including funny-looking hats that no owl could actually wear. One of these had become the "sacred ash bin" for the cold ashes scraped from the ember's container. Mags also had brought scraps of ermine that Madame Plonk immediately claimed. "Ceremonial, dear! Them's the robes of state," Mags kept saying. "Yes, I really lucked out this time. One of them queens or kings of the

Others had kept a stash in this place." Souvenirs from cor-
onations, from rituals of the Others' churches, piles of
cloth stitched with silver and gilt thread provided enough
to start yet another guild among the nest-maid snakes, a
fine embroidery and sewing guild. Mags had hired a dozen
helpers to transport all the loot. She had helpfully brought
along some pictures of a queen and her attendants as well
as many of the Others' church leaders all dressed up for
celebrations of their own Glaux, so that the owls of the
tree could see the costume and pomp of the Others.

Oh, how Otulissa rued the day Mags had arrived with
all this junk! What would that sweet-faced queen with her
kind blue eyes have thought of a bunch of owls flapping
through the air wearing all her royal trappings? *We're owls,
for Glaux's sake, not Others!* Again Otulissa clamped her beak
shut for fear the words might escape.

The procession was quite a spectacle. She saw a small
company of Northern Saw-whets and Pygmy swoop down
from above. On their heads the owls wore ivory thimbles,
like the one that Primrose had flown with. They depos-
ited the thimbles in a row near the ember. Some ashes
were poured into the thimbles. Near them was a set of
decorated teacups and some more ashes were placed in
these. Analysis of the ember's sparks and ashes had become
a favorite field of study for many owls, especially among the

GGE. A ritual had even been invented that involved the dusting of ashes on the wing tips of those owls about to be Elevated to the position of High Owls of the Ember. It was all just too ridiculous to even imagine owls doing. But the problem was someone had imagined it. And not just one owl, but several. Were they so bored in these times of peace and prosperity that their minds had turned to this senseless veneration, this worship of a coal? Of course Otulissa knew that it was no mere coal. Indeed, it was an ember that possessed great powers that could be used for good or for evil. That was the lesson of the legends. And it was true that one must be vigilant not to let a graymalkin get close, an owl like Nyra, to be precise. But nowhere did legends suggest anything more than vigilance. How had all this *veneration* come about? And so quickly? The Band and Coryn had barely been gone a moon cycle. How she wished they would come back soon. Then perhaps all this would end. But would it? Otulissa felt her gizzard tremble.

CHAPTER NINE

Coryn Sneaks Out

Luckily for Coryn, the hollow where he and the Band had settled was not that far from the Shadow Forest. And the winds had eased up. So he hoped he could make quick work of this. He would go back to the region near the pond where he had spent the better part of a winter after escaping from Nyra and the Pure Ones. It was there that he had first encountered the rabbit. As he flew in the broad light of day, he kept a sharp lookout for crows but so far had seen none. And as he approached the old fallen tree trunk where he had lived, he felt a flutter in his gizzard. Would the rabbit still be there? It seemed almost impossible that a rabbit in these woods thick with owls could have survived so long — even a mystic one. The scene was still so vivid in Coryn's mind. He had seen the plump, succulent rabbit, sitting perfectly still, as if transfixed, in front of a beautiful spiderweb. The rabbit was studying the designs in the web, "reading" them, he said. Their conversation came back to Coryn now.

"I'm a mystic of sorts," the rabbit had begun to explain when Coryn asked him what he was doing. "I see certain things where others don't."

"In a spiderweb?"

"Precisely. I'm a web reader."

But right now as Coryn flew across the pond, the rabbit was nowhere in sight. Coryn spent several hours scouring the surrounding region. He knew time was running out. To fly back to the hollow in the fir tree in Silverveil he would now have to fly against the rising wind. The Band would be worried, possibly furious. The sun was sinking fast. He knew he could not spend any more time. He made one more circle around the pond. Still no sign of the rabbit. So he climbed high above the forest, turned toward Silverveil, and flew on.

He had not been flying long when he picked up a raucous din on the edges of the wind. *By Glaux, that sounds like a grog tree.* Soren had told him that grog trees had begun to reappear in the Southern Kingdoms shortly after the Battle of the Burning in the canyonlands. He had never been to one and he thought this might just be the time. What better place to pick up gossip? But would he be recognized? Most assuredly so. The scar that slashed across his face was a mirror image of Nyra's. They knew that he was not Nyra, but they also knew that he was a king and the inheritor of the ember. *Gadfeathers!* The word exploded in his brain and sent his gizzard into a tizzy. Hadn't Soren also said that gadfeathers were returning? Maybe he could disguise himself!

Gadfeathers, known for their singing as well as their garish ways, festooned themselves with all manner of discarded feathers from other birds, twigs, strands of ivy — whatever was available. *But what if they ask me to sing?* Coryn blinked. He had no idea if he could sing. He wasn't a Snowy or a Boreal Owl, who were known for their fine voices. He supposed he could try. The whole idea was a bit overwhelming. Then a strange quiver moved through his gizzard as he remembered that in the last of the legends, King Hoole had gone in gadfeather disguise.

He alighted in an oak tree overgrown with lovely ever-ivy, a variety that stayed green year round. He could drape some over his head to disguise the scar. There were even some scarlet winter berries growing on a vine as well. But could he sing? He shut his eyes tight and tried to remember one of the old songs from the legends that the Snow Rose, a very famous gadfeather, had sung. It was about wandering and freedom and might appeal to the crowd at a grog tree. He tried a few lines of the song.

> *I'll find a feather for your ruff,*
> *fly away with me till dawn.*

Fly away then we'll be gone,
Hollows we shall leave behind,
fly to places they'll never find.

For a Barn Owl, he didn't sound all that bad. Granted, he was no Madame Plonk — but he wasn't a total disaster either. *Well, here goes,* he thought as he tore off a length of ivy and draped it across his face and tucked bright red winter berry twiglets into his tail feathers. He launched himself off the oak branch, feeling ridiculous but resolved, and headed toward the grog tree. The north side of the tree, a sycamore with dozens of low-spreading limbs, was vacant. All the owls had congregated in the lower branches on the south side of the tree. He soon saw why. Sparkling in the setting sun were the bright and gaudy wares of none other than Trader Mags. She had spread her goods on a deep purple velvet cloak. "Oh, yes, dearie," he heard her saying, "this here represents my new discovery. Bubbles, go fetch them ermine trimmings like I sold Madame Plonk."

"Oh, Madame Plonk bought some of these?" Coryn heard an owl ask. Madame Plonk was known throughout the owl kingdom not only for her magnificent voice but for her glamour.

"Yes, darlin', and this purple cloth with the tufts of ermine would look fabulous on you."

"She's getting on — ain't she now? I'm surprised she can haul this stuff around on her back while she sings."

"She ain't as young as you, darlin'." Trader Mags was loathe to bad-beak her most devoted client. "She mostly wears it in her apartment for high tea. Speaking of which, some time ago I sold her my last coronation teacup. But I might have a line on where I can get another."

Coryn hid in the shadows of the tree. He had a perfect view of the goods and it was not the "gewgaws," as Otulissa called Trader Mags's glittery wares, that attracted him but a tattered old book off to one side. The cover was made from lemming skins. There was only one place where lemmings lived and that was in the Northern Kingdoms, or the N'yrthghar, as it had once been called. On the front of the book an odd design had been etched. Coryn's gizzard grew still and then twisted violently. It was the image of a strange bird — a cross between an owl and a puffin. A puffowl! The result of a monstrous experiment — the creation of that supreme hagsfiend — Kreeth. That was her book! *The Book of Kreeth!*

CHAPTER TEN

The Nature of Hagsfiends Is Discussed

Look, I know you are all angry with me for sneaking off," Coryn turned his head and looked slyly at the Band, "but it isn't as if I invented sneaking off. Didn't I spend my first day of this expedition listening to stories about the four of you sneaking off from the great tree?"

"Point well made," Soren conceded.

"But why? Why did you do this and leave us all worried to death?" Gylfie pressed. "You're not just any owl, Coryn. You are the king."

"Yes, exactly. I am not just any owl." He hesitated. "But it had nothing to do with my being king."

Soren suddenly wilfed and felt an alarming tremor in his gizzard. *He's not going to tell them . . . is he?* At that moment Coryn seemed to almost read Soren's mind and spun his head toward his uncle. "They have to know, Soren. It's time."

"Have to know what? Time for what?" Digger asked. Digger, Twilight, and Gylfie nervously exchanged glances.

Soren closed his eyes and tried to still his gizzard. Perhaps Coryn was right. Perhaps they did have to know, and maybe bringing it out in the open would lessen Coryn's obsession with his mother.

"I think my mother, Nyra, is a hagsfiend."

Digger, Twilight, and Gylfie wilfed. Even burly Twilight was a mere misty shadow of his former self. "That can't be true," he whispered hoarsely.

Soren stepped forward. He had to say something.

"Don't deny it, Soren!" Coryn said. There was a sharpness in his voice that the others had never heard before.

"It's not a question of denying. We have no proof — only suspicions. It is more complicated than Coryn suggests," Soren spoke softly.

"I am sure it is," Digger said. Digger was the most philosophical of the Band. He did not accept the surface meaning of things but, as his name suggested, seemed compelled to dig deeper to find an unexpected truth.

"If Nyra's a hagsfiend, then you . . . well, look, you either are or you aren't!" snapped Twilight. Then suddenly the Great Gray was taken aback by his own words. "I mean, it's not like we don't like you."

"Oh, shut up, Twilight!" Digger barked in a most unphilosophical tone of voice.

"I'm only saying it's action not words that count. And Coryn doesn't act haggish."

Digger blinked. "Why, Twilight. That's an astounding insight. I couldn't have said it better myself."

"Well, then quit telling me to shut up. I said it in half the words you would have used, Digger."

"But is there more, Coryn?" Digger added.

"Tell them," Soren said in a quiet voice that he hoped belied his desperation.

"The nature of hagsfiends as we know them has changed over hundreds and thousands of years. Most of us in this modern age have had an encounter with one, but they are powerless wisps that appear but rarely, usually when we are flying and are extremely tired. They are the crows of the night, which makes some kind of sense, since it was originally proposed that they were some sort of mistake of natural history appearing millions of years ago when birds first separated into different species — a mishmash of things that never quite sorted itself out. In the ancient times of nachtmagen, they were quite dangerous."

Soren coughed. "If I might interrupt. That is precisely my point. This is a different era. There is no evidence that

Nyra is anything more than a bad, evil owl. My own brother, your father, Kludd, was a bad, evil owl."

"But my mother's face is monstrously large, unusually large for a Barn Owl, and so is mine."

"It is not faces, not color, not appearances that matter. That was the essence of the Pure Ones' stupidity. They believed that Barn Owls were a superior species of owls. Such reasoning discounted everything else," Soren said fiercely.

Coryn now blinked his eyes tightly shut for several seconds. "All right. I will agree with you that there is no evidence. And until now, or at least very recently, I was wrongly obsessed with my identity. Had I inherited this terrible legacy? It haunted me constantly. I realize now that was wrong of me. It was self-indulgent and inappropriate for a leader, let alone a king. But there is something else that I discovered when I sneaked off."

Soren's gizzard had just started to settle down, but a new turmoil now roiled within in it. "What is it?" he said. Dread seemed to tremble on the edge of those three simple words.

"There is a book. It is in the possession of Trader Mags."

"Yes, and what is the book?" Gylfie said slowly.

"On its cover is a design."

"A design of what, for Glaux's sake?" Twilight fumed.

"A puffowl."

The four members of the Band were suddenly struck dumb.

"Listen to me carefully, now," Coryn said.

Soren blinked and looked at his nephew. *This is a king speaking. Not a self-absorbed young owl having an identity crisis.*

"We know from reading the legends that Kreeth died in that last battle, in the battle for the Ice Palace. Duncan MacDuncan, the wolf, killed her. We know that she never mated. Never had offspring. Therefore her line of hags-fiends died out. But we all know that ideas, good or evil, have longer lives than we mere mortals. It is proven by our libraries, and the libraries at the Palace of Mists. And so this book in which Kreeth wrote her formulas and her fiendish thoughts exists and has existed throughout the centuries." Coryn paused. He saw a mixture of fear and confusion in the four owls' eyes. "I would have tried to bargain for it. But it's a big book. And I didn't have my botkin. There was no way I could have carried it by myself."

"But it's just words," Twilight said defiantly.

"Words, as you well know, can be powerful," Digger replied. "What are you getting at, Coryn?"

"You are right. If Kreeth's words have managed to

survive all these years, even if this book had remained unknown, hidden away, lost, might not some monstrous remnant of her experiments survived in some form or another? And now that the ember has been retrieved we all know that with it comes the possibility for good magic and bad, or nachtmagen. Yes, those hagsfiends that we have all encountered like wisps from a bad dream are impotent. However, they are but one form. Now that the ember is back, there is the possibility that nachtmagen will strengthen these impotent, powerless hagsfiends."

Especially, Soren thought, *if they had the book of the arch hagsfiend, Kreeth.*

"So you are saying that Nyra could be transformed — if indeed she lives." Soren looked hard at his nephew.

"Wasn't she bad enough already?" Twilight asked.

"Maybe," Coryn said, "haggishness is like a disease, which lies dormant for years upon years and when the conditions are right begins to flourish again."

Flourish, thought Soren. He was beginning to despise the word. The great tree now so often called the Golden Tree was said to flourish magnificently. But when Soren thought of those shimmering limbs with their sparkling leaves, he imagined them reaching up to and piercing the ether veil of the owl universe.

Oh, how Soren longed for the days when the Golden Tree was just the great tree. Was that wrong? Was it treasonous to think this way? The world had seemed so dangerous back then. But it was a danger one could see. Pure Ones were Pure Ones. Flecks were flecks. St. Aggie's thugs were ... well ... St. Aggie's thugs. You knew who the enemy was. You had an idea of where it might lurk. But this was entirely different. Nyra was not really the enemy. She was merely an agent, the instrument through which an ancient kind of evil, nachtmagen, could be made possible. Nachtmagen itself was the enemy, and how could you fight that?

CHAPTER ELEVEN
The Ether Veil

Soren flew in a luminous golden light. He felt his white face gilded by it, and when he looked down he saw that his white-feathered legs appeared to have been dipped in gold. At that moment he noticed a tiny silver glint like a minuscule fracture in the golden light all about him. He felt his gizzard freeze. His wings grow heavy. *A slit! A tiny slit in the ether veil.* Then he saw another and another. The slits widened, the tips of haggish black feathers began to push through. Suddenly, the golden light bristled with black points. *This is not budging. This is not the same as when our primaries begin to emerge. This is the ether veil shredding!* "Don't wait for me!" a familiar voice screamed. "I am beyond all help! Go! Go! They're back!"

Who? Who is that screaming in my dream? Soren thought. Then, *I am going yeep. Yeep in my own dream. The owl world dies!*

"Soren, wake up! Wake up!" Gylfie was flying up and down in front of his face and batting the air with her tiny wings trying to bring him out of his dream. *How many times have I done this?* she thought. But since he was known to have starsight, Soren and his dreams were not to be ignored. The owls were now all awake. Gylfie turned to them as she continued to fan Soren with her wings. "Bad dream."

"Uh-oh!" Twilight said. He shook his head violently, spinning it this way and that, as if to clear his head of grogginess. "Like we haven't had enough bad news already."

"Just put a mouse in it, Twilight." Gylfie scowled. Then she turned to Soren. "You awake now?"

"Yes." Although as was usually the case he could not remember any details of the dream. "We have to find that book." This was the only thing he could say.

"Where do we start?" Digger asked.

"Find Trader Mags, of course," Coryn said.

"She doesn't like visitors," Gylfie said. "She always thinks they're trying to get a discount."

"Yeah, well, she adds on such a huge transport charge. It's ridiculous," Twilight huffed.

"Is she still in that chapel ruin?" Digger asked.

"I would imagine so," Soren replied. "What time is it now?" he said, peering out of the hollow. The sun flared red through the trees.

"Still a while until tween time and then another half hour till First Black."

Soren peered out. "We'll go at First Lavender."

Owls were keenly aware of every shade in the changing spectrum of a rising and setting sun for each season of the year. Tween time was the last drop of sun before first shadows of twilight, which at this time of year were a frail lavender color. The owls waited impatiently in silence as they watched the sun set.

"All right!" Soren said. "We're off."

Five owls flew out of the fir tree hollow, Soren with Coryn at his side. As soon as they were clear of the tree they rearranged themselves into a tightly packed formation. Twilight flew point, Coryn to starboard, Soren to port, Digger flew tail position, and Gylfie was in the center. Twilight was always the lead owl in conditions of dramatically changing light. He had an extraordinary ability to see in that silvery border between day and night — at twilight when the boundaries became dim and the very shapes of things seemed to melt away.

Coryn could not help but think how different this was from their flight across the Sea of Hoolemere when they had told wet poop jokes, laughed, and even sung. *It's all so different now*, Coryn thought. How horrible to think that the terrible book was in the same world as they were. What was happening? He was king, but how could he fight hagsfiends or whatever monstrosities had slipped through the ether veil? He knew in his gizzard that was what Soren had dreamed of. It must have been a terrible dream. Why, he wondered, had this not happened when Hoole was king? Had he, Coryn, done something wrong? Was it because he was the child of Nyra and Kludd? All these thoughts ran through Coryn's head as they flew on toward the chapel of Trader Mags.

CHAPTER TWELVE
A Visit with Trader Mags

B ook? What book? You know I deal with so many arti-cles. I got me a large inventory these days, Soren, dearie."

Twilight stepped forward, his plumage bristling so much that he seemed to swell to half again his normal size. "Drop the dearies, sweetheart. We know you ain't no scholar. You don't get that many books running through this outfit of yours."

"Oh, beggin' your pardon, sir." Bubbles, a smaller mag-pie, lighted down on the stone floor next to her boss. "Them books don't run. Don't fly, neither. No, they more or less flutter. Their pages, that is."

"Shut your frinkin' beak!" Trader Mags' shrill squawk echoed through the chapel, rousing the last clutch of snoozing bats from the rafters. Soren felt a slight tremor pass through his gizzard. Ever since that one bloody night in St. Aggie's long before his flight feathers had fledged, the sight of bats had made him feel weak. The owls of St. Aggie's had a savage practice in which they would summon flocks of vampire bats to suck the blood from young owls on the brink of fledging. The bats would take just enough blood to quell the owls' desire to fly. Now Soren, Twilight, and Trader Mags, purveyor of fine goods, stood in a pool of crimson light reflected from the remains of a rose-colored stained-glass window through which the moon shined. The light, the leathery flap of the bats' wings transported him back to that bloody night so long ago. He shook his head. His patience with Mags was wearing thin.

"Look, Mags, enough of this. We know you had the book. It was reported seen at a grog tree."

"By a slipgizzle?" she said in a more timid voice now.

"Precisely," Digger said, walking forward on his long featherless legs. "A slipgizzle of the king's."

"Oh, I see," Trader Mags said primly, and readjusted the jaunty bandanna that covered one eye.

The king perched, unnoticed, in a shadowy corner of the chapel.

"Yes," she said, sighing, "there was a book. Big old thing despite the fact that some of its pages were missing. An old soldier, I think, wanted it. He had to carry it off in a botkin." Coryn felt a twinge in his gizzard. *Soldier? What soldier?*

"What soldier?" Soren said aloud, echoing Coryn's thoughts.

"Well, soldier or hireclaw, not sure. But hireclaw most likely," Mags replied.

"What did he look like?" Twilight asked.

Mags hesitated. Twilight swelled now until he looked like a feathery cloud-streaked moon rolled down from the sky. "C'mon! C'mon! Make it snappy."

Any trace of composure Trader Mags possessed now vanished. Her beak began clacking nervously. "I c-c-can't say. I can't say," she stammered.

"Can't or won't?" Twilight said sharply.

Mags wheeled around to Soren and looked at him beseechingly with her tiny, piercing black eyes. Soren remained impassive. In a flash, Twilight tore off the bandanna. The owls gasped. A bald spot in the magnificent glistening black plumage was revealed. Trader Mags shrieked.

"Cover her up. Give her back the bandanna! For Glaux's sake," Soren ordered.

"Don't be such a thug, Twilight," Gylfie scolded.

"We need some answers here," Twilight shot back.

"Oh, that hireclaw, he was a thug all right," Trader Mags muttered.

"Oh, ma'am, I be so sorry," Bubbles broke in, gushing with sympathy. "Never knew you got the feather blight. And on your head! How unfortunate," she said, picking up the bandanna to give to her boss.

"Better bald than brainless, you twit!" Trader Mags lashed out at the smaller magpie with one wing and swatted her across the floor. She then turned to Soren. "He didn't give a name. I can only tell you that he was an unusually large Barn Owl."

Coryn felt a turbulence mounting in his gizzard. "Any distinguishing characteristics? Marks?" *Don't say it! Don't say it!* he thought.

"Yes, as a matter of fact. A large nick out of his beak."

She had said it. She might as well have shouted his name out loud. *Stryker!* One of Nyra's top lieutenants. Lieutenant Major Stryker of the Pure Ones, and he had received that wound in the Battle of the Burning. Trader Mags, of course, did not know his name or much else about him aside from the nick in his beak.

"I don't know," she said repeatedly to each question as it was asked. "I don't know where he flew in from. . . . No, Gylfie, no idea where he was going."

"Did he talk much?"

"Not really."

"Did he know Krakish?" Digger asked.

"What in hagsmire is Krakish?" Trader Mags asked.

"The language of the Northern Kingdoms," Soren replied.

"I don't know if he knew it," she paused. "But . . ."

"But what?" Twilight pressed.

She looked at him nastily. Then spat the words out. "He didn't have to know much freakish."

"Krakish," Gylfie corrected. "Why not?"

"'Cause there wasn't many words in that book. Mostly pictures. Worst, ugliest pictures you ever seen. To tell the truth, I was glad to get rid of the frinkin' thing."

"Well." Soren sighed, realizing that getting more information was a lost cause. "You've been most helpful, Mags. I'm sorry about the bandanna." She had retied it on her head and looked up beseechingly. "You won't go telling now about me bald spot, will ya, Soren? It'd just tear me up somethin' fierce."

"No, of course not."

"You know, Mags, if you took off that bandanna some of the time and let the air get at it, your feathers might come back," Gylfie offered.

"I'm attached to it," she said without a trace of sentiment in her voice, and looked furiously at Twilight with her beady black eyes. Then she turned to the others. "Are you sure I can't interest you in something? You know, I found this new site. And I got me some lovely porcelain things back in the sacristy. Bubbles, go fetch them demitasse cups."

Soren felt obliged to at least look at the wares after having caused her so much trouble and embarrassment. Maybe he could bring back a present for the three Bs, as his chicks were sometimes called. They were always wanting presents when he came back from hunting. It seemed like just bringing in a vole was not quite sufficient these days. Bubbles arrived with a botkin, and Mags drew from it several little cups.

"They ain't teacups exactly. They calls them demitasses. At least, so Madame Plonk tells me. Now, mind you, they ain't as big and as fancy as that lovely coronation teacup of Madame Plonk's. But they be awfully pretty. So dainty, ain't they?"

Soren could imagine Basha, Blythe, and Bell eating dried caterpillars out of them. "What'll you take for them?" he asked.

"Oh, let's see. I've had a hankering for some yoick

stones." Yoick stones were small rocks with traces of both gold and silver that could be smashed by a Rogue smith and then fired to release the silver and gold, even though it was an inferior grade of these two metals.

"Don't have any," Soren said. "How about a fine rabbit skin?"

"Perhaps."

"Digger, will you get the botkin with the skin?

Digger went out, returning quickly, and spread the skin on the stone floor.

"Killed him myself," Twilight said.

"I don't doubt it," Mags said as she carefully stepped around the skin, examining it.

"It was an artistic kill if I do say so." Twilight's voice brimmed with pride.

Trader Mags stopped in her tracks. "There ain't no such thing, you brute, as an artistic kill!" She then looked up at Soren. "I'll take it."

So the deal was made and the owls were off. The night was still long. "I'd say," Digger began, "that you, Twilight, are not high on Trader Mags' list of favorite creatures."

"That's the least of our problems," Gylfie said. "Where in the world are we going to find this owl with the book? We don't even know his name."

"His name is Stryker and he was my mother's top lieutenant."

"Our worst fear," Gylfie moaned.

"Not exactly," Coryn said cryptically. The other four owls spun their heads to look at Coryn. "Our worst fear is a half-made hagsfiend with a book on how to finish the job."

"But the book," Digger said. "What little we know from reading the legends did not tell how to make a hagsfiend but how to create new monsters. Hagsfiends were born, not made."

Now all the owls peered at Digger. "That is small comfort, Digger!" Gylfie said. "A monster? A hagsfiend? Not exactly delightful company."

"Words, just words," muttered Twilight.

"Quit squabbling!" Coryn barked. He was trying to think how they might find Stryker. Where he might be. For a long time, the Pure Ones had been encamped in the canyonlands. But they had been routed by war and must have moved by now. If he could get some coals from a Rogue smith's forge they could kindle a fire. Just a small one that might yield a few hints as to where the old lieutenant might be. But Coryn knew from past experience that his firesight never seemed to work very well when he sought specific answers. The images were often vague and confusing. The flames did not like to be forced. They yielded what they would at their own whim and not on demand. As he was thinking about this, he caught a glimpse of something sparkling beneath them. Like diamonds strung through winter grass, a spiderweb hung in the night. And then a rapid heartbeat. *The rabbit!*

CHAPTER THIRTEEN

The Coronation Teacup

Otulissa had been busy in the library for at least half the day and had not yet slept. As she flew back to her hollow through the strands of golden milkberry vines and heard the soft susurrus of stirring leaves, she thought how wrong all this felt. *It's the time of the white rain, for Glaux's sake. It's winter. Winter everyplace but here,* she thought miserably. The golden strands should be withered and white. The berries should be shriveled and even whiter and there should be no leaves. The tree should loom dark, stripped of the splendors of summer or autumn. That was the way it was supposed to be. Was she the only owl feeling this way, she wondered. She was pretty sure that Soren's mate was not all that pleased with this perpetual summer. But of course, Pelli was so busy with her three owlets she barely had time to worry. *Fine thing, Soren going off like that just when the Bs were about to learn how to fly! Males!* She'd never mate. *Well,* she thought, *one should never say never.* She felt a little squeeze in her gizzard as she thought of Cleve. A gizzard squeeze was the closest an owl came to blushing.

Cleve was a dear friend whom she had met in the Northern Kingdoms. He lived at the Glauxian retreat on the island in the Bitter Sea. He was a healer and was continuing his study of medicine. So far he had not taken vows. *I'll smack him if he does!* Otulissa thought. *Cancel that! What a terrible thing to even think of dear Cleve.* But she knew that if they mated, there would be a mess of hatchlings, and guess who would get stuck taking care of them? Otulissa wasn't really mother material. She loved young-'uns. But how could she raise chicks in a proper manner, head up the Ga'Hoology chaw, fly weather and colliering, teach the history of the tree, and give special seminars in higher magnetics, all on her own? She was one of the busiest rybs in the entire tree. No, it was out of the question.

But then she returned to her original question: Was she the only one disturbed by the unchanging nature of the tree, this so-called Golden Tree that seemed condemned to a perpetual summer, that shed very few of its leaves? And those leaves that did drop left behind odd golden traceries like some sort of scroom. *A scroom tree?* she wondered. Taking one more look at the branches of the tree before she entered her own hollow, she thought for perhaps the thousandth time how peculiar everything felt.

She was fairly sure that Eglantine didn't think things were normal. And Eglantine had hemmed and hawed and not yet given an answer about participating in one of the endless rituals that the GGE was always dreaming up. But Primrose, Eglantine's best friend, seemed most enthralled with all the ceremonies and had agreed to become an acolyte at the altar of the ashes that were collected from the ember.

Otulissa alighted on the branch outside her hollow. There was a cross fire of brilliance that almost hurt her eyes as the midday sun reflected off the golden vines and limbs of the tree. Years before they would have called this a perfect late-summer day — the milkberries approaching the copper rose color of early fall would indeed have a special luminosity on a day like this. Owls would even get up from their daytime sleep for a glimpse of such splendor. But now it did not seem splendid. Too much of a good thing and, alas, even beauty becomes quite ordinary. *Even vulgar. Yes, vulgar. The tree is vulgar.* Otulissa sniffed. "Vulgar" was one of her favorite words. Tawdry, vulgar, coarse, gaudy, ostentatious, flashy — like Madame Plonk. Madame Plonk was all of those words.

"Oh, great Glaux, Madame Plonk! You scared the living nightlights out of me!" Otulissa gasped as the Great Snowy entered her hollow. Indeed, none other than Madame

Plonk perched just inside Otulissa's hollow. She looked in all her frippery about as out of place among Otulissa's simple furnishings — books, maps, and such — as golden milkberries in winter.

"I know we've had our differences but . . ." Madame Plonk began.

"We *are* different." Otulissa blinked. There was no owl who could be more different from herself than Madame Plonk. Right now, however, Otulissa had to admit she had never seen Madame Plonk look so sad — indeed, devastated. "Whatever is the problem, Madame Plonk?" And she was tempted to add, *How could I ever help you with any problem you might have?*

"It's my teacup." Madame Plonk's eyes welled up with tears.

"Your teacup?" Otulissa was bewildered. *What in Glaux's name is she talking about?* And the way she was scratching her breast with one talon suggested that her teacup was some vital organ that had begun to act up. "Madame Plonk, I am not quite following you. Your teacup?"

"My coronation teacup. I've had it for years." She sobbed and collapsed now from the guest perch into a small mountain of white feathers.

"Pull yourself together, Madame Plonk. This is most unseemly. Get a grip!"

The Snowy picked up her large head. "You don't remember? You helped me read the numbers and the name. I'm not as smart as you and you were so kind."

Aahh, the pellet drops! Otulissa thought. but did not say so out loud. It was a crude expression for finally remembering something. She did remember the teacup now. It was another gewgaw that Plonk had gotten from Trader Mags. Yes, there was a picture of a female Other wearing a crown gazing out with great dignity, a dignity that far exceeded anything Madame Plonk could ever aspire to. And there were numbers. "One-nine-five-three. Yes, of course."

"Queen E, you remember?"

"Yes, I can't imagine why anyone would give a one-letter name to a queen. One must assume the rest of the letters were worn away though time. So what is the problem?"

The very question threw Madame Plonk into a new fit of sobs. She was beating her wings now on the floor of the hollow. To Otulissa, she seemed like an actress who was enjoying her own performance a bit too much. But then again, there was something rather gizzard-rending when she began to speak. "You cannot imagine how, over all these years as the dark fades from the day, after I have sung 'Night Is Done' and all the owls go to rest, how wonderful it is to settle on the branch just outside my hollow with my coronation cup filled with milkberry tea. So restorative to not only the voice but the spirits. I watch the sun creep up over the horizon."

Great Glaux, she's waxing absolutely poetic! Otulissa thought as Madame Plonk wiped away a tear.

"And now would you believe it?"

"Believe what, Madame Plonk?" Otulissa said gently.

"They want, no, they demand, my coronation teacup."

She flopped down again with a huge sob. *Great Glaux in glaumora, what am I going to do with this ... this ... thing?* Otulissa thought as she regarded the heaving heap of white fluff. She sighed deeply and then spoke calmly. "Who precisely wants the teacup?"

Madame Plonk raised her head and said crossly, "Not just any teacup, the coronation teacup of Queen E."

"All right, who wants the coronation teacup of Queen E, and why?"

"The acolytes of the altar."

"Oh, racdrops!" Otulissa exploded. "Whatever for?"

"The sacred ashes of the ember."

"Oh, now they've really gone too far," Otulissa said. And apparently they truly had, for Madame Plonk, who had enjoyed until now all the ridiculous vulgar ritual of what was being called the "cult of the ember," was fed up.

Otulissa spoke briskly. "I don't know when this

stupidity will end, but surely Primrose could help you out. She's an acolyte, isn't she?"

"She is, but she is . . . I don't know how to put it. . . . She is really enjoying being one. She's changed. Even Eglantine says so. And you know she's writing plays now."

"Yes, I heard that. I heard that she's quite good."

"Yes, odd, isn't it? All of us in some way have been able to do so much more. Why, I never thought that I could ever reach those high notes in the moonlight cantata with hardly taking a breath but since the ember arrived I can." She paused and raised her head. Her yellow eyes turned hard. "BUT I DON'T WANT TO DO THIS! I WON'T GIVE UP MY CORONATION TEACUP."

"But what can I do about it, Madame Plonk?"

"Hide it, please, Otulissa. No one would ever suspect that such a rare and beautiful thing would be kept here." She looked about the spare hollow not so much with disdain as pity.

Otulissa would never know quite what made her agree to take the teacup, but she did. Perhaps it was just the wrongness of the tree and the stupidity of all this ritual. What, indeed, gave these idiot owls the right to commandeer personal possessions for their ridiculous rituals? Acolytes of the ashes! And that Primrose, a very sensible owl, a responsible member of the search-and-rescue chaw, had bought into it! *Well, I shall have a very serious talk with her*, Otulissa thought. But then she thought again. She knew she wouldn't. Teacups might be hidden, but words could be overheard, could leak out, and she had noticed that for the first time in all the years she had been at the Great Ga'Hoole Tree, the owls in this golden era had become more guarded. They were frightened to say what they really thought. Indeed, what was considered a great flourishing of the Golden Tree could be the beginning of its death. How she longed for a true season of white rain, when the berries would turn the color of dried bones and the tree, leafless, would look grim and dignified with its dark limbs spreading like a black skeleton against a wintry sky.

CHAPTER FOURTEEN
The Rabbit at Last

Coryn motioned to the Band to hold back and remain on the limb where they had just lighted down while he settled silently on the ground near the rabbit. In a pool of moonlight, it stood seemingly frozen in front of a spiderweb. As rabbits went, this was not an especially impressive one. Small of stature, with an undistinguished brownish-gray pelt, it was completely unremarkable except for the white crescent on its forehead. This, in fact, was the signifying mark of a web reader, a mystic rabbit who could read in the webs of spiders "tidings," as the rabbit called them, from the present, the future, and the past. But the information was most often incomplete and vague. It came in fragments, the rabbit had explained to Coryn, much like the pieces of a puzzle.

There was no greeting, and the rabbit did not deflect its gaze from the web. It merely took up as if there had been no interruption between that first time it had met

Coryn and now. "A dark feather, ashes, bone. Is it now? Was it then? Or is it yet to come?"

Coryn knew better than to ask a specific question. If he did, the rabbit would give him a very confusing answer. But he could not help it. "Is it something about me?"

The rabbit finally turned slowly toward him. "Me . . . me . . . me. Aaah, youth! Even with kings, it's all about me, me, me."

The four other owls fluttered down and stood in a circle around the rabbit. "I wish I could help you more. You're looking for her, aren't you?" Nyra's name did not need to be mentioned. All five owls nodded. "And I can only come up with these three things — a dark feather, ashes, and bone. Coryn has explained to you that I can only offer pieces. I cannot put the puzzle together. And these pieces are very difficult. I am not sure if they are real or just . . . confusing!" the rabbit exclaimed. "What I see in the web is either a wisp or a whisper."

"You can *see* a whisper?" asked Twilight.

"Shhh," said Digger. "You're being too literal."

"If it's a wisp, it is just an escaped thread from a dream. But if it is a whisper, well, it might be real. What I am seeing has the — how should I put it? — the cloudiness of a dream, but there is also an echo."

"Do whispers have echoes?" Twilight asked.

"I asked myself the same question. One does not think of whispers as having echoes. Does one?" The five owls shook their heads. "Unless that is a whisper in a cave."

It was as if a bolt of lightning had shot through Coryn's gizzard. "Bones! Feather! Ashes! Cave! She's in a cave!"

"There are a lot of caves, Coryn," Gylfie said softly.

"No, not just any cave. *The* cave."

The four other owls exchanged skeptical glances.

"The cave of my father's Final ceremony in the canyonlands. She wants his bones, or rather the ashes of his burned bones!"

"Great Glaux!" Digger blurted. "Ashes from a Final ceremony. Kreeth lusted for them. They were a most powerful ingredient for her monstrous experiments."

Twilight had grown very still. He looked toward Coryn. The moonlight glanced off his head, turning his gray feathers silvery. "The cave," he said quietly, "the cave where I killed Kludd in the Battle of the Burning, is that where they had the Marking?" The Final ceremony for a fallen leader was called the Marking.

Coryn nodded. "They had guarded his body day and night so scavengers wouldn't get it and then when there were only bones, they burned them."

"That is odd," Soren said. "For a Final ceremony most owls burn the entire body. Why wait for the bones?"

Coryn opened his eyes wide at his uncle's question and then blinked. Blinked not in surprise but with a strange knowingness. Soren felt a quiver pass through his gizzard. "As I told you before we left, Soren, my mother had a fondness for peculiar rituals, rituals of violence and blood that have roots in a haggish legacy. We know from the legends the power of ashes from bones."

"But she hadn't read the legends," Gylfie said. There was a note of quiet despair in her voice.

"She didn't need to. She *felt* them," Coryn replied evenly.

"So," the rabbit said, turning to the spiderweb again, "it is not a wisp, but a whisper."

"It's real." Twilight said. "Let's fly!"

And as the five owls lofted themselves into the winter night, Twilight had but one thought: *I killed him once. If she conjures him up I'll kill him again . . . and Nyra, too!*

In a distant cave in the canyonlands, an owl hunched over a book. The night was almost moonless; only a thin sliver hung in the sky. But it seemed that the rest of that moon had come down to Earth and sought refuge in this cave, for in the darkness a face like a glistening orb appeared suspended, its surface slashed and cratered with battle wounds.

"I haven't given up on the ember, Stryker," she told her lieutenant. "I was hatched on the night of an eclipse, as was my son, Nyroc." *Never, never shall I call him Coryn,* she silently swore. The years had not done Nyra any favors. Once considered a great beauty, a magnificent specimen of a *Tyto alba,* the loveliest of all Barn Owls, at least as far as the Pure Ones were concerned, she had not weathered well. Her dark eyes had lost their luster. The scar that ran diagonally down her face, a wound from long ago, had widened, leaving an ugly red slash. The unique heart shape of a Barn Owl's face was perhaps its most alluring feature. The contours of the heart usually fringed in short tawny golden feathers had darkened on Nyra's face to a deep muddy brown and grown shaggy, blurring the elegance of the heart shape. In several places, her feathers had grown thin, revealing unsightly patches of skin.

She now looked up at Stryker as if expecting a response. "Yes, General Mam, I know that. I was there — well, not when you were hatched — but I remember quite well the eclipse when Nyroc hatched!"

"And do you know the significance of being born on the night of an eclipse?" Stryker, though no mental giant of a bird, was a survivor, and he knew how to play the game to jolly the General Mam. He knew that she was eager to impart some tidbit of profound knowledge. Ever since he had gotten the book for her she had spent long days studying rather than sleeping. "Well, I'll tell you." She sighed happily. Indeed, this was the happiest he had seen Nyra in a long time. Most of the Pure Ones were dead or gone. Some fled to the Northern Kingdoms—they thought they would be safer in those vast ice-shrouded regions of glaciers and endless winter. Some had vanished into the Beyond and still others had hoped simply to start over, and never to hear the words "Pure Ones" again. In all, there were only five of the original Pure Ones left: Nyra, Stryker, Wortmore, Spyke, and Gebbles.

And there was a new recruit. Hardly a young one and not a Barn Owl, but an ancient Whiskered Screech from the Northern Kingdoms — Ifghar. He claimed that he was the brother of the legendary Ezylryb and he arrived with a Kielian snake named Gragg who, if he could be kept off the bingle juice, was fairly intelligent. They were both frightfully old. Ifghar could barely fly. But they knew war. They knew about fighting, and most important, they knew about ice weapons. The Guardians of Ga'Hoole had won the great battle in the canyonlands, the Battle of the Burning, often called the Battle of Fire and Ice because of the ice weapons that came with the reinforcement troops from the Northern Kingdoms. Since then, they had improved their skills with these weapons and sent regular expeditions to harvest new ones. Stryker hoped this Ifghar and his snake would sooner or later prove useful.

"Let me tell you about the significance of an eclipse." Nyra cocked her head and began to speak in an almost professorial manner. "You see, dear Stryker, when an owl hatches on the night of a lunar eclipse an enchantment can be cast on that creature, a charm that gives that creature unusual powers. Hoole, considered by some the first great king, was hatched on such a night, as was I and my son, Nyroc. An eclipse is coming and with this book that you fetched for me, well . . . I think I can accomplish great things."

"Capture the ember?"

"No, you fool, re-create a creature already hatched. Except I shall make him better this time . . . much better. . . ." Her dull eyes began to glisten ever so slightly, as if deep within them a spark that had long lain dormant had been rekindled.

CHAPTER FIFTEEN

The First Prisoner

Otulissa looked through the bars of the hollow. It was all so unbelievable. A prison at the Great Ga'Hoole Tree! And she, Otulissa, was the first prisoner! She gazed out the window at the wintry sky. It was just First Lavender and in the distance she could see three tiny specks and then a larger one. Her breath caught. It was Pelli and her chicks, Basha, Blythe, and Bell. It was their First Flight ceremony. Otulissa could tell by the configurations they were flying. But why would they be doing it before tween time at First Lavender? How odd. It wasn't as if there were a danger of crows out here on the island. Crows rarely flew across the Sea of Hoolemere. They hated salt water, almost as much as the hagsfiends had in the legends. Then it came to her. A new rule had been instituted that all First Flight ceremonies were supposed to be flown around the altar of the ember and the ashes. *How wrong is that — to have one's First Flight indoors, around some stupid altar and not under a starry sky.* Otulissa sighed and worry stirred her gizzard. "Oh, dear! I hope Pelli knows what she's doing. This could be dangerous for her and the chicks," Otulissa murmured to herself.

Elyan and Gemma had pronounced that certain things were considered *glimpox* — or slanderous — a violation of the sacred nature of the ember. This would certainly be considered glimpox. They'd have to build a new jail. There certainly wasn't room in this one. What was truly glimpox was a jail in the great tree. What could be a worse, a more horrendous violation of the nature of this tree than making a hollow into a jail? It was outrageous, unbelievable. And it had all happened because of that foolish coronation teacup she had agreed to hide for Madame Plonk. Otulissa shut her eyes tight, reliving the horrible moments leading up to her arrest.

Gemma had arrived at her hollow. Her rather skimpy ear tufts stuck up as high as she could manage and twitched as if to add some sort of accent of authority to what she was about to say. "It has been reported that you have in your possession an article that was requisitioned for the vigil of the ashes." Otulissa would not even deign to inquire what in hagsmire was the vigil of the ashes. She didn't care.

"Of what article are you speaking?" Otulissa asked politely.

"The coronation teacup of Madame Plonk."

Otulissa immediately decided to own up to having the teacup and silently cursed Madame Plonk. At least she would not be accused of lying. "Yes, right here."

She fetched the teacup from a cubby in her hollow so quickly that Gemma seemed almost surprised. "Take it," she said, shoving it toward the Whiskered Screech. "I have no use for it."

"Then why did you hide it for Madame Plonk?"

"She merely requested that I keep it for her. I had no idea why." *A tiny lie*, she thought. "But you're more than welcome to it."

Gemma had seemed visibly upset. This had obviously been too easy. "But you were hiding it in that cubby."

"I don't have a lot of room in here, as you can see," Otulissa had said, gesturing with a small sweeping arc of one wing. "I put it out of harm's way."

"Aha!" Gemma screeched, and lofted herself directly into the air. "So you consider myself and the rest of the order of the Guardians of the Guardians of the Ember to be 'harm'?"

"I never said such a thing!"

"Yes, you did, just now. I arrest you for un-emberish glimpox activity. Article One, Section B of the Glimpox Statutes for Protection of the Ember."

With that, three other members of the order, who must have been waiting outside on a close branch, stormed into Otulissa's hollow, and the next thing she knew she was in a prison that she didn't even know existed in the great tree.

She ran her talons over the bars and mused that Bubo himself must have made them. *What must he have thought?* At just that moment, as if reading her mind, there was a flare of ruddy red outside the opening and the old blacksmith appeared.

"Otulissa!" he said in a raw, desperate voice. "I thought I was making rods for still another cage for the ember. I swear, Otulissa. I would have never done it had I known." The Great Horned looked an absolute wreck. His yellow eyes flickered madly.

"Bubo, I know you couldn't have known. No need for an apology."

The light of the setting sun flashed off the bars, tingeing them gold. Bubo squinted and blinked. "It's a terrible time, ain't it?" He shook his head wearily. "What with this Golden Tree and all."

"I'm starting to hate gold," Otulissa said.

"I even think Plonkie's getting a bit disgusted with it all."

"As well she should!" Otulissa scowled.

"Look, don't go too hard on her. She feels terrible about the whole thing."

"Yes, but look who's in prison."

"But she's under 'tree arrest,' as they call it."

"Tree arrest! What will they think of next? What does that mean?"

"She can't leave the tree, but they have to have her around to sing all them new chants for them ceremonies." The very words caused a deep twinge in Otulissa's gizzard as she saw the three Bs completing their First Flight ceremony. *What has happened to the real ceremonies that mark growth and the passages in an owl's life? Ceremonies for an ember — racdrops!* "What are we going to do?" Otulissa sighed. "When will Soren and the Band and the king get back? Coryn would have a fit if he saw this nonsense with the ember."

"I'm thinking, Otulissa, we got to get word to them!"

"But we don't even know where they are."

At that moment, a song began to rise in the tree as Madame Plonk's unearthly voice spiraled up into the soft purple of the twilight. It was a new song that had replaced the old one that hailed the coming of First Black. This one hailed the glow of the ember.

Eternal ember, strong and glowing,
let your light suffuse our tree.

Most holy spirit of the fires,
deliver us from fate most dire.

On the word "dire," there was an ear-shattering crack that resounded throughout the tree. A high flutter could be heard as hundreds of owls flew out from their hollows. The golden leaves of the tree shivered and a few even fell off, drifting lazily toward the ground.

And then the word swirled through the tree. A burly Short-eared Owl flew by the bars of her prison. "Matron! Matron! What is it?" Otulissa called out.

Barely turning around, the matron called back. "It's Madame Plonk. Her voice has cracked!"

CHAPTER SIXTEEN

Cracked

Listen to me, Bubo," Madame Plonk spoke in a low, hoarse voice. Each word was like a rough-edged shard grating against the next. "I got her into this. I've got to get her out of it."

"But not you, Plonkie, dear. You know nothing about flying around out there. When was the last time you crossed Hoolemere? You know nothing about tracking. I should go."

"They're not going to let you go for a minute, Bubo. They got you working that forge all hours. And they'd suspect you. They know how close you are to Coryn and to Soren and the Band." Madame Plonk fixed her old friend in a steady gaze. "Look, even when I hid that cup they didn't really want to punish me because they needed my voice. Same way they need your smithing. Tree arrest. That's a laugh. I was planning this before my voice cracked. It hurts to talk so don't make me explain too much. Just listen. I'm the first to admit that I'm a vain old owl. 'The first singer of the tree' was what they used to call a gadfeather. She was a Snowy like me and my line is descended from hers. Her name was Snow Rose. She not only sang, but she was a heroic owl. She helped save the life of Hoole's mother, Siv, then joined Siv's troops in the Battle in the Beyond when Hoole retrieved the ember." Madame Plonk paused. "I didn't know any of this until I took the cup to Otulissa and had, well, I had my last spot of tea in the coronation cup, and she joined me and told me this part of the old stories. The ones they call the legends. But imagine this Snow Rose, a warrior singer! A soldier singer! It's true. All written down it is in them old books of Ezylryb's. I can do it, too, Bubo. I can be a warrior singer. I know I can."

Bubo looked at her with some alarm. Madame Plonk had led a rather comfortable life, indeed one might say cushy, in that tricked-out hollow of hers that was almost frothy with its trimmings of lace, tassels, gewgaws, and baubles. She was Trader Mags' best customer. The various doodads that Mags stripped from the castles, manor houses, churches, and abbeys of the Others found their way into Madame Plonk's hollow. There were plump cushions stuffed with her own discarded feathers covered in velvet from a prince's cloak. "Gemma and Elyan are so worried about me now since my voice cracked because without it they can't have their stupid rituals. They're smothering me with kindness."

"You're not under tree arrest?"

"No. I told them that I had to be entirely alone if my voice was to come back, that it made me too nervous to have all these matrons and owls checking on me all the time. I can get away, Bubo. I can."

"But, Plonkie."

"Bubbie?" She turned her yellow eyes on him, batted them a few times in a sad yet still flirtatious manner, and implored. "You've got to understand. No one will suspect me if I go."

"But how will you find them? No one knows where they might be."

"I'll go to these grog trees I've heard about. A lot of gossip swirls about in grog trees. If my voice is back, I might sing. Singers in olden days were always welcome at grog trees, Otulissa told me." She shut her eyes for a long time. A very long time, and did not open them when she began to speak. "And it will come back, Bubo, it will. As soon as I get away." She opened her eyes now and looked straight into the Great Horned's eyes. "There is something wrong with the tree, Bubo. You know it as well as I do. It ain't right. Everything looks all gold and glorious but something's amiss It shames me now to think of meself singing away at all those stupid ceremonies for the frinkin' ember."

"Hush, Plonkie. Mind your beak. They got slipgizzles all over. Can hardly breathe without them listening in."

"Oh, Bubo, but all that nonsense — acolytes of the ashes, the ember procession, the sacred this, the blah-blah that — and I was actually enjoying it for a while. I got to wear that scrap of purple velvet tufted with ermine, and I felt so special."

"You *are* special, Plonkie."

"It's my voice that was special and now it's cracked."

There was a fluttering outside the hollow and the shadow of wings passed through the stream of moonlight. Bubo looked around nervously and then leaned in close to the Snowy so that his beak was almost touching her ear slit. "Plonkie, are you *really* set on doing this?"

"I am, Bubo."

CHAPTER SEVENTEEN
The Shape of the Flames

A wing and a whisper, thought Soren. *Is that all we've got? Yes.* That seemed to be what he, the Band, and Coryn were flying on. It was all too vague. He wanted to be able to trust the strange rabbit's mystic web readings, but it just all seemed so . . . so . . . he searched for the word . . . so *wispy.* So insubstantial. And if Nyra was really there in this cave with whatever remnants of the Pure Ones there might be, things needed to be firmer. They had to plan a strategy. What were they to do? Just fly in and seize the book? Even if they were successful in taking the book, would that be the end of their troubles? It wasn't really the book that was the problem. It was, Soren supposed, the ideas in the book. But ideas could be dangerous just the way the ember could be dangerous in the talons of the wrong owl. He supposed they must fly on. Within a split second of having that thought, he knew he was dead wrong. And as if to confirm his next thought he saw the dark tendrils of smoke rising in the distance.

Soren lifted a port wing giving the signal to land. They had flown fast from Silverveil and were now on the border between The Barrens and Ambala.

"What are we stopping for? I'm not tired," Coryn asked as they settled into one of the rather puny trees in The Barrens. But Gylfie took one look at Soren and realized immediately that something was disturbing him deeply. The spindly branch could barely support the weight of the five owls and bowed toward the ground.

"Brushfire over there half a league away." Digger nodded toward the rolling smudge of smoke on the horizon.

"I know," Soren said. "That's part of the reason we've stopped."

"What's the other part?" Gylfie asked. She fixed her old friend with a knowing look.

"We're rushing into this."

"What do you mean?" Coryn asked. His voice was slightly strained. "That was one of the clearest readings I've ever gotten from the rabbit."

"You've encountered that rabbit all of two times, Coryn," Soren said. "We need more information. I want to dive into that brushfire. Get some coals and build a small fire here."

Coryn looked somberly at his uncle. "You know I can't just simply ask a fire. That's not how it works."

"I know, Coryn, I know. I don't want you to ask any-thing. I only want you to watch — just watch. There are hot coals in these brushfires. They'll give you good flames."

Gylfie sighed. "Except for you and Coryn, the rest of us won't be much help in harvesting coals. We're hardly colliers. Too bad Otulissa isn't here."

Soren jerked his head up. He felt a sharp ping in his gizzard and blinked at Gylfie. The moment she said the words "too bad Otulissa isn't here" it reminded him of something.

"What's wrong, Soren?" Gylfie asked.

He shook his head as if to dislodge a thought that had become wedged deep in his brain. "When you said 'Otulissa' it reminded me of something." *Another wisp? A wisp of a dream perhaps?*

An hour later, the five owls backed away from a small fire that they had built with the half dozen or so coals that Soren and Coryn had retrieved. Coryn stood the closest to the fire. He felt clumsy, even stupid. The flames looked so ordinary. This wasn't right. He spun his head around finally. "I don't mean to be rude, but the rest of you get out of here. Scram. I can't do it when you're watching me."

"Of course," Soren said. "We'll go hunting."

Once they were gone, Coryn relaxed. He let the heat

of the flames lick his face. He closed his eyes and watched the red shadows dance jigs on the inside of his eyelids, then opened them again. The moon was rising. More than halfway through its newing, it appeared slightly lopsided, as if it were about to tumble off the horizon. When it was full in a few more days, there would be an eclipse according to Gylfie, who knew the ways of the stars and the planets because she was the navigation ryb. Coryn had been hatched on the night of an eclipse. And so had Hoole, the king of the legends, and so had Nyra. He felt a shiver pass through him. How could the world contain such good and such bad?

And what was he? What if the blood of a hagsfiend really did run through his veins? His mind wandered. The flames cast red silhouettes against the moon that trembled now on the darkening horizon. Odd, but he suddenly realized that he had never seen the flames in just this manner — their silhouettes as opposed to looking directly at them. He could not look into them as deeply, but their contours, their shapes had a new clarity. He saw the shape of an owl. A Whiskered Screech, he was certain. He could tell by the small tuft of feathers that hung from his face. He was not especially strong nor a steady flier, and what was that — a nest-maid snake coiled on his back? A wind stirred the fire and the flames leaped suddenly to one side, stretching, nearly galloping across the silver of the moon. His gizzard gave a small jump. Something so familiar in that shape, but just then low clouds brushed across the moon. "Racdrops!" Coryn muttered, and dropped his gaze to the flames in the fire. Could he find it there? It was the second shape, the second silhouette that intrigued him, and not that of the Whiskered Screech. There was something in that shape, and he was sure that it was not an owl this time that tugged at his very gizzard. He felt a longing, a deep and anguished longing — for a place? For a creature? He peered deeply into the flames. *There are so many different colors in a fire no one would believe it,* thought Coryn. *There is never just red or orange.* Coryn had heard that there were no two snowflakes exactly alike, and he believed that no two flames were alike, either. He had once tried to count the shades of orange, but at some imperceptible point the orange seemed to melt into yellow, and then within the yellow . . . . Coryn's gizzard flinched. *A lovely shade of cream!* Soren was right — they were rushing into things. They should not be flying toward the canyonlands at all. They needed an immediate course correction. Coryn had only seen that peculiar cream color once before, and not in a fire but in the Beyond. It was on the glossy coat of a dire wolf. "Gyllbane!"

CHAPTER EIGHTEEN
Most Distressing News

It was a long way to the Beyond, but luckily once again the wind blew from behind and gave them a hefty push north and west. The night was thinning. The moon had slipped away into another world, and it was becoming that hazy time before the dawn. As they shifted positions in their flight formation so that Twilight could fly point in this murky light streaked with false shadows and blurred horizons, Soren could feel the tremor of excitement that coursed through their gizzards. They were at last to meet Gyllbane, the courageous she-wolf, who had turned on her own clan, the notorious MacHeaths, and befriended Coryn. Her own pup had been maimed by Lord MacHeath in hopes that this would qualify the young wolf to become a member of the Sacred Watch.

Once more, Soren felt a strange little ping in his gizzard. Otulissa! Had he dreamed of her? Had he seen something in a dream? Had his starsight revealed something he could not quite grasp? It seemed odd to him that now for the first time he was flying to the Beyond. Otulissa, of course, had been in the Beyond. That was where she had first found Coryn and taught him to collier and then . . . *Well*, thought Soren, *as they say, the rest is history.*

"Fire in the sky! Volcanoes! Dead ahead!" Twilight shouted back.

The Band blinked as they perched atop a ridge. It was a strange and wonderful place, the Beyond. A trio of wolves approached them. The noble Gyllbane and her son, Cody, and the faithful Hamish, Coryn's best friend from his time in the Beyond. Hamish, born with a crippling deformity, had qualified for the Sacred Watch in which he had briefly served. But one of the true blessings of the ember was that once it was recovered, the wolves of the Watch were restored. What was broken in their bodies was mended. What was deformed was made to grow straight. What was crippled gained strength. When Coryn saw his dear friend Hamish come bounding up the rocky escarpment, sleek and powerful, he experienced an unspeakable thrill. And though he was far from the ember he felt a shimmering within him, a glow at the very core of his gizzard that he knew could only be that of the ember. It was strange, but for the first time he began to get a glimmering that one did not need to have the ember to possess it. He realized this as Hamish stepped closer and he touched his beak to Hamish's wet nose in greeting. Coryn saw the deep burnish of green in his wolf eyes, the same flickering green found in what they had come to think of as the gizzard of the Ember of Hoole. That glimpse of green in the wolf's eyes seemed to kindle a sympathetic response, a shimmering heat within Coryn.

Soren, although he had read about the wolf clans in the legends and heard from Coryn about their peculiar and elaborate codes of conduct, was nonetheless astonished. Despite Coryn's protests, the three wolves scraped the rough ground as they kneeled, then crouched and sunk to their bellies, twisting their necks in all sorts of odd contortions, then flattened their ears and flashing the whites of their eyes. This was the conduct required of a creature of low rank when approaching one of high rank. Coryn was a king and not for one minute would these wolves let him forget it.

After the introductions were made and the greetings exchanged, Gyllbane, one of the most beautiful wolves imaginable, turned to Coryn and said, "So, friend, what brings you here, so far from your island in the middle of the sea?"

Coryn turned his head toward the circle of the five volcanoes that made what was called the Sacred Ring. It all looked so different now. Colliers still plunged in steep dives to harvest the coal slopes that spilled from the volcanoes' craters, and there was the usual traffic on the fringes of the circle between the colliers and Rogue smiths as they haggled over the price of coals and whether one was truly bonk or not. But the immense piles of gnaw bones surrounding the five volcanoes seemed bare without the wolves of the watch keeping their vigil from the tops.

Finally, Coryn answered. "I began this journey for the most selfish of reasons. I feared that I bore the traces of a vile heritage. I could not put my obsession with my mother, Nyra, to rest."

Gyllbane blinked. In her own way, she understood this. She had met Nyra and knew her power, and she herself had once been a victim of ruthlessness. It had been hard for her to forget MacHeath and his abuse of her and her pup.

"And now?" Hamish asked. "Why have you come, old friend? Have you found out what you want to know?"

"Not really, but I have found out that she still lives and that in her possession is a book that is very dangerous. You've heard of hagsfiends?" The three wolves exchanged glances. Although it was fairly clear that the word was unfamiliar to them, they seemed disturbed. The hackles on the backs of their necks suddenly were erect, their eyes narrowed to green slits.

"Let us not talk out here. Follow me to my cave."

The cave shook with the thunderous eruptions of the volcanoes, and outside the night flinched with the red light of flames that scoured the sky. "And you say," Hamish spoke slowly, "that these creatures are no more?"

"Yes, they are extinct, yet not entirely gone," Gylfie said.

"I don't understand," Gyllbane said. "Either something is or it isn't, correct?"

Soren now spoke. "These hagsfiends that your ancestors — and ours — fought alongside Hoole, these creatures in their ancient forms are dead and gone. But they have left behind dim shadows...." *How to explain it?* Soren thought. "Like whispers from another world they come to us, fragments from a bad dream. But it is not a dream. We have all had brushes with them. Haven't any of you dire wolves ever been haunted by such?"

Gyllbane shook her head. "Never. My old chief, MacHeath, was trouble enough. I surely didn't need a hagsfiend or even a dim shadow of one to cause more." Coryn felt a slight tremor reverberate in his gizzard when she spoke of the wrathful old wolf who had maimed her son, Cody, when he was just a pup. "What are these dim shadows of hagsfiends like?"

Soren continued. "Somewhat like scrooms, yet far less powerful." There was an undeniable nervous reaction among the three wolves in the cave when they heard this.

"We have not read the legends as you have and we need to know more about the ancient forms of the hagsfiends. Describe them to us." Then Gyllbane asked with a sudden urgency, "What do they look like, wherein lie their powers, and what exactly could they do to ordinary creatures?"

"You have to begin," Gylfie said, "with magen, for it was a time of magen in those ancient days — both good magen and evil magen." So Gylfie, the rest of the Band, and Coryn described as best they could what they had learned from reading the legends. But it was when they came to the peculiar yellow light that emanated from the hagsfiends' eyes that the three wolves stood up with every bit of their coats bristling, their eyes flashing white in a terror that Coryn had never in his time in the Beyond witnessed.

"Fyngrot, you call it?!" Gyllbane asked in a trembling voice.

"Yellow? Yellow pouring from their eyes?" Cody asked in nearly strangled words.

Soren explained in detail how the hagsfiends used fyngrot.

Hamish stepped forward. This time there were no gestures of homage. Rank was forgotten. "We have something similar among dire wolves. Vyrwolves," he said in a low growl. "We thought they were gone, too. A relic of our past, as I suppose you thought the hagsfiends were." A cold silence fell upon them all. *Great Glaux,* thought Soren, *can there be some connection between the two — between hagsfiends and vyrwolves?* Soren sensed that the same thought was occurring to Coryn. For indeed, once there had been a connection between the most evil wolf — MacHeath — and the most evil owl — Nyra.

"And they're not gone?" Coryn asked.

"We fear not," Gyllbane said.

"But I don't understand." Soren spoke now, his black eyes flickering with confusion. "How can they possibly be like hagsfiends? Wolves are not birds."

"Think of them as wingless hagsfiends." It was Digger who said this. They all spun their heads toward him and the three wolves regarded him with a measure of surprise.

"Precisely," Hamish said. "Wingless. But still very dangerous and sharing much in common with these hagsfiends that you described."

"This fyngrot," Gyllbane whispered tremulously. The incoherent roar of the erupting volcanoes mingled with the pounding of eight creatures' hearts. "It is like the jaunyx."

"The jaunyx?" the five owls asked in unison.

"Our eyes," Hamish said. "Our eyes are naturally green."

"A bright intense green, the same as the rim of the ember's center," Soren said.

The owls' gizzards were all astir now, for each one of them was remembering the passages from the legends in which King Hoole had, with the help of the bright beams from the wolves' eyes, broken through a powerful fyngrot and brought down a troop of hagsfiends in the Desert of Kuneer.

"They are still green," Gylfie whispered almost desperately. "Tell them, Soren, tell them of the passages from the legends where the wolves broke the fyngrot of the hagsfiends with the green of their eyes."

There was now a stirring among the wolves. They rose and turned in tight circles, then settled down again. "Is this true?" Gyllbane asked. "If so, we have lost this part of the tale as it was passed down since the first Fengo."

"Are legends true?" Soren asked no one in particular. "It was written down." He left the rest of what he was about to say unspoken. *But legends can inspire,* he thought. Soren knew that inspiration could not be told, or preached. It must be felt truly to be acted upon.

Gyllbane sighed. "Dunleavy MacHeath, the lord of my clan before I left it, his eyes began to fade soon after Coryn retrieved the coal." She paused.

"And?" Coryn asked.

Gyllbane turned toward her son. "Cody can tell you what happened."

"He'd always been a brute, Lord MacHeath. Thanks to him I am lame with two half paws, bitten off by my own chieftain in the hope that this would qualify me to become a gnaw wolf of the Sacred Watch."

"He lusted so for that ember, he maimed a defenseless pup," Gyllbane added, "just to be close to it. Then when the right owl came, he thought that owl would . . ." Her voice dwindled off.

"And Nyra was the right owl," Coryn said.

"Yes, but you, Coryn, retrieved the ember instead," Cody continued. "For a while he thought all was lost. He became increasingly deranged and then fell into a distemper that was worse than the foaming disease. He staggered into the far southwestern range of hills and went deep into a cave somewhere there. For a long time we thought he had died. Many of the clan hoped and prayed and watched the spirit trail of stars that led to the soul cave where dead wolves go upon death, though few thought he deserved a place there. Then one day he came back with a new mate — Brygdylla. He looked ragged and his eyes had faded to almost no color — at least none that could be named. His new mate looked equally ragged and had the same colorless eyes. We thought she had suffered from the same illness. But then one night shortly after he had returned, he called a meeting of the clan in the Gadderheal. It was the night of a full moon, and he told us to follow him out of the Gadderheal cave and to stand across from him. As the moon rose and cast a perfect pool of silver light on the ground, he and Brygdylla stood in the center. A strange transformation began to occur."

There was a pause in the thunderous eruptions, and a quiet engulfed the cave that in its own way seemed as loud as the roar of the volcanoes. Cody continued. "MacHeath and his mate grew to three times their normal size, their dull, shaggy coats turned a dark glistening bluish-black, and their eyes were suddenly yellow. They pulled back their lips in a grimace not of fear but threat, revealing fangs — fangs the likes of which none of us had ever seen and twice their normal size, their edges no longer smooth but jagged with sharp little points."

"They had become vyrwolves," Hamish said. "And those MacHeaths who would not join them were slaughtered."

"But what about you, Cody? Why not you?"

"I never thought I would thank my lameness for this." He held up one of his mangled paws. "But since I'm maimed, I was of no use to them. Easily overlooked. And what was there to brag about in killing a maimed young wolf barely out of his puppy days?"

"And then what happened?" Soren asked. He did not like the sound of this at all. It had an eerie familiarity, a resonance with a dark legendary past. This must have been why Ezylryb had insisted on his deathbed that Soren, the Band, and the young king read the legends.

"And then MacHeath, Brygdylla, and a small remnant of the MacHeath clan — the ones he spared — went with him."

"But where?" Gylfie asked.

"To that cave in the southwestern hills."

"That cave!" Digger stepped forward. "I think I know of that cave." They all blinked and looked toward the Burrowing Owl.

"What?" Gylfie asked in a hoarse whisper.

"I think that cave leads to what is known among Burrowing Owls as the Tunnel of Despair." He paused. "A place where strange transformations took place. But none of us thought it was a real place. We thought —" He stopped, his voice almost broken. He peered down at his strong featherless legs, which had dug plenty of burrows and tunnels over the years in some of the hardest, most scrabbly earth imaginable. "We thought that it was just a mythical place, a legend." Digger paused, then began again. "But as we now know, legends have a way of revealing truth."

CHAPTER NINETEEN
An Owl with a Mission

How miserable can this get? Madame Plonk thought as icy slop from the Sea of Hoolemere dashed her in the face. She was wedged in between head-buffeting winds above and a tumultuous sea below. If she flew high to avoid the sea slop, the winds were too strong, at least for her, a frankly fat Snowy who had not been on a serious flight in years. Flying too low she encountered the rowdy breaking waves, which she felt took absolute delight in drenching her. Madame Plonk had to admit she was definitely out of shape. But she flew on. She had gotten Otulissa into this mess back at the tree and she would get her out of it. She felt terrible about asking Otulissa to hide the frinkin' coronation teacup, which she hoped she never laid eyes on again. But most of all she felt deeply ashamed for ever partaking of, and lending her voice, her most precious possession, to these yoickish rituals dreamed up by the GGE. She was as fed up with the frinkin' ember as she was with the teacup.

All these thoughts assailed her as she flew on. Despite her vanity and frivolous habits, she was in many ways a practical owl. She knew that it would do her no good to dwell on the past. She must not squander her strength, but conserve it and fly on. A fuzzy line began to break through the thick vapors of mist and fog and spume-tossed air. *Land!* she thought. Then the fuzzy line grew bolder and assumed a shape. *It must be Cape Glaux.* She hadn't seen it in years and although it was a barren windswept promontory, to Madame Plonk it seemed like the most welcoming place in the world. She would only allow herself a short rest, for night was now falling and to fly in the daylight would be dangerous. Crows! How long had it been since she even had to consider the foul creatures? But it wouldn't do to become the victim of a mobbing. She had to find Soren, the Band, and the young king. Bubo had told her the whereabouts of a grog tree. "When you get to the Cape, fly off the bottom port star of the Golden Talons, not the starboard star."

"Port? Starboard? What do I know of such things? Tell me plain, Bubo," she had demanded.

"All right. Go to the Cape, turn left, fly straight for two hours. You'll get to Silverveil, and that forest on its far western side meets up with the Shadow Forest. If you fly a straight course, on the border between the two forests you'll find the grog tree in a stand of sycamores."

She was absolutely starving by the time she arrived on the Cape, and luckily a rock rat was perched almost smack dab beneath her in a thicket of coarse winter grass. She looked about for a tree and a hollow even though she knew it was foolish, but it had been so long since she had holed up in a ground scrape, although this was the customary shelter of her kind. She had grown accustomed to more luxuriously appointed residences during her time at the tree. Indeed, she did not even call her hollow a hollow but an apartment and had lined it with the plushest of mosses, and all manner of decorations she had acquired through her dealings with Trader Mags.

"Aaah, dear Mags!" She realized that she would be flying right through Mags' home territory in Silverveil. How she would love . . . She cut off the thought almost immediately. *How can I be thinking about shopping at a time like this?!* She gave herself a stern talking-to: "Time to shape up, old gal! You're on a mission. You sybaritic hunk of feathers, you gluttonous, high-living lowlife of a fat owl." She looked down at the rock rat she had just killed and felt her hunger vanish. *Well, maybe I'll get thin.* But she knew she had to eat something, for soon she would have to fly on. Not a drop of the night could be wasted. She tore off the rat's head, then swallowed the rest. Normally, she would have eaten the head but she knew there was little nutritional value in it, so why take on the extra weight? It would only make flying into a headwind — *Pardon the pun*, she thought — more difficult. For exactly five seconds she felt proud of her willpower, but she suddenly burst into tears. "I'm such a fool, a vain old fool." She crammed herself into a shallow ground scrape beneath a rock shelf overhang, collapsed in an exhausted heap, and instantly fell sound asleep.

Madame Plonk was dreaming of bars, vertical iron bars, and behind them the dignified face of a Spotted Owl. "Sorry! So sorry! Stupid teacup!" Her own sobbing woke her up and then her eyes flinched in the blinding white light. "Great Glaux, I've slept into the day! How could I! How could I!" She was hysterical now. She would have to wait until night, and even though these winter days were short, any delay was risky not just to the well-being of Otulissa but of the entire tree. The Band had to come back as quickly as possible. Shaking and awash with a mix of anger at herself and fear, she was dissolving into a complete panic. The glare of the sun was a scorching mockery. But through her panic she saw something even whiter than the sun. Whiter than the sun but with a sudden dash of black, a black that looked rather crowish . . .

Oh, great Glaux! I'm done for! she screeched, and swooned, collapsing, in a heap.

Madame Plonk was not sure how long she was out, but when she came to an astonishing sight met her eyes. It was a Snowy bending over her: a large male, pure white except for a black feather tucked into the plumage behind his head. *How very odd.* Madame Plonk blinked.

"Madame, may I be of service? You seem most distressed." It was a gentleman speaking, no doubt about that, Madame Plonk thought. She tried to compose herself before she spoke. "I was having a bad dream," she began and then blurted out, "but I deserve it. I'm a terrible owl. I have done a terrible thing!"

"Now, now, madame, I'm sure it can't be all that bad."

"Oh, but it is!" Between sobs and gulps, Madame Plonk spilled out her story. It was a jumbled tale of teacups, ashes, cracked voices, a Spotted Owl named Otulissa, and Coryn.

"Coryn!" the male Snowy exclaimed.

"Yes, Coryn, the king of the great tree."

"So that is where you are from."

Madame Plonk nodded.

"You must be the famed singer of the tree."

"Once," she replied cryptically.

He blinked, not quite understanding her, but went on. "Oh, yes, I know about you and the great tree and the new king, Coryn." He paused. "You see, I knew him when he was still called Nyroc."

"You did?" Madame Plonk blinked.

"Well, I am rather ashamed of how I came to know him, but yes, I did make his acquaintance briefly."

"I must find him. I must find him and the Band."

"Oh, you shall, Madame Plonk. You see you have come upon the right owl. I am Doc Finebeak, the finest tracker in the Southern Kingdoms. Once upon a time, I was hired by Nyra to track down her errant son. I know this young owl. I know his flight track. If anyone can find him and this Band you speak of, it's me. We can leave immediately."

"What? It's broad daylight. Are you yoicks? What about crows?"

"What about crows?" He cocked his head so that the black feather showed. "The crows and I, well, how shall I put it? The crows and I have an arrangement. This crow feather I wear — it's a long story how I got it, but basically it gives me a free passage for daytime flight — a get-out-of-mobbing-free feather, so to speak."

"Oh . . ." That was all Madame Plonk could say. Just "oh" and deep in her chest she felt a shimmering flutter in her gizzard. She hadn't felt that in years! *My, my! I mustn't be distracted. Just think* mission, *you old fool!*

CHAPTER TWENTY
The Tunnel of Despair

Gylfie was chosen for the mission of exploring the Tunnel of Despair for two reasons. First, she was small and could thread her way undetected through the bizarre underground twisting channel that sometimes narrowed to the width of a Barn Owl's wingspan; second, she was the premier navigator of the great tree. Of any of them, she would never get lost. Take away every starry reference point, take away the sky, as indeed was the case, and it mattered not to Gylfie.

Stone flowers bloomed in the dense shadows as Gylfie flew through the twisting maze of passages. A lesser owl, one of inferior intelligence or unsteady gizzard, might have found these weird contortions of rock frightening. They seemed to grow magically from the floor, ceiling, and sides of the tunnel in myriad shapes ranging from needlelike protuberances to blossoms locked in an eternal spring. But Gylfie was no lesser owl. Her mind buzzed with star charts and the configurations of the constellations in the sky above. Her brain and gizzard tingled with the minute vibrations of the Earth's magnetic poles. Within her were both chart and compass.

Still, Gylfie was not used to being underground. Although she was flying, she felt as if she were being buried alive because with each wing beat she was moving deeper into the Earth. *Earth is not a place for a winged creature,* she thought. The damp smell of clay, rock, and soil offended her sensibilities. She hated not seeing the sky. That's how it had been at St. Aggie's when they were imprisoned deep in the stone maze, exposed to the full shine of the moon for moon blinking. She felt her gizzard grow squishy with dread and her heartbeat accelerate. *Keep calm! Keep calm! The sky is there. You just can't see it. I've had worse experiences — like when I was captured by kraals in the Northern Kingdoms. I have to do this for the Band. For the tree. For owlkind, birdkind, animalkind. Don't be some weak-gizzard moon calf, freak gizzle, idiotic owl.* Gylfie kept up the self-scolding. She would fly on. She had flown in battle, through hurricanes, and through fires. She could fly through this frinkin' stupid tunnel!

The only other owl of the Band who would have possibly been adequate for the job, despite his lack of celestial navigation abilities, was Digger. As a Burrowing Owl he had an extensive knowledge of caves and tunnels and the topography of the underground; not only the topography but the cave dwellers, the peculiar animals that lived in caves. But with a wingspan of nearly two feet, Digger was too big. He told Gylfie as much as he could about the natural history of caves and tunnels in general. However there was not much time. For the moon had long passed its dwenking and was well into its newing, growing fatter and fatter each night. The strange transformation of the dire wolves into vyrwolves took place, they had been told, on the night of a full moon. But even before they were told this, Coryn had been nervous about the newing moon because this time there would be an eclipse. Coryn's words now flowed back to Gylfie as she flew the twisting channels of the earth: *"Do you know the significance of an eclipse?"* Coryn had asked with a quaver in his voice.

Neither Coryn nor the Band had known that at the very same moment he had spoken these words, his own mother was speaking nearly the same words to Stryker, her top lieutenant. Still, Coryn's obvious agitation over the coming eclipse coupled with what they now knew of the effect of the full moon on vyrwolves added an acute urgency to her mission.

Aside from the navigational information Gylfie was continuously processing as she flew, she kept in mind Digger's stories of the tunnel. The legend of the place interlocked with its natural history in a remarkable manner. The tunnel, which meandered off into caves of varying sizes, was perforated with thousands of holes, cracks, and crevices through which rainwater seeped. On its journey downward, this water dissolved the rock in its path, leaving these many cave flowers and strange formations. And as the water collected, it turned fizzy and bubbled not with heat but odd gases. The oldest caves and pools were closest to the Earth's surface. As water continued to leak down, cutting more passageways, the newer caverns were formed. It was in the oldest caves, however, with their burbling gaseous pools, that strange creatures lived. Eyeless fish and shrimp, blind albino crayfish, and all manner of strange spiders. Certain kinds of eels and catfish also found their way from aboveground streams into those of the Tunnel of Despair. And finally there were trogloxenes — cave visitors or cave guests — crickets, bats, rats, and flying insects, and, Gylfie supposed, herself. There was in the Tunnel of Despair an unnatural history as well and it, too, had its source in the pools and lakes. For it was the deep water of certain pools that gave rise to vyrwolves. By drinking deeply from these pools, a wolf — not an ordinary wolf but a vicious or depraved one with a touch of evil — could be transformed into a wolf with the potential for extraordinary evil, and on nights of the full moon become a vyrwolf.

Gylfie's mission was to find any trace of these wolves and to locate this pool of potent waters. She was also to explore and see where the tunnel ended. Coryn knew that Nyra had collaborated with MacHeath to try to seize the ember. If they were together again, the destruction they could wreak was gizzard-freezing, unthinkable. With the full moon and its eclipse fast approaching, it was as if heaven and earth were conspiring to inexorably arrange themselves in a deadly design. A dance of death was about to commence.

Gylfie was not sure how long she had been flying, but she knew she had covered several leagues with all the twists and turns. She had rarely stopped to rest, but now just ahead there was a welcoming niche and she thought she would fetch up in it. The tunnel, of course, was windless and Gylfie had never felt more cut off from all the things that had meaning for an owl — the billowing thermal drafts of air rising from earth warmed by the sun, the coolness of the night, the moon scattering its silver on her wings, the stars — the dear, dear stars in their familiar transits across the velvet of the night. She slipped into the niche. A flatworm was crawling by and she peeled him off the stone ledge with her tiny talons and popped him in her mouth, then settled in for a short snooze.

It was the smell that first woke her — deeply rank, wet, wet fur! *And they say owls can't smell!* And then she became aware of a loud panting. *I'm near!* she thought. She shut her eyes tight and told herself not to panic. *I must stay calm. I must find out as much as I can.* She stepped out onto the ledge. Her talons clicked against the stone. She froze. She would have to fly. And she wasn't the most silent of fliers. Still, it would be more silent than trying to creep up on them with her talons striking the rock surfaces. She flew close to the wall. Suddenly, there was light! Gylfie blinked. A moon hung in the darkness of the tunnel. For a second she felt completely disoriented and faltered in flight, recovering just before colliding with a stone flower. She lighted down. *The moon? Impossible!*

And then she realized that through an opening in the cave's roof the moon was reflected in a large pool of water. Still water. All the pools she had seen so far were fizzing with tiny bubbles, but not this one. And it was not only the moon she saw reflected in its dark surface but the faces of a half dozen wolves.

"Drink, drink deeply," one wolf counseled. "It has been a whole moon cycle since last we met to drink of the vyr. Our strength has waned but it will come back. Yes, it will!" As the wolf said this, he lifted his head and swung it in Gylfie's direction. His eyes hung in the blackness like two yellow flames. Gylfie felt a coldness in her gizzard. Her wings drooped. It was like every fyngrot she had imagined when they had read the legends. This was a hagwolf if there ever was one. She wilfed and grew thinner. She heard in the distance a fluttering of wings, large wings. And then there was a second moon! A scarred moon. There was only one owl with such a face. Nyra!

CHAPTER TWENTY-ONE
Race the Moon

"So you're sure, Gylfie, that the cave over there is where you would have emerged if you had been able to go to the very end of the tunnel?" Soren cocked his head in the direction to which he was referring. The owls had flown to the canyonlands as soon as Gylfie had reported back to them at their prearranged meeting place in the Shadow Forest.

"Absolutely." The tiny Elf Owl nodded firmly. "Somehow I managed to fly out of it while the wolves were still drinking at that pool just before the tunnel widened into the cave. No one saw me."

"And this is the cave of Kludd's Final ceremony?" Twilight looked at Coryn.

"It is. And just over there in those cliffs beyond the next ridge is the stone hollow where I was raised." Coryn swiveled his head around. This place was filled with bad memories. His First Flight ceremony. His mother's rage, his own despair over his friend Phillip, the terrible fear when he had experienced his first visions in the fires of his father's Final ceremony and realized that he had been lied to since the moment of his hatching.

It seemed an uncanny twist of fate that the Tunnel of Despair had ended in the very same cave in which Kludd had been killed. The Band, Coryn, Gyllbane, and the other wolves who traveled with her were gathered on a ridge in the canyonlands. Gyllbane and the wolves she could muster had traveled in a byrrgis at a speed they called "press paw"— not as fast as attack or chase speed but fast enough to cover long distances quickly.

It had been hard to get more wolves, for it was mating season and the clans were scattered. But Hamish had known where to find Duncan MacDuncan and his lieutenant. Gyllbane had prevailed upon Fitzmore McFang, who had kindly taken her in after she had left the MacHeaths. McFang had come with his powerful mate, Adair, who was as fearless as she was strong. Their son, Fitzy, had also come. In addition to these, there were three from the MacNamara clan, a clan traditionally headed up by a female always called Namara. And because MacNamara she-wolves were known for their toughness and great intelligence, males vied for them. But only one male would be chosen and, contrary to all custom, he would drop his birth clan name and assume that of

MacNamara. So Namara came with her mate Cormag and their son, Airilla, and daughter, Morag. In all, there were a dozen wolves. But they were dire wolves — not vyrwolves. It remained to be seen if it would be an even match.

"Are the vyrwolves all in the cave now?" Twilight whispered.

"I think so," Namara answered. She lifted her nose. "The scent marks are old out here. They have not been out for some time."

The owls and the wolves knew that they had to strike before the moon rose, but cave battles were difficult. Even in a large cave, space would be tight if they fought with fire. And they did plan to do just that. There were other considerations that made the cave far from ideal: It led into a long, long tunnel. The last thing they wanted was for the vyrwolves to scatter down the intricate maze of passages. They had to assume that the vyrwolves and Nyra and her remnant Pure Ones knew the terrain of the tunnel better than they did. That meant that Nyra and the wolves would be fighting on familiar territory. This would give them a distinct advantage. But if they rushed them in the cave — before the moonlight shone on them — the wolves would still be just wolves and not vyrwolves. For that transformation, they needed to expose themselves to the moon. It was a very hard call to make.

They say owls can't smell, Stryker thought to himself. But he could. He could smell the fetid stink of these wolves to whom his commander, General Mam, had allied them. There was no choice, really. Their own ranks had been shattered, and he had to admit these wolves had powers — powers that Nyra felt were akin in some mysterious ways to the powers that she hoped to attain. She was saying the words again now.

"The book, the transforming waters, these ashes of my dear Kludd." She ran her beak through the ashes and seemed to inhale them as if savoring their scent. "These ashes, my friends" — she swiveled her head to look at the congregation of wolves and remaining Pure Ones — "are the key to what the ancients called nachtmagen. With them, you will see, I shall transform my son — and, with that, the ember shall be ours. "

"Does the book say that, General Mam?" Stryker asked.

"You doubt me, Stryker?" It was as if a stream of yellow heat glared from Nyra's eyes.

"Never, my general." He raised his right talon in the salute that Nyra had recently begun insisting upon when being addressed. It seemed that since their numbers had been depleted, Nyra had become increasingly obsesssed with these formal gestures indicating acknowledgment of her exalted state. She greatly admired the elaborate codes of conduct that the wolves required between the lower and the higher ranks and wished that owls could scrape the ground as effectively as the wolves did when they cowered on their bellies in front of MacHeath, rolling their eyes back until they flashed white. But this was simply not how owls were constructed.

She lowered her voice and spoke in a close, intimate tone. "You see, my dear Stryker, I feel a kinship with this ancient bird named Kreeth." She would not admit that the words from the book were hard for her to read. The diagrams and the pictures were really enough. She sensed their meaning. "I understand the science of nachtmagen. These are deep things that only a chosen few can comprehend. And Kreeth and I are among them. Or she was . . ."

Stryker, though not very bright, was mulling over some troubling thoughts. The Pure Ones' entire philosophy was based upon Barn Owls being the most superior breed of all owls. And yet this Kreeth was not even a true owl. She was a hagsfiend, a strange cross between owl and crow. He himself had encountered those ragtag remnants that came like dark wisps of bad dreams as one flew through the night. Their hauntings, although startling, were harmless. But here was Nyra, claiming kinship with an archfiend from some distant past who was as far from pure as one could imagine. He dared not question her, though. No, never. He regarded her now, as she once again ran her beak through the ashes, and observed that there seemed to be a darkening of the white feathers at the edges of her face.

Always just before a battle there were those quiet thoughts one had — random notions that often had nothing to do with the attack, with strategy, or even with premonitions of death. Soren was experiencing such thoughts as he perched on the ridge and swiveled his head toward his nephew. Coryn appeared to almost bristle with readiness and gallgrot for this fight. But would he be strong enough to face his mother? To fight her to the death if need be? To kill her? Soren vowed that he would spare Coryn that horrendous task. He would kill Nyra. A son, even the son of one as terrible as Nyra, should not be required to fight his mother to the death.

How odd, Soren thought, that it had been his intention to set out on this journey with his nephew to distract him from his obsession with Nyra and his own haggishness. Instead he must face her. Then for perhaps the thousandth time, Soren wished that Otulissa were here. The Spotted Owl was a superb strategist. He closed his eyes and tried to think of how she would have planned the attack. Once again he felt that deep twinge in his gizzard. *Why is it that every time I think of Otulissa I feel something like dread?*

It was a race with the moon. When the wolves came out under the full-shine moonlight they would become monsters. But with the eclipse, would they lose their power or would a worse one arise? If Soren could have flown up and stopped the moon he would have. He looked up and blinked at it. Two great forces were coming together on their inevitable course. Would he try if he could to stop the moon or stop the Earth? Stay the night or wish for the day? For it was the night of a lunar eclipse when the Earth in its orbit would come between the moon and the sun. He imagined that first bite that the Earth's shadow would take from the moon as the eclipse began. He imagined . . . and in that instant his dream came back. The slits in the ether veil! The black feathers piercing through. *"Don't wait for me!"* That voice — it was Otulissa's! *"Go! Go!"*

Soren turned to Coryn. "We go now!" Behind them in a shallow trough in the rocks were dozens of smoldering coals. Nearby were neatly stacked dried twigs and limbs gathered from the Shadow Forest. When Gylfie had met up with the Band and the wolves in the Shadow Forest and given her report, with the help of the wolves the owls had begun to gather their arsenal, for they knew that trees were sparse in the canyonlands, especially since the Battle of the Great Burning. From the Beyond they had brought coals in their botkins and buckets.

Coryn watched nervously as the Band chose their weapons — two light spruce twigs with fine tufts of needles on their tips for Gylfie; a larger limb for Twilight, who could handle the heft of the well-seasoned oak branch that would burn slowly and maintain a glowing, fiery tip. Soren chose a pliant limb from a fir tree. He knew firs, and this particular limb had an abundance of needle clusters. It would be the most strategic weapon of all. With his superb flying skills, Soren would be able to clear a path as if he were brandishing a comet. Digger, who had the strongest legs of any of them, would carry a double-fired birch limb. With flames at each end of the branch, he would grip the limb from the middle and wield it like a stave. After selecting the right weapon, with a near ritualistic serenity each owl would dip it into the coals to ignite it. The Band had all been tested in battle. But Coryn, though he had survived more than his fair share of tests of courage, had never really been tried in full battle. And although he was perhaps one of the greatest colliers who ever lived he had never fought with fire. How the young king envied the four owls of the Band their confidence, their single-mindedness, their unswerving determination. From the smallest to the largest, they seemed so resolute, so ready. And yet who had more at stake than himself? He was about to face the mother who once tried to kill him. He was the king of the Great Ga'Hoole Tree. But did he have Ga', that elusive spirit he had read about in the legends? Hoole's mother, Queen Siv, was said to have had it. Coryn suspected that his uncle Soren possessed Ga'. He looked at his uncle now as he stepped forward to ignite his branch. Coryn would be next. Would something fire within him to steady his nerves, to trim his gizzard for this battle? Yes, he had retrieved the ember, but did he have Ga'? That was the question.

CHAPTER TWENTY-TWO

The Book, the Battle, and the Band

There were two thoughts in their minds as they flew with their burning branches toward the cave: Don't let the wolves or Nyra leave the cave and don't let them go deeper into the tunnel. That was their strategy, coupled with the element of surprise. There was one other thing that they had to accomplish, and indeed, this was the entire purpose of the attack: to take *The Book of Kreeth*. Gylfie had managed to see where Nyra had put the book. It was in a niche just above the fire pit where Kludd's bones had been burned. The ashes of those bones were still there in a small pile encircled by stones — an altar to a tyrant.

And now, deep in the bowels of the earth, Nyra perched near the tyrant's ashes, hoping with Kreeth's book of charms and spells, to re-create herself as a hagsfiend and ultimately regain and re-create her son. And then — *the ember*.

Outside the cave the twelve wolves were crouching on top of boulders, ready to pounce should a vyrwolf charge from the cave. The Band had remembered how in the legends Hoole had used the wolves and the intense green light of their eyes to cut through the fyngrot of the hagsfiends. If the wolves in the cave escaped into the light of the full moon, could this weapon of green light be used now? Would it work? They all hoped that there would be no need to find out, that the vyrwolves would be contained within the cave and be brought to a quick end.

The moon was slipping up over the horizon in its unstoppable ascent. Another thought flitted through the minds of both Soren and Gylfie. How deadly the moon could be! Years before as near hatchlings — when they were both imprisoned not far from this very spot in the canyonlands in St. Aggie's — they had been forced to remain under the light of the full moon as part of those tyrannical owls' attempts to moon blink them. Somehow they had survived and now the memory emboldened them.

"Hi-yiiiiii!!" Soren gave the shrill shriek of a Barn Owl as he whizzed into the cave with his burning firebrand. A fiery blizzard of sparks crackled through the darkness. He flew in steep, ascending and plunging loops until the cave was crisscrossed with trails of sparks. The wolves began to howl. Nyra and her owls screeched and flew for their battle claws.

Under the cover of this fiery melee, Gylfie flew with two ignited spruce twigs, one in each talon. *Steady, steady,* she told herself as directly ahead she saw a wolf's jaw drop, opening a pink cavern that could easily swallow her whole. She flew right for the throat and crammed one of her flaming twigs down the wolf's gullet. A tremendous gagging howl ripped through the cave. One twig gone but she still had one left. She wheeled around and saw Nyra come toward her. Nyra had only had time to put on one battle claw. It shot out toward Gylfie, but it merely raked the air as Gylfie darted out of Nyra's path. Because of the single battle claw Nyra was flying unbalanced. Gylfie realized that this was to her own advantage. She must continue to distract Nyra by leading her away from the niche where the book was hidden. It was Cody's job to retrieve the book. With her remaining twig, Gylfie feinted and jabbed at Nyra, who was maddened by the little owl. She then wheeled around to come in for a new, angled attack. That was when Nyra spotted Coryn. He was backing a snarling wolf into a corner with a double-fired branch similar to Digger's.

"You!" Nyra screeched.

And then a searing taunt seized the air. It was Twilight bellowing at the top of his lungs.

General Mam, she don't scare me,
she ain't gonna make me flee.
General Mam, she so dumb,
she don't know which way to run.
Fly by night, fly by day —
she ain't gonna get away.
She so ugly, that frinkin' face,
she ain't nothing but a fat disgrace.
Disgrace in word, disgrace in deed,
Monster Mam is what I see!

Nyra staggered in flight, then tore off her battle claw and, seizing it like a flail, began to swing it wildly at Twilight. Suddenly, blood and sparks flew through the air. Twilight began to plummet. "No!" An anguished cry tore through the cave.

"Yes! The mighty Twilight falls!" Nyra screeched. There was a blur as Nyra flew toward the back of the cave. "Death to Twilight, killer of Kludd!"

"Stop her!" someone cried out.

The Tunnel, the Tunnel of Despair. They can't go in! That was all that Digger could think of as he tried, with his double-fired staves, to block the part of the cave that led into the tunnel. Digger was quick but not quick enough. Nyra slipped by him and now three wolves were charging him. He clipped one, setting its tail on fire. But he knew he had failed to block the tunnel.

"I'm after them!" Coryn shouted as he flew by with his fir branch spitting fire.

Furious, Digger cracked his long stave on a sharp edge of a rock, splitting it in half so he could fly down the narrow passageways of the tunnel. He had to go. Despite their narrowness, he knew best how to navigate the twisting channels of the cave. Gylfie had been there before, of course, but she was occupied with helping Cody retrieve the book. So he flew in the wake of Coryn, a burning stump of stave in each talon. The defense of blocking the tunnel entrance had failed. This was a battle that was going to be carried deep into the earth.

But perhaps not deep enough. Through a slit in the rock, a filament of moonlight seeped, a sliver of light no bigger than the thread of a plummel.

CHAPTER TWENTY-THREE

Mysticus!

S trange!" Doc Finebeak muttered as he alighted on a rock outcropping a short distance from the cave where the fighting had erupted.

"What?" Madame Plonk asked.

"I had the trail. I mean, we're still on their track but I get the oddest feeling that it has doubled back . . . back to where we are right here."

"But how could that be?" Madame Plonk hesitated. She was not sure exactly how to address this handsome, distinguished Snowy. They had been flying together for more than two nights. To call him Doc Finebeak seemed rather formal, and also was a beakful. He had not given her any other name, however. "Doc" seemed too casual. Beakie? Too familiar. Madame Plonk blinked and blinked again. Something was visible above a depression in the very rugged terrain not far ahead. "What in the world is that?" she whispered. In the light of the moon, two bright yellow slashes seemed to float just above the ground.

They rose and winged cautiously closer.

"It's . . . it's . . ." Doc Finebeak hesitated, then whispered, "a wolf!" There was more movement close to the ground and then a plume of sparks. *A volcano, here?* Finebeak wondered. It was not a volcano, but the earth seemed to be erupting. Sparks, wolves, and owls spouted from the ground. "A cave battle!" Doc Finebeak exclaimed. Some owls were fighting each other with burning branches, some were chasing the wolves and were brandishing fire as well. The battle was both above and below ground now.

"It's Coryn!" Madame Plonk gasped. "Coryn, our king." They watched in stunned silence. But now something even more peculiar was happening. Some of the wolves stopped fighting and were gamboling in the moonlight. They were growing larger before Madame Plonk's and Doc Finebeak's very eyes. They were becoming enormous.

"Great Glaux!" Madame Plonk exclaimed.

"They need our help!" Doc Finebak said. Four simple little words, but nearly incomprehensible to Madame Plonk. *What?* What in the world could she possibly do in a situation like this? *Me, fight? Fight with fire? Fight with anything?*

Ahead of them two Barn Owls rose higher, above the fray — Nyra and Coryn.

Doc Finebeak roared, spread his great wings even

wider and powered forward. "I let this female almost kill her own son once. I shall not stand by this time! Never again!"

Me? Madame Plonk thought desperately again. Panic welled in the back of her throat. *I'm a fat owl with a cracked voice.* She opened her beak to protest her helplessness. And from it a note came pealing into the night. Madame Plonk had sung many high notes before in her life. High C was an ordinary vocal experience for the singer of the great tree but right now in this moment, under the full moon with the shadow of the Earth creeping in front of it, she hit an unbelievable note. It was not simply high C. It was C-sharp in the eighth octave, the note sometimes referred to by other singers as *mysticus.* High enough to shatter glass. And now its vibrations shimmered out into the night. The wolves who had been yelping and howling fell to the ground writhing in pain. Chips of mica split off rocks. But the moon was not stayed.

Digger flew up. "Plonk, keep singing, but go to Twilight. He's ... he's dying."

"What!" she shreed, and a vyrwolf fell dead. Gyllbane and her pack fought on and above the writhing vyrwolves, who seemed vastly more affected by the mysticus than the dire wolves, Coryn and Nyra began to circle each other in flight. The merest sliver of the moon disappeared as the shadow of the Earth began to slide across it. Nyra swung her head toward her son and hissed. "We belong together, Nyroc. We were both hatched on a night such as this. Our power is great and will become greater tonight."

"That is no longer my name. I am Coryn."

"You are Nyroc and you are nothing without me." The night was growing dimmer as the Earth's shadow ate away at the moon, gnawing it like a fanged animal tearing flesh from bone. Nyra held the single battle claw in her two talons, and Coryn knew she could swing and attack with great accuracy. He still had the drops of Twilight's blood splattered on his face, and he would never forget the sight of the Great Gray plummeting in a fiery red rain of blood and sparks. Coryn's own double-fired branch was losing its heat. One end was nearly extinguished. If only the wind would rise and breathe some life into the remaining fire. *If only . . . my life is filled with "if onlys."*

Suddenly, Nyra was nearly upon him. She now had the battle claw in her teeth and a flaming branch in her talons. She was advancing upon him, pressing him against a sheer cliff wall. He hovered, backstroking as she continued to advance. He could feel his tail feathers graze the wall. He was alone. There was no Twilight to begin a taunting chant. Where was Soren? That excruciatingly high note continued to scratch the night and the flames of Nyra's branch were singeing his breast feathers. He could feel their heat. But it was not the heat of flame he felt. What heat was that? It was coming from within him. His gizzard felt on fire.

Nyra suddenly stopped advancing. She blinked. *What is this?* she thought. *My son's eyes are burning green, green like those of a wolf, but not a vyrwolf.* The light flowing like a liquid green flame from Coryn's eyes was overpowering. Deep within that light was a flicker of orange with a lick of blue at its center. But the mysterious light was coming from that ring of green. The orange, the blue, the green — was not that like the Ember of Hoole? Coryn saw Nyra begin to go yeep. Yet he hardly noticed. He just felt this overpowering glow within him. *Impossible,* he thought. He was here and the ember was far away.

The world went black and silence filled the night. The singing stopped. Coryn looked around. There was no one. Nyra had vanished. She was not on the ground or in the air. He flew down to have a closer look. No sign of her. In the back of his mind, there was a fleeting thought: Could she have fallen into one of the openings of the Tunnel of Despair? The wolves, too, seemed to have vanished. Were they in the tunnel as well? Had the earth opened to swallow this evil? *May it stay in the tunnel forever,* he thought. In the distance close to the ground, Coryn glimpsed a puff of white. He flew toward it. As he flew, he noticed beneath him a carnage of wolves, but so far no bodies of owls, and although he did not recognize the wolves as the ones who had come with them from the Beyond, they certainly did not look like vyrwolves. They were of normal size, their different colors ranging from gray to brown to cream. Was this like that desert battle of the hagsfiends he had read about in the legends when the hagsfiends, finally vanquished, looked no bigger than ordinary crows? As he drew closer, his gizzard stilled. Something awful was ahead. His mind, his heart, his gizzard railed against it. *No, not Twilight. Not Twilight . . .*

CHAPTER TWENTY-FOUR
Not Twilight

It wasn't Twilight. It was Cody. Gyllbane's sobs racked the night. The young wolf barely beyond being pup lay atop *The Book of Kreeth*, his throat slashed. "He saved the book," Gyllbane sobbed. "He saved it, but for what?" She raised her head. Coryn's gizzard was wrenched. Here was a mother who truly loved her son.

Near Cody's body lay Twilight. Madame Plonk was hovering over him, fanning him with her large wings. The Band crowded in close. He had lost a great deal of blood. He seemed shrunken and his gaze wandered deliriously.

"How will we ever get him back to the great tree?" Coryn asked.

"We won't," said Digger solemnly. Coryn blinked. Was Digger saying that Twilight would die here? He didn't understand. This wasn't like the Band. Not at all like the Band — and where was Soren?

"Where's Soren? He isn't hurt, is he?"

"No." Gylfie stepped forward. "Soren is on his way to

Ambala with Doc Finebeak. They will fly through the rest of the night and through the day."

"Why?" asked Coryn. But the rest of them really weren't hearing Coryn's questions. They were all staring at his eyes as the last telltale reflections of the Ember of Hoole faded from them. "Why?" demanded Coryn more forcefully. "Why, at a time like this, is he flying to Ambala?"

Gylfie stepped forward closer now and looked up into the young king's eyes, still searching for what she thought she had glimpsed. "He has gone to Ambala to seek Slynella and Stingyll."

"Slynella and Stingyll!" Coryn felt his gizzard stir with happiness because these were the two flying snakes, companions of Mist, who lived with her in the eagle's nest high in the mountaintops of Ambala. Their poisonous venom could also cure, if properly dispensed from the two prongs of their ivory-and-crimson forked tongues. The snakes had befriended Coryn after he had left his mother and the Pure Ones, when Coryn had been treated as an outcast and forced to flee nearly every forest in the Southern Kingdoms.

If only Twilight could live until they arrived. Soren was a fast flier, and with Doc Finebeak's free pass through crow territory, perhaps there was a chance. Coryn crouched down on the ground near the Great Gray.

"Twilight," Coryn whispered. "Live. Please live." The other owls huddled in closer. They, too, began to speak encouraging words despite their worst fears. Gylfie and Digger were dazed. They had been the Band forever. They had been four. *And now with Twilight on the brink of death, and Soren away, we feel . . .* Gylfie thought, *like an owl with one wing. Halved. Diminished.*

For the rest of the night and through the next day they all spoke encouraging words to the Great Gray, and Madame Plonk continued to fan Twilight tirelessly with her enormous white wings. A vole was caught, killed, and its blood squeezed into Twilight's parched throat. Twilight had been thrashing and restless, but now as tween time approached, he grew quieter. Digger and Gylfie and Madame Plonk glanced nervously at one another. What did this mean? They all knew this was the hour that Twilight had been named for. It was that silvery edge of time that truly was Twilight's hour. He was an owl who could see things that other birds could not when the boundaries between day and night became dim and shapes melted away, when the edges of time and space, of earth and sky, became uncertain. How often had they heard the Great Gray say, "I live on the edge and I love it"? But what edge was that dear, brash owl teetering on now?

Was it truly the edge between being and not being, between sky and glaumora, between life and death? For Twilight to die at twilight, for him to draw his last breath as the evening shadows gathered seemed so wrong.

So very wrong, Gylfie thought.

"Look!" Hamish said. "Look to the east." Two glowing scrolls of green unfurled through a low-flying cloud.

"It's Slynella!" Gylfie shrieked.

"And Stingyll!" Digger gasped in relief. The two flying snakes were flanked by Soren and Doc Finebeak.

"Hang on!" Gylfie crouched close to Twilight's ear slits. "Hang on! Remember how they saved Soren that time, Twilight?"

The venomous green flying snakes of Ambala, elixirs for life and poisons for death in their forked tongues, could cure the most grievously wounded, but they could not bring back the dead. Gylfie glanced at Gyllbane, who had dragged herself to her feet and looked longingly as the snakes coiled themselves around the barely breathing body of Twilight. Gylfie flew back and lighted down in the ruff of Gyllbane's neck fur. "I am so sorry, Gyllbane. So very sorry."

"Can nothing be done?"

"I'm afraid not. The snakes are good but they cannot perform miracles."

Gyllbane shut her eyes tight. "Cody and I, we escaped

MacHeath and that was a miracle, and our time together seems like another sort of miracle. But it is over." The sky was growing darker. The stars were breaking out and Gyllbane looked up as if searching for something. Then she rose and walked away. Gylfie fluttered off her back, sensing that the wolf needed to be alone for a while, alone and apart. She went over to where the owls were still clustered around Twilight. The snakes' jaws were stretched so wide open that they appeared to be unhinged. Their forked tongues were flickering in the night like strange pink lightning as they dabbed their venom in the still-bleeding wounds of Twilight. Soren looked up. "I think they're stanching the flow of blood. He seems better. His breathing is more even. But the gash on his port wing is bad. I don't know how he'll fly with it ever again."

A ragged voice cut through the evening air. "I'll teach myself. I'm from the Orphan School of Tough Learning. Flew when I was barely fledged. Nobody taught me then. Had to figure it out for myself. Lived with foxes in Kuneer. Learned how to drill a hole in a tree from woodpeckers in Ambala. I'll teach myself to fly with this wing, you can bet on it. Now, scram, all of you. I need my sleep. I'll be ready to fly by tomorrow's First Black." He paused and churred. "With a little help from my friends."

*   *   *

Twilight was ready not by First Black but two days later, which was miracle enough. The Band arranged themselves into a loose rectangle known as a krokenbot, which was a flight vacuum for transporting wounded owls. It was a formation they had learned from the owls of the Northern Kingdoms and it had proven as effective as the more traditional vine hammocks they often brought to the battlefield. The seven owls, the Band plus Doc Finebeak, Coryn, and Madame Plonk, rose now into the night with Twilight in the middle of the rectangle, who gingerly flapped his wings every few seconds. As they flew, Gylfie spun her head back to look for Gyllbane. The beautiful wolf had climbed to the very top of the rock formation known as the Great Horns, which were two peaks that rose like the tufts of a Great Horned Owl into the sky. The wolf had camped there for a night and a day and now into this night. Like a sentry of the night sky, she kept watch on a track of stars that the wolves called the spirit trail, which led to a constellation known to wolves as the cave of souls. She was waiting for the lochinmorrin, when Cody's spirit would begin to climb the spirit trail to find his peace in the cave of souls. Gyllbane would know it deep within her when it finally happened and she would wait patiently until that moment.

CHAPTER TWENTY-FIVE

Other-ish

Primrose!" Otulissa said, shocked as the tiny Pygmy Owl was shoved into the prison hollow of the great tree. "What in the world are you doing here?"

"Blasphemy." Primrose sighed.

"Blasphe . . . W-w-w-w-what? What in the world does that mean?" Otulissa asked.

Primrose blinked. "You mean you don't know?" She was stunned. She thought Otulissa, the most learned owl in the tree, would know the meaning of this word. How could Elyan and Gemma know and not Otulissa? They weren't half as smart.

"Well, I am familiar with the word in certain contexts. It comes from the Others and has something to do with their gods and their churches, but it is certainly not an owl word. I can't imagine it being an owl anything."

"Well, it is and I've done it."

"What have you done?"

"Nothing that I am aware of. So I can't really tell you."

"Primrose, Primrose." Otulissa sighed. "Does this have something to do with the ember?"

"Yes, but I didn't cause it."

"I'm sure you didn't. Just begin at the beginning."

"I was on watch. You know I'm" — she paused — "or *was*, an acolyte of the ashes. My duties were to remove the ashes from the chalice."

"The chalice? What in hagsmire is that?"

"You know, the container that Bubo made."

"Since when are they calling it the chalice? We always just called it the container or the pot — or the cask. Another one of those frinkin' Others' words. We're owls, for Glaux's sake, not Others. Well, go on."

"It was shortly after I removed the ashes that the ember started to grow dimmer, lose its glow. To make a long story short, they all got nervous. They were sure that somehow I hadn't done it right, hadn't said the right words."

"What words?"

"Just words. Gemma made them up, I think. She said I'd done something, said them wrong. Saying them wrong is blasphemy. But I swear I said them the way I always did when I remove the ashes. I didn't do anything differently. The ember just started to kind of fade. I didn't make blaswhatever." And with that, the little Pygmy Owl began to weep.

Otulissa hopped over and began running her beak through the feathers on Primrose's tiny wings. "Of course you didn't." She paused and pitched her voice low and very rough. "You want to hear blasphemy? I wish they'd chuck that frinking ember into the Sea of Hoolemere and I'd yarp a pellet on it for good measure!"

Primrose jerked up her head. "Don't speak that way, Otulissa. You'll really get in trouble."

"Trouble? I'm in *prison*. It's the whole frinking tree that's in trouble."

Primrose blinked again. She'd never heard such language coming from Otulissa. She was swearing worse than a seagull.

The prison hollow was not commodious and there had even been talk of putting bars in another hollow as there were apparently more blasphemers. But on this particular morning as a weak winter sun trickled in, Otulissa, who could not sleep, got up to stretch her wings as best she could without disturbing Primrose. Normally, she would have been happy to see this late-winter sun, for that would mean that spring could not be more than a moon cycle away, that the tree would be coming out of the season of the white rain and begin to turn silvery and then with summer golden and then in the final flush of the yearly cycle, copper rose. But for moon cycle after moon cycle, it had not changed. It was still summer gold. *How boring life is when nothing changes*, Otulissa thought as she peered out through the bars. *Gold! I hate it!* Just then in the pale dawn sky that was streaked with a pink as delicate as the inside of seashells, she saw a spot of white — two spots of white. *Not clouds*, she thought. Her thoughts came slowly but with a crispness, a clarity as she watched the two spots grow larger.

It can't be. She hasn't flown out from the island in years. But I swear I'd recognize that fat head anyplace. And Soren! Her gizzard leaped.

In the next moment, a great triumphal chord sounded from the grass harp. The great tree throbbed with a fluttering of wings, and owls could be heard crying, "The Band is back! The king is returning." Hundreds of owls swarmed out of their hollows. The air around the tree was laced with cries of "Hail Coryn, king of the Great Ga'Hoole Tree. The ember will glow once more." Then the sound of things crashing, shattering.

"What was that? What is it?" Primrose awoke with a start.

"Coryn is back. The Band is back," Otulissa said breathlessly.

"But that noise. Is it a fight? What is happening?"

"I don't know." Otulissa blinked. Fear threaded through her gizzard. "I can't imagine."

And Otulissa really couldn't have imagined what was going on in the Great Hollow. The Band, Madame Plonk, Coryn, and Doc Finebeak swept through the immense hollow where the owls shared many of their most solemn and most festive occasions. In their absence, the Great Hollow had been rendered unrecognizable — draped with all sorts of embroidered cloth and tapestries made by the nest-maids' sewing guild. The ember itself had been placed on an altar that was strung with beads and pearls obviously acquired through Trader Mags.

"It looks like a church!" Gylfie squealed in dismay.

"It's so OTHER!" Soren gasped.

"It sure ain't owl!" Twilight raged. Twilight, who had much of his strength back, now seemed suddenly to regain the rest as he flew directly at the tapestry that hung behind the altar and, with his beak, tore it down.

"Blasphemy!" an owl cried. "Arrest that owl!"

"Shut up!" Bubo roared. "Or I'll knock yer block off!"

"Bubo," Coryn commanded, "go immediately and release Otulissa and then take your strongest hammer and tongs and destroy those prison bars."

The Band and Coryn tore through the Great Hollow,

ripping down tapestries, scattering ashes from small cups and bowls. The Guardians of the Guardians of the Ember perched in a confused silence, wilted, slender shadows of their former selves. They mumbled to one another, blinking and wondering. And when all the gilt and glittering ornamentation had been removed, the Great Hollow stripped bare of its elaborate decoration, the acolytes and the choirs told to shut their beaks and stop the maddening songs and prayers of praise to an ember, Coryn called the owls of the great tree to order.

"The parliament!" the young king commanded. "I want the parliament perched directly before me." The owls of the parliament gathered on a perch. "Now this group, the . . . the . . ." Coryn resisted calling them a mob. "The Guardians of the Guardians of the Ember, please fly forth."

Six owls flew up and lighted down in front of Coryn: Elyan, Gemma, and Yeena; Penfold, a Northern Saw-whet; Humbert, a Spotted Owl; and a Great Gray called Felix.

"Disgrace to the species!" Twilight muttered, eyeing Felix.

Elyan stepped forward. "We meant no harm. We only intended to protect."

"You did nothing of the sort," Coryn fumed. "You violated the very meaning, the essence of this tree. A prison!

What twisted gizzard came up with the horrendous notion of a prison? How dare you!" Coryn flew directly at the six owls, dropped his beak open, and hissed his fury at them. The tiny Northern Saw-whet was toppled by the wash of Coryn's wings flapping in rage. "And this ember!" He seized the iron cask and shook it so the ember glowed more fiercely. "This ember is not a living thing. It has heat, yes, and peculiar powers, and must be kept from the likes of Nyra. But it is not noble. You Guardians are noble. And I set the Great Ga'Hoole Tree and its noble owls above any ember. It is your loyalty, your love of this tree and its values that I esteem above any riches in the owl kingdoms. For that is invaluable and knows no price. I shall take the ember back to the Beyond if it becomes a false god to you. We are owls. We value each other. We celebrate our owlness and not the heat and the glow of an ember. You have done shameful things, committed heinous acts in the name of this ember. You have imprisoned one of our most trusted and revered owls, the ryb Otulissa. You have forced Bubo to make bars for a prison. Arrest!" Coryn spat out the word. "We have no room for such words in our good and Great Tree of Ga'Hoole."

"What will you do to us?" Felix asked. "What is our punishment?" Coryn blinked at the six owls. They all were waiting for him to mete out some punishment. But that would be too easy. "What would you want me to do? Put you in prison?" he said with a contempt that made every owl's gizzard shrink in shame. "What has happened here?" he wondered aloud. "You have become so Other-ish. Perhaps you should go to a place where Others might live. But they live no longer, as I understand. Now go to your hollows. We will deal with you later."

The offending owls filed out.

Coryn picked up the teacup and looked at the picture of the dignified queen with her serene blue eyes. Queen E. "Here, Madame Plonk, this belongs to you, I believe."

"I don't want it any longer, Your Majesty."

"No, Plonkie," Coryn called to her affectionately. "Take it. It is yours. You have never confused being an owl with being an Other. You're owl, through and through."

"Take it, my dear," Doc Finebeak urged.

Coryn motioned the Band and Otulissa to follow him to his hollow.

Otulissa's eyes immediately fell on the tattered book. She walked up to it slowly as she might cautiously approach a poisonous snake she was not quite sure was dead.

"It's not *The Book of Kreeth*? Great Glaux!" she whispered.

"It is," Soren replied quietly. "Nyra had it."

Otulissa jerked her head up in horror and blinked rapidly. "Let's hope she didn't learn too much."

"We want you to take a look at it," Coryn said. "You, of all of us, understand Krakish best."

Hesitantly, she opened the book as if she expected venom to shoot from it. The minutes slipped by silently, slowly. The owls almost dared not breathe. Finally, Otulissa looked up. "Well, the good news is that Nyra could not have understood a word of this. The bad news is that I can't, either. It is very ancient Krakish. We don't even have the dictionaries here that might help me with translation."

"Where would you find them?" Twilight asked.

Otulissa looked at Coryn and then Soren. "Does Coryn know about Bess?" she whispered.

"The Knower?" Coryn asked excitedly. "The Boreal Owl in the Palace of Mists?"

"I guess you do," Otulissa said matter-of-factly. "She is the only one who could decipher this. Some of it, I daresay, is written in code. But Bess is experienced with codes."

"You mean we have to go to the Palace of Mists?" Gylfie said.

"In time, I imagine," Otulissa replied. "But for now let's keep the book a secret."

"Ezylryb's secret library," Soren suggested.

"Maybe," Otulissa said. "But first I think we need to hide the ember." Its reddish light danced on the walls. The glow had been restored to an even greater intensity. Red shadows sprang across the walls as if in a wanton and wild dance to unheard music.

"And you have some ideas about that?" Coryn asked.

"Yes, come closer, all of you — not a word beyond this hollow."

Then in the ear slits of the Band, Otulissa whispered her plan.

Epilogue

On another part of the Island of Hoole, not far from the great tree, as the sun rode high in the lengthening days of early spring and the inhabitants of the tree slept the thick sleep of midday, Coryn, the Band, and Otulissa gathered deep in the cave of Bubo the blacksmith.

"This here be where I keep them." Bubo the Great Horned nodded at pits in the cave floor that glowed with heaps of coals. "I got me bonks right here." He pointed with a sooty talon. "And then the others — grade A, grade B, I don't go lower than C. Below C, they ain't much good for anything."

He paused and chuckled. "'Course, with colliers like Soren and Otulissa, Ruby and Martin, it be mostly bonks and grade A I get." This was not flattery but the truth. The colliering chaw was extraordinarily talented. Not only were they good at retrieving coals, they were excellent teachers. Soren's mate, Pelli, was bringing in a fair share of bonk coals recently, as was a young Saw-whet that Martin was teaching to work the lower layers of forest fires. "So, you be thinking of keeping the Ember of Hoole in here?"

"It was Otulissa's idea and I think it is a good one," Soren said.

"The idea is that the ember should never again become an object of . . . of . . . of fascination, of worship." Gylfie's voice was urgent as she spoke these words.

"We know it is not like other coals or embers," Coryn continued. "It affects owls who come into its presence differently." *And sometimes even those who are not in its presence,* he thought. He would never forget the extraordinary heat that began to burn within him as Nyra advanced against him, pressing him into that sheer rock wall in the canyonlands. He remembered the shock when he realized that the green light that he was seeing was actually coming from his own eyes. No one else had witnessed this, no one except Nyra, and she had appeared to have gone yeep and then simply vanished.

By careful questioning of Primrose, Coryn had figured out that it was exactly at the moment of this confrontation with Nyra that the ember's glow had begun to fade and this was what had led to Primrose's arrest. Through some mystical transference, the ember's energy had briefly become his. And although he had survived, as far as he knew his mother was not dead. Merely vanished. No body, no bones, no remains to be burned. He had peered into a few fires since he had returned, attempting to scour the flames for clues to what had happened to her. It was foolish, of course, because Coryn knew that he could never go to a fire and demand such specific information. He coughed a bit now as if to clear his head of the thought. "But Bubo, you do not seem to be affected by the ember."

"I been around so many most all me life, maybe it's . . . it's . . ."

"Like an immunity," Otulissa added. "You know, if you have had mite blight three or four times, your feathers somehow grow used to it and pretty soon the mites just dry up and don't hurt your feathers at all."

"Maybe that's it," Bubo said. "But you're welcome to keep the ember here. I can't think of a better place to hide it than in plain sight with a mess of other coals. No special container."

"Well, it was a brilliant idea, thanks to Otulissa." Soren nodded at the Spotted Owl. "Coryn, why don't you remove it now and put it in with the rest of Bubo's bonk coals?"

"Happily," Coryn said.

He plucked open the latch of the teardrop-shaped container with his talons. The ember had regained its glow since their return. It looked as it always had, fiercely orange with the glimmer of green surrounding the lick of blue at its center. Except for the green it was not so different from any of the other bonk coals in the pit. And that was exactly how the owls in Bubo's cave wanted it. There would be no more special groups or orders or societies or Guardians of the Guardians of the Ember. Coryn tipped the container over the pit and the Ember of Hoole tumbled in, lodging amid a cluster of embers in the top layer. Then it dropped down until it was almost out of sight among the others. All of the owls felt a gentle stirring like the softest breeze passing through their gizzards. They looked slowly at one another and knew at last that their world had been restored, their great tree put to rights — owls among owls and an ember among embers.

That evening as the owls began to rouse themselves from their sleep, across the Sea of Hoolemere, in the canyonlands, a beautiful wolf cast her wild untamed song into a night that flowed with stars as she saw a gathering of soft mist, the creamy golden color of her own coat.

"Cody!" she whispered. The mist wolf turned his head and raised its muzzle as if to say good-bye. "Go on! Go on!" she urged, and she felt something in her let go. Gyllbane could rest now; her pup was on the star trail and had nearly reached the cave of souls.

OWLS
and others from the

GUARDIANS OF GA'HOOLE SERIES

The Band

SOREN: Barn Owl, *Tyto alba,* from the Forest Kingdom of Tyto; escaped from St. Aegolius Academy for Orphaned Owls; a Guardian at the Great Ga'Hoole Tree and close advisor to the king

GYLFIE: Elf Owl, *Micrathene whitneyi,* from the Desert Kingdom of Kuneer; escaped from St. Aegolius Academy for Orphaned Owls; Soren's best friend; a Guardian at the Great Ga'Hoole Tree and ryb of navigation chaw

TWILIGHT: Great Gray Owl, *Strix nebulosa,* free flier, orphaned within hours of hatching; Guardian at the Great Ga'Hoole Tree

DIGGER: Burrowing Owl, *Athene cunicularia,* from the Desert Kingdom of Kuneer; lost in the desert after attack in which his brother was killed by owls from St. Aegolius; a Guardian at the Great Ga'Hoole Tree

The Leaders of the Great Ga'Hoole Tree

CORYN: Barn Owl, *Tyto alba*, the new young king of the great tree; son of Nyra, leader of the Pure Ones

EZYLRYB: Whiskered Screech Owl, *Otus trichopsis*, Soren's former mentor; the wise, much-loved, departed ryb at the Great Ga'Hoole Tree (also known as LYZE OF KIEL)

The Others at the Great Ga'Hoole Tree

OTULISSA: Spotted Owl, *Strix occidentalis*, chief ryb, and ryb of Ga'Hoology and weather chaws; an owl of great learning and prestigious lineage

MARTIN: Northern Saw-whet Owl, *Aegolius acadicus*, member of the Chaw of Chaws; a Guardian at the Great Ga'Hoole Tree

RUBY: Short-eared Owl, *Asio flammeus*, member of the Chaw of Chaws; a Guardian at the Great Ga'Hoole Tree

EGLANTINE: Barn Owl, *Tyto alba*, Soren's younger sister

MADAME PLONK: Snowy Owl, *Nyctea scandiaca*, the elegant singer of the Great Ga'Hoole Tree

MRS. PLITHIVER: blind snake, formerly the nest-maid for Soren's family; now a member of the harp guild at the Great Ga'Hoole Tree

OCTAVIA: Kielian snake, nest-maid for many years for Madame Plonk and Ezylryb (also known as BRIGID)

GEMMA: Whiskered Screech Owl, *Otus trichopsis*, a pompous member of the Great Ga'Hoole Tree

ELYAN: Great Gray Owl, *Strix nebulosa*, a member of the parliament who is unwholesomely in thrall to the Ember of Hoole

Characters from the Time of the Legends
GRANK: Spotted Owl, *Strix occidentalis*, the first collier; friend to young King H'rath and Queen Siv during their youth; first owl to find the ember

HOOLE: Spotted Owl, *Strix occidentalis*, son of H'rath; retriever of the Ember of Hoole; founder and first king of the great tree

H'RATH: Spotted Owl, *Strix occidentalis*, King of the N'yrthghar, a frigid region known in later times as the Northern Kingdoms; father of Hoole

SIV: Spotted Owl, *Strix occidentalis*, mate of H'rath and Queen of the N'yrthghar, a frigid region known in later times as the Northern Kingdoms; mother of Hoole

KREETH: Female hagsfiend with strong powers of nachtmagen; friend of Ygryk; conjured Lutta into being

Other Characters

DUNLEAVY MacHEATH: treacherous dire wolf, once leader of the MacHeath clan in Beyond the Beyond

GYLLBANE: courageous member of the MacHeath clan of dire wolves; her pup, Cody, was maimed by clan leader Dunleavy MacHeath

BESS: Boreal Owl, *Aegolius funerus*, daughter of Grimble, who was a guard at St. Aegolius Academy for Orphaned Owls; keeper of the Palace of Mists (also known as THE KNOWER)

DOC FINEBEAK: Snowy Owl, *Nyctea scandiaca*, famed freelance tracker once in the employ of the Pure Ones

"Sorry ... sorry, I'm late," Ruby said, landing in the hollow.

Otulissa looked at Soren. "Do you want to begin?"

Where to begin? Soren thought. Ruby and Martin didn't even know about the Palace of Mists. So first that had to be explained.

Soren began slowly. "There is this place, Ruby and Martin, that we discovered when we were youngsters. It is called the Palace of Mists."

"Palace of Mists," Ruby said with wonder. Soren went on to explain that they had promised Bess they would keep it a secret, except for telling Otulissa. Bess was a scholar and she had agreed to share the library and what she knew with the two most scholarly owls of the Great Tree — Otulissa and the late Ezylryb. Soren then turned to Otulissa. "I think you should tell them about the letter from Bess."

"I committed the letter to memory," she said, "so I will just recite it." Otulissa felt the tension in the hollow mounting, and then she arrived at those astounding three sentences:

"But such is not the case. These star maps were not created by the Others, but by owls. There is in fact a sixth kingdom of owls. It is called the Middle Kingdom, and I believe it is within wing-reach."

One could have heard a feather drop, or a thread of down from a plummel for that matter. There was complete and utter silence. And then everyone started talking at once. "A sixth kingdom?" "So far?" "How do we get there?" "When do we go?" "Do we tell the rest of the tree?" "What do we tell them?"

"Quiet!" Coryn ordered. They all turned to him. "We have to take things in an orderly fashion." Despite his measured tone and careful words, they all could see that Coryn was as excited as they were. He had never been to the Palace of Mists. He had heard about it from the Band and longed to go there and meet the mysterious Bess. And now perhaps to travel to this sixth kingdom — but who would be in charge of the tree? The last time they had left, near disaster had ensued. "Right now, it's not so much a question of when we leave, but how."

Ruby blinked and thought, *How? Fly! How else?*

"Do we tell the parliament right now?" Coryn asked.

Digger stepped forward. "First, I think we have to go to the Palace of Mists. Second, we must review the fragments and discuss all this with Bess. Finally, if indeed we decide to go on and seek the sixth kingdom across the Unnamed Sea   which in itself is a staggering thought — I think someone must know where we have gone. We also must tell that someone of Bess and the Palace of Mists — in case we do not return within one moon cycle."

Soren interjected, "If we do not return within a moon's cycle, there should be arrangements to send a contingent to the Palace of Mists." He paused. "And I think Eglantine would be a good choice. Eglantine along with Primrose. I will speak with them about it."

"All right, I think we've got the beginning of a plan. Tweener will be soon," Coryn said. "I know we're all very excited but, please, not a word about this in the dining hollow. No one must know anything yet."

"Yes, Coryn is right." Soren nodded solemnly. "Not a word to anyone."

Out past the reach
of the Ga'Hoole Tree,
where survival is the
only law, live the
Wolves of the Beyond.

New from Kathryn Lasky

WOLVES OF THE BEYOND

In the harsh wilderness beyond
Ga'Hoole, a wolf mother hides in
fear. Her newborn pup has a twisted
paw. The mother knows the rigid
rules of her kind. The pack cannot
have weakness. Her pup must be
abandoned—condemned to die. But
the pup, Faolan, does the unthinkable.
He survives. This is his story—the story
of a wolf pup who rises up to change
forever the Wolves of the Beyond.

SCHOLASTIC

www.scholastic.com

WOLVES

BEAUTIFUL REDEMPTION

BY

KAMI GARCIA &
MARGARET STOHL

LITTLE, BROWN AND COMPANY
New York • Boston

Copyright © 2012 by Kami Garcia, LLC, and Margaret Stohl, Inc.
Excerpt from *Icons* copyright © 2013 by Margaret Stohl, Inc.
Excerpt from *Unbreakable* copyright © 2013 by Kami Garcia, LLC

Little, Brown and Company

Hachette Book Group
237 Park Avenue, New York, NY 10017
Visit our website at www.lb-teens.com

Little, Brown and Company is a division of Hachette Book Group, Inc.
The Little, Brown name and logo are trademarks of Hachette Book Group, Inc.

The publisher is not responsible for websites (or their content)
that are not owned by the publisher.

First Paperback Edition: October 2013
First published in hardcover in October 2012 by Little, Brown and Company

Library of Congress Cataloging-in-Publication Data

Garcia, Kami.
Beautiful redemption / by Kami Garcia & Margaret Stohl.
p. cm. — (Beautiful creatures ; 4)
Summary: When Ethan wakes after the chilling events of the Eighteenth Moon, his one goal is to return to Lena and his loved ones, while back in Gatlin, Lena vows to do whatever it takes to bring Ethan home—even trusting old enemies and risking the lives of those Ethan left to protect.
ISBN 978-0-316-12353-2 (hardback) / ISBN 978-0-316-12356-3 (paperback)
[1. Supernatural—Fiction. 2. Psychic ability—Fiction. 3. Love—Fiction.
4. South Carolina—Fiction.] I. Title.
PZ7.G155627Bfr 2012 [Fic]—dc23 2012022870

10 9 8 7 6 5 4 3 2 1
RRD-C
Printed in the United States of America

For our fathers,
Robert Marin and Burton Stohl,
who taught us to believe
we could do anything,
and
our husbands,
Alex Garcia and Lewis Peterson,
who made us do the one thing
we never thought we could.

Death is the beginning of Immortality.

— MAXIMILIEN ROBESPIERRE

Beginning Again

Other people had flying dreams. I had falling nightmares. I couldn't talk about it, but I couldn't stop thinking about it either.

About him.

Ethan falling.

Ethan's shoe dropping to the ground, seconds before.

It must have come off when he fell.

I wondered if he knew.

If he'd known.

I saw that muddy black sneaker dropping from the top of the water tower every time I closed my eyes. Sometimes I hoped it was a dream. I hoped I'd wake up, and he'd be waiting out in the driveway, in front of Ravenwood, to take me to school.

Wake up, sleepyhead. I'm almost there. That's what he would've Kelted.

I'd hear Link's bad music coming through the open window, before I even saw Ethan behind the wheel.

That's how I imagined it.

I'd had nightmares about him a thousand times before. Before I knew him, or at least knew he was going to be Ethan. But this wasn't like anything I'd ever seen in any nightmare.

It shouldn't have happened. It wasn't how his life was supposed to be. And it couldn't be how my life was supposed to be.

That muddy black sneaker wasn't supposed to drop.

Life without Ethan was something worse than a nightmare.

It was real.

So real that I refused to believe it.

———

February 2nd
Nightmares end.
That's how you know they're nightmares. This—
Ethan— everything—it isn't ending, has no sign
of ending.
I felt—I feel—like I'm stuck.

Like it's my life that shattered when he—when
everything else ended.
It broke into a thousand tiny pieces.
When he hit the ground.

I couldn't stand to look at my journal anymore. I couldn't write poetry; it hurt to even read it.

It was all too true.

The most important person in my life died jumping off the Summerville water tower. I knew why he did it. Knowing why didn't make me feel any better.

Knowing he did it for me only made me feel worse.

Sometimes I didn't think the world was worth it.

Saving.

Sometimes I didn't think I was worth it either.

Ethan thought he was doing the right thing. He knew it was crazy. And he didn't want to go, but he had to anyway.

Ethan was like that.

Even if he was dead.

He saved the world, but he shattered mine.

What now?

BOOK ONE

Ethan

⊰ CHAPTER 1 ⊱

Home

A blur of blue sky over my head.

Cloudless.

Perfect.

Just like the sky in real life, only a little more blue and a little less sun in my eyes.

I guess the sky in real life isn't actually perfect. Maybe that's what makes it so perfect.

Made it.

I squeezed my eyes shut again.

I was stalling.

I wasn't sure I was ready to see whatever was out there to

see. Of course the sky looked better—Heaven being what it was and all.

Not to assume that's where I was. I'd been a decent guy, as far as I could tell. But I had seen enough to know that everything I thought about everything had pretty much been wrong so far.

I had an open mind, at least by Gatlin's standards. I mean, I'd heard all the theories. I had sat through more than my share of Sunday school classes. And after my mom's accident, Marian told me about a Buddhism class she took at Duke taught by a guy named Buddha Bob, who said paradise was a teardrop inside a teardrop inside a teardrop, or something like that. The year before that, my mom tried to get me to read Dante's *Inferno*, which Link told me was about an office building that caught fire, but actually turned out to be about a guy's voyage into the nine circles of Hell. I only remember the part my mom told me about monsters or devils trapped in a pit of ice. I think it was the ninth circle of Hell, but there were so many circles down there that after a while they all sort of ran together.

After what I'd learned about underworlds and otherworlds and sideways worlds, and whatever else came in the whole triple-layer cake of universes that was the Caster world, that first glimpse of blue sky was fine by me. I was relieved to see there was something that looked like a cheesy Hallmark card waiting for me. I wasn't expecting pearly gates or naked cherub babies. But the blue sky, that was a nice touch.

I opened my eyes again. Still blue.

Carolina blue.

A fat bee buzzed over my head, climbing high into the sky—until he banged into it, just as he had a thousand times before.

Because it wasn't the sky.

It was the ceiling.

And this wasn't Heaven.

I was lying in my old mahogany bed in my even older bedroom at Wate's Landing.

I was home.

Which was impossible.

I blinked.

Still home.

Had it been a dream? I desperately hoped so. Maybe it was, just like it had been every single morning for the first six months after my mom died.

Please let it have been a dream.

I reached down and searched the dust under my bed frame. I felt the familiar pile of books and pulled one out.

The Odyssey. One of my favorite graphic novels, though I was pretty sure Mad Comix had taken a few liberties with the version Homer wrote.

I hesitated, then pulled out another. *On the Road.* The first sight of the Kerouac was undeniable proof, and I rolled to one side until I could see the pale square on my wall where, until a few days ago—was that all it had been?—the tattered map had hung, with the green marker lines circling all the places from my favorite books I wanted to visit.

It was my room, all right.

The old clock on the table next to my bed didn't seem to be working anymore, but everything else looked about the same. It must be a warm day, for January. The light that came flooding in from the window was almost unnatural—sort of like I was in one of Link's bad storyboards for a Holy Rollers music video. But aside from the movie lighting, my room was exactly the way I'd left it. Just like the books under my bed, the shoe boxes holding my whole life story were still there lining my walls. Everything that was supposed to be there was there, at least as far as I was concerned.

Except Lena.

L? You there?

I couldn't feel her. I couldn't feel anything.

I looked at my hands. They seemed all right. No bruises. I looked at my plain white T-shirt. No blood.

No holes in my jeans or my body.

I went to my bathroom and looked at myself in the mirror above my sink. There I was. Same old Ethan Wate.

I was still staring at my reflection when I heard a sound from downstairs.

"Amma?"

My heart felt like it was pounding, which was pretty funny, since when I woke up, I wasn't even sure it was beating. Either way, I could hear the familiar sounds of my house, coming

10

from down in the kitchen. Floorboards creaked as someone moved back and forth in front of the cupboards and the burners and the old kitchen table. Same old footsteps, going about the same old business as usual in the morning.

If it was morning.

The smell of our old frying pan on the burner came wafting up from downstairs.

"Amma? That's not bacon, is it?"

The voice was clear and calm. "Sweetheart, I think you know what I'm cooking. There's only one thing I know how to cook. If you can call it that."

That voice.

It was so familiar.

"Ethan? How much longer are you going to make me wait to give you a hug? Been down here a long time, darling."

I couldn't understand the words. I couldn't hear anything except the voice. I'd heard it before, not that long ago, but never like this. As loud and clear and full of life as if she was downstairs.

Which she was.

The words were like music. They chased all the misery and confusion away.

"Mom? Mom!"

I raced down the stairs, three at a time, before she could answer.

◄ CHAPTER 2 ►

Fried Green Tomatoes

There she was, standing in the kitchen in her bare feet, her hair the same as I remembered—half up, half down. A crisp white button-down shirt—what my dad used to call her "uniform"—was still covered with paint or ink from her last project. Her jeans were rolled at her ankles like always, whether or not it was in style. My mom never cared about stuff like that. She was holding our old, black iron frying pan filled with green tomatoes in one hand and a book in the other. She had probably been cooking while she read, without looking up. Humming some part of a song she didn't even realize she was humming and probably couldn't hear.

That was my mom. She seemed exactly the same.

Maybe I was the only one who had changed.

I took a step closer, and she turned toward me, dropping the book. "There you are, my sweet boy."

I felt my heart turning inside out. Nobody else called me that; they wouldn't want to and I wouldn't let them. Just my mom. Then her arms caught me, and the world folded around us as I buried my face in her hug. I breathed in the warm smell and the warm feeling and the warm everything that was my mom to me.

"Mom. You're back."

"One of us is." She sighed.

That's when it hit me. She was standing in my kitchen, and I was standing in my kitchen, which meant one of two things: Either she had come back to life, or...

I hadn't.

Her eyes filled with something—tears, love, sympathy— and before I knew it, her arms were around me again.

My mom always understood everything.

"I know, sweet boy. I know."

My face found its old hiding place in the crook of her shoulder.

She kissed the top of my head. "What happened to you? It wasn't supposed to be like this." She pulled back so she could see me. "None of it was supposed to end this way."

"I know."

"Then again, it's not like there's a right way to end a person's life, is there?" She pinched my chin, smiling down into my eyes.

I had memorized it. The smile, her face. Everything. It was all I had left during the time she was gone.

I'd always known she was alive somewhere, in some way. She had saved Macon and sent me the songs that shepherded me through every strange chapter of my life with the Casters. She'd been there the whole time, just like she had when she was alive.

It was only one moment, but I wanted to keep it that way as long as I could.

I don't know how we got to the kitchen table. I don't remember anything except the solid warmth of her arms. But there I sat, in my regular chair, as if the past few years had never even happened. There were books everywhere—and from the looks of it, my mom was partway through most of them, as usual. A sock, probably fresh from the laundry, was stuck in *The Divine Comedy*. A napkin poked halfway out of *The Iliad*, and on top of that a fork marked her place in a volume of Greek mythology. The kitchen table was full of her beloved books, one pile of paperbacks higher than the next. I felt like I was back in the library with Marian.

The tomatoes sizzled in the pan, and I breathed in the scent of my mother—yellowing paper and burnt oil, new tomatoes and old cardboard, all laced through with cayenne pepper.

No wonder libraries made me so hungry.

My mom slid a blue and white china platter onto the table between us. Dragonware. I smiled because it had been her favorite. She dropped hot tomatoes onto a paper towel, sprinkling pepper across the plate.

"There you go. Dig in."

I tucked my fork into the nearest slice. "You know, I haven't eaten one of these since you—since the accident." The tomato was so hot it burned my tongue. I looked at my mom. "Are we—is this—?"

She returned the look blankly.

I tried again. "You know. Heaven?"

She laughed, pouring sweet tea into two tall glasses—tea being the only other thing my mom knew how to make. "No, not Heaven, EW. Not exactly."

I must have looked worried, like I thought we had somehow ended up in the other place. But that couldn't be right either, because—as cheesy as it sounded—being with my mom again was Heaven, whether or not the universe thought of it that way. Then again, the universe and I hadn't agreed on much lately.

My mom pressed her hand against my cheek and smiled as she shook her head. "No, this isn't any kind of final resting place, if that's what you mean."

"Then why are we here?"

"I'm not sure. You don't get a user's manual when you check in." She took my hand. "I always knew I was here because of you—some unfinished business, something I needed to teach you or tell you or show you. That's why I sent you the songs."

15

"The Shadowing Songs."

"Exactly. You kept me plenty busy. And now that you're here, I feel like we were never apart." Her face clouded over. "I always hoped I would get to see you again. But I hoped I would be waiting a lot longer. I'm so sorry. I know it must be terrible for you right now, leaving Amma and your father. And Lena."

I nodded. "It sucks."

"I know. I felt the same way," she said.

"About Macon?" The words came tumbling out of my mouth before I could stop them.

Her cheeks went red. "I guess I deserved that. But not everything that happens in a mother's life is something she needs to discuss with her seventeen-year-old son."

"Sorry."

She squeezed my hand. "You were the person I didn't want to leave, most of all. And you were the person I worried about leaving, most of all. You and your father.

"Your father, thankfully, is in the exceptional care of the Ravenwoods. Lena and Macon have him under some power-ful Casts, and Amma's spinning stories of her own. Mitchell has no idea what's happened to you."

"Really?"

She nodded. "Amma tells him you're in Savannah with your aunt, and he believes it." Her smile wavered, and she looked past me into the shadows. I knew she must be worried about my dad, despite whatever Casts he was under. My sudden departure from Gatlin was probably hurting her as much as it was me—standing by and watching it all happen, without being able to do anything about it.

"But it's not a long-term solution, Ethan. Right now everyone is just doing the best that they can. That's usually how it is."

"I remember." I'd been through it once before.

We both knew when.

She didn't say anything after that, just picked up a fork of her own. We ate together in silence for the rest of the afternoon, or for a moment. I couldn't tell which was which anymore, and I wasn't sure it mattered.

We sat out on the back porch picking shiny-wet cherries out of the colander and watching the stars come out. The sky had faded to a darkish blue, and the stars appeared in crazy bright clusters. I saw stars from the Caster sky and the Mortal sky. The split moon hung between the North Star and the Southern Star. I didn't know how it was possible to see two skies at once, two sets of constellations, but it was. I could see everything now, like I was two different people at the same time. Finally, an end to the whole Fractured Soul thing. I guess one of the perks of dying was having both halves of my soul back together.

Yeah, right.

Everything had come together now that it was over, or

maybe because it was over. I guess life was like that some-times. It all looked so simple, so easy from here. So unbeliev-ably bright.

Why was this the only solution? Why did it have to end like this?

I leaned my head against my mom's shoulder. "Mom?"

"Sweetheart."

"I need to talk to Lena." There it was. I'd finally said it. The one thing that had kept me from being able to exhale all day. The thing that had made me feel like I couldn't sit down, like I couldn't stay. Like I had to get up and go somewhere, even if I had nowhere to go.

As Amma used to say, the good thing about the truth is it's true, and there's no arguing with the truth. You may not like it, but that doesn't make it any less true. That's all I had to hold on to right about now.

"You can't talk to her." My mom frowned. "At least, it's not easy."

"I need to tell her I'm okay. I know her. She's waiting for a sign from me. Just like I was waiting for a sign from you."

"There's no Carlton Eaton to run your letter over to her, Ethan. You can't send a letter from this world, and you can't get to hers. And even if you could, you wouldn't be able to write one. You don't know how many times I wished it was possible."

There had to be a way. "I know. If it was, I would've heard from you more."

18

She looked up toward the stars. Her eyes shone with reflected light as she spoke. "Every day, my sweet boy. Every single day."

"But you found a way to talk to me. You used the books in the study, and the songs. And I saw you that night I was at the cemetery. And in my room, remember?"

"The songs were the Greats' idea. I suppose because I had been singing to you since you were a baby. But everyone's different. I don't think you can send anything like a Shadowing Song to Lena."

"Even if I knew how to write one." My songwriting skills made Link look like one of the Beatles.

"It wasn't easy for me, and I'd been kicking around here a whole lot longer than you have. And I had help from Amma, Twyla, and Arelia." She squinted up at the twin skies. "You have to remember, Amma and the Greats have powers that I know nothing about."

"But you were a Keeper." There had to be things she knew that they didn't.

"Exactly. I was a Keeper. I did what the Far Keep asked me to do, and I didn't do what the Far Keep didn't want me to do. You don't mess with them, and you don't mess with their record of things."

"*The Caster Chronicles?*"

She picked a cherry from the bowl, examining it for spots. She took so long to answer, I was starting to think she hadn't heard me. "What do you know about *The Caster Chronicles?*"

"Before Aunt Marian's trial, the Council of the Far Keep came to the library, and they brought the book with them."

She put the old metal colander down on the step beneath us. "Forget about *The Caster Chronicles*. All of that doesn't matter anymore."

"Why not?"

"I'm serious, Ethan. We're not out of danger, you and I."

"Danger? What are you talking about? We're already—you know."

She shook her head. "We're only partway home. We've got to find out what's keeping us here, and move on."

"What if I don't want to move on?" I wasn't ready to give up. Not as long as Lena was waiting for me.

Once again, she didn't answer for a long time. When she did, my mom sounded about as dark as I'd ever heard her. "I don't think you have a choice."

"You did," I said.

"It wasn't a choice. You needed me. That's why I'm here—for you. But even I can't change what happened."

"Yeah? You could try." I found myself crushing a cherry in my hand. The juice ran red between my fingers.

"There's nothing to try, Ethan. It's over. It's too late." She barely whispered, but it felt like she was shouting.

Anger welled up inside me. I hurled a cherry across the yard, then another, then the whole bowlful. "Well, Lena and Amma and Dad need me, and I'm not just going to give up. I feel like I shouldn't be here—like this is all a huge mistake." I looked at the empty bowl in my hands. "And it's not cherry season. It's winter." I looked up at her, my eyes blurring with tears, though all I could feel was anger. "It's supposed to be winter."

My mom put her hand on mine. "Ethan."

I pulled away. "Don't try to make me feel better. I missed you, Mom. I did. More than anything. But as happy as I am to see you, I want to wake up and have this not be happening. I understand why I had to do it. I get it. Fine. But I don't want to be stuck here forever."

"What did you think was going to happen?"

"I don't know. Not this." Was that the truth? Had I really thought I could get out of sacrificing my own good for the good of the world? Did I think the One-Who-Is-Two thing was a joke?

I guess it was easier to play the hero. But now that it was real—now that I had to own up to an eternity of what and who I'd lost—suddenly it didn't seem so easy.

My mom's eyes welled up, worse than mine. "I'm so sorry, EW. If there was a way I could change things, I would." She sounded as miserable as I felt.

"What if there is?"

"I can't change everything." My mom looked down at her bare feet on the step below her. "I can't change anything."

"I'm not ready for some stupid cloud, and I don't want to get my wings when some stupid bell rings." I threw the metal bowl. It went clattering down the stairs, rolling across the back lawn. "I want to be with Lena and I want to live and I want to go to the Cineplex and eat popcorn until I'm sick and drive too fast and get a ticket and be so in love with my girlfriend that I make a total fool out of myself every day for the rest of my life."

"I know."

"I don't think you do," I said, louder than I'd intended. "You had a life. You fell in love—twice. And you had a family. I'm seventeen. This can't be the end for me. I can't wake up tomorrow and know that I'm never going to see Lena again."

My mother sighed, sliding her arm around me and pulling me close.

I said it again because I didn't know what else to say. "I can't."

She rubbed my head like I was a sad, scared little kid. "Of course you can see her. That's the easy part. I can't guarantee you can talk to her, and she won't be able to see you, but you can see her."

I looked at her, stunned. "What are you talking about?"

"You exist. We exist here. Lena and Link and your father and Amma, they exist in Gatlin. It's not that one plane of existence is more or less real. They're just different planes. You're here and Lena's there. In her world, you'll never be fully present. Not like you were. And in our world, she'll never be like us. But that doesn't mean you won't be able to see her."

"How?" At that moment, it was the only thing I wanted to know.

22

"It's simple. Just go."

"What do you mean, go?" She was making it sound easy, but I had a feeling there was more to it.

"You imagine where you want to go, and then you just go."

It didn't seem possible, even though I knew my mom would never lie to me. "So if I just wish myself to Ravenwood, I'll be there?"

"Well, not from our back porch. You have to leave Wate's Landing before you can go anywhere. I think our homes have the Otherworld equivalent of a Binding on them. When you're at home, you're here with me and nowhere else."

A shiver went down my spine as she said the words. "The Otherworld? Is that where we are? What it's called?"

She nodded, wiping her cherry-stained hand on her jeans.

I knew I wasn't anywhere I'd been before. I knew it wasn't Gatlin, and I knew it wasn't Heaven. Still, something about the word seemed farther away than anything I'd ever known. Farther even than death. Even though I could smell the dusty concrete of our back patio and the fresh cut grass stretching beyond it. I could feel the mosquitoes biting and the wind moving and the splinters of the old wooden steps at my back. All it felt like was loneliness. It was just us now. My mom, and me, and my backyard full of cherries. Some part of me had been waiting for this ever since her accident, and another part of me knew, maybe for the first time, it would never be enough.

"Mom?"

"Yes, sweet boy?"

"Do you think Lena still loves me, back in the Mortal realm?"

She smiled and tousled my hair. "What kind of silly question is that?"

I shrugged.

"Let me ask you this. Did you love me when I was gone?"

I didn't respond. I didn't have to.

"I don't know about you, EW, but I knew the answer to that question every day we were apart. Even when I didn't know anything else about where I was or what I was supposed to be doing. You were my Wayward, even then. Everything always brought me back to you. Everything." She smoothed my hair out of my face. "You think Lena's any different?"

She was right.

It was a stupid question.

So I smiled and took her hand and followed her inside. I had things to figure out and places to go—that much I knew. But some things I didn't have to figure out. Some things hadn't changed, and some things never would.

Except me. I had changed, and I would give anything to change back.

CHAPTER 3

This Side or the Next

Go on, Ethan. See for yourself."

I didn't look back at my mom when I reached for the doorknob.

Even though she was telling me to go, I was still uneasy. I didn't know what to expect. I could see the painted wood of the door, and I could feel the smooth iron of the handle, but I had no way of knowing if Cotton Bend was on the other side.

Lena. Think about Lena. About home. This is the only way.

Still.

This wasn't Gatlin anymore. Who knew what was behind that door? It could be anything.

I stared down at the knob, remembering what the Caster Tunnels had taught me about doors and Doorwells.

And portals.

And seams.

This door might look normal enough—any Doorwell looked pretty much like the next—but that didn't mean it was. Like the *Temporis Porta*. You never knew where you were going to end up. I'd learned that the hard way.

Quit stalling, Wate.

Get on with it.

What are you, chicken? What do you have to lose now?

I closed my eyes and turned the knob. When I opened them, I wasn't staring at my street—not even close.

I found myself on my front porch in the middle of His Garden of Perpetual Peace, Gatlin's cemetery. Right in the middle of my mother's plot.

The cultivated lawns stretched out in front of me, but instead of headstones and mausoleums decorated with plastic cherubs and fawns, the graveyard was full of houses. I realized I was looking at the homes of the people buried in the cemetery, if that's even where I was. Old Agnes Pritchard's Victorian was planted right where her plot should have been, with the same yellow shutters and crooked rosebushes that hung over the walkway. Her house wasn't on Cotton Bend, but her little rectangle of grass in Perpetual Peace was directly across from my mom's plot—the spot where Wate's Landing was sitting now.

Agnes' house looked almost exactly as it had in Gatlin, except her red front door was gone. In its place was her weathered cement headstone.

AGNES WILSON PRITCHARD
BELOVED WIFE, MOTHER & GRANDMOTHER
MAY SHE SLEEP WITH THE ANGELS

The words were still etched into the stone, which fit perfectly into the painted white doorframe. It was the same at every house as far as I could see—from Darla Eaton's restored Federal to the peeling paint of Clayton Weatherton's place. All the doors were missing, replaced by the gravestones of the dearly departed.

I turned around slowly, hoping to see my own white door with the haint blue trim. But instead I was staring at my mother's headstone.

LILA EVERS WATE
BELOVED WIFE AND MOTHER
SCIENTIAE CUSTOS

Above her name, I saw the Celtic symbol of Awen—three lines converging like rays of light—carved into the stone. Aside from being large enough to fill the doorway, the headstone was the same. Every nicked edge, every faded crack. I ran my hand over the face of it, feeling the letters beneath my fingers.

27

My mom's headstone.

Because she was dead. I was dead. And I was pretty sure I had just stepped out of her grave.

That's when I started to lose it. I mean, can you blame a guy? The situation was a little overwhelming. There's not much you can do to prepare for something like that.

I pushed on the gravestone, pounding on it as hard as I could until I felt the stone give way, and I stepped back inside my house—slamming the door behind me.

I stood against the door, breathing in as much air as I could. My front hall looked exactly the same as it had a moment ago.

My mom looked up at me from the front stairs. She had just opened *The Divine Comedy*; I could tell by the way she was still holding her sock bookmark in one hand. It was almost like she was waiting for me.

"Ethan? Changed your mind?"

"Mom. It's a graveyard. Out there."

"It is."

"And we're—" The opposite of alive. It was just starting to sink in.

"We are." She smiled at me because there wasn't really anything else she could say. "You stand there as long as you need to." She looked back down at her book and flipped a page. "Dante agrees. Take your time. It is only"—she flipped a page—"'*la notte che le cose ci nasconde.*'"

"What?"

" 'The night that hides things from us.' "

I stared at her as she continued to read. Then, seeing as there weren't that many options, I pulled the door open and stepped out.

It took me a while to take it all in, the way it takes your eyes a while to adjust to sunlight. As it turns out, the Otherworld was just that—an "other world"—a Gatlin right in the middle of the cemetery, where the dead folks in town were having their own version of All Souls Day. Except it seemed like this one lasted a lot longer than a day.

I stepped off my porch and onto the grass just to be sure it was really there. Amma's rosebushes were planted where they had always been, but they were blooming again, safe from the record-breaking heat that had killed them when it hit town. I wondered if they were blooming in the real Gatlin, too.

I hoped so.

If the Lilum kept her promise, they were. I believed she did. The Lilum wasn't Light or Dark, right or wrong. She was truth and balance in their purest forms. I didn't think she was capable of lying, or she would've sugarcoated the truth for me a little. Sometimes I wished she would have.

I found myself wandering across the freshly trimmed lawns, weaving between the familiar houses scattered throughout the cemetery like a tornado had lifted them right

out of Gatlin and dropped them here. And not just houses—
there were people here, too.

I tried heading toward Main Street, instinctively looking
for Route 9. I guess I wanted to hike to the crossroads, where I
could take a left up the road to Ravenwood. But the Otherworld didn't work that way, and every time I reached the
end of the rows of graveyard plots, I found myself back where
I started. The graveyard just kept going in circles. I couldn't
get out.

That's when I realized I needed to stop thinking in terms of
streets and start thinking in terms of graves and plots and
crypts.

If I was going to find my way back to Gatlin, I wasn't going to
walk there. Not on any kind of Route 9. That was pretty clear.

What had my mom said? *You imagine where you want to
go, and then you just go.* Was that really all that was standing
between Lena and me? My imagination?

I closed my eyes.

L—

"Whatcha doin' there, boy?" Miss Winifred looked up
from sweeping her porch a few houses away. She was in the
pink-flowered housecoat she wore most days back when she
was alive. When *we* were alive.

I stared. "Nothing. Ma'am."

Her headstone was behind her, a magnolia tree etched
above her name and underneath the word *Sacred*. There were
a lot of those around here, magnolias. I guess the magnolia

carvings were the red doors of the Otherworld. You were nobody without one.

Miss Winifred noticed me staring and stopped sweeping for a second. She sniffed. "Well, get on with it, then."

"Yes, ma'am." I could feel my face turning red. I knew I wouldn't be able to imagine myself anywhere else with those sharp old eyes on me.

Turns out, even in the streets of the Otherworld, Gatlin was no place for the imagination.

"And stay off my lawn, Ethan. You'll trample my begonias," she added. That was all. As if I had wandered onto her property back home.

"Yes, ma'am."

Miss Winifred nodded and went back to sweeping her porch like it was just another sunny day on Old Oak Road, where her house was sitting right now back in town.

But I couldn't let Miss Winifred stop me.

I tried the old concrete bench at the end of our row of plots. I tried the shadowy place behind the hedges along the edge of Perpetual Peace. I even tried sitting with my back up against the railing of our own plot for a while.

I was no closer to imagining my way to Gatlin than I was to imagining myself back into the grave.

Every time I closed my eyes, I got this spirit-killing, bone-crushing fear that I was dead in the ground. That I was gone and that I would never be anywhere again, except at the bottom of a water tower.

Not back home.

Not with Lena.

Finally, I gave up. There had to be another way.

If I wanted to get back to Gatlin, there was someone who just might know how.

Someone who made it her business to know everything about everyone and, for about the last hundred years, always had.

I knew where I needed to go.

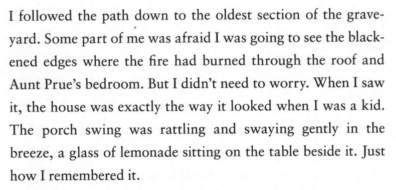

I followed the path down to the oldest section of the grave-yard. Some part of me was afraid I was going to see the black-ened edges where the fire had burned through the roof and Aunt Prue's bedroom. But I didn't need to worry. When I saw it, the house was exactly the way it looked when I was a kid. The porch swing was rattling and swaying gently in the breeze, a glass of lemonade sitting on the table beside it. Just how I remembered it.

The door was carved out of good Southern blue granite; Amma had spent hours choosing it herself. "A woman as right as your aunt deserves the right marker," Amma had said. "And anyhow, if she isn't happy, I'll never hear the end a it." Both were probably true. At the top of the gravestone, a deli-cate angel with outstretched hands was holding a compass. I was willing to bet there wasn't another angel in all of Perpet-ual Peace, or maybe any cemetery in the South, that was holding a compass. Carved angels in the Gatlin graveyard held on to every kind of flower, and some even held on to the gravestones like they were life vests. None held a compass—never a compass. But for a woman who had spent her life secretly mapping the Caster Tunnels, it was right.

Under the angel was an inscription:

PRUDENCE JANE STATHAM
THE BELLE OF THE BALL

Aunt Prue had picked out the inscription herself. Her note said she wanted another "e" on *Ball*—making it *Balle*, which wasn't even a word. According to Aunt Prue, it sounded more French that way. But my dad made the point that Aunt Prue, being a patriot, shouldn't have minded having her last words written out in plain old Southern American English. I wasn't so sure, but I also wasn't about to enter into that particular conversation. It was just one part of the extensive instructions she'd left for her own funeral, along with a guest list that required a bouncer at the church.

Still, it made me smile just looking at it.

Before I even had the chance to knock, I heard the sound of dogs yipping, and the heavy front door swung open. Aunt Prue was standing in the doorway, her hair still in pink plastic curlers, one hand on her hip. There were three Yorkshire terriers weaving around her legs—the first three Harlon Jameses.

"Well, it's 'bout time." Aunt Prue grabbed me by the ear

quicker than I had ever seen her move when she was alive, and yanked me into the house. "You were always stubborn, Ethan. But what you did this time ain't right. I don't know what in the Good Lord's Myst'ry got inta you, but I've got a mind ta send you out front ta get me a switch." It was a charming custom from Aunt Prue's day, to let a kid pick the switch you planned to whip them with. But I knew as well as Aunt Prue did that she would never hit me. If she was going to, she would have already done it years ago.

She was still twisting my ear, and I had to bend down because she was only half my height. The whole posse of Harlon Jameses were still yipping, trailing after us as she dragged me toward the kitchen. "I didn't have a choice, Aunt Prue. Everyone I loved was going to die."

"You don't have ta tell me. I watched the whole thing, and I was wearin' my good spectacles!" She sniffed. "And ta think, folks used ta say I was the mell-o-dramatic one!"

I tried not to laugh. "You need your glasses here?"

"Just used ta them, I guess. Feel nekkid without 'em now. Hadn't figured on that." She stopped walking and pointed a bony finger at me. "Don't you try changin' the subject. This time you've made a bigger mess than a blind housepainter."

"Prudence Jane, why don't you stop hollerin' at that boy?" An old man's voice called from the other room. "What's done is done."

Aunt Prue pulled me back into the hall, without loosening

her grip on my ear. "Don't you tell me what ta do, Harlon Turner!"

"Turner? Wasn't that—" As she yanked me into the living room, I found myself face to face with not one but all five of Aunt Prue's husbands.

Sure enough, the three younger ones—most likely her first three husbands—were eating corn nuts and playing cards, the sleeves of their white button-down shirts rolled up to the elbows. The fourth one was sitting on the couch reading the newspaper. He looked up and acknowledged me with a nod, shoving the little white bowl toward me. "Car nut?"

I shook my head.

I actually remembered Aunt Prue's fifth husband, Harlon— the one Aunt Prue had named all her dogs after. When I was a kid, he used to carry around sour lemon hard candy in his pocket, and he'd sneak me a couple during church. I ate them, too, lint and all. There was no telling what you'd eat in church, bored out of your skull. Link once drank a whole mini-bottle of Binaca breath spray during a talk on the atonement. Then he spent the whole afternoon and part of the evening atoning for that, too.

Harlon looked exactly the way I remembered. He threw his hands up, a sure sign of surrender. "Prudence, you're near 'bout the most ornery woman I've ever met in my en-tire life!"

It was true, and we all knew it. The other four husbands looked up, a mixture of sympathy and amusement on their faces.

Aunt Prue let go of my ear and turned to face her latest late husband. "Well, I don't recollect askin' you ta marry me, Harlon James Turner. So I reckon that makes you the most foolish man I've ever met in *my* en-tire life!" The ears of the three tiny dogs perked up at the sound of their name.

The man reading the paper stood up and patted poor old Harlon on the shoulder. "I think you ought ta let our little firecracker have some time ta herself." He dropped his voice. "Or you may end up passin' on a second time."

Aunt Prue seemed satisfied and marched back to the kitchen with the three Harlon Jameses and me following dutifully. When we reached the kitchen, she pointed to a chair at the table and busied herself pouring two tall glasses of sweet tea. "If I had known I'd have ta live with the five a those men, I'd have thought twice 'bout gettin' married at all."

And here they were. I wondered why—until I figured out it was better not to. Whatever unfinished business she had with her five husbands and about as many dogs, I sure didn't want to know.

"Drink up, son," Harlon said.

I glanced at the tea, which looked pretty appealing even though I wasn't the least bit thirsty. It was one thing when my mom was cutting me up a fried tomato. I hadn't thought twice about eating anything she handed me. Now that I had passed through the graveyard to visit my dead aunt, it occurred to me that I didn't know the rules, or anything about the way things worked over here—wherever *here* was. Aunt Prue noticed me staring at the glass. "You can drink it, not that you need ta. But it's different on the other side."

"How?" I had so many questions that I didn't know where to start.

"Can't eat or drink over there, back in the Mortal realm, but you can move things. Just yesterday, I hid Grace's dentures. Dropped 'em right down in the Postum jar." It was just like Aunt Prue to find a way to drive her sisters crazy from the grave.

"Wait—you were over there? In Gatlin?" If she could go see the Sisters, then I could get back to Lena. Couldn't I?

"Did I say that?" I knew she'd have the answer. I also knew she wouldn't tell me a thing if she didn't want me to know.

"Yeah, actually. You did."

Tell me how I can find my way back to Lena.

"Well now, just for the teeniest minute. Nothin' ta get all hopped up 'bout. Then I skee-daddled back ta the Garden here, lickety-split."

"Aunt Prue, come on." But she shook her head, and I gave up. My aunt was every bit as stubborn in this life as she'd been in the last. I tried a new subject. "The Garden? Are we really in His Garden of Perpetual Peace?"

"Darn tootin'. Every time they bury someone, a new house shows up on the block." Aunt Prue sniffed again. "Can't do a thing ta stop 'em from comin' either, even if they ain't your kind a folks."

I thought about the headstones instead of doors, all the

cemetery plot houses. I'd always thought the layout of His Garden of Perpetual Peace was kind of like our town, what with the good plots all lined up one way and the questionable graves pushed out near the edges. Turns out the Otherworld wasn't any different.

"Then why don't I have one, Aunt Prue? A house, I mean."

"Young 'uns don't get houses a their own unless their parents outlive 'em. And after seein' that room a yours, I don't see as how you could keep a whole house clean anyway." I couldn't really argue with her on that.

"Is that why I don't have a gravestone?"

Aunt Prue looked away. There was something she didn't want to tell me. "Maybe you should ask your mamma 'bout that."

"I'm asking you."

She sighed heavily. "You aren't buried at Perpetual Peace, Ethan Wate."

"What?" Maybe it was too soon. I didn't even know how much time had passed since that night on the water tower. "I guess they haven't buried me yet."

Aunt Prue was wringing her hands, which was only making me more nervous.

"Aunt Prue?"

She took a sip of her sweet tea, stalling. At least it gave her hands something to do. "Amma isn't takin' your leavin' well, and Lena's no better. Don't think I don't keep an eye on them two. Didn't I give Lena my good old rose necklace, so I can get a feel for her every now and again?"

38

The image of Lena sobbing, of Amma screaming my name right before I jumped, flashed through my mind. My chest tightened.

Aunt Prue kept on talking. "None a this was supposed ta happen. Amma knows it, and she and Lena and Macon are havin' a heap a trouble with your passin'."

My passing. The words sounded strange to me.

A horrible thought surfaced in my mind. "Wait. Are you saying they didn't bury me?"

Aunt Prue put her hand to her heart. "Of course they buried you! They did it straightaway. They just didn't bury you in the Gatlin cemetery." She sighed, shaking her head. "Didn't even have a proper memorial, I'm 'fraid. No ushers, no sermons. No Psalms or Lamentations."

"No Lamentations? You sure know how to hurt a guy, Aunt Prue." I was kidding, but she only nodded, grim as the grave.

"No program. No funeral potatoes. Nothin' so much as a supermarket biscuit. Not even a book a remembrances. Might as well a stuck you in one a them shoe boxes in your bedroom."

"Then, where did they bury me?" I was starting to get a bad feeling.

"Over at Greenbrier, by the old Duchannes graves. Stuck you in the mud like a possum-bitten house cat."

"Why?" I looked at her, but Aunt Prue glanced away. She was definitely hiding something. "Aunt Prue, answer me. Why did they bury me at Greenbrier?"

39

She looked right at me, crossing her arms over her chest defiantly. "Now, don't get yerself all bowed up. It was jus' the tiniest excuse for a service. Nothin' ta write home 'bout." She sniffed. "On account a none a the folks in town knowin' you passed."

"What are you talking about?" There was nothing folks in Gatlin came out for like a funeral.

"Amma told everyone there was an E-mergency with your aunt in Savannah, and you went on down there to help her."

"The whole town? They're pretending I'm still alive?" It was one thing for Amma to try to convince my grieving dad I was still around. For her to try to convince the whole town was more than crazy, even for Amma. "What about my dad? Won't he figure out something's going on, when I never come home? He can't think I'm down in Savannah forever."

Aunt Prue stood up and walked over to the counter, where a Whitman's Sampler was already opened. She turned the lid over, inspecting the diagram that listed the type of chocolate nestled in each brown wrapper. Finally, she chose one and took a bite.

I looked at her. "Cherry Cordial?"

She shook her head, showing me. "Messenger Boy." The rectangular chocolate boy was missing his head now. "I'll never know why folks waste their money on fancy candy. If you ask me, these are the best durned chocolates on this side or the other."

"Yes, ma'am."

Sugared up on drugstore candy, she laid the truth on me. "The Casters put a Charm on your daddy. He doesn't know you're a bit dead either. Every time it looks like he might be sniffin' 'round ta the truth, the Casters double up that Charm till he doesn't know up from down. It ain't natural, if ya ask me, but not much 'round Gatlin is. Whole place's gone downright cattywampus." She held out the half-eaten box of candy. "Now have yourself somethin' sweet. Chocolate makes everything better. Molasses Chew?"

I was buried at Greenbrier so Lena and Amma and my friends could keep it a secret from everyone, including my father— who was under the influence of a Cast so powerful that he didn't know his own son was gone, just like my mom said.

There wasn't enough chocolate in the world to make this better.

⊰ CHAPTER 4 ⊱

Catfish Crossin'

Getting Aunt Prue to say the one thing you wanted her to say, right when you wanted her to say it, was like thinking you could ask the sun to shine. At some point, and probably sooner than later, you had to admit you were at her mercy. I had to, anyway.

Because I was.

I couldn't stomach one more waxy chocolate, washed down with one more glass of sweet tea, while one more little dog stared at me, to get at the one thing I needed to know. All I could do was start begging.

"I have to go to Ravenwood, Aunt Prue. You have to help me. I have to see Lena."

My aunt sniffed and tossed the box of chocolates back down on the counter. "Oh, I see, now I *have ta have ta have ta?* Someone died and made you the Gen'ral? Next you'll be thinkin' you need a statue and a green all your own." She sniffed again.

"Aunt Prue—" I gave up. "I'm sorry."

"I reckon you are."

"I just need to know how to get to Ravenwood." I knew I sounded desperate, but it didn't matter, because I was. I hadn't been able to walk there or imagine myself there. There had to be another way.

"You know you get more bees with honey, sugar. Crossin' over from one side ta the next hasn't done much ta improve your manners, Ethan Wate. Bossin' an old woman like that."

I was losing patience with my aunt. "I said I'm sorry. I'm kind of new at this, remember? Can you please help me? Do you know anything about how to get from here to Ravenwood?"

"Do you know I'm bone tired a this conversation?"

"Aunt Prue!"

She clamped her teeth shut and stuck out her chin, the way Harlon James did when he got a lock on a bone.

"There has to be a way I can see her. My mom came to visit me twice. Once in a fire Amma and Twyla made in a graveyard, and once in my own room."

"Pretty powerful stuff, crossin' like that. Then again, your mamma's always been stronger than most folks. Why don'tcha ask her?" She looked irritated.

"Crossing?"

"Crossin' over. Not for the faint a heart. For most a us, you just can't get there from here."

"What's that supposed to mean?"

"It means you can't make preserves till you learn how ta boil water, Ethan Wate. Gotta put in the time. Get used ta the water 'fore you jump in." Not that Aunt Prue could ever bottle anything that wouldn't burn a hole in your bread, according to Amma.

I crossed my arms, annoyed. "Why would I jump into boiling water?"

She glared at me, fanning herself with a folded piece of paper the way she had on the thousand Sundays when I drove her to church.

The rocker stopped. Bad sign.

"I mean, *ma'am.*" I held my breath until the rocker started to squeak again. This time I lowered my voice. "If you know something, please help me. You said you went to see Aunt Grace and Aunt Mercy. And I know I saw you when I was at your funeral."

Aunt Prue twisted her mouth like her dentures were hurting. Or like she was trying to keep her thoughts to herself. "You had your whole mess a split-up souls back then. You could see all sorts a things a Mortal ain't supposed ta see. I ain't seen Twyla since that day either, and she's the one who crossed me over in the first place."

"I can't figure this out on my own."

" 'Course you can. You can't just show up 'round here and 'spect ta do whatcha like, easy as bad pie in a box. That's all part a crossin'. It's like fishin'. Why would I just hand you the catfish when I should be teachin' you how ta fish?"

I put my head in my hands. At that particular moment, I would have been plenty fine with bad pie in a box. "And where can a guy learn to catch a catfish around here?"

There was no answer.

I looked up to see Aunt Prue dozing in her rocking chair, the folded paper she'd been fanning herself with resting in her lap. There was no waking Aunt Prue from one of her naps. Not before, and probably not now.

I sighed, gently taking the makeshift fan out of her hand. It unfolded partway, revealing the edge of a drawing. It looked like one of her maps, only half-drawn, more of a doodle than anything else. Aunt Prue couldn't sit still long without starting to sketch out her whereabouts, even in the Otherworld.

Then I realized it wasn't a map of His Garden of Perpetual Peace—or if it was, the graveyard world was bigger than I thought.

This wasn't just any map.

It was a map of the *Lunae Libri*.

———

"How can there be a *Lunae Libri* in the Otherworld? It's not a grave, right? Nobody died there?"

My mom didn't look up from her copy of Dante. She hadn't looked up when I swung open the front door either. She couldn't hear a word anyone said when she was lost in those pages. Reading was her own version of Traveling.

I stuck my hand between her face and the yellowed pages, wiggling my fingers. "Mom."

"What?" My mom looked as startled as a person could look when you hadn't actually snuck up on them.

"Let me save you some time. I saw the movie. The office building catches fire." I closed the book and held out Aunt Prue's folded paper. My mom took it, smoothing it out in her hands.

"I knew Dante was ahead of his time." She smiled, turning over the paper.

"Why was Aunt Prue drawing this?" I asked, but she didn't answer. She just kept staring at the paper.

"If you're going to start asking yourself why your aunt does anything, you'll be busy for the rest of eternity."

"Why did she need a map?" I asked.

"What your aunt needs is to find someone else to talk to besides you."

That was all she said. Then she gave up, standing and slipping her arm around my shoulders. "Come on. I'll show you."

I followed my mom right down the street that wasn't a street, until we came to a plot that wasn't just a plot, and a familiar grave that wasn't even a grave. I stopped walking as soon as I saw where we were.

My mom laid her hand on Macon's gravestone, a wistful smile creeping across her face. She pushed on the stone, and it swung open. Ravenwood's front hall stood there, ghostly and deserted, as if nothing had changed except that Lena's family had gone to Barbados or something.

"So?" I couldn't bring myself to step inside. What use was Ravenwood without Lena or her family? It almost made me feel worse to be here in her home and still so far away.

My mom sighed. "So. You're the one who wanted to go to the *Lunae Libri*."

"You mean the secret stairway into the Tunnels? Will it lead into the *Lunae Libri*?"

"Well, I don't mean the Gatlin County Library." My mom smiled.

I pushed past her into the hallway and took off running. By the time she caught up to me, I had made it all the way to Macon's old room. I flipped up the carpet and yanked open the trapdoor.

There they were.

The invisible stairs leading down into the Caster darkness.

And beyond, the Caster Library.

⊰ CHAPTER 5 ⊱

Another Lunae Libri

Darkness, it turns out, is about as dark as usual no matter what world you're in. The invisible steps beneath the trapdoor—the same ones I'd stumbled and climbed and half-fallen my way down so many times before—were every bit as invisible as they'd ever been.

And the *Lunae Libri*?

Nothing had changed about the moss-covered, rocky passageways that led us there. The long rows of ancient books, scrolls, and parchments were hauntingly familiar. Torches still threw unsteady flickering shadows across the stacks.

The Caster Library looked the same as always, even though now I was far, far away from every living Caster.

Especially the one I loved most.

I grabbed a torch from the wall, waving it in front of me. "It's all so real."

My mom nodded. "It's exactly as I remember it." She touched my shoulder. "A good memory. I loved this place."

"Me too." This was the only place that had offered me any hope when Lena and I faced the hopeless situation of her Sixteenth Moon. I looked back at my mom, half-hidden in the shadows.

"You never told me, Mom. I didn't know anything about you being a Keeper. I didn't know anything about this whole side of your life."

"I know. And I'm so sorry. But you're here now, and I can show you everything." She took my hand. "Finally."

We made our way into the darkness of the stacks, with only the torch between us. "Now, I'm no reference librarian, but I know my way around these stacks. On to the scrolls." She looked at me sideways. "I hope you never touched any of these. Not without gloves."

"Yeah. I got that down, the first time I burned all my skin off." I grinned. It was strange to be here with my mom, but now that I was, I could tell the *Lunae Libri* had been every bit hers, as much as it was Marian's.

She grinned back. "I guess that's not a problem anymore."

I shrugged. "Guess not."

She pointed to the nearest shelf, her eyes bright. It was good to see my mom back in her natural habitat.

She reached for a scroll. "C, as in *crossing*."

After what seemed like hours, we had made zero headway.

I groaned. "Can't you just tell me how to do this? Why do I have to look it up for myself?" We were surrounded by piles of scrolls, stacked all around us on the stone table at the very center of the *Lunae Libri*.

Even my mom seemed frustrated. "I already told you. I just imagine where I want to go, and I'm there. If that doesn't work for you, then I don't know how to help you. Your soul isn't the same as mine, especially not since it was fractured. You need help, and that's what books are for."

"I'm pretty sure this isn't what books are for—visitations from the dead." I glared at her. "At least, that's not what Mrs. English would say."

"You never know. Books are around for lots of reasons. As is Mrs. English." She yanked another stack of scrolls into her lap. "Here. What about this one?" She pulled open a dusty scroll, smoothing it with her hands. "It's not a Cast. It's more like a meditation. To help your mind focus, as if you were a monk."

"I'm not a monk. And I'm not any good at meditating."

"Clearly. But it wouldn't hurt you to try. Come on, focus. Listen."

She leaned over the parchment scroll, reading aloud. I read along over her shoulder.

> "In death, lie.
> In living, cry.
> Carry me home
> to remember
> to be remembered."

The words hovered in the air, like a strange silvery bubble. I reached out to touch them, but they faded out of sight as quickly as they had appeared.

I looked at my mom. "Did you see that?"

My mom nodded. "Casts are different in this world."

"Why isn't it working?"

"Try it in the original Latin. Here. Read it for yourself." She held the paper closer to the torch, and I leaned toward the light.

My voice shook as I said the words.

> "*Mortuus, iace.*
> *Vivus, fle.*
> *Ducite me domum*
> *ut meminissem*
> *ut in memoria tenear.*"

I closed my eyes, but all I could think about was how far I was from Lena. How her curling black hair twisted in the

Caster breeze. How the green and the gold flecks lit her eyes, as bright and dark as she was.

How I'd probably never see her again.

"Oh, come on, EW."

I opened my eyes. "It's no use."

"Concentrate."

"I'm concentrating."

"You're not," she said. "Don't think about where you are now. Don't think about what you've lost—not the water tower or anything that came after it. Keep your head in the game."

"I am."

"No, you're not."

"How do you know?"

"Because if you were, you wouldn't be standing here. You would be halfway home, with one foot back in Gatlin."

Would I? It was hard to imagine.

"Close your eyes."

I closed them obediently.

"Repeat what I say," she whispered.

In the silence, I heard her words inside my mind, like she was speaking aloud to me.

We were Kelting, my mother and I. In death, from the grave, in a faraway world. It seemed familiar between us, something from long ago, something we had lost.

Carry me home.

Carry me home, I said.

Ducite me domum.

Ducite me domum, I said.
To remember.
Ut meminissem, I said.
And be remembered.
Ut in memoria tenear, I said.
You remember, my son.
I remember, I said.
You will remember.
I will always remember, I said.
I am the one, I said.
You will—
I will—
Remember . . .

⊰ CHAPTER 6 ⊱

Silver Button

I opened my eyes.

I was standing in the front hallway of Lena's house. It worked. I had crossed. I was back in Gatlin, in the world of the living. I was overwhelmed with relief; it was still here.

Gatlin remained. Which meant Lena remained. Which meant everything I'd lost—everything I'd done—hadn't been for nothing.

I leaned against the wall behind me. The room stopped spinning, and I lifted my head and looked around at the old plaster walls.

The familiar flying staircase. The shining lacquered floors.

Ravenwood.

The real Ravenwood. Mortal, solid, and heavy beneath my feet. I was back.

Lena.

I closed my eyes and fought away the prickling tears.

I'm here, L. I did it.

I don't know how long I stood frozen in place, waiting for a response, like I thought she was going to come running around the corner and into my arms.

She didn't.

She didn't even feel me Kelting.

I drew in a deep breath. The enormity of it all was still hitting me.

Ravenwood looked different than the last time I was here. It wasn't really a surprise—Ravenwood was always changing—but even so, I could tell from the black sheets hanging over all the mirrors and windows that this time things had changed for the worse.

It wasn't just the sheets. It was the way the snow fell from the ceiling, even though I was inside. The cold white drifts piled in the doorways and filled the fireplace, swirling into the air like ash. I looked up to see the ceiling crowded with storm clouds that wound all the way up the stairwell to the second floor. It was pretty cold even for a ghost, and I couldn't stop shivering.

Ravenwood always had a story, and that story was Lena's. She controlled the way the house looked with her every mood. And if Ravenwood looked like this...

Come on, L. Where are you?

I couldn't help but listen for her to answer, even though all I heard was silence.

I made my way through the slick ice of the front hall until I reached the familiar sweep of the grand front stairwell. Then I climbed the white steps, one at a time, all the way to the top.

When I turned to look down, there were no footprints at all.

"L? You in there?"

Come on. I know you can feel me here.

But she didn't say anything, and as I slipped through the cracked doorway into her bedroom, it was almost a relief to see she wasn't inside. I even checked the ceiling, where I had once found her lying along the plaster.

Lena's bedroom had changed again, like it always did. This time the viola wasn't playing by itself, and there wasn't writing everywhere, and the walls weren't glass. It didn't look like a prison, the plaster wasn't cracked, and the bed wasn't broken.

Everything was gone. Her bags were packed and neatly stacked in the center of the room. The walls and the ceiling were completely plain, like an ordinary room.

It looked like Lena was leaving.

I got out of there before I could think what that would mean for me. Before I tried to figure out how I would visit her in Barbados, or wherever she was going.

It was almost as hard to think about as leaving her the first time around.

I found my way out through the massive dining room where I had sat on so many other strange days and nights. A thick layer of frost covered the table, leaving a dark, wet rectangle on the carpet immediately below. I slipped through an open door and escaped out to the back veranda, the one that faced the sloping green hill leading to the river—where it wasn't snowing at all, just overcast and gloomy. It was a relief to be back outside, and I followed the path behind the house until I came to the lemon trees and the crumbling stone wall that told me I was at Greenbrier.

I knew what I was looking for the second I saw it.

My grave.

There it was, among the bare branches of the lemon trees, a mound of fresh soil lined with stones and covered with a sprinkling of snow.

It didn't have a headstone, only a plain old cross made of wood. The new dirt hill looked like something less than a final resting place, which actually made me feel better, rather than worse, about the whole thing.

The clouds overhead shifted, and a glimmer from the grave caught my eye. Someone had left a charm from Lena's necklace on the top of the wooden cross. The sight of it made my stomach flip over.

It was the silver button that had fallen off her sweater the night we first met in the rain on Route 9. It had gotten caught in the cracked vinyl of the Beater's front seat. In a way, it felt like we had come full circle now, from the first time I saw her to the last, at least in this world.

Full circle. The beginning and the end. Maybe I really had picked a hole in the sky and unraveled the universe. Maybe there was no kind of slipknot or half hitch or taut-line that could ever keep it all from coming undone. Something connected my first glimpse of the button to this one, even though it was just the same old button. Some small bit of universe had stretched from Lena to me to Macon to Amma to my dad and my mom—and even Marian and my Aunt Prue—back to me again. I guess Liv and John Breed were in there somewhere, and maybe Link and Ridley. Maybe all of Gatlin was.

Did it matter?

When I saw Lena for the very first time at school, how could I possibly have known where this was all headed? And if I had, would I have changed a single thing? I doubted it.

I picked up the silver button carefully. The second my fingers touched it they moved more slowly, as if I had plunged my hand to the bottom of the lake. I felt the weight of the worthless tin like it was a pile of bricks.

I put it back on the cross, but it rolled off the edge, falling onto the mounded dirt of the grave. I was too tired to try to move it again. If someone else was here, would they have seen the button move? Or did it only seem like that to me? Either way, that button was hard to look at. I hadn't thought about what it would feel like to visit my own grave. And I wasn't ready to rest, in peace or not.

I wasn't ready for any of this.

I'd never really thought past the whole dying-for-the-sake-of-the-world part of things. When you're alive, you don't dwell on how you're going to spend your time once you're dead. You just figure you're gone, and the rest will pretty much take care of itself.

Or you think you're not really going to die. You're going to be the first person in the history of the world who doesn't have to. Maybe that's some kind of lie our brains tell us to keep us from going crazy while we're alive.

But nothing's that simple.

Not when you were standing where I was.

And nobody's any different from anyone else, not when you come right down to it.

These are the kinds of things a guy thinks about when he visits his own grave.

I sat down next to my headstone and flopped back on the hard soil and grass. I plucked a single blade poking through the scattering of snow. At least it was coming in green. No dead, brown grass and lubbers now.

Thank the Sweet Redeemer, as Amma liked to say.

You're welcome. That's what I'd like to say.

I looked at the grave next to me and touched the fresh, cold soil with my hand, letting it fall through my fingers. Not a bit dry either. Things really had changed around Gatlin.

I was brought up a good Southern boy, and I knew better than to disturb or disrespect any grave in town. I had walked circles around graveyards, trailing my mom carefully to avoid accidentally putting a stray foot on someone's sacred plot.

It was Link who didn't know better than to lie on top of the graves and pretend to sleep where the dead were resting. He wanted to practice—that's what he said. A dry run. "I want to see what the view is like from down there. You wouldn't want a guy to head out for the rest a his life without knowin' where it was all takin' him in the end, would you?"

But when it came to graves, it was a different thing to worry about disrespecting your own.

That's when a familiar voice caught in the wind, surprising me with how close it was. "You get used to it, you know."

I followed the voice a few graves over, and there she was, red hair blowing wild. Genevieve Duchannes. Lena's ancestor, the first Caster who had used *The Book of Moons* to try to bring back someone she loved—the original Ethan Wate. He was my great-great-great-great-uncle, and it hadn't worked out any better for him than it had for me. Genevieve failed, and Lena's family was cursed.

The last time I saw Genevieve, I was digging up her grave with Lena, looking for *The Book of Moons*.

"Is that—Genevieve? Ma'am?" I sat up.

She nodded, curling and uncurling a loose strand of hair with her hand. "I thought you might be coming around. I wasn't sure when. There's been a lot of talk." She smiled.

"Though your kind tends to stay in Perpetual Peace. Casters, we go where we like. Most of us stay in the Tunnels. I feel better here."

Talk? I bet there was, though it was hard to imagine a town full of ghostly Sheers doing the talking. More like my Aunt Prue, probably.

Her smile faded. "But you're just a boy. It's worse, isn't it? That you're so young."

I nodded in Genevieve's direction. "Yes, ma'am."

"Well, you're here now, and that's what matters. I suppose I owe you, Ethan Lawson Wate."

"You don't owe me anything, ma'am."

"I hope to repay the debt one day. Returning my locket meant the world to me, but I don't think you'll see much gratitude from Ethan Carter Wate, wherever he may be. He always was a bit stubborn that way."

"What happened to him? If you don't mind my asking, ma'am." I'd always wondered about Ethan Carter Wate— after he came back to life for only a second. I mean, he was the beginning of all of this, everything that had happened to Lena and me. The other end of the thread we pulled, the one that had unraveled the entire universe.

Didn't I have a right to know how his story ended? It couldn't have been much worse than mine, could it?

"I don't really know. They took him away to the Far Keep. We couldn't be together, but I'm sure you know that. I learned it myself, the hard way," she said, her voice sad and far away.

Her words caught in my mind, snagging on others I'd tried to push off until now. The Far Keep. The Keepers of *The Caster Chronicles*—the same ones my mom refused to talk about. Genevieve didn't look like she wanted to elaborate either.

Why didn't anyone want to talk about the Far Keep? What were *The Caster Chronicles* really about?

I looked from Genevieve to the lemon trees. Here we were, at the site of the first big fire. It was the place where her family's land had burned, and where Lena tried to face off against Sarafine for the first time.

Funny how history repeated itself around here.

Funnier still how I was about the last person in Gatlin to figure that out.

But I had learned a few things the hard way myself. "It wasn't your fault. *The Book of Moons* sort of plays tricks on people. I don't think it was ever meant for Light Casters. I think it wanted to turn you—" She shot me a look, and I stopped talking. "Sorry, ma'am."

She shrugged. "I don't know. For the first hundred years or so, I felt that way. Like that book had stolen something from me. Like I'd been duped..." Her voice trailed off.

She was right. She had gotten the short stick.

"But good or bad, I made my own choices. They're all I have now. It's my cross to bear, and I'll be the one to bear it."

"But you did it out of love." So did Lena and Amma.

"I know. That's what helps me bear it. I just wish my Ethan

didn't have to bear it, too. The Far Keep is a cruel place." She looked down at her grave. "What's done is done. There's no cheating death any more than you can cheat *The Book of Moons*. Someone always has to pay the price." She smiled sadly. "I guess you know that, or you wouldn't be here."

"I guess I do."

I knew it better than anyone.

A twig snapped. Then a voice called out, even louder.

"Stop following me, Link."

Genevieve Duchannes disappeared at the sound of the words. I didn't know how she did it, but I was so startled that I felt myself start slipping away, too.

I clung to the voice—because it was familiar, and I would've recognized it anywhere. And because it sounded like home, chaos and all.

It was the voice that anchored me in the Mortal realm now, the same way it had kept my heart bound to Gatlin when I had been alive.

L.

I froze. I couldn't move, even though she couldn't see me.

"You tryin' to give me the slip?" Link was stomping around behind Lena, trying to catch up with her as she made her way through the lemon trees. Lena shook her head like she was trying to shake Link.

Lena.

She pushed through the brush, and I caught a glimpse of gold and green eyes. That was it; I couldn't help myself.

"Lena!" I shouted as loud as I could, my voice ringing across the white sky.

I took off running across the stubbly frozen ground, through the weeds and all the way down the rocky path. I flung myself into her arms...and went flying to the ground behind her.

"I'm not just trying. I'm *giving* you the slip." Lena's voice floated over me.

I had almost forgotten. I wasn't really here, not in a way she could feel. I lay back on the ground, trying to catch my breath. Then I propped myself up on my elbows, because Lena was really there, and I didn't want to miss a second of it.

The way she moved, the tilt of her head, and the soft lilt of her voice—she was perfect, full of life and beauty and everything I couldn't have anymore.

Everything that didn't belong to me.

I'm here. Right here. Can you feel me, L?

"I wanted to check on him. I haven't been out here all day. I don't want him to be lonely, or bored, or mad. Whatever he's feeling." Lena knelt next to my grave, next to me, grabbing at handfuls of cold grass.

I'm not lonely. But I miss you.

Link rubbed his hand through his hair. "You just went to check on his house. Then you checked on the water tower and your bedroom, and now you're checkin' on his grave. Maybe you should find somethin' to do other than checkin' on Ethan."

"Maybe you should find something to do other than bothering me, Link."

"I promised Ethan I'd look after you."

"You don't understand," she said.

Link looked as annoyed as Lena seemed frustrated. "What are you talkin' about? You think I don't understand? He was my *best friend* since kindergarten."

"Don't say it like that. He's still your best friend."

"Lena." Link wasn't getting anywhere.

"Don't Lena me. Out of everyone, I thought you would understand how things work around here." Her face was pale, and her mouth looked funny, like she was about to smile or cry, only she couldn't decide which.

Lena, it'll be okay. I'm right here.

But even as I thought about it, I knew nobody could fix this. The truth was, the moment I stepped off that water tower everything changed, and nothing was going to change back.

Not anytime soon.

I never knew how bad it would feel from this side. At least for me. Because I could see it all, but I couldn't do a thing to change it.

I reached for her hand, sliding my fingers around hers. My hands slipped right through, but if I really concentrated, I could still feel them, heavy and solid.

For the very first time, nothing shocked me. No burning. It wasn't like sticking my fingers in an electrical outlet.

I guess being dead will do that for you.

"Lena, help me out here. I don't speak chick—you know that—and Rid isn't here to translate."

"*Chick?*" Lena shot him a withering look.

"Aw, come on. I barely speak English, unless we're talkin' about the Lowcountry kind."

"I thought you went looking for Ridley," Lena said.

"I did, all through the Tunnels. Everywhere Macon sent me and a few places he'd never let me go. Holy hell—I haven't found anyone who's seen her."

Lena sat down and straightened the line of rocks around my grave. "I need her to come back. Ridley knows how it all works. She'll help me figure out what to do."

"What are you talkin' about?" Link sat down next to her, and next to me.

Just like old times, when the three of us would sit together on the bleachers at Jackson High. They just didn't know it.

"He's not dead. Just like Uncle Macon wasn't dead. Ethan will come back—you'll see. He's probably trying to find me right now."

I squeezed her hand. She was right about that, at least.

"Don't you think you'd be able to tell, if he was?" Link sounded a little doubtful. "If he was here, don't you think he'd give us a shout-out or somethin' like that?"

I tried her hand again, but it was no use.

Will you two pay attention?

Lena shook her head, oblivious. "It's not like that. I'm not saying he's sitting here next to us or something."

But I was. Sitting next to them or something.

Guys? I'm right here?

Even though I was Kelting, I felt like I was shouting.

"Yeah? How do you know where he is or isn't? If you're so sure and all?" Link's Sunday school background wasn't helping him out here. He was probably busy imagining houses made of clouds, and cherubs with wings.

"Uncle Macon said that new spirits don't know where they are or what they're doing. They barely know how they died or what happened to them in real life. It's upsetting, suddenly finding yourself in the Otherworld. Ethan might not even know who he is yet, or who I am."

I knew who she was. How could I forget something like that?

"Yeah? Well, say you're right. If that's the case, you have nothin' to worry about. Liv told me that she'd find him. She has that watch a hers all tweaked up, like some kind a Ethan Wate–ometer."

Lena sighed. "I wish it was that simple." She reached for the wooden cross. "This thing's crooked again."

Link looked frustrated. "Yeah? Well, there's no merit badge for grave diggin'. Not in Gatlin's pack meetin's."

"I'm talking about the cross, not the grave."

"You're the one who wouldn't let us get a stone," Link said.

"He doesn't need a gravestone when he's not—"

Then her hand froze, because she noticed. The silver button wasn't where she'd left it.

Of course it wasn't. It was where I dropped it.

67

"Link, look!"

"It's a cross. Or two sticks, dependin' on how you look at it." Link squinted. He was starting to tune out; I could tell by the glazed look in his eyes, the one I'd seen on every school day.

"Not that." Lena pointed. "The button."

"Yep. It's a button, all right. Any way you slice it." Link was staring at Lena like she was suddenly the dense one. It was probably a terrifying thought.

"It's my button. And that's not where I put it."

Link shrugged. "So?"

"Don't you get it?" Lena sounded hopeful.

"Not usually."

"Ethan's been here. He moved it."

Hallelujah, L. It's about time. We were making some progress here.

I held my arms out to her, and she threw her arms around Link and hugged him tight. Figures.

She pulled back from Link, excited.

"Hey now." Link looked embarrassed. "It could have been the wind. It could have been—I don't know—wildlife or somethin'."

"It wasn't." I knew the mood she was in. There was nothing anyone could say to change her mind, no matter how irrational it seemed.

"Seem pretty sure a that."

"I am." Lena's cheeks were pink, and her eyes were bright. She opened her notebook, unclipping the Sharpie from her

68

charm necklace with one hand. I smiled to myself, because I'd given her that Sharpie at the top of the Summerville water tower, not so long ago.

I winced at the thought now.

Lena scribbled something and ripped out the page of her notebook. She used a rock to hold the note on top of the cross.

The paper fluttered in the cool breeze but remained where she'd left it.

She wiped a stray tear and smiled.

The paper had only one word on it, but we both knew what it meant. It was a reference to one of the first conversations we'd ever had, when she told me what it said on the poet Bukowski's grave. Only two words: *Don't try.*

But the torn piece of paper on my grave was christened with only one word, in all caps. Still damp and still smelling like Sharpie.

Sharpie and lemons and rosemary.

All the things that were Lena.

TRY.

I will, I..
I promise.

CHAPTER 7

Crosswords

As I watched Link and Lena disappear toward Ravenwood, I knew there was one more place I needed to go, one person I had to see before I went back. She owned Wate's Landing more than any Wate ever would. She haunted that place even in full flesh and blood.

Part of me was dreading it, imagining how torn up she must be. But I needed to see her, all the same.

Bad things had happened.

I couldn't change that, no matter how much I wanted to.

Everything felt wrong, and even seeing Lena didn't make it feel right.

As Aunt Prue would say, things had gone cattywampus.

Whether in this realm or any other, Amma was always the one person who could set me straight.

I sat on the curb across the street, waiting for the sun to go down. I couldn't get myself to move. I didn't want to. I wanted to watch the sun dip behind the house, behind the clotheslines and the old trees and the hedge. I wanted to watch the sunlight fade and the lights in the house go on. I watched for the familiar glow in my dad's study, but it was still dark. He must be teaching at the university, as if nothing had happened. That was probably good, better even. I wondered if he was still working on his book about the Eighteenth Moon, unless restoring the Order had brought an end to that, too.

There was a light in the kitchen bay window, though.

Amma.

A second light flickered through the small square window next to it. The Sisters were watching one of their shows.

Then, in the dwindling light, I noticed something strange. There were no bottles on our old crepe myrtle. The one where Amma hung empty, cracked glass bottles to trap any evil spirits that happened to float our way and to keep them from getting in our house.

Where could the bottles have gone? Why wouldn't she need them now?

I stood up and walked a little closer. I could see through

the kitchen window to where Amma sat at our old wooden table, probably doing a crossword. I could imagine the #2 pencils scratching, could almost hear them.

I crossed the lawn and stood in the driveway, just outside the window. For once I figured it was a good thing no one could see me, because peeping in windows at night in Gatlin is what made even decent folks want to get out their shotguns. Then again, there were lots of things that made folks around here want to get out their shotguns.

Amma looked up and out into the darkness, like a deer in the headlights. I could have sworn she saw me. Then real headlights flashed behind me, and I realized it wasn't me Amma was looking at.

It was my dad, driving my mom's old Volvo. Pulling right through me and into the driveway. As if I wasn't there.

Which, in a whole lot of ways, I wasn't.

I stood in front of the house that I had spent so many summers repainting, and reached out to touch the brushstrokes next to the door. My hand slipped partway through the wall.

It disappeared inside, kind of like when I shoved it through the Charmed door of the *Lunae Libri*, the one that only looked like a regular old grating.

I pulled my hand out and stared at it.

Looked fine to me.

I stepped closer, into the side wall of the house, and found myself trapped. It kind of burned, like walking into a lit fireplace. I guess slipping my hand through was one thing, but getting my body into the house was another.

I went around to the front door. Nothing. I couldn't even kick a foot partway through. I tried the window above the kitchen table, and the one over the sink. I tried the back windows and the side windows and even the cat door that Amma had installed for Lucille.

No luck.

Then I figured out what was going on, because I went back to the kitchen window and saw what Amma was doing. It wasn't the *New York Times* crossword puzzle, or even *The Stars and Stripes* one. She had a needle, not a pencil, in one hand, and a square of cloth instead of paper in the other. She was doing something I'd seen her do a thousand times, and it wasn't going to improve anyone's vocabulary or keep anyone's mind New York City sharp.

It had to do with keeping people's souls safe—Gatlin County safe.

Because Amma was sewing a little bundle of ingredients into one of her infamous charm bags, the kind I had found in my drawers and beneath my mattress and sometimes even in my own pockets. Considering that I couldn't step foot in the house, she must have been sewing them nonstop since I jumped off the water tower.

As usual, she was using her charms to protect Wate's Landing, and there was no getting past any one of them. The salt snaking its way across the windowsill was even thicker than usual. For the first time, there was no doubt that her crazy protections kept our house haint-free. For the first time, I noticed the strange glow of the salt, as if whatever powered it leaked into the air around the windowsills.

Great.

I was rattling the screen out back, when I caught a glimpse of the stairwell leading down to Amma's canning pantry. I thought about the secret door at the back of that little room of storage shelves, the one that had probably been used for the Underground Railroad. I tried to remember where the tunnel came out—the one where we'd found the *Temporis Porta*, the magical door that opened into the Far Keep. Then I remembered the tunnel's trapdoor opening to the field across Route 9. It had gotten me out of the house before; maybe it could get me in this time.

I closed my eyes and thought about that spot, as hard as I could. It didn't work before, when I'd tried to imagine myself somewhere. But that didn't mean I couldn't try again. My mom said that's how it worked for her. Maybe all I had to do was picture myself somewhere hard enough, and I'd find my way there. Kind of like the ruby slippers in *The Wizard of Oz*—only without the actual slippers.

I thought about the fairgrounds.

I thought about the cigarette butts and the old weeds and the hard dirt with the imprints of long-gone carnival booths and trailer hitches.

Nothing happened.

I tried again. Still nothing.

I wasn't sure how your average Sheer did it. Which left me ten kinds of stuck. I almost gave up and walked, figuring if I could make it out to Route 9, I could hitch a ride on the back of an unsuspecting pickup truck.

Just when it seemed impossible, I thought about Amma. I thought about wanting to get inside my house so badly I could taste it, like a whole plate of Amma's pot roast. I thought about how much I missed her, how I wanted to hug her, take a good scolding, and untie her apron strings, like I had my entire life.

The minute those thoughts formed clearly in my mind, my feet started to buzz. I looked down, but I couldn't see them. I felt like a seltzer tablet someone had dropped into a glass of water, like everything around me was starting to bubble and fizz.

Then I was gone.

I found myself standing in the tunnel, right across from the *Temporis Porta*. The ancient door looked as forbidding to me in death as it had in life, and I was happy to leave it behind as I made my way through the tunnel and toward Wate's Landing. I knew where I was going, even in the dark.

I ran the whole way home.

I kept running until I shoved my way through the pantry door, up the stairs, and into the kitchen. Once I got past the problem of the salt and the charms, the walls didn't seem like a big deal—or feel like much of one either.

It was like walking in front of one of the Sisters' endless slide shows, where you step in front of the projector during the hundredth photo of the cruise ship, and suddenly you look down and the ship is cruising right over you. That's what a wall felt like. Just a projection, as unreal as a photograph from someone else's trip to the Bahamas.

Amma didn't look up as I approached. The floorboards didn't squeak for the first time ever, and I thought about all the times I would've appreciated that—when I was trying to sneak out of that kitchen or my house, out from beneath Amma's watchful eye. It required a miracle, and even then it usually didn't work.

I could have used a few Sheer skills back when I was alive. Now I would give anything for someone to know I was actually here. Funny how things work out like that. Like they say, I guess you really do have to be careful what you wish for.

Then I stopped in my tracks. Actually, the smells coming from the oven stopped me.

Because the kitchen smelled like Heaven, or the way Heaven should smell—since I was thinking about it a lot more these days. The two greatest smells on earth. Pulled pork with Carolina Gold, that was one of them. I'd know Amma's famous golden mustard barbeque sauce anywhere, not to mention the slow-cooked pork that gave up and fell to pieces at the first touch of a fork.

The other smell was chocolate. Not just chocolate, but the densest, darkest chocolate around, which meant the inside of Amma's Tunnel of Fudge cake, my favorite of all her desserts. The one she never made for any contest or fair or family in need—just for me, on my birthday or when I got a good report card or had a rotten day.

It was my cake, like lemon meringue was Uncle Abner's pie.

I sank into the nearest chair at the kitchen table, my head in my hands. The cake wasn't for me to eat. It was for her to give, an offering. Something to take out to Greenbrier and leave on my grave.

The thought of that Tunnel of Fudge cake laid out on the fresh dirt by the little wooden cross made me want to throw up.

I was worse than dead.

I was one of the Greats, but a whole lot less great.

The egg timer went off, and Amma pushed back her chair, spearing the charm bag with her needle one last time and letting it drop to the table.

"Don't want your cake to dry out now, do we, Ethan Wate?" Amma yanked open the oven door, and a blast of heat and chocolate shot out. She stuck her quilted mitts in so far I worried she was going to catch fire herself. Then she yanked out the cake with a sigh, almost hurling it onto the burner.

"Best let it cool a bit. Don't want my boy burnin' his mouth."

Lucille smelled the food and came wandering into the kitchen. She leaped onto the table, just like always, getting the best vantage point possible.

When she saw me sitting there, she let out a horrible howl. Her eyes caught me in a fixed glare, as if I'd done something deeply and personally offensive.

Come on, Lucille. You and me, we go way back.

Amma looked at Lucille. "What's that, old girl? You got somethin' to say?"

Lucille yowled again. She was ratting me out to Amma. At first I thought she was just trying to be difficult. Then I realized she was doing me a favor.

Amma was listening. More than listening—she was scowling and looking around the room. "Who's there?"

I looked back at Lucille and smiled, reaching out to scratch her on the top of her head. She twitched beneath my hand.

Amma swept the kitchen with her eagle eye. "Don't you be comin' in my house. Don't need you spirits comin' around. There's nothin' here left to take. Just a lot a broken-down old ladies and broken hearts." She reached slowly toward the jar sitting on the counter and took hold of the One-Eyed Menace.

There it was. Her death-defying, all-powerful wooden spoon of justice. The hole in the middle looked even more like an all-seeing eye tonight. And I had no doubt it could see, maybe as well as Amma. In this state—wherever I was—I could see plain as day that the thing was strangely powerful. Like the salt, it practically glowed, leaving a trail of light where she waved it in the air. I guess things of power came in all shapes and sizes. And when it came to the One-Eyed Menace, I'd be the last one to doubt anything it could do.

I shifted uncomfortably in my chair. Lucille shot me another look, hissing. Now she was getting bratty. I wanted to hiss right back at her.

Stupid cat. This is still my house, Lucille Ball.

Amma looked my way, as if she was seeing straight into my eyes. It was eerie, how close she came to knowing right where I was. She raised the spoon high above the both of us.

"Now you listen. I don't take kindly to you stickin' your nose inta my kitchen, uninvited. You either get outta my house, or you make yourself known, you hear? I won't have you intrudin' on this family. Been through nearabout enough already."

I didn't have much time. The smell from Amma's charm bag was making me kind of sick, to tell the truth, and I didn't have a whole lot of experience at haunting—if this even qualified. I was completely out of my league.

I stared at the Tunnel of Fudge cake. I didn't want to eat it, but I knew I had to do something with it. Something to make Amma understand—just like Lena and the silver button.

The more I thought about that cake, the more I knew what I had to do.

I took a step toward Amma and her cake, ducking around the defensive spoon—and stuck my hand into the fudge, as far as I could. It wasn't easy—it felt like I was trying to grab a handful of cement minutes before it hardened into actual pavement.

But I did it anyway.

I scooped out a big piece of chocolate cake, letting it topple off the side and slide onto the burner. I might as well have taken a bite out of it—that's pretty much what the gaping hole in the side of the cake looked like.

One giant ghostly bite.

"No." Amma stared, wide-eyed, holding the spoon in one hand and her apron in the other. "Ethan Wate, is that you?"

I nodded, even though she couldn't see me. She must have felt something, though, because she lowered the spoon and dropped into the chair across from me, letting the tears flow like a baby in the cry room at church.

Between the tears I heard it.

Just a whisper, but I heard it as clearly as if she had shouted my name.

"My boy."

Her hands were shaking as she held on to the edge of the old table. Amma might be one of the greatest Seers in the Lowcountry, but she was still a Mortal.

I had become something else.

I moved my hand over hers, and I could have sworn she slipped her fingers between mine. She rocked in her chair a little, the way she did when she was singing a hymn she loved or was just about to finish a particularly hard crossword.

"I miss you, Ethan Wate. More than you know. Can't bear to do my puzzles. Can't recall how to cook a roast." She wiped her hand across her eyes, leaving it on her forehead like she had a headache.

I miss you, too, Amma.

"Don't go too far from home, not just yet. You hear me? I've a few things to tell you, one a these days."

I won't.

Lucille licked her paw and rolled it over her ears. She hopped down from the table and howled one last time. She started to walk out of the kitchen, stopping only to look back at me. I could hear what she was saying, as clearly as if she was speaking to me.

Well? Come on, already. You're wasting my time, boy.

I turned and gave Amma a hug, reaching my long arms all the way around her tiny frame, as I had so many times before.

Lucille stopped and cocked her head, waiting. So I did what I'd always done when it came to that cat. I got up from the table and followed.

⊰ CHAPTER 8 ⊱

Broken Bottles

Lucille scratched at the door to Amma's room, and it slid open. I slipped through the crack in the door right after the cat.

Amma's room looked better and worse than it did the last time I saw it, the night I jumped off the water tower. That night, the jars of salt, river stones, and graveyard dirt—the ingredients in so many of Amma's charms—were missing from their places on the shelves, along with at least two dozen other bottles. Her "recipe" books had been scattered across the floor, without so much as a single charm or doll in sight.

The room had been a reflection of Amma's state of mind—lost and desperate, in a way that hurt to remember.

Today it looked completely different, but as far as I could

tell, the room was still full of what she was feeling on the inside, the things she didn't want anyone to see. The doors and windows were laden with charms, but if Amma's old charms were as good as they come, these were even better—stones intricately arranged around the bed, bundles of hawthorn tied around the windows, strands of beads decorated with tiny silver saints and symbols looped around the bedposts.

She was working hard to keep something out.

The jars were still crowded together the way I remembered them, but the shelves weren't bare anymore. They were lined with cracked brown, green, and blue glass bottles. I recognized them immediately.

They were from the bottle tree in our front yard.

Amma must have taken them down. Maybe she wasn't afraid of evil spirits anymore. Or maybe she just didn't want to catch the wrong one.

The bottles were empty, but each one was stopped up with a cork. I touched a small bluish-green one with a long crack down one side. Slowly, and with about as much ease as if I was pushing the Beater all the way up the hill to Ravenwood on a summer day, I edged the cork out from the rim of the bottle, and the room began to fade....

The sun was hot, swamp mist rising like ghosts over the water. But the little girl with the neat braids knew better. Ghosts were made of more than steam and mist. They were as real as she was, waiting for her

ancient grandmamma or her aunties to call them up.
And they were just like the living.

Some were friendly, like the girls who played hop-
scotch and cat's cradle with her. And others were
nasty, like the old man who paced around the grave-
yard in Wader's Creek whenever there was thunder.
Either way, the spirits could be helpful or ornery,
depending on their mood and what you had to offer.
It was always a good idea to bring a gift. Her great-
great-great-grandmamma had taught her that.

The house was just up the hill from the creek, like
a weatherworn blue lighthouse, leading both the dead
and the living back home. There was always a candle
in the window after dark, wind chimes above the
door, and a pecan pie on the rocker in case someone
came calling. And someone always came calling.

Folks came from miles and miles to see Sulla the
Prophet. That's what they called her great-great-
great-grandmamma, on account of how many of her
readings came to pass. Sometimes they even slept on
the little patch of grass in front of the house, waiting
for the chance to see her.

But to the girl, Sulla was just the woman who told
her stories and taught her to tat lace and make a but-
ter piecrust. The woman with a sparrow that would
fly in the window and sit right on her shoulder, like it
was a branch on an old oak.

When she reached the front door, the girl stopped and smoothed her dress before she went in.

"Grandmamma?"

"I'm in here, Amarie." Her voice was smooth and thick—"Heaven and honey," the men in town called it.

The house was only two rooms and a small cooking space. The main room was where Sulla worked, reading tarot cards and tea leaves, making charms and roots for healing. There were glass canning jars all over, full of everything from witch hazel and chamomile to crows' feathers and graveyard dirt. On the bottom shelf was one jar Amarie was allowed to open. It was full of buttery caramels, wrapped in thick wax-coated paper. The doctor who lived in Moncks Corner brought them whenever he came by for ointments and a reading.

"Amarie, you come on over here now." Sulla was fanning a deck of cards out on the table. They weren't the tarot cards the ladies from Gatlin and Summerville liked her to read. These were the cards Grandmamma saved for special readings. "You know what these are?"

Amarie nodded. "Cards a Providence."

"That's right." Sulla smiled, her thin braids falling over her shoulder. Each one was tied with a colored string—a wish someone who visited her was hoping would come true. "Do you know why they're different from tarot cards?"

Amarie shook her head. She knew the pictures were different—the knife stained with blood. The twin figures facing each other with palms touching.

"Cards a Providence tell the truth—the future even I don't want to see some days. Dependin' on whose future I'm readin'."

The little girl was confused. Didn't tarot cards show a true future if a powerful reader was interpreting the spread? "I thought all cards show the truth if you know how to make sense a them."

The sparrow flew in from the open window and perched on the old woman's shoulder. "There's the truth you can face and the truth you can't. You come over here and sit down, and I'll show you what I mean." Sulla shuffled the cards, the Angry Queen disappearing into the deck behind the Black Crow.

Amarie walked around to the other side of the table and sat down on the crooked stool where so many folks waited to see their fate.

Sulla flicked her wrist, fanning the cards out in one swift motion. Her necklaces tangled together at her throat—silver charms etched with images Amarie didn't recognize, hand-painted wooden beads strung between bits of rock, colored crystals that caught the light when Sulla moved. And Amarie's favorite—a smooth black stone threaded through a piece of cord that rested on the hollow of Sulla's neck.

Grandmamma Sulla called it "the eye."

"Now pay attention, Little One," Sulla instructed.
"One day you'll be doin' this on your own, and I'll be
whisperin' to you from the wind."

Amarie liked the sound of that.
She smiled and pulled the first card.

The edges of the vision blurred, and the row of colored bottles came back into view. I was still touching the cracked bluish-green one and the cork that had unleashed the memory—one of Amma's, trapped like a dangerous secret she didn't want to escape into the world. But it wasn't dangerous at all, except maybe to her.

I could still see Sulla showing her the Cards of Providence, the cards that would one day form the spread that showed her my death.

I pictured the faces of the cards, especially the twins, face to face. The Fractured Soul. My card.

I thought about Sulla's smile and how small she looked compared to the giant she seemed to be as a spirit. But she wore the same intricate braids and heavy strands of beads snaking around her neck in both life and death. Except the cord with the black stone—I didn't remember that one.

I looked down at the empty bottle, pushing back the cork and leaving it on the shelf with the others. Did all these bottles hold Amma's memories? The ghosts that were haunting her in ways the spirits never would?

I wondered if the night of my death was in one of those bottles, shoved down deep where it couldn't escape.

I hoped so, for Amma's sake.

Then I heard the stairs creak.

"Amma, you in the kitchen?" It was my dad.

"I'm in here, Mitchell. Right where I always am before supper," Amma answered. She didn't sound normal, but I didn't know if my dad could tell.

I followed the sound of their voices back through the hall. Lucille was sitting at the other end waiting for me, her head tilted to the side. She sat straight like that until I was inches away from her, and then she stood up and sauntered off.

Thanks, Lucille.

She'd done her job, and she was through with me. Probably had a saucer of cream and a fluffy pillow waiting for her in front of the television.

I guessed I wasn't going to be able to spook her again.

As I rounded the corner, my dad was pouring himself a glass of sweet tea. "Did Ethan call?"

Amma stiffened, her cleaver poised over an onion, but my dad didn't seem to notice. She started chopping. "Caroline has him busy waitin' on her. You know how she is, classy and sassy, just like her mamma was."

My dad laughed, his eyes crinkling in the corners. "That's true, and she's a terrible patient. She must be driving Ethan crazy."

My mom and Aunt Prue weren't kidding. My dad was under the influence of a serious Cast. He had no idea what had happened. I wondered how many of Lena's family members it took to pull this off.

Amma reached for a carrot, lopping the end off before she even got it on the cutting board. "A broken hip's a lot worse than the flu, Mitchell."

"I know—"

"What's all that racket?" Aunt Mercy called from the living room. "We're tryin' ta watch *Jeopardy!*"

"Mitchell, get on in here. Mercy's no good at the music questions." It was Aunt Grace.

"You're the one who thinks Elvis Presley is still alive," Aunt Mercy shot back.

"I most certainly do. He can dance himself a mean jive," Aunt Grace shouted, catching every third word at best. "Mitchell, hurry on up. I need a witness. And bring some cake with you."

My dad reached for the Tunnel of Fudge cake on the counter, still warm from the oven. When he disappeared down the hall, Amma stopped chopping and rubbed the worn gold charm of her necklace. She looked sad and broken, cracked like the bottles lined up on the shelves in her bedroom.

"Be sure and let me know if Ethan calls tomorrow," my dad shouted from the living room.

Amma stared out the window for a long time before she spoke, barely loud enough for me to hear. "He won't."

⇥ CHAPTER 9 ⇤

The Stars and Stripes

Leaving Amma behind was like stepping away from a fire on the coldest night of winter. She felt like home, safe and familiar. Like every scolding and every supper I'd ever had, everything that had been me. The closer I was to her, the warmer I felt—but in the end, it made the cold feel that much colder when I walked away.

Was it worth it? Feeling better for a minute or two, knowing that the cold would still be out there waiting?

I wasn't sure, but for me it wasn't a choice. I couldn't stay away from Amma or Lena—and deep down, I didn't think either one of them wanted me to.

Still, there was a silver lining, even if it was a little

tarnished. If Lucille could see me, that was something. I guess it was true what people said about cats seeing spirits. I just never figured I would be the one to prove it.

And then there was Amma. She hadn't exactly seen me, but she'd known I was there. It wasn't much, but it was something. I had been able to show her, just like I'd been able to show Lena I was at my grave.

It was exhausting, taking a chunk out of a cake or moving a button a few inches. But it had gotten the message across.

In a way, I was still here in Gatlin, where I belonged. Everything had changed, and I didn't have the answers for how to fix that. But I hadn't gone anywhere, not really.

I was here.

I existed.

If only I could find a way to say what I really wanted to say. There was just so much I could do with a Tunnel of Fudge cake and an old cat and a random charm on Lena's necklace.

To tell you the truth, I was feeling downright woebegone. As in, stuck in the doldrums without a map, Ethan Wate.

W. O. E. B. E. G. O. N. E.

Nine across.

That's when it came to me. Not so much an idea as a memory—of Amma sitting at our kitchen table, all hunched over her crossword puzzles with a bowl of Red Hots and a pile of extra-sharp #2 pencils. Those puzzles were how she kept things right, figured things out.

In that moment it all came together. The way I saw an

opening on the basketball court or figured out the plot at the beginning of a movie.

I knew what I had to do, and I knew where I had to go. It was going to require a little more than scooping out a cake or pushing around a button, but not much more.

More like a few strokes of a pencil.

It was time I paid a visit to the office of *The Stars and Stripes*, the best and only newspaper in Gatlin County.

I had a crossword puzzle to write.

There wasn't a single grain of salt lining any window at *The Stars and Stripes* office, any more than there was a single grain of truth in the paper itself. There were, however, swamp coolers in every window. More swamp coolers than I had ever seen in one building. They were all that remained of a summer so hot that the whole town had almost dried up and blown away, like dead leaves on a magnolia tree.

Still, no charms, no salt, no Bindings or Casts or even a cat. I slipped in as easy as the heat had. A guy could get used to this kind of access.

Inside the office, there wasn't much more than a few plastic plants, a reenactment calendar that hung crookedly on the wall, and a high linoleum counter. That's where you stood with your ten dollars when you wanted to put an ad in the paper to hawk your piano lessons or new puppies or the old plaid couch that had been sitting in your basement since 1972.

That was about it until you got behind the counter, where three little desks stood in a row. They were covered with papers—exactly the papers I was looking for. This was what *The Stars and Stripes* looked like before it became an actual newspaper—when it was still something closer to the town gossip.

"What are you doing in here, Ethan?"

I turned around, startled, my hands up at my sides as if I'd just been busted for breaking and entering—which, in a way, I had.

"Mom?"

She was standing behind me in the empty office, on the other side of the counter.

"Nothing." It was all I could say. I shouldn't have been surprised. She knew how to cross. After all, she was the one who'd helped me find my way back to the Mortal realm.

Still, I hadn't expected to find her here.

"You're not doing 'nothing,' unless you've decided to become a journalist and report on life from the Great Beyond. Which, considering how many times I tried to get you to join the staff of *The Jackson Stonewaller*, doesn't seem likely."

Yeah, okay. I had never wanted to eat my lunch in there with the school newspaper staff. Not when I could be in the lunchroom with Link and the guys from the basketball team.

The things I thought were important back then seemed so stupid now.

"No, ma'am."

"Ethan, please. Why are you here?"

"I guess I could ask you the same question." My mom shot me a look. "I'm not looking for a job at the paper. I just want to help out on one little section."

"That's not a good idea." She spread her hands on the counter in front of me.

"Why not? You were the one sending me all those Shadowing Songs. It's practically the same thing. This is just a little more—direct."

"What are you planning to do? Write Lena a want ad and publish it in the paper? 'Wanted, one Caster girlfriend. Preferably named Lena Duchannes'?"

I shrugged. "That wasn't exactly what I had in mind, but it could work."

"You can't. You can barely pick up a pencil in this realm. You don't have physics working on your behalf as a Sheer. Around here, picking up a feather is harder than dragging a two-by-four down the street with your pinkie."

"Can *you* do it?"

She shrugged. "Maybe."

I looked at her meaningfully. "Mom, I want her to know I'm all right. I want her to know I'm here—like you wanted to let me know when you left the code in the books in the study. Now I have to find a way to tell her."

My mom walked around the counter slowly, without saying a word for a long minute. She watched as I moved across
the room toward the piles of newsprint.

"Are you sure about this?" She sounded hesitant.

"Are you going to help me or not?"

She came and stood next to me, which was her way of
answering. We began to read the next issue of *The Stars and
Stripes*, laid out all over every surface. I leaned over the papers
on the nearest desk. "Apparently, the Ladies Auxiliary of Gatlin County is starting a book club called the Read & Giggle."

"Your Aunt Marian is going to be thrilled to hear that; the
last time she tried to start a book club, nobody could agree on
a book, and they had to disband after the first meeting." My
mom had a wicked glint in her eye. "But not until they voted
to spike the lemonade with a big box of wine. Just about
everyone agreed on that."

I kept going. "Well, I hope the Read & Giggle doesn't end
up the same way, but if it does, don't worry. They're also starting a table tennis club called the Hit & Giggle."

"And look at that." She pointed over my arm. "Their supper club is called the Dine & Giggle."

I stifled a laugh, pointing. "You missed the best one.
They're renaming the Gatlin Cotillion to—wait for it—the
Wiggle & Giggle."

We went through the rest of the paper, having about as
good a time as two Sheers stuck in a small-town newspaper
office could ask for. It was like a scrapbook of our life together,

all glued onto a whole bunch of newsprint. The Kiwanis Club was getting ready for its annual pancake breakfast, where the pancakes were raw and liquid in the middle, the way my dad liked them best. Gardens of Eden had won Main Street Window of the Month, which it did pretty much every month, since there weren't all that many windows on Main anymore.

It only got better as we read on. A wild hen was roosting in the Santa's sled that Mr. Asher had put up as part of his light-up lawn display, which was awesome, because the Ashers' holiday displays were infamous. One year Mrs. Asher even put lipstick on Emily's Baby Cuddles Jesus because she didn't think his mouth showed up well enough in the dark. When my mom tried to ask her about it with a straight face, Mrs. Asher said, "You can't just expect to shout hosannas and have everyone get the message, Lila. Lord have mercy, half the folks around here don't even know what hosanna means." When my mom pressed her further, it was obvious Mrs. Asher didn't either. After that, she never invited us to her house again.

The rest of it was the news you'd expect around here, the kind that never changed even when it always changed. Animal Control had picked up a lost cat; Bud Clayton had won the Carolina Duck-Calling Contest. The Summerville Pawnshop was running a special, Big B's Vinyl Siding and Windows was shutting down, and the *Quik-Chik* Leadership Scholarship competition was heating up.

Life goes on, I guess.

Then I saw the page for the crossword puzzle and slid it toward me as quickly as I could. "There."

"You want to do the crossword puzzle?"

"I don't want to do it. I want to write one for Amma. If she saw it, she'd tell Lena."

My mom shook her head. "Even if you could manage to get the letters the way you want them on the page, Amma won't see it. She doesn't take the paper anymore. Not since you— left. She hasn't touched one of her puzzles in months."

I winced. How could I have forgotten? Amma had said it herself while I was standing in the kitchen at Wate's Landing.

"What about a letter, then?"

"I've tried it a hundred times, but it's nearly impossible. You can only use what's already on the page." She studied the paper in front of us. "Actually, it might work because you can drag the letters around on the draft. See, how they're laying it out on the table?"

She was right. The way the puzzle worked, the letters were cut into a thousand tiles, like a Scrabble board. All I had to do was move the paper around.

If I was even strong enough to do that.

I looked at my mom, more determined than ever. "Then we'll use the crossword, and I'll make Lena see it."

Moving the letters into place was like digging up a rock from the Sisters' garden, but my mom helped me. She shook her head as we stared at the page. "A crossword puzzle. I don't know why I didn't think of that."

I shrugged. "I'm just not very good at writing songs."

In its current state, the crossword was barely half-finished, but the staff around here probably wouldn't mind too much if I helped them along. After all, it looked like the Sunday edition, the biggest day for *The Stars and Stripes*—at least for the crossword. Between the three of them, they'd probably be relieved that someone else had taken it on this week. I was surprised they didn't have Amma in here writing the puzzles for them already.

The only hard part would be getting Lena to take an interest in this puzzle at all.

Eleven across.

P. O. L. T. E. R. G. E. I. S. T.

As in, apparition or phantasm. A spectral being. A spirit from another world. A ghost. The vaguest shadow of a person, the thing that comes to you in the night when you think no one is looking.

In other words, the thing you are, Ethan Wate.

Six down.

G. A. T. L. I. N.

As in, parochial. Local. Insular. The place we're stuck, whether in the Otherworld or the Mortal one.

E. T. E. R. N. A. L.

As in, endless, without stopping, forever. The way you feel about a certain girl, whether you're dead or alive.

L. O. V. E.

As in, how I feel about you, Lena Duchannes.

T. R. Y.

As in, as hard as I can, every minute of every day.

As in, I got your message, L.

Then I felt overwhelmed by the thought of how much I'd lost, of everything that stupid fall off the water tower had cost me, and I lost control and loosened my grip on Gatlin. First my eyes filled, and then the letters blurred away, drifting into nothing as the world vanished beneath my feet and I was gone.

I was crossing back. I tried to remember the words from the scroll—the ones that had brought me here—but my mind couldn't focus on anything at all.

It was too late.

Darkness surrounded me, and I felt something like wind whipping across my face, howling in my ears. Then I heard my mother's voice—steady as the grip of her cool hand on mine.

"Ethan, hold on. I've got you."

⊰ CHAPTER 10 ⊱

Snake Eyes

I felt my feet touch something solid, like I had just stepped off a train and onto the platform at the station. I saw the floorboards of our front porch, then my Chucks standing on them. We'd crossed back, leaving the living world behind us. We were back where we belonged, with the dead.

I didn't want to think about it like that.

"Well, it's 'bout time, seein' as I finished watchin' all your mamma's paint dry more than an hour ago."

Aunt Prue was waiting for us in the Otherworld, on the front porch of Wate's Landing—the one in the middle of the cemetery.

I still wasn't used to the sight of my house here instead of the mausoleums and weeping angel statues that dominated

Perpetual Peace. But standing by the railing, with all three Harlon Jameses sitting at attention around her feet, Aunt Prue looked pretty dominant, too.

More like mad as a hornet.

"Ma'am," I said, scratching my neck uncomfortably.

"Ethan Wate, I've been waitin' on you. Thought you'd only be gone a minute." The three dogs looked just as irritated. Aunt Prue nodded at my mother. "Lila."

"Aunt Prudence." They regarded each other warily, which seemed strange to me. They had always gotten along when I was growing up.

I smiled at my aunt, changing the subject. "I did it, Aunt Prue. I crossed. I was...you know, on the other side."

"You might a let a person know, so they didn't wait on your porch for the best part a the day." My aunt waved her handkerchief in my general direction.

"I went to Ravenwood and Greenbrier and Wate's Landing and *The Stars and Stripes*." Aunt Prue raised an eyebrow at me, as if she didn't believe it.

"Really?"

"Well, not by myself. I mean, with my mom. She might have helped some. Ma'am."

My mom looked amused. Aunt Prue did not.

"Well, if you want a preacher's chance in Heaven ta get yourself back there, we need ta talk."

"Prudence," my mom said in a strange tone. It sounded like a warning.

I didn't know what to say, so I just kept talking. "You mean about crossing? Because I think I'm starting to get the hang—"

"Stop yappin' and start listenin', Ethan Wate. I'm not talkin' 'bout practicin' any crossin'. I'm talkin' 'bout crossin' back. For good, ta the old world."

For a second, I thought she was teasing me. But her expression didn't change. She was serious—at least as serious as my crazy great-aunt ever was. "What are you talking about, Aunt Prue?"

"Prudence." My mom said it again. "Don't do this."

Don't do what? Give me a chance to get back there?

Aunt Prue glared at my mother, easing herself down the stairs one orthopedic shoe at a time. I reached out to help her, but she waved me off, stubborn as ever. When she finally made it to the carpet of grass at the base of the stairs, Aunt Prue stepped in front of me. "There's been a mistake, Ethan. A mighty big one. This wasn't supposed ta happen."

A tremor of hope washed over me. "What?"

The color drained out of my mom's face. "Stop." I thought she was going to pass out. I could barely breathe.

"I won't," said Aunt Prue, narrowing her eyes behind her spectacles.

"I thought we decided not to tell him, Prudence."

"You decided, Lila Jane. I'm too old not ta do as I please."

"I'm his mother." My mom wasn't giving up.

"What's going on?" I tried to wedge myself between them, but neither one of them would look my way.

Aunt Prue raised her chin. "The boy's old enough ta decide somethin' that big on his own, don'tcha think?"

"It's not safe." My mom folded her arms. "I don't mean to be firm with you, but I'm going to have to ask you to go."

I'd never heard my mother talk to any of the Sisters like that. She might as well have declared World War III for the Wate family. It didn't seem to stop Aunt Prue, though.

She just laughed. "Can't put the molasses back in the jar, Lila Jane. You know it's the truth, and you know you got no right keepin' it from your boy." Aunt Prue looked me right in the eye. "I need you ta come on with me. There's someone you need ta meet."

My mom just looked at her. "Prudence…"

Aunt Prue gave her the kind of look that could wilt and wither a whole flower bed. "Don't you *Prudence* me. You can't stop this thing. And where we're goin' you can't come, Lila Jane. You know well as I do that we both got nothin' but the boy's best interest at heart."

It was a classic Sisters' face-off, the kind where before you blinked, you were already past the point where nobody came out ahead.

A second later, my mom backed off. I would never know what happened in that silent exchange between them, and it was probably better that way.

"I'll wait for you here, Ethan." My mom looked at me. "But you be careful."

Aunt Prue smiled, victorious.

One of the Harlon Jameses began to growl. Then we took off down the sidewalk so fast I could barely keep up.

_____ ᘓ

I followed Aunt Prue and the yipping dogs to the outer limits of Perpetual Peace—past the Snows' perfectly restored Federal-style manor house, which was situated in exactly the same spot their massive mausoleum occupied in the cemetery of the living.

"Who died?" I asked, looking at my aunt. Seeing as there wasn't anything on earth powerful enough to take down Savannah Snow.

"Great-great-grandpappy Snow, 'fore you were even half-way inta diapers. Been here a long time now. Oldest plot in the row." She picked her way down the stone path that led around back, and I followed.

We headed toward an old shed behind the house, the rotted planks barely holding up the crooked roof. I could see tiny flecks of faded paint clinging to the wood where someone had scraped it clean. There was no amount of scraping that could disguise the shade that trimmed my own house in Gatlin—haint blue. The one shade of blue meant to keep the spirits away.

I guess Amma was right about the haints not caring much for the color. As I looked around, I could already see the difference. There wasn't a graveyard neighbor in sight.

"Aunt Prue, where are we going? I've had enough of the Snows to last more than one lifetime."

She glowered at me. "I told you. We're goin' ta call on someone who knows more than me 'bout this mess." She reached for the splintered handle of the shed. "You just be thankful I'm a Statham, and Stathams get on with all kinds a folks, or we wouldn't have a soul ta help us sort things out." I couldn't look at my aunt. I was too scared I would start laughing, considering she got along with just about no kinds of folks, at least not in the Gatlin I was from.

"Yes, ma'am."

She stepped inside the shed, which didn't look like anything more than an ordinary shed. But if I'd learned anything from Lena and my experiences in her world, it was that things aren't always what they seem.

I followed Aunt Prue—and the Harlon Jameses—inside and closed the door behind us. The cracks in the wood let in just enough light for me to see her turn around in the shed. She reached for something in the dim light, and I realized it was another handle.

A hidden Doorwell, like the ones in the Caster Tunnels.

"Where are we going?"

Aunt Prue paused, her hand still resting on the iron pull. "Not all folks are lucky enough ta be buried in His Garden of Perpetual Peace, Ethan Wate. The Casters, I reckon they got as much right ta the Otherworld as we do, don'tcha think?"

Aunt Prue pushed the door open easily, and we stepped out onto a rocky coastline.

There was a house balancing dangerously on the edge of a cliff. The weathered wood was the same sad shade of gray as the rocks, as if it had been painstakingly carved from them. It was small and simple and hidden in plain sight, like so many things in the world I'd left behind.

I watched as the waves crashed against the face of the cliff, reaching toward the house but ultimately failing. This place had stood the test of time, defying nature in a way that seemed impossible.

"Whose house is that?" I offered Aunt Prue my arm, helping her navigate the uneven ground.

"You know what they say about curiosity and cats. May not kill ya, but it'll get ya inta a heap a trouble around here, too. Though trouble seems ta find you even when you ain't lookin' for it." She gathered her long flowered skirt in her other hand. "You'll see soon enough."

She wouldn't say another word after that.

We climbed a treacherous stairway carved into the side of the cliff. Where the rock wasn't reinforced with splintering boards, it crumbled away under my feet, and I almost lost my footing. I tried to remind myself that I wasn't about to go plummeting to my death, seeing as I was already dead. Still, it didn't help as much as you'd think it would. That was another thing I'd learned from the Caster world: There always seemed to be something worse around the next corner. There was always something to be afraid of, even if you hadn't figured out exactly what it was yet.

When we reached the house, all I could think was how much it reminded me of Ravenwood Manor, though the two buildings didn't resemble each other in any way. Ravenwood was a Greek Revival–style mansion, and this was a single-story clapboard. But the house seemed aware of us as we approached, alive with power and magic, like Ravenwood. It was surrounded by crooked trees with slanted branches that had been beaten into submission by the wind. It looked like the kind of twisted drawing you'd find in a book meant to terrify children into having nightmares. The kind of book where kids were trapped by more than just witches and devoured by more than wolves.

I was thinking it was a good thing I no longer needed to sleep, when my aunt marched up the walk. Aunt Prue didn't hesitate. She walked right up to the door and pounded the oxidized brass ring three times. There was writing carved around the doorframe. It was Niadic, the ancient language of Casters.

I backed up, letting all the Harlon Jameses go in front of me. They growled their tiny dog growls at the door. Before I had a chance to examine the writing more closely, the door creaked open.

An old man stood in front of us. I assumed he was a Sheer, but that wasn't a distinction worth making here—we were all spirits of one kind or another. His head was shaved and scarred, faint lines overlapping in a vicious pattern. His white beard was cut short, his eyes covered by dark wraparound glasses.

A black sweater hung from his skinny frame, which was partially hidden behind the door. There was something frail and worn out about him, like he had escaped from a work camp, or worse.

"Prudence." He nodded. "Is this the boy?"

"'Course it is." Aunt Prue shoved me forward. "Ethan, this here is Obidias Trueblood. Go on in."

I extended my hand. "It's nice to meet you, sir."

Obidias held up his right hand, which had been hidden behind the door. "I'm sure you'll understand if we don't shake." His hand was severed at the wrist, a black line marking the place where it had been cut. Above the mark, his wrist was severely scarred, as if it had been punctured over and over again.

Which it had.

Five writhing black snakes extended from his wrist to the point where his fingers would normally have reached. They were hissing and striking at the air, curling around one another.

"Don't worry," Obidias said. "They won't hurt you. It's me they enjoy tormenting."

I couldn't think of anything to say. I wanted to run.

The Harlon Jameses growled even more loudly, and the snakes hissed back. Aunt Prue scowled at all of them. "Puh-lease. Not you, too."

I stared at the snake hand. Something about it was familiar.

How many guys with snakes for fingers could there be? Why did I feel like I knew him?

It hit me, and I realized who Obidias was—the guy Macon had sent Link to see in the Tunnels. Last summer, right after the Seventeenth Moon. The guy who'd died right in front of Link after Hunting bit him, in his house, this house—at least the Otherworld version of it. Back then I thought Link was exaggerating, but he wasn't.

Not even Link could have made this up.

The snake that replaced Obidias' thumb wrapped itself around his wrist, stretching its head toward me. Its tongue flicked in and out, the little fork flying.

Aunt Prue pushed me across the threshold, and I went stumbling, only inches from the snakes. "Go on in. You aren't afraid of a few itty-bitty little garden snakes, are you?"

Was she kidding? They looked like pit vipers.

I turned awkwardly toward Obidias. "I'm sorry, sir. It— they just caught me off guard."

"Don't give it another thought." He waved off the apology with a twist of the wrist on his good hand. "It's not something you see every day."

Aunt Prue sniffed. "I've seen a stranger thing or two." I stared at my aunt, who looked as smug as if she shook a new snake hand every day of her life.

Obidias closed the door behind us, but not before checking the horizon in every direction. "You came alone? You weren't followed?"

Aunt Prue shook her head. "Me? Nobody can follow me."
She wasn't kidding.

I looked back to Obidias. "Can I ask you something, sir?" I
had to know for sure if he'd met Link, if he was the same guy.

"Of course."

I cleared my throat. "I think you met a friend of mine.
When you were alive, I mean. He told me about someone who
looked like you."

Obidias held out his hand. "You mean a man with five
snakes for a hand? There probably aren't many of us."

I wasn't sure how to say the next part. "If it was my friend,
he was there when you—you know. Died. I'm not sure it matters, but if it does, I'd like to know."

Aunt Prue looked at me, confused. She didn't know any of
this. Link had never told anyone but me, as far as I knew.

Obidias was watching me, too. "Did this friend of yours
happen to know Macon Ravenwood?"

I nodded. "He did, sir."

"Then I remember him well." He smiled. "I saw him deliver
my message to Macon after I passed. You can see a great deal
from this side."

"I guess so." He was right. Because we were dead, we could
see everything. And because we were dead, it didn't matter
what we could see. So the whole seeing-things-from-the-grave
concept? Majorly overrated. All you ended up seeing was
more than you wanted to in the first place.

I'm pretty sure I wasn't the first guy who would've traded

seeing a little less for living a little more. I didn't say that to Edward Snakehands, though. I didn't want to think about how much I had in common with a guy whose fingers had fangs.

"Why don't we make ourselves more comfortable? We have a lot to talk about." Obidias ushered us further into the living room—really the only room I could see, except for a small kitchen and a lone door at the end of the hall, which must have led to the bedroom.

It was basically one gigantic library. Shelves extended from the floor to the ceiling, a battered brass library ladder attached to the highest shelf. A polished wooden stand held a huge leather volume, like the dictionary we had in the Gatlin County Library. Marian would've loved this place.

There was nothing else in the room aside from four threadbare armchairs. Obidias waited for Aunt Prue and me to sit down before he chose a chair opposite ours. He removed the dark glasses he was wearing, and his eyes locked on mine.

I should have known.

Yellow eyes.

He was a Dark Caster. Of course.

That made sense, if he really was the guy from Link's story. But still, now that I thought about it, what was Aunt Prue doing, taking me to see a Dark Caster?

Obidias must have realized what I was thinking. "You didn't think there were Dark Casters here, did you?"

I shook my head. "No, sir. I guess I didn't."

"Surprise." Obidias smiled grimly.

Aunt Prue swooped in to save me. "The Otherworld's a place for unfinished business. For folks like me and you and Obidias here, who aren't ready ta move on just yet."

"And my mom?"

She nodded. "Lila Jane more than anyone. She's been kickin' around here longer than the whole lot a us."

"Some can cross freely between this world and others," Obidias explained. "We all eventually get to our destination. But those of us whose lives were cut short before we could right the wrongs haunting us, we remain here until we find that moment of peace."

He didn't have to tell me. I already knew it for myself—crossing was complicated business. And I hadn't felt anything remotely peaceful. Not yet.

I turned to Aunt Prue. "So you're stuck here, too? I mean, when you aren't crossing back to visit the Sisters? Because of me?"

"I can leave if I set my mind ta it." She patted my hand, as if to remind me I was silly to think there was ever anyone or anything that could keep my aunt from a place she wanted to go. "But I'm not goin' anywhere till you're back home, where you belong. You're a part a my unfinished business now, Ethan, and I 'cept that. I mean ta make things right." She patted my cheek. "Besides, what else am I gonna do? I got myself Mercy and Grace ta wait for, don't I?"

"Back home? You mean to Gatlin?"

"Ta Miss Amma, and Lena, and all our kin," she answered.

"Aunt Prue, I could barely cross to visit Gatlin, and even then nobody could see me."

"That's where you're wrong, boy." Obidias spoke up, and one of his angry-looking snakes sank its fangs into his wrist. He winced, pulling a piece of black material shaped like a mitten out of his pocket. He dropped the hood over the hissing snakes, using two pieces of cord at the bottom to tighten it. The snakes shifted and thrashed beneath the fabric. "Now, where was I?"

"Are you okay?" I was a little distracted. It's not every day that a guy, or even a Sheer, gets bitten by his own hand. At least I hoped it wasn't.

But Obidias didn't want to talk about himself. "When I heard about the circumstances that brought you to this side of the veil, I sent word to your aunt immediately. Your aunt and your mother."

My Aunt Prue clicked her tongue impatiently.

That explained my aunt wanting to bring me here—and my mother not wanting her to. Just because you told any two people in my family the same piece of news, that didn't mean they'd agree about what they'd heard. My mom used to say the people in the Evers family were about the most hog-minded, mule-stuck bloodline you could find—and the Wates were worse. A pack of wasps fighting over the nest—that's what my dad called the Wate family reunions.

"How did you hear about what happened?" I tried not to stare at the snakes twisting beneath the black hood.

"News travels fast in the Otherworld," he said, hesitating. "More importantly, I knew it was a mistake."

"I told you, Ethan Wate." Aunt Prue looked mighty satisfied.

If it was a mistake—if I wasn't supposed to be here— maybe there was a way to fix it. Maybe I really could go home.

I wanted so badly for it to be true, the same way I had wanted this to be a dream I could wake up from. But I knew better.

Nothing was ever how you wanted it to be. Not anymore. Not for me.

They just didn't understand.

"It wasn't a mistake. I chose to come, Mr. Trueblood. I worked it out with the Lilum. If I didn't, the people I loved, and lots of others, were going to die."

Obidias nodded. "I know all of that, Ethan. Just like I know about the Lilum and the Order of Things. I'm not questioning what you did. What I'm saying is that you never should've had to make that choice. It wasn't in the *Chronicles*."

"*The Caster Chronicles?*" I had only seen the book once, in the archive when the Council of the Far Keep came to question Marian, yet it was the second time I'd heard the subject come up since I got here. How did Obidias know about it? And whatever any of it meant, my mom hadn't exactly wanted to elaborate.

"Yes." Obidias nodded.

"I don't understand what that has to do with me."

He was silent for a moment.

"Go on, tell him." Aunt Prue was giving Obidias True-blood the same forceful look she always gave me right before she made me do something crazy, like bury acorns in her yard for baby squirrels. "He deserves ta know. Set it right."

Obidias nodded at Aunt Prue and looked back at me with those golden-yellow eyes that made my skin crawl almost as much as his snake hand did. "As you know, *The Caster Chronicles* is a record of everything that has happened in the world. But it is also a record of what might be—possible futures that have not come to pass."

"The past, the present, and the future. I remember." The three weird-looking Keepers I saw in the library and during Marian's trial. How could I forget?

"Yes. In the Far Keep, those futures can be altered, transforming them from *possible* futures to *actual* ones."

"Are you saying the book can change the future?" I was stunned. Marian had never mentioned any of this.

"It can," Obidias answered. "If a page is altered, or one is added. A page that was never intended to be there."

A shiver moved up my back. "What are you saying, Mr. Trueblood?"

"The page that tells the story of your death was never part of the original *Chronicles*. It was added." He looked up at me, haunted.

"Why would someone do that?"

"There are more reasons for people's actions than the number of actions that are actually set in motion." His voice was distant, full of regret and sorrow I would never have expected from a Dark Caster. "The important thing is that your fate— this fate—can be changed."

Changed? Could you save a life once it was over?

I was terrified to ask the next question, to believe there was a way I could get back to everything I lost. To Gatlin. To Amma.

Lena.

All I wanted was to feel her in my arms and hear her voice in my head. I wanted to find a way back to the Caster girl I loved more than anything in this world, or any world.

"How?" The answer didn't actually matter. I would do whatever I had to, and Obidias Trueblood knew it.

"It's dangerous." Obidias' expression was a warning. "More dangerous than anything in the Mortal world."

I heard the words, but I couldn't believe them. There was nothing more terrifying than staying here. "What do I have to do?"

"You'll have to destroy your own page in *The Caster Chronicles*. The one that describes your death."

I had a thousand questions, but only one mattered. "What if you're wrong, and my page was there all along?"

Obidias stared down at what was left of his hand, the snakes rearing and striking even under the cloth. A shadow passed across his face.

He raised his eyes to meet mine.

"I know it wasn't there, Ethan. Because I'm the one who wrote it."

◄ CHAPTER 11 ►

Darker Things

The room went quiet, so quiet you could hear the house creak as the wind pushed against it. So quiet you could hear the snakes hiss almost as loudly as Aunt Prue's asthma and my pounding heart. Even the Harlon Jameses slunk away, whimpering behind a chair.

For a second, I couldn't think. My mind was completely blank.

There was no way to process this—to understand why a man I had never met would change the course of my life, so irreparably and violently.

What the hell did I do to this guy?

I finally found the words, at least some of them. There were others I couldn't say in front of Aunt Prue, or she'd wash my mouth out with more than soap and probably make me suck down a bottle of Tabasco, too. "Why? You don't even know me."

"It's complicated—"

"Complicated?" My voice started rising, and I pulled myself up out of my chair. "You ruined my life. You forced me to choose between saving the people I loved and sacrificing myself. I hurt everyone I care about. They had to put a Cast on my own father to keep him from going crazy!"

"I'm sorry, Ethan. I wouldn't have wished this on my worst enemy."

"No. You just wished it on some seventeen-year-old kid you'd never met." This guy wasn't going to help me. He was the reason I was stuck in this nightmare in the first place.

Aunt Prue reached out and took my hand. "I know you're angry, and you've got more right than anyone ta be. But Obidias can help us get you back home. So you need ta sit down here and listen ta what he's got ta say."

"How do you know we can trust him, Aunt Prue? Every word that comes out of his mouth is probably a lie." I pulled my hand away.

"You listen here, and you listen good." She yanked on my arm harder than I would've expected, and I sank back down into the chair next to her. She wanted me to look her in the eye. "I've known Obidias Trueblood since before he was Light or Dark, before he'd done wrong or right. Spent the better part a my days walkin' the Caster Tunnels with the Truebloods and my daddy." Aunt Prue paused and glanced at Obidias. "And he saved me a time or two down there. Even if he wasn't smart enough ta save himself."

I didn't know what to think. Maybe my aunt had charted the Tunnels with Obidias. Maybe she could trust him.

But that didn't mean I could.

Obidias seemed to know what I was thinking. "Ethan, you may find this hard to believe, but I know what it's like to feel helpless—to be at the mercy of decisions that you didn't make."

"You have no idea how I feel." I heard the anger in my voice, but I didn't try to hide it. I wanted Obidias Trueblood to know I hated him for what he'd done to me and the people I loved.

I thought about Lena leaving the button on my grave. He didn't know what that felt like—for me or Lena.

"Ethan, I know you don't trust him, and I don't blame you." Aunt Prue was playing hardball now. This meant something to her. "But I'm askin' you ta trust me and hear him out."

I locked eyes with Obidias. "Start talking. How do I get back?"

Obidias took a long breath. "As I said, the only way to get your life back is to erase your death."

"So if I destroy the page, I go home—right?" I wanted to be sure there were no loopholes.

No calling a moon out of time, no splitting the moon in half. No curses that kept me from leaving, once the page was gone.

He nodded. "Yes. But first you have to get to the book."

"You mean from the Far Keep? The Keepers had it with them when they came for my Aunt Marian."

"That's right." He looked at me, startled. I guess he hadn't expected me to know anything about *The Caster Chronicles*.

"So what are we doing sitting around here talking? Let's get on with it." I was halfway out of my chair before I realized Obidias wasn't moving.

"And you think you'll just walk in there and take the page?" he asked. "It's not that easy."

"Who's going to stop me? A bunch of Keepers? What do I have to lose?" I tried not to think about how terrifying they had seemed when they came for Marian.

Obidias pulled the hood off his hand, and the snakes hissed and struck one another. "Do you know who did this to me? A 'bunch of Keepers' who caught me trying to steal my page from the *Chronicles*."

"Lord have mercy," Aunt Prue said, fanning herself with her handkerchief.

For a second, I didn't know if I believed him. But I recognized the emotion playing out on his face, because I was feeling it myself.

Fear.

"Keepers did that to you?"

He nodded. "Angelus and Adriel. On one of their more generous days." I wondered if Adriel was the big one who had shown up in the archive with Angelus and the albino woman. They were the three strangest-looking people I'd seen in the Caster world. At least until today.

I looked at Obidias and his snakes.

"Like I said, what can they do to me now? I'm already dead." I tried to smile, even though it wasn't funny. It was the opposite of funny.

Obidias held out his hand, the snakes jerking and stretching as they tried to reach me. "There are things worse than death, Ethan. Things that are darker than the Dark Casters. I should know. If you are caught, the Keepers will never let you leave the library at the Far Keep. You will be their scribe and their slave, forced to rewrite the futures of innocent Casters... and Mortal Waywards who are Bound to them."

"Waywards are supposed to be pretty rare. How many can there be to write about?" I had never met another one, and I'd met Vexes and Incubuses and more kinds of Casters than I ever wanted to.

Obidias leaned forward in his chair, cloaking his cruelly deformed hand once again. "Perhaps they aren't as rare as you think. Maybe they just don't live long enough for the Casters to find them."

There was an undeniable truth in his words that I couldn't explain. I guess there was some part of me that knew a lie would have sounded different. Another part knew I'd always been in danger, one way or another—with or without Lena.

Whether I was meant to jump off a water tower or not.

Either way, the fear in his voice should've been proof enough.

"Okay. So I won't get caught."

Aunt Prue's face was filled with concern. "Maybe this isn't the best idea. We should go on back ta my house and think on it. Talk ta your mamma about it. She's waitin' on us, I reckon."

I squeezed her hand. "Don't worry, Aunt Prue. I know a way in. There's a *Temporis Porta* in an old tunnel beneath Wate's Landing. I can get in and out before the Keepers ever realize I was there."

If I could walk through walls in the Mortal realm, I was pretty sure I could step through the *Temporis Porta*, too.

Obidias broke the end off a thick cigar. His hand was shaking as he lit the match and held it up. He took a few puffs, until it glowed a steady orange. "You can't enter the library at the Far Keep through the Mortal realm. You have to enter through the seam." He delivered the news as calmly as if he was giving me directions to the local Stop & Steal, to pick up some milk.

"You mean the Great Barrier?" It seemed like a strange place for a door to the Far Keep's inner sanctum. "I can handle it. I did it once, and I can do it again."

"What you've done is nothing compared to what you're about to do. The Great Barrier is just one place you can get to from the seam," Obidias explained. "You can cross into other worlds from there that will make the Barrier feel like home."

"Just tell me how to get there." We were wasting time, and every second we sat around talking was another second away from Lena.

"You have to cross the Great River. It runs through the Great Barrier, all the way to the seam. It forms the border between the realms."

"Like the River Styx?"

He ignored me. "And you can't cross unless you have the river eyes—two smooth black stones."

"Are you kidding?"

He shook his head. "Not at all. They're very rare and hard to come by."

"River eyes. Got it. I can find a couple rocks."

"*If* you get across the river, and that's a big if, you'll still have to make it past the Gatekeeper before you can get into the library."

"How do I do that?"

Obidias took a puff from the cigar. "You have to offer him something he can't refuse."

"What exactly would that be?" Aunt Prue asked, as though she might have whatever it was tucked in her pocketbook. Like the Gatekeeper would be interested in three linty breath mints, some nondairy creamer, and a wad of folded-up Kleenex.

"It's always different. You'll have to figure it out when you get there," Obidias said. "He has...eclectic taste." He didn't say any more on the subject.

An offering. Eclectic taste. Whatever the hell that meant.

"Okay. So I have to find the black stones and get across the Great River," I said. "Figure out what the Gatekeeper guy wants and give it to him to get inside the library. Then find *The Caster Chronicles* and destroy my page." I paused, because the question I was about to ask was the most important detail, and I wanted to get it straight. "If I do all that and don't get caught, I'll get back home—my real home? How do I do that? What happens after I destroy the page?"

Obidias looked at Aunt Prue and back to me. "I'm not sure. It's never happened, as far as I know." He shook his head. "It's a chance, nothing more. And not even a good one..."

"Nothin's certain, Ethan Wate, 'cept for that you had a shot at a life a your own, and the Keepers stole it from you."

I stood up before they could finish talking.

Lena was waiting, in my room or hers, by the crooked cross stuck in the grass at my gravesite or somewhere else. But she was waiting—that's what mattered.

If I had a chance in hell to get back home, I'd take it.

I'm trying, L. Don't give up on me.

"I need to get going, Mr. Trueblood. I have a river to cross."

Aunt Prue opened her pocketbook and pulled out a faded map, covered with shapes that didn't represent any continent, country, or state I'd ever seen. This was more than a doodle on the back of an old church program. I knew what Aunt Prue's maps were like, and I knew how important they had been to me before—the last time I found my way to the seam, for Lena's Seventeenth Moon.

"I've been workin' on it since I got here, jus' a little bit here and there. Obidias told me you'd be needin' it." She shrugged. "Reckoned it was the least I could do."

I leaned down and hugged her. "Thanks, Aunt Prue. And don't be worried."

"I'm not," she lied. But she didn't need to be.

I was worried enough for both of us.

⚔ CHAPTER 12 ⚔

Still Here

After we got back to our side of the Otherworld—Harlon Jameses and all—I didn't go home. I left Aunt Prue at her house and walked the streets—more like the rows—of His Garden of Perpetual Peace.

Peace wasn't exactly what I was feeling.

I stopped in front of Wate's Landing. It looked every bit the same as when I left, and I knew my mom was inside. I wanted to talk to her. But there were other things I had to do first.

I sat down on the front steps, closing my eyes.

"Carry me home."

What was it?

To remember. And be remembered.

Ducite me domum.

Ut meminissem.

Ut in memoria tenear.

I remember Lena.

Not the water tower.

What came before.

I remember Ravenwood.

Let Ravenwood remember me.

Let Ravenwood—

Carry me—

I was lying in the dirt in front of Ravenwood, half-stuck beneath a rosebush and an overgrown camellia hedge. I had crossed again—and this time, all on my own.

"I'll be damned." I laughed, relieved. I was getting pretty good at this whole being-dead thing.

Then I practically ran up the old veranda steps. I had to see if Lena had gotten the message—my message. My only problem was that no one bothered to do the crossword in *The Stars and Stripes*, not even Amma. I had to find a way to get them to look at that paper, if they hadn't already.

Lena wasn't in her room, and she wasn't at my grave either. She wasn't in any of the usual places we used to go.

Not in the lemon grove or the crypt, where I'd died the first time.

I even looked in Ridley's old room, where Liv was asleep in Ridley's creaking four-poster bed. I was hoping she'd be able to sense that I was there with her Ethan Wate-ometer. No such luck. That's when I realized it was nighttime in Gatlin, the real Gatlin, and there was absolutely no correlation between time that passed in the Otherworld and Mortal time. I felt like I'd only been gone a few hours—and here it was, the middle of the night.

I didn't even know what day it was, come to think of it.

Worse yet, when I leaned over Liv's face in the moonlight, it looked like she had been crying. I felt guilty, since there was a strong possibility I was the reason for the tears, unless she and John had had a fight.

But that was unlikely, because when I looked down, I was standing right in the middle of John Breed's chest. He was curled up next to the bed, on the worn pink shag carpeting.

Poor guy. As many times as he had screwed up in the past, he was good to Liv, and for a while he believed he was the One Who Is Two. It's hard to hold a grudge against a guy who tried to give his life to save the world. If anyone understood that, it was me.

It wasn't his fault the world wouldn't have him.

So I stepped off his chest as quickly as I could, and vowed to be a little more careful where I put my feet in the future. Not that he'd ever know.

As I moved through the rest of the house it seemed completely vacant. Then I heard the crackling of a fireplace and followed the sound. At the bottom of the stairs, straight off the front hall, I found Macon sitting in his cracked leather chair by the fire. True to form, where there was Macon, there was also Lena. She was sitting at his feet, leaning against the ottoman. I could smell the Sharpie she was writing with. Her notebook lay open on her lap, but she was barely looking at it. Drawing circles over and over, until the page looked like it was ripping apart.

She wasn't crying—far from it.

She was plotting.

"It was Ethan. It had to be. I could feel him there with us, like he was standing right next to his grave."

Had she seen the crossword? Maybe that was why she was so fired up. I looked around the study, but if she'd read the paper, there was no sign of it. A stack of old newspapers filled a brass bin next to the fireplace; Macon used them for kindling. I tried to lift a single page of newsprint, and I could barely make a corner flutter.

I wondered if I would've been able to figure out the crossword without a more experienced Sheer like my mom helping me.

Amma didn't need to worry so much about the haint blue and the salt and the charms. This whole haunting thing wasn't as easy as it was cracked up to be.

Then I noticed how sad Macon looked, studying Lena's face. I gave up on the newspaper and focused harder on their conversation.

"You may have felt the essence of him, Lena. A burial site is a powerful place, no doubt."

"I don't mean I felt something, Uncle Macon. I felt him. Ethan, the Sheer. I'm sure of it."

The smoke from the fire curled out from the grating. Boo lay with his head in Lena's lap, the flames reflecting in his dark eyes.

"Because a button fell onto his grave?" Macon's voice didn't change, but he sounded tired. I wondered how many of these conversations he'd endured since I died.

"No. Because he moved it." Lena didn't give up.

"What about the wind? What about someone else? Wesley could have bumped it off, considering he is not the most graceful of creatures."

"It was only a week ago. I remember it perfectly. I know it happened." She was even more stubborn than he was.

A week ago?

Had that much time passed in Gatlin?

Lena hadn't seen the paper. She couldn't prove I was still here, not to herself or my family or even my best friend. There was no way to explain about Obidias Trueblood and all the complications in my life, not while she didn't even know I was in the room with her.

"What about since then?" Macon asked.

She looked troubled. "Maybe he's gone. Maybe he's up to something. I don't know how it works in the Otherworld." Lena stared into the fire as if she was looking for something. "It's not just me. I went to see Amma. She said she felt him in the house."

"Amma's feelings are not to be trusted when it comes to Ethan."

"What's that supposed to mean? Of course Amma can be trusted. She's the most trustworthy person I know." Lena looked furious, and I wondered how much she actually knew about that night at the water tower.

He didn't say a word.

"Isn't she?"

Macon closed his book. "I can't see the future. I'm not a Seer. All I know is Ethan did what needed to be done. The whole realm—Dark and Light—will always be grateful to him."

Lena stood up, ripping the ink-stained page from her notebook. "Well, I'm not. I understand he was very brave and noble and whatever, but he left me here, and I'm not sure it was worth it. I don't care about the universe and the realm and saving the world, not anymore. Not without Ethan."

She tossed the ripped page into the fire. The orange flames leaped up around it.

Uncle Macon spoke as he watched the fire. "I understand."

"Really?" Lena didn't seem to believe him.

"There was a time when I put my heart above all else."

"And what happened?"

"I don't know. I got older, I suppose. And I learned that things often are more complicated than we think."

Leaning against the mantel, Lena stared into the fire.

"Maybe you just forgot what it feels like."

"Perhaps."

"I won't." She looked at her uncle. "I won't ever forget."

She twisted her hand, and the smoke rose up until it curled around her and took shape. It was a face. It was my face.

"Lena."

My face disappeared at the sound of Macon's voice, fading away into streaks of gray cloud.

"Leave me alone. Let me have what little I can, what I have left of him." She sounded fierce, and I loved her for it.

"Those are only memories." There was sadness in Macon's voice. "You have to move on. Trust me."

"Why? You never did."

He smiled sadly, staring past her into the fire. "That's how I know."

—☙

I followed Lena up the stairs. Though the ice and snow had melted away since my last visit to Ravenwood, a thick gray fog hung throughout the house, and the air was colder.

Lena didn't seem to notice or care what was going on around her, even though her breath was curling up toward her face in a quiet white cloud. I noticed the dark rings under her eyes, the way she looked as thin and as frail as she had when Macon died. She wasn't the same person she had been then, though—she was someone much stronger.

She had believed Macon was gone forever, and we found a way to bring him back. I knew deep down she couldn't hold out for any less of a fate for me.

Maybe Lena didn't know I was here, but she knew I wasn't gone. She wasn't giving up on me yet. She couldn't.

I knew, because if I was the one left behind, I couldn't have either.

Lena slipped into her room, past the pile of suitcases, and crawled into bed without even taking off her clothes. She waved her fingers, and her door slammed shut. I lay down next to her, my face on the edge of her pillow. We were only inches apart.

The tears began to roll down her face, and I thought my heart would break, just watching her.

I love you, L. I always will.

I closed my eyes and reached for her. I wished, desperately, that there was something I could do. There had to be some way I could let her know I was still here.

I love you, Ethan. I won't forget you. I'll never forget you, and I'll never stop loving you.

I heard her voice uncurl inside my head. When I opened my eyes, she was staring right through me.

"Never," she whispered.

"Never," I said.

I wrapped my fingers in the curls of black hair and waited until she fell asleep. I could feel her nestled up next to me.

I had to make sure she found that newspaper.

As I followed Lena down the stairs the next morning, I was starting to feel a) like some kind of stalker and b) like I was losing my mind. Kitchen sent out as big a breakfast as ever—but thankfully, now that the Order wasn't broken and the world wasn't about to end, the food wasn't so raw that the sight of it made you want to throw up.

Macon was waiting for Lena at the table, and he was already digging in. I still wasn't used to the sight of him eating. There were biscuits this morning, baked with so much butter it came bubbling up through cracks in the dough. Thick slices of bacon crowded against an Amma-sized mountain of scrambled eggs. Berries piled inside a big piece of pastry crust that Link, before his Linkubus days, would have swallowed whole in one bite.

Then I saw it. *The Stars and Stripes* was folded at the bottom of a whole stack of newspapers—from about as many countries as I could name.

I reached for the paper just as Macon reached for the coffeepot, shoving his hand right through my chest. It felt cold and strange, like I'd swallowed a piece of ice. Maybe like brain freeze from an ICEE, only in my heart rather than in my head.

I grabbed the paper with both hands and pulled on it as hard as I could. One edge slowly peeked out from beneath the pile.

Not good enough.

I looked up at Macon and Lena. Macon had his head buried

in a newspaper called *L'Express*, which looked like it was written in French. Lena had her eyes glued to her plate, like the eggs were going to reveal an important truth.

Come on, L. It's right here. I'm right here.

I yanked the paper harder, and it slid all the way out from the pile and fluttered onto the floor.

Neither one of them looked up.

Lena stirred milk into her tea. I reached for her hand with mine, squeezing it until she dropped the spoon, splashing tea onto the tablecloth.

Lena stared at her teacup, flexing her fingers. She leaned down to blot the tablecloth with her napkin. Then she noticed the paper on the floor, where it had landed next to her foot.

"What's this?" She picked up *The Stars and Stripes*. "I didn't know you subscribed to this paper, Uncle M."

"I do. I find it's helpful to know what's going on in town. You wouldn't want to miss, I don't know, the latest diabolical plan of Mrs. Lincoln and the Ladies Auxiliary." He smiled. "Where would the fun be in that?"

I held my breath.

She tossed it over, facedown on the table.

The crossword was on the back. The Sunday edition, just like I'd planned it back in the office of *The Stars and Stripes*.

She smiled to herself. "Amma would do this crossword in about five minutes."

Macon looked up. "Less than that, I'm sure. I believe I could do it in three."

"Really?"

"Try me."

"Eleven across," she said. "Apparition or phantasm. A spectral being. A spirit from another world. A ghost."

Macon looked at her, his eyes narrowing.

Lena leaned over the paper, holding her tea. I watched as she began to read.

Figure it out, L. Please.

It was only when the teacup began to shake and fell to the carpet that I knew she'd gotten it—not the crossword but the message behind it.

"Ethan?" She looked up. I leaned closer, holding my cheek against hers. I knew she couldn't feel it; I wasn't back with her, not yet. But I knew she believed I was there, and for now that's all that mattered.

Macon stared at her, surprised.

The chandelier above the table began to sway. The room brightened until it was blindingly white. The enormous dining room windows began to crack into hundreds of glass spiderwebs. Heavy drapes flew against the walls like feathers in the wind.

"Darling," Macon began.

Lena's hair curled in every direction. I closed my eyes as window after window began to shatter like fireworks.

Ethan?

I'm here.

Above everything, that was all I needed her to know.

Finally.

⊰ CHAPTER 13 ⊱

Where the Crow Carries You

Lena knew I was there. It was hard to drag myself away, but she had figured out the truth. That was the main thing. Amma and Lena. I was two for two. It was a start.

And I was exhausted.

Now I had to find my way back to her for good. I crossed back in about ten seconds flat. If only the rest of the way was that easy.

I knew I should go home and tell my mom everything, but I also knew how worried she'd be about me going to the Far Keep. From what Genevieve and my mom and Aunt Prue and Obidias Trueblood had said, the Far Keep seemed like the last place a person would voluntarily go.

Especially a person with a mother.

I cataloged everything I needed to do, everywhere I needed to go. The river. The book. The river eyes—two smooth black stones. That's what Obidias Trueblood said I needed. My mind kept going back to it, over and over.

How many smooth black stones could there be in the world? And how was I going to know which ones happened to be the eyes of the river, whatever that even meant?

Maybe I'd find them on the way. Or maybe I'd already found them, and I didn't even know it.

A magical black rock, the eye of the river.

It sounded strangely familiar. Had I heard it before?

I thought back to Amma, to all the charms, every tiny bone, every bit of graveyard dirt and salt, every piece of string she'd given me to wear.

Then I remembered.

It wasn't one of Amma's charms. It was from the vision I saw when I opened the bottle in her room.

I had seen the stone hanging around Sulla's neck. Sulla the Prophet. In the vision Amma had called it "the eye."

The river's eye.

Which meant I knew where to find it and how to get there—as long as I could figure out how to find my way to Wader's Creek on this side.

It couldn't be avoided, intimidating as it was. It was time to pay a visit to the Greats.

I unfolded Aunt Prue's map. Now that I knew how to read the map, it wasn't that hard to see where the Doorwells were marked. I found the red X on the Doorwell that led to Obidias' place—the one at the Snow family crypt—so after that I went looking for every red mark I could find.

There were plenty of red Xs, but which of those Doorwells would take me to Wader's Creek? Their destinations weren't exactly marked like exits on the interstate—and I didn't want to stumble into any of the surprises that could be waiting for a guy behind Otherworld door number three.

Snakes for fingers might be getting off easy.

There had to be some kind of logic. I didn't know what connected the Doorwell behind the Snow family plot to the rocky path that had taken me to Obidias Trueblood, but there had to be something. Seeing as we were all related to one another around here, that something was probably blood.

What would connect one of these plots in His Garden of Perpetual Peace to the Greats? If there was a liquor store in the graveyard—or a buried coffin full of Uncle Abner's Wild Turkey, or the ruins of a haunted bakery known for lemon meringue pie—he wouldn't have been far behind me.

But Wader's Creek had its own graveyard. There wasn't a crypt or a plot for Ivy, Abner, Sulla, or Delilah in Perpetual Peace.

Then I found a red X behind what my mom had said was one of the oldest tribute markers in the graveyard, and I knew it had to be the one.

So I folded up the map and decided to check it out.

Minutes later, I found myself staring at a white marble obelisk.

Sure enough, the word SACRED was carved into the crumbling veined stone, right above a gloomy-looking skull with empty eyes that stared at you straight on. I never understood why a single creepy skull marked a handful of Gatlin's oldest graves. But we all knew about this particular tribute, even though it was tucked away on the far edge of Perpetual Peace, where the heart of the old graveyard sat, long before the new one was built up around it.

The Confederate Needle—that's what folks around Gatlin called it, not because of its pointed shape but because of the ladies who had put it there. Katherine Cooper Sewell, who founded the Gatlin chapter of the Daughters of the American Revolution—probably not long after the Revolution itself— had seen to it that the DAR raised enough money for the obelisk before she died.

She had married Samuel Sewell.

Samuel Sewell had built and run the Palmetto Brewery, the first distillery in Gatlin County. Palmetto Brewery made one thing and one thing only.

Wild Turkey.

"Pretty smart," I said, circling to the back of the obelisk, where the twisted wrought iron fencing bowed and broke into pieces. I didn't know if I would've been able to see it back home, but here in the Otherworld, the trapdoor of a Doorwell cut into the base of the rock was plain as day. The rectangular outline of the entrance snaked between rows of engraved shells and angels.

I pressed my hand against the soft stone and felt it give way beneath me, swinging from sunlight into shadow.

A dozen uneven stone steps later, I found myself on what sounded like a gravel pathway. I made my way around a turn in the passage and caught sight of light pooling in the distance. As I got closer, I smelled swamp grass and waterlogged palmettos. There was no mistaking that smell.

This was the right place.

I reached a warped wooden door, propped halfway open. Nothing could keep out the light now—or the hot, sticky air, which only got hotter and stickier as I climbed the steps on the other side of the door.

Wader's Creek was waiting for me. I couldn't see past the first fringe of tall cypress trees, but I knew it was there. If I followed the muddy path in front of me, I would find my way to Amma's home away from home.

I pushed through the palmetto branches and saw a row of tiny houses, just off the edge of the water.

The Greats. It had to be.

As I made my way down the path, I heard voices. On the nearest veranda, three women were crowded around a table with a deck of cards. They were fussing and swatting at one another the way the Sisters did when they played Scrabble.

I recognized Twyla from a distance. I suspected she was going to join the Greats when she died on the night of the Seventeenth Moon. Still, it was strange to see her here, hanging out on the porch and playing cards with them.

"Now, you can't throw that card, Twyla, and you know it. You think I can't see you cheatin'?" A woman in a colorful shawl pushed the card back toward Twyla.

"Now, Sulla. You may be a Seer, *cher*. But there's nothin' there to see," Twyla responded.

Sulla. That's who she was. Now I recognized her from the vision—Sulla the Prophet, Amma's most famous ancestor of all.

"Well, I think you're both cheatin'." The third woman tossed her cards down and adjusted her round glasses. Her shawl was bright yellow. "And I don't want ta play with either one a you." I tried not to laugh, but the scene was too familiar; I might as well be home.

"Don't you be such a sourpuss, Delilah." Sulla wagged her head.

Delilah. She was the one in the glasses.

A fourth woman was sitting in a rocking chair at the edge of the porch, with a hoop in one hand and a needle in the other. "Why don't you go on in and cut your old Aunt Ivy a slice a pie? I'm busy with my stitchin'."

Ivy. It was weird to finally see her in person after the visions.

"Pie? Ha!" An old man laughed from his rocking chair—a bottle of Wild Turkey in one hand and a pipe in the other.

Uncle Abner.

I felt like I knew the man personally, though we'd never met. After all, I'd been in the kitchen when Amma made him more than a hundred pies over the years—maybe a thousand.

The giant crow flew down and landed on Uncle Abner's shoulder. "Won't find any pie in there, Delilah. We're runnin' low."

Delilah stopped, one hand on the screen door. "Why would we be runnin' low, Abner?"

He nodded in my direction. "I'm guessin' Amarie's busy bakin' for him now." He emptied his pipe, tapping the old tobacco over the side of the porch railing.

"Who, me?" I couldn't believe Uncle Abner was actually talking to me. I took a step closer to all of them. "I mean, hello, sir."

He ignored me. "I'm guessin' I won't be seein' another lemon meringue unless it's the boy's favorite, too."

"Are you gonna stand there starin' or come on over here already?" Sulla had her back to me, but she still knew I was there.

Twyla squinted into the sunlight. "Ethan? That you, *cher*?"

I walked toward the house, as much as I felt like staying where I was. I don't know why I was so nervous. I hadn't expected the Greats to seem so regular. They could've been any group of old folks, hanging out on the porch on a sunny afternoon. Except that they were all dead.

"Yeah. I mean, yes, ma'am. It's me."

Uncle Abner stood up and walked over to the railing to get a better look. The enormous crow was still perched on his shoulder. It flapped its wings, and he didn't even flinch. "Like I said, we won't be gettin' any pie—or much else—now that the boy's up here with us."

Twyla waved me over. "Maybe he'll share a bit a his with you."

I climbed up the scuffed wooden steps, and the wind chimes tapped against one another. There wasn't so much as a breeze.

"He's a spirit, all right," Sulla said. There was a tiny brown bird hopping around the table. A sparrow.

"'Course he is." Ivy sniffed. "Wouldn't be up here otherwise."

I gave Uncle Abner and his scavenger a wide berth.

When I was close enough, Twyla jumped up and threw her arms around me. "Can't say I'm happy you're here, but I am happy to see you."

I hugged her back. "Yeah, well, I'm not all that happy to be here either."

Uncle Abner took a swig of whiskey. "Then why'd you go and jump off that fool tower?"

I didn't know what to say, but Sulla answered before I had to think of anything. "You know the answer to that, Abner, about as well as you know your own name. Now stop givin' the boy a hard time."

The crow flapped its wings again. "Somebody should," Uncle Abner said.

Sulla turned and gave Uncle Abner the look. I wondered if that was where Amma had learned it. "Unless you were strong enough to stop the Wheel a Fate yourself, you know the boy didn't have a choice."

Delilah brought a wicker chair over for me. "Now, you come on and sit down here with us."

Sulla was still flipping cards, but these were ordinary playing cards.

"Can you read those, too?" It wouldn't have surprised me.

She laughed, and the sparrow chirped. "No, we're just playin' gin." Sulla slapped down her cards. "Speakin' a that—gin."

Delilah pouted. "You always win."

"Well, I've won again," Sulla said. "So why don't you sit down here, Ethan, and tell us what brings you 'round our way."

"I'm not sure how much you know."

She lifted her eyebrows.

"Okay, so you probably already know that I went to see Obidias Trueblood, this old—"

"Mmm hmm." She nodded.

"And if he's telling the truth, there's a way I can get back home." I was stumbling over my words. "I mean, to the home where I was alive."

"Mmm hmm."

"I have to get my page from—"

"*The Caster Chronicles*," she finished for me. "I know all that. So why don't you go on and say what you need from us."

I was sure she knew, but she wanted me to ask anyway. It was only proper.

"I need a stone." I thought about the best way to describe it. "This will probably sound strange, but I saw you wearing it once, in kind of a dream. It's shiny and black...."

"This one?" Sulla held out her palm. There it was. The black stone I saw in my vision.

I nodded, relieved.

"Darn right you do." She pressed the rock into my hand, closing my fingers around it. It pulsed with a kind of strange warmth that seemed to come from inside.

Delilah looked at me. "You know what that is?"

I nodded. "Obidias said it's called a river's eye, and I need two of them to get across the river."

"Then I reckon you're one short," Uncle Abner said. He hadn't moved from the railing. He was busy packing his pipe with dry leaf tobacco.

"Oh, there's another one." Sulla smiled knowingly. "Don't you know?"

I shook my head.

Twyla reached over and took my hand. A smile spread across her face, her long braids slipping over her shoulder as she nodded. "*Un cadeau*. A gift. I remember when I gave it to Lena," she said in her heavy French Creole accent. "River's eye is a powerful stone. Brings luck and a safe journey." As she spoke, I saw the charm from Lena's necklace. The smooth black rock she always wore hanging from the chain.

Of course.

Lena had the second stone I needed.

"You know how to get to the river and get on your way?" Twyla asked, dropping my hand.

I pulled Aunt Prue's map out of my back pocket. "I have a map. My aunt gave it to me."

"Maps are good," Sulla said, looking it over. "But birds are better." She made a clicking noise with her tongue, and the sparrow fluttered onto her shoulder. "A map can lead you astray if you don't read it right. A bird always knows the way."

"I wouldn't want to take your bird." She had already given me the stone. It felt like I was taking too much. Plus, birds made me nervous. They were like old ladies but with sharper beaks.

Uncle Abner took a long puff of his pipe and walked toward us. Even though he wasn't looming over me from the sky, he was still taller than me. He had a slight limp, and I couldn't help but wonder what caused it.

He hooked his finger around one of the suspenders attached to his loose brown pants. "Then take mine."

"Excuse me, sir?"

"My bird." He cocked his shoulder, and the huge crow's feathers ruffled. "If you don't wanna take Sulla's bird—which I understand, since it's not much bigger than a field mouse—then take mine."

I was scared to stand next to that vulture-sized crow. I definitely didn't want to take it anywhere with me. But I had to

146

be careful, because he was offering me something he valued, and I didn't want to insult him.

I *really* didn't want to insult him.

"I appreciate it, sir. But I don't want to take your bird either. It seems…" The crow squawked loudly. "Really attached to you."

The old man waved off my concern. "Nonsense. Exu is smart, named for the god of the crossroads. He watches the doors between worlds and knows the way. Don't you, boy?"

The bird sat proudly on the man's shoulder as if he knew Uncle Abner was singing his praises.

Delilah walked over and held out her arm. Exu flapped his wings once, dropping down to land on her. "The crow is also the only bird that can cross between the worlds—the veils between life and death, and places far worse. That old heap a feathers is a powerful ally, and a better teacher, Ethan."

"Are you saying he can cross over to the Mortal realm?" Was that really possible?

Uncle Abner blew the thick pipe smoke in my face as he spoke. "'Course he can. There and back, there and back again. Only place that bird can't go is underwater. And that's only 'cause I never taught him to swim."

"So he can show me the way to the river?"

"He can show you a lot more than that if you pay attention." Uncle Abner nodded at the bird, and it took off into the sky, circling above our heads. "He behaves best if you give a gift every now and again, just like the god I named him after."

I had no idea what kinds of gifts to offer a crow, a voodoo god, or a crow named after one. I got the feeling regular birdseed wasn't going to cut it.

But I didn't have to worry, because Uncle Abner made sure I knew. "Take some a this." He poured whiskey into a dented flask and handed me a small tin. It was the same one he had opened to fill his pipe.

"Your bird drinks whiskey and eats tobacco?"

The old man frowned. "Just be glad he doesn't like eatin' scrawny boys that don't know their way 'round the Otherworld."

"Yes, sir." I nodded.

"Now you get outta here and take my bird and that stone." Uncle Abner shooed me away. "I won't get any a Amarie's pie with you hangin' 'round here."

"Yes, sir." I put the tobacco tin and the flask in my pocket with the map. "And thank you."

I started down the stairs and stepped off the porch. I turned back to take one last look at the Greats, gathered around a card table, sewing and fussing, scowling and drinking whiskey, depending on which one of them you were talking about. I wanted to remember them this way, like regular people who were great for reasons that had nothing to do with seeing the future or scaring the hell out of Dark Casters.

They reminded me of Amma and everything I loved about her. The way she always had the answers and sent me off with something strange in my pocket. The way she scowled at me when she was worried, and reminded me of all the things I still didn't know.

Sulla stood up and leaned over the porch rail. "When you see the River Master, you be sure to say I sent ya, you hear?"

She said it like I should know what she was talking about. "River Master? Who is that, ma'am?"

"You'll know him when you see him," she said.

"Yes, ma'am." I started to turn away.

"Ethan," Uncle Abner called, "when you get home, tell Amarie I'm expectin' a lemon meringue and a basket a fried chicken. Two big, fat drumsticks.... Make that four."

I smiled. "I will."

"And don't forget to send my bird back. He gets ornery after a while."

The crow circled above me as I made my way down the stairs. I had no idea where I was going, not even with a map and a tobacco-eating bird that could cross over between worlds.

It didn't matter if I had my mom, Aunt Prue, a Dark Caster who had escaped from the very place I was trying to break into, and all the Greats, with Twyla thrown in for good measure.

I had one stone now, and the more I thought about Lena, the more I realized I'd always known where to find the other one. She never took it off her charm necklace. Maybe that's why Twyla had given it to her when she was a little girl—for some kind of protection. Or for me.

After all, Twyla was a powerful Necromancer. Maybe she'd known that I'd need it.

I'm coming, L. As soon as I can.

I knew she couldn't hear me Kelting, but I listened for her voice in the back of my mind anyway. As if the memory of it could somehow replace hearing her.

I love you.

I imagined her black hair and her green and gold eyes, her beat-up Chucks and her chipped black nail polish.

There was only one thing left to do, and it was time for me to do it.

⊰ CHAPTER 14 ⊱

Messed-Up Things

It didn't take me long to retrace my steps to the Confederate Needle, and I found my own way to *The Stars and Stripes* this time around. I was crossing like an old Sheer now. Once I got the hang of it—a certain way of letting my mind do the work for me without focusing on anything at all—it seemed as easy as walking. Easier, since I wasn't actually walking.

And once I was there, I knew what to do, and I could do it myself. In fact, I was actually looking forward to it. I'd done a little thinking ahead of time. I could see why Amma liked crossword puzzles so much. Once you got the right mind-set, they were sort of addictive.

When I found my way into the office—past Swamp Cooler

City—the mock-up of the current issue was on one of the three little desks, right where it had been last time. I fanned open the papers. This time I found the crossword puzzle without much trouble.

This puzzle was even less finished than the last one. Maybe the staff was getting lazy, now that they knew there was a chance someone else would do it for them.

Either way, Lena would be reading the crossword puzzle. I picked up the nearest letter and pushed it into place.

Four down.

O. N. Y. X.

As in, a black stone.

Nine across.

T. R. I. B. U. T. A. R. Y.

As in, a river.

Six down.

O. C. U. L. U. S.

As in, an eye.

Eight across.

C. H. A. R. I. S. M. A.

As in, charm.

M. A. T. E. R.

As in, my own. Lila Jane Evers Wate.

S. E. R. I. O. U. S.

As in, grave.

That was the message. I need the black stone—the eye of a river, and the one you wear on your charm necklace. And I need you to leave it for me at my mother's grave. I couldn't spell it out any clearer than that.

At least not in this edition of the paper.

By the time I finished, I was exhausted, as if I'd been running sprints all afternoon on the basketball court. I didn't know how much time would need to pass in the Otherworld before Lena got my message in this one. I only knew that she'd get it.

Because I was as sure of her as I was of myself.

When I got home to the Otherworld—to my house, or my mom's grave, whatever you wanted to call it—there it was, waiting for me on the doorstep.

She must have left it on my mother's grave, like I asked.

I couldn't believe it had worked.

Lena's black-rock charm from Barbados, the one she always wore around her neck, sat in the middle of the doormat.

I had the second river stone.

A wave of relief settled over me. It lasted about five seconds, until I realized what the stone also meant.

It was time to go. Time to say good-bye.

So why couldn't I bring myself to say it?

"Ethan." I heard my mom's voice, but I didn't look up.

I was sitting on the floor of the living room, my back to the couch. I had a house and a car in my hands, stray pieces of my mom's old Christmas town. I couldn't take my eyes off the car.

"You found the lost green car. I never could."

She didn't answer. Her hair looked even messier than usual. Her face was streaked with tears.

I don't know why the town was set out on the coffee table like that, but I put down the house and moved the tiny green tin car farther along the table. Away from the toy animals, the church with the bent steeple, and the pipe-cleaner tree.

Like I said, time to go.

Part of me wanted to take off running the second I heard about what I had to do to get back to my old life. Part of me didn't care about anything but seeing Lena again.

But as I sat there, all I could think about was how much I didn't want to leave my mom. How much I'd missed her, and how quickly I had gotten used to seeing her in the house, hearing her in the next room. I didn't know if I wanted to give that up again, no matter how badly I needed to go back.

So all I could do was just sit there and look at that old car and wonder how something that had been lost for so long could be found again.

My mom took a breath, and I closed my eyes before she could say a word. It didn't stop her. "I don't think it's wise, Ethan. I don't think it's safe, and I don't think you should be going. No matter what your Aunt Prue says." Her voice wavered.

"Mom."

"You're only seventeen."

"Actually, I'm not. What I am now is nothing." I looked up at her. "And I hate to break it to you, but it's a little late for that speech. You have to admit that safety might not be my biggest concern at the moment. Now that I'm dead and everything."

"Well, if you say it like that." She sighed and sat down on the floor next to me.

"How do you want me to say it?"

"I don't know. Passed on?" She tried not to smile.

I half-smiled back. "Sorry. Passed on." She was right. Folks didn't like saying *dead*, not where we were from. It was impolite. As if saying it somehow made it true. As if words themselves were more powerful than anything that could actually happen to you.

Maybe they were.

After all, that's what I had to do now, wasn't it? Destroy the words on a page in some book in a library that had changed my Mortal destiny. Was it really so far-fetched to think that words had a way of shaping a person's whole life?

"You don't know what you're getting yourself into, sweetheart. Maybe if I had figured it out for myself, before all this, you wouldn't even be here. There wouldn't have been a car accident, and there wouldn't have been a water tower—" She stopped.

"You can't keep things from happening to me, Mom. Not even these things." I leaned my head back along the edge of the couch. "Not even messed-up things."

"What if I want to?"

"You can't. It's my life, or whatever this is." I turned to look at her.

She leaned her head on my shoulder, holding the side of my face close with her hand. Something she hadn't done since I was a kid. "It's your life. You're right about that. And I can't make a decision like this for you, however much I want to. Which is very, very much."

"I kind of figured that part out."

She smiled sadly. "I just got you back. I don't want to lose you again."

"I know. I don't want to leave you either."

Side by side, we stared at the Christmas town, maybe for the last time. I put the car back where it belonged.

I knew then that we would never have another Christmas together, no matter what happened. I would stay or I would go—but either way, I would move on to somewhere that wasn't here. Things couldn't be like this forever, not even in this Gatlin-that-wasn't-Gatlin. Whether I was able to get my life back or not.

Things changed.

Then they changed again.

Life was like that, and even death, I guess.

I couldn't be with both my mom and Lena, not in what was left of one lifetime. They would never meet, though I had already told them everything there was to tell about the other. Since I got here, my mom had me describe every charm on

Lena's necklace. Every line of every poem she'd ever written. Every story about the smallest things that had happened to us, things I didn't even know I remembered.

Still, it wasn't the same as being a family, or whatever we could have been.

Lena and my mom and me.

They would never laugh about me or keep a secret from me or even fight about me. My mom and Lena were the two most important people in my life, or afterlife, and I could never have both of them together.

That's what I was thinking when I closed my eyes. When I opened them, my mom was gone—as if she'd known I couldn't leave her. As if she'd known I wouldn't be able to walk away.

Truthfully, I didn't know if I could have done it, myself.

Now I'd never find out.

Maybe it was better that way.

I pocketed the two stones and made my way down the front steps, closing the door carefully behind me. The smell of fried tomatoes came wafting out the door as it shut.

I didn't say good-bye. I had a feeling we'd see each other again. Someday, somehow.

Aside from that, there wasn't anything I could tell my mom that she didn't already know. And no way to say it and still walk out the door.

She knew I loved her. She knew I had to go. At the end of the day, there wasn't much more to say.

I don't know if she watched me go.

I told myself she did.

I hoped she didn't.

CHAPTER 15

The River Master

As I stepped inside the Doorwell, the known world gave way to the unknown world more quickly than I expected. Even in the Otherworld, there are some places that are noticeably more other than others.

The river was one of them. This wasn't any kind of river I'd seen in the Mortal Gatlin County. Like the Great Barrier, this was a seam. Something that held worlds together without being in any one of them.

I was in totally uncharted territory.

Luckily, Uncle Abner's crow seemed to know the way. Exu flapped overhead, gliding and hanging in circles above me, sometimes landing on high branches to wait for me if I fell too far behind. He didn't seem to mind the job either; he tolerated our quest with only the occasional squawk. Maybe he enjoyed getting out for a change. He reminded me of Lucille that way, except I didn't catch her eating little mice carcasses when she was hungry.

And when I caught him looking at me, he was really looking at me. Every time I started to feel normal again, he would catch my eye and send shivers down my spine, like he was doing it on purpose. Like he knew he could.

I wondered if Exu was a real bird. I knew he could cross between worlds, but did that make him supernatural? According to Uncle Abner, it only made him a crow.

Maybe all crows were just creepy.

As I walked farther, the swamp weeds and cypress trees jutting out of the murky water led to greener grass beyond the bank, grass so tall I could barely see over it in places.

I wove through the grass, following the black bird in the sky, trying not to remember too much about where I was going or what I was leaving behind. It was hard enough not to imagine the look on my mother's face when I walked out the door.

I tried desperately not to think about her eyes, about the way they lit up when she saw me. Or her hands, the way she waved them in the air as she talked, as if she thought she could pull words out of the sky with her fingers. And her arms, wrapping around me like my own house, because she was the place where I was from.

I tried not to think about the moment the door closed. It would never open again, not for me. Not like that.

It's what I wanted. I said it to myself as I walked. It's what she wanted for me. To have a life. To live.

To leave.

Exu squawked, and I beat back the tall brush and the grass.

Leaving was harder than I ever could've imagined, and part of me still couldn't believe I had done it. But as much as I tried not to think about my mom, I tried to keep Lena's face in my mind, a constant reminder of why I was doing this— risking everything.

I wondered what she was doing right now.... Writing in her notebook? Practicing the viola? Reading her battered copy of *To Kill a Mockingbird*?

I was still thinking about it when I heard music in the distance. It sounded like... the Rolling Stones?

Part of me expected to push through the grass and see Link standing there. But as I edged closer to the chorus of "You Can't Always Get What You Want," I realized it was the Stones, but it definitely wasn't Link.

The voice wasn't bad enough, and too many of the notes were right.

It was a big guy, wearing a faded bandanna tied around his head, and a Harley-Davidson T-shirt with scaly wings across the back. He was sitting at a plastic folding table like the ones the bridge club used back in Gatlin. With his black shades and long beard, he looked like he should be riding an old chopper instead of sitting next to a riverbank.

Except for his lunch. He was spooning something out of a plastic Tupperware container. From where I was, it looked like intestines or human remains. Or . . .

The biker belched. "Best chili-ghetti this side a the Mississippi." He shook his head.

Exu cawed and landed on the edge of the folding table. An enormous black dog lying on the ground next to it barked but didn't bother to get up.

"What're you doing around here, bird? Unless you're looking to make a deal, there's nothing for you here. An' don't even think I'm letting you get into my whiskey this time." The biker shooed Exu off the table. "Go on. Shoo. You tell Abner I'm ready to deal when he's ready to play."

As he waved the crow off the table, and Exu disappeared into the blue sky, the biker noticed me standing at the edge of the grass. "You out sightseeing, or are you looking for something?" He tossed the remains of his lunch into a small white Styrofoam cooler and picked up a deck of playing cards.

He nodded my way, shuffling the cards from hand to hand.

I swallowed hard and stepped closer as "Hand of Fate" started playing on the old transistor radio sitting in the dust. I wondered if he listened to anything besides the Rolling Stones, but I wasn't about to ask. "I'm looking for the River Master."

The biker laughed, dealing a hand as if someone was sitting on the other side of the table. "River Master. I haven't heard that one in a while. River Master, Ferryman, Water Runner—I go by a lot of names, kid. But you can call me Charlie. It's the one I answer to *when* I feel like answering."

I couldn't imagine anyone getting this guy to do anything he didn't feel like doing. If we were in the Mortal realm, he would probably be a bouncer at a biker bar or a pool hall where people were dragged out for breaking bottles over one another's heads.

"Nice to meet you...Charlie," I choked. "I'm Ethan."

He waved me over. "So what can I do for you, Ethan?"

I walked over to the table, careful to give the giant creature on the ground a wide berth. It looked like a mastiff, with its square face and wrinkled skin. Its tail was bandaged with white gauze.

"Don't mind old Drag," he said. "He won't get up unless you're carrying some raw meat." Charlie grinned. "Or unless you *are* raw meat. Dead meat like you, kid—you're off the hook."

Why didn't that surprise me?

"Drag? What kind of name is that?" I reached out toward the dog.

"Dragon. The kind that breathes fire and chews your hand off if you try to pet him."

Drag looked at me, growling. I moved my hand back to my pocket.

"I need to cross the river. I brought you these." I laid the river eyes on the padded card table. It really did look like the ones at the bridge club.

Charlie glanced at the stones, unimpressed. "Good for you. One for the way there, one for the way back. That's like showin' a bus driver your bus ticket. Still don't make me want to get on no bus."

"It doesn't?" I swallowed. So much for my plans. Somehow I had thought this was all working out too easily.

Charlie looked me over. "You play blackjack, Ethan? You know, twenty-one?"

I knew what he meant. "Um, not really." Which wasn't entirely true. I used to play with Thelma, until she started cheating as badly as the Sisters did at Rummikub.

He pushed my cards toward me, flipping a nine of diamonds on top of the first one. My hand. "You're a smart boy—I bet you can figure it out."

I checked my card, a seven. "Hit me." That's what Thelma would have said.

Charlie seemed like a risk-taker. If I was right, he probably respected other people who did the same. And what did I have to lose?

He nodded approvingly, flipping a king. "Sorry, kid, that's twenty-six. You're over. But I would've taken the hit, too."

Charlie shuffled the deck and dealt us each another hand.

This time I had a four and an eight. "Hit me."

He flipped a seven. I had nineteen, which was hard to beat. Charlie had a king and a five sitting in front of him. He had to take a hit, or I would win for sure. He pulled a card from the top of the deck. A six of hearts.

"Twenty-one. That's blackjack," he said, shuffling again.

I wasn't sure if this was some kind of test or if he was just bored out here, but he didn't seem anxious to get rid of me anytime soon. "I really need to get across the river, si—" I stopped myself before I called him "sir." He lifted an eyebrow. "I mean, Charlie. See, there's a girl—"

Charlie nodded, interrupting. "There's always a girl." The Rolling Stones started crooning "2,000 Light Years from Home." Funny.

"I need to get back to her—"

"I had a girl once. Penelope was her name. Penny." He leaned back in his chair, smoothing his scraggly beard. "Eventually she got tired of hanging around here, so she took off."

"Why didn't you go with her?" The second I asked the question, I realized it was probably too personal. But he answered anyway.

"I can't leave." He said it matter-of-factly, flipping cards for both of us. "I'm the River Master. It's part of the gig. Can't run out on the house."

"You could quit."

"This isn't a job, kid. It's a sentence." He laughed, but there was a bitterness that made me feel sorry for him. That and the folding card table and the lazy dog with the messed-up tail.

Then "2,000 Light Years from Home" faded out, replaced by "Plundered My Soul."

I didn't want to know who was powerful enough to sentence him to sit by what, for the most part, looked like a pretty

165

unimpressive river. It was slow and calm. If he wasn't hanging out here, I probably could've swum across.

"I'm sorry." What else could I say?

"It's okay. I made my peace with it a long time ago." He tapped on my cards. An ace and a seven. "You want a hit?"

Eighteen again.

Charlie had an ace, too.

"Hit me." I watched as he turned the card between his fingers.

A three of spades.

He took off his shades, ice blue staring back at me. His pupils were so light, they were barely visible. "You gonna call it?"

"Blackjack."

Charlie pushed back his chair and nodded toward the riverbank. There was a poor man's ferry waiting, a crude raft made of logs that were bound together with thick rope. It was just like the ones that lined the swamp in Wader's Creek. Dragon stretched and ambled after him. "Let's go before I change my mind."

I followed him to the rickety platform and stepped onto the rotting logs.

Charlie held out his hand. "Time to pay the Ferryman." He pointed toward the brown water. "Come on. Hit me."

I tossed the stone and it hit, without so much as a splash.

The moment he lowered the long pole to push against the river bottom, the water changed. A putrid odor rose from the surface—swamp rot, spoiled meat—and something else.

I looked down into the shadowy depths beneath me. The water was clear enough to see all the way to the bottom now, except I couldn't, because there were bodies everywhere I looked, only inches below the surface. And these weren't the writhing forms from myths and movies. They were corpses, bloated and waterlogged, still as death. Some faceup, some facedown—but what faces I could see had the same blue lips and terrifyingly white skin. Their hair fanned out around them in the water as they floated and bumped against one another.

"Everyone pays the Ferryman sooner or later." Charlie shrugged. "Can't change that."

The taste of bile rose in my throat, and it took every ounce of energy I had to keep from throwing up. The revulsion must have registered on my face, because Charlie's tone was sympathetic. "I know, kid. The smell's hard to take. Why do you think I don't make many trips across?"

"Why did it change? The river." I couldn't drag my eyes away from the waterlogged bodies. "I mean, it wasn't like this before."

"That's where you're wrong. You just couldn't see it. There are lots of things we choose not to see. Doesn't mean they aren't there, even if we wish they weren't."

"I'm tired of seeing everything. It was easier back when I didn't know anything. I barely even knew I was alive."

Charlie nodded. "Yeah. So I hear."

The wooden platform smacked against the opposite bank. "Thanks, Charlie."

He leaned on the pole, his unnaturally blue, pupil-less eyes staring right through me. "Don't mention it, kid. I hope you find that girl."

I reached my hand out cautiously and scratched Dragon behind the ears. I was happy to see my hand didn't burn off.

The huge dog barked at me.

"Maybe Penny will come back," I said. "You never know."

"The odds are against it."

I stepped onto the bank. "Yeah, well. If you're going to look at it that way, I guess you could say they're against me, too."

"You may be right. If you're headed where I think."

Did he know? Maybe this side of the river only led to one place, though I doubted it. The more I learned about the world I thought I knew and all the ones I didn't, the more everything threaded together, leading everywhere and nowhere at the same time.

"I'm going to the Far Keep." I didn't think he'd get the chance to tell any of the Keepers, since he couldn't leave this spot. Besides, there was something about Charlie I liked. And saying the words only made me feel more like they were true.

"Straight ahead. You can't miss it." He pointed into the distance. "But you have to get past the Gatekeeper."

"I heard." I had been thinking about it since my visit to Obidias' house with Aunt Prue.

"Well, you tell him he owes me money," Charlie said. "I won't wait around forever." I looked at him, and he sighed. "Well, say it anyway."

"You know him?"

He nodded. "We go way back. There's no telling how long it's been, but I'd guess a lifetime or two."

"What's he like?" Maybe if I knew more about this guy, I would have a better chance of convincing him to let me into the Far Keep.

Charlie smiled, pushing off with the pole and sending the poor man's ferry floating back into the sea of corpses.

"Not like me."

⊰ CHAPTER 16 ⊱

A Rock and a Crow

Once I left the river behind, I realized the road to the Gates of the Far Keep wasn't a road at all. It was more of a crude, winding path, hidden within the walls of two towering black mountains that stood side by side, creating a natural gate more ominous than anything that could've been made by Mortals—or Keepers. The mountains were slick, with razor-sharp corners that reflected the sun, as if they were made of obsidian. They looked like they were cutting black slits into the sky.

Great.

The idea of navigating a path through those jagged knife-blade cliffs was a little more than intimidating. Whatever the Keepers were up to, they definitely didn't want anyone to know about it.

Big surprise there.

Exu circled overhead now, as if he knew exactly where he was going. I picked up my pace to follow his shadow on the trail in front of me, feeling grateful for the creepy bird that was even bigger than Harlon James. I wondered what Lucille would think about him. Funny how a supernatural crow borrowed from the Greats could seem like the one familiar thing in the landscape.

Even with the help of Uncle Abner's crow, I kept stopping to consult Aunt Prue's map. Exu definitely knew the general direction of the Far Keep, but he disappeared from view every mile or so. The cliffs were high, the trail was twisted, and Exu didn't have to worry about navigating those mountains.

Lucky bird.

On the map, my path was outlined in Aunt Prue's shaky hand. Every time I tried to trace where it would lead, the path disappeared a few miles ahead. I was starting to worry that her hand had shaken a little too far in the wrong direction. Because the directions on the map didn't have me going over the mountains or between them—I was supposed to go *through* one of them.

"That can't be right."

I stared from the paper up to the sky. Exu glided from tree to tree in front of me, though now that we were closer to the mountains, the trees were that much farther apart. "Sure. Go ahead. Rub it in. Some of us have to walk, you know."

He squawked again. I waved the whiskey flask over my head. "Just don't forget who has your dinner, eh?"

He dove at me, and I laughed, sliding the flask back into my pocket.

It didn't seem so funny after the first few miles.

When I reached the sheer cliff face, I double-checked the map. There it was. A circle drawn in the hillside—marking some sort of cave entrance or a tunnel. It was easy enough to find on the map. But when I lowered the paper and tried to find the cave, there was nothing.

Just a rocky cliff face, so steep it rose into a straight vertical, cutting the trail off right in front of me. It pushed up into the clouds so high that it looked like it never ended.

Something had to be wrong.

There had to be an entrance to the tunnel somewhere around here. I felt along the cliff, stumbling over broken pieces of the shiny black rock.

Nothing.

It wasn't until I stepped back from the cliff and noticed a patch of dead brush growing along the stones that I put it together.

The brush grew in what was vaguely the shape of a circle.

I grabbed the dead overgrowth with both hands, yanking as hard as I could—and there it was. Sort of. Nothing could've prepared me for the reality of what that circle drawn on the mountain actually represented.

A small, dark hole—and by *small*, I mean *tiny*—barely big enough for a man. Barely big enough for Boo Radley. Maybe Lucille, but even that would have been cutting it tight. And it was pitch-dark inside. Of course it was.

"Aw, come on!"

According to the map, the tunnel was the only way to the Far Keep, and to Lena. If I wanted to get home, I was going to have to crawl through it. I felt sick just thinking about it.

Maybe I could go around. How long would it take to reach the other side of the mountain? Too long, that was for sure. Who was I kidding?

I tried not to think about what it would feel like to have a whole mountain fall on you while you were crawling through the middle of it. If you were already dead, could you be crushed to death? Would it hurt? Was there anything left to hurt?

The more I told myself not to think about it, the more I thought about it, and soon I was almost ready to turn back.

But then I imagined the alternative—being trapped here in the Otherworld without Lena for "infinity times infinity," as Link would say. Nothing was worth that risk. I took a deep breath, wedged my way inside, and started to crawl.

The tunnel was smaller and darker than I ever could've imagined. Once I squeezed inside, I had only a few inches of free space above me and on either side. This was worse than the time Link and I got locked in the trunk of Emory's dad's car.

I had never been scared of small spaces, but it was impossible not to feel claustrophobic in here. And it was dark—worse than dark. The only light came from cracks in the rock, which were few and far between.

Most of the time, I was crawling in complete darkness, only the sound of my breathing echoing off the walls. Invisible dirt filled my mouth, stung my eyes. I kept thinking that I was going to hit a wall—that the tunnel would just stop and I'd have to backtrack to get out. Or that I wouldn't be able to.

The ground beneath me was made of the same sharp black stone as the mountain itself, and I had to move slowly to avoid bearing down on the exposed edges of razored rubble. My hands felt like I'd shredded them to pieces; my knees, like two sacks of shattered glass. I wondered if dead people could bleed to death. With my luck, I would be the first guy to find out.

I tried to distract myself—counting to a hundred, humming the off-key tunes of some of the Holy Rollers' songs, pretending I was Kelting with Lena.

Nothing helped. I knew I was alone.

It only strengthened my resolve not to stay that way.

It's not much farther, L. I'm going to make it and find the Gates. We'll be back together soon, and then I'll tell you about how much this really sucked.

I fell silent after that.

It was too hard to pretend to Kelt.

174

My movements slowed, and my mind slowed with them, until my arms and legs moved in some kind of stiff syncopation, like the driving beat to one of Link's old songs.

Back and forth. Back and forth.

Lena. Lena. Lena.

I was still Kelting her name when I saw the light at the end of the tunnel—not a metaphoric light but a real one.

I heard Exu cawing in the distance. I felt the beginnings of a breeze, the stir of air in my face. The cold dampness of the tunnel began to give way to the warm light of the outside world.

I was almost there.

I squinted when the sunlight hit the mouth of the hole. I hadn't hauled my body out yet. But the tunnel was so dark that my eyes were having a hard time adjusting to even the smallest amount of light.

When I was only halfway out, I dropped onto my stomach with my eyes still closed, the black dirt pressing against my cheek. Exu was calling loudly, probably angry that I was taking a break. At least that's what I thought.

I opened my eyes to see the sun glinting off a pair of black-laced boots. Then the bottom of a matching wool robe came into focus.

Great.

I raised my head slowly, prepared to see a Keeper towering over me. My heart began to pound.

It looked like a man—in a way. If you ignored the fact that he was completely bald, with impossibly smooth grayish-black skin and enormous eyes. The black robe was tied at the waist with a long cord, and he—if you could call it a he—looked like some kind of miserable alien monk.

"Did you lose something?" he asked. The voice sounded so much like a man's. Like an old man, sort of sad or maybe kind. It was hard to reconcile the human features and voice with the rest of what I was staring at.

I pulled against the rock opening, yanking my legs out from the tunnel, trying to avoid bumping into whatever he was. "I—I'm trying to find the way to the Far Keep," I stammered. I tried to remember what Obidias had said. What was I looking for? Doors? Gates? That was it. "I mean, the Gates of the Far Keep." I got to my feet and tried to step back, but there was nowhere to go.

"Really?" He looked interested. Or maybe sick. Honestly, I wasn't sure it was really even a face I was looking at, so it was hard to tell what the expression meant.

"That's right." I tried to sound confident. When I stood tall, I was almost his height, which was reassuring.

"Are the Keepers expecting you?" His strange, dull eyes slitted.

"Yes," I lied.

He turned abruptly on his heel to go, his robe swinging after him.

Wrong answer.

"No," I called out. "And they'll torture me if they find me. At least that's what everyone seems to think. But there's this girl—it was all a mistake—I'm not supposed to be here—and then the lubbers came, and the Order broke, and I had to jump." My words died out, once I realized how crazy I sounded. There was no point trying to explain. It barely made sense even to me.

The creature stopped, tilting his head to the side, as if he was considering my words. Me. "Well, you've found them."

"What?"

"The Gates of the Far Keep."

I looked past him. There was nothing around but shiny black rock and clear blue sky. Maybe he was crazy. "Um, I don't see anything but mountains."

He turned and pointed. "There."

The sleeve of his robe slid down, and I caught a glimpse of an extra fold of skin flapping away from his body and disappearing under the robe.

It looked like the wing of a giant bat.

I remembered the crazy story Link told me over the summer. Macon had sent him into the Caster Tunnels to deliver a message to Obidias Trueblood. That much I'd already put together. But there was another part, about how Link was attacked by some kind of creature he ended up stabbing with his garden shears—it was grayish black and bald, with the features of a man, and deformed black bands of skin that Link was convinced were wings. "Seriously," I remembered

177

him saying. "You don't want to face that thing in an alley at night."

I knew it couldn't be the same creature, because Link said the monster he saw had yellow eyes. And the one standing here was staring back at me with green eyes—almost Caster green. Then there was the other thing. The whole gardening-shears-to-the-chest thing.

This couldn't be him.

Green eyes. Not gold. I didn't need to be afraid, right? He couldn't be Dark, could he?

Still, it wasn't anything I'd ever seen before—and I had seen more than my share.

The creature turned around, lowering his arm that wasn't an arm. "Do you see them?"

"What?" The wings? I was still trying to figure out what he was—or wasn't.

"The Gates." He seemed disappointed by my stupidity. I guess I'd be disappointed, too, if I were him. I was feeling pretty stupid myself.

I searched in the direction he had pointed a moment ago. There was nothing there. "I don't see anything."

A satisfied smile spread across his face, as if he had a secret. "Of course you don't. Only the Gatekeeper can see them."

"Where's the—" I stopped, realizing I didn't need to ask the question. I already knew the answer. "You're the Gatekeeper." There was a River Master and a Gatekeeper. Of course there was. There was also a snake man, a whiskey-drinking crow that could fly from the land of the living to the land of the dead, a river full of bodies, and a dragon dog. It was like waking up in the middle of a game of *Dungeons & Dragons*.

"The Gatekeeper." The creature nodded, obviously pleased with himself. "I am that, among other things."

I tried not to fixate on the word *thing*. But as I looked at his charcoal-colored skin and thought about those awful wings, I couldn't stop imagining him as some terrifying cross between a person and a bat.

A real-life Batman, sort of.

Only not the kind who saves anyone. Maybe the reverse.

What if this thing doesn't want to let me in?

I took a deep breath. "Look, I know it's crazy. I left crazy behind about a year ago. But there's something I need in there. And if I don't get it, I won't be able to go home. Is there any way you can show me where the Gates are?"

"Of course."

I heard the words before I saw his face. And I smiled, until I realized I was the only one smiling.

The creature frowned, his huge eyes narrowing. He put his hands together in front of his chest, tapping his crooked fingertips. "But why would I do that?"

Exu shrieked in the distance.

I looked up to see the massive black shape circling above our heads, as if he was prepared to swoop down and attack.

Wordlessly, without looking up, the creature held up his hand.

Exu descended and landed on the Gatekeeper's fist, nuzzling his arm as if reunited with an old friend.

Maybe not.

The Gatekeeper looked even more frightening with Exu at his side. It was time to face facts. The creature was right. He had no reason to help me.

Then the bird squawked, almost sympathetically. The creature made a low, throaty sound—almost a chuckle—and raised a hand to smooth the bird's feathers. "You are lucky. The bird is a good judge of character."

"Yeah? What does the bird say about me?"

"He says—slow on the switchbacks, cheap with the whiskey, but a good heart. For a dead man."

I grinned. Maybe that old crow wasn't so bad.

Exu squawked again.

"I can show you the Gates, boy."

"Ethan."

"Ethan." He hesitated, repeating my name slowly. "But you have to give me something in return."

I was almost afraid to ask. "What do you want?" Obidias had mentioned that the Gatekeeper would expect some kind of gift, but I hadn't really put much thought into it.

He looked at me thoughtfully, considering the question. "Trade is a serious matter. Balance is a key principle within the Order of Things."

"The Order of Things? I thought we didn't have to worry about that anymore."

"There is always Order. Now more than ever, the New Order must be carefully maintained."

I didn't understand the details, but I understood the importance. Wasn't that how I got into this mess in the first place?

He kept talking. "You say you need something to take you home? The thing you desire most? I say, what brought you here? That is what I desire most."

"Great." It sounded simple, but he might as well have been speaking in riddles or randomly written Mad Libs.

"What do you have?" His eyes glinted greedily.

I stuffed my hands in my pockets and pulled out the one remaining river stone and Aunt Prue's map. The whiskey and the tobacco—Exu's stash—were long gone.

The Gatekeeper lifted his hairless brows. "A rock and an old map? Is that all?"

"That's what brought me here." I pointed at Exu, still perched on his shoulder. "And a bird."

"A rock *and* a crow. That is difficult to pass up. But I already have both of those things in my collection."

Exu pushed off from his shoulder and flew back up into the sky, like he was offended. Within seconds the crow disappeared.

"And now you have no bird," the Gatekeeper said matter-of-factly.

"I don't understand. Is there something specific you want?" I tried to hide the frustration in my voice.

The Gatekeeper seemed delighted by the question. "Specific, yes. Specifically, a fair trade is what I prefer."

"Could you be a *little* more specific than that?"

He tilted his head. "I don't always know what will interest me until I see it. The things that are the most valuable are often the ones you don't even know exist."

That was helpful.

"How am I supposed to know what you have already?"

His eyes lit up. "I can show you my collection if you would like to see it. There isn't another one like it anywhere in the Otherworld."

What could I say? "Yeah. That would be great."

As I followed him along the sharp black stones, I could hear Link's voice in my head. "Bad move, man. He's gonna kill you, stuff you, and add you to his collection of idiots who followed him back to his creepy cave."

This was one time I was probably safer dead than alive.

How fair and balanced was that?

The Gatekeeper slid through a narrow crack in the wall of slick black stone. It was bigger than the hole, but not by much. I moved along sideways because there wasn't enough room to turn around.

I knew this could be some kind of trap. Link had described the creature he encountered as an animal—dangerous and crazed. What if the Gatekeeper was no different, just better at hiding it? Where was that stupid crow when I needed him?

"We're almost there," he called back to me.

I could see a faint light ahead, flickering in the distance.

His shadow passed in front of it, momentarily darkening the passage as the narrow space opened into a cavernous room. Wax dripped from an iron chandelier bolted directly into the glossy stone ceiling. The walls sparkled in the candlelight.

If I hadn't just crawled through a whole mountain of the stuff, I might have been more impressed. As it was, the closeness of the cavern walls just made my skin crawl.

But when I glanced around, I realized this place was more like a museum—with an even crazier collection than what you'd find if you dug up the Sisters' whole backyard. Glass cases and shelves lined the walls, filled with hundreds of objects. It was the randomness of the collection that intrigued me, like a child had done not only the collecting but the cataloging. Intricately carved silver and gold jewelry boxes sat next to a collection of cheap children's music boxes. Shiny black vinyl records were piled in towering stacks next to one of those old-fashioned record players with a funnel speaker, like the one the Sisters used to have. A Raggedy Ann doll curled in a rocking chair, a huge green jewel the size of an apple resting in her lap. And on a center shelf, I saw an opalescent sphere similar to the one I had carried in my hand the past summer.

It couldn't be . . . an Arclight.

But it was. Exactly like the one Macon had given my mom, except milky white instead of midnight black.

"Where did you get that?" I walked toward the shelf.

He darted in front of me, snatching the sphere. "I told you. I'm a collector. You could say a historian. You mustn't touch anything in here. The treasures in this room cannot be replaced. I've spent a thousand lifetimes collecting them. They are all equally valuable," he breathed.

"Yeah?" I looked at a Snoopy lunch box full of pearls.

He nodded. "Priceless."

He replaced the Arclight. "All sorts of things have been offered to me at the Gates," he added. "*Most* people, and non-people, know it is only polite to bring me a gift when they come knocking." He stole a look at me. "No offense."

"Yeah, sorry. I mean, I wish I had something to give you—"

He lifted a hairless eyebrow. "Besides a rock and a crow?"

"Yeah." I scanned the rows of leather books lined up neatly on the shelves, the spines inscribed with symbols and languages I didn't recognize. The spine of a black leather book caught my eye. It looked like it said . . . "*The Book of Stars*?"

The Gatekeeper looked pleased and rushed to pull it down from the shelf. "This is one of the rarest books of its kind." Niadic, the Caster language I had come to recognize, looped around the edges of the cover. A cluster of stars was embossed in the center. "There is only one other like it—"

"*The Book of Moons*," I finished for him. "I know."

His eyes widened, and he clutched *The Book of Stars* to his chest. "You know about the Dark half? No one in our world has seen it for hundreds of years."

"That's because it isn't in your world." I looked at him for a long moment before correcting myself. "Our world."

He shook his head in disbelief. "How could you possibly know that?"

"Because I was the one who found it."

For a moment, he didn't say a word. I could tell he was trying to decide if I was lying or crazy. There was nothing in his expression that made it seem like he actually believed me, but like I said, there wasn't really too much to go on—his face not really being a face and all.

"Is this a trick?" His dull green eyes narrowed. "It wouldn't serve you well to play games with me if you ever expect to find the Gates of the Far Keep."

"I didn't even know *The Book of Moons* had another half, or whatever you said. So how would I know to lie about it?"

It was true. I had never heard anyone mention it—not Macon or Marian or Sarafine or Abraham.

Is it possible they didn't know?

"As I said, balance. Light and Dark are both part of the invisible scale that is always tipping as we hang on to the edges." He ran his crooked fingers over the cover of the book. "You can't have one without the other. Sad as that might be."

After everything I had learned about *The Book of Moons*, I couldn't imagine what was within the covers of its counterpart.

Did *The Book of Stars* yield the same kind of devastating consequences?

I was almost afraid to ask. "Is there a price for using that one, too?"

The Gatekeeper walked to the far end of the room and sat down in an intricately carved chair that looked like a throne from an old castle. He lifted a Mickey Mouse Thermos, pouring a stream of amber liquid into the plastic cup, and drank half of it. There was a weariness in his movements, and I wondered how long it had taken him to amass the collection of intangibly valuable and valueless items within these walls.

When he finally spoke, he sounded like he'd aged a hundred years.

"I have never used the book myself. My debts are too steep to risk owing anything more. Though there is not much left for them to take, is there?" He threw back the rest of his drink and slammed the plastic cup on the table. Within seconds, he was pacing again, nervous and agitated.

I followed him to the other side of the room.

"Who do you owe?"

He stopped walking, pulling his robe tighter, as if he was protecting himself from an unseen enemy. "The Far Keep, of course." There was a mix of bitterness and defeat in his voice. "And they always collect their debts."

CHAPTER 17

The Book of Stars

The Gatekeeper turned his back to me, moving instead to a glass case behind him. He examined a collection of charms—amulets hanging from long leather cords, crystals and exotic rocks that reminded me of the river stones, runes with markings I didn't recognize. He opened the cabinet and took out one of the amulets, rubbing the silver disk between his fingers. It reminded me of the way Amma touched the gold charm she wore around her neck, whenever she got nervous.

"Why don't you just leave?" I asked. "Take all this stuff and disappear?" I knew the answer even as I asked the question.

Nobody would stay here unless they had to.

He spun a large enamel globe on a tall stand next to the

cabinet. I watched as it turned, strange shapes spinning past me. They weren't the continents I was used to seeing in history class.

"I can't leave. I'm Bound to the Gates. If I venture too far from them, I'll continue to change."

He stared down at his bent, gnarled fingers. A chill rushed up my back.

"What do you mean?"

The Gatekeeper turned his hands over slowly, as if he had never seen them before. "There was a time when I looked like you, dead man. A time when I was a man."

The words were swimming around in my head, but I couldn't find a way to make them true. Whatever the Gatekeeper was—however reminiscent his features were of a man's—it wasn't possible.

Was it?

"I—I don't understand. How—?" There was no way to say what I was thinking without being cruel. And if he was a man somewhere inside there, he had suffered more than enough cruelty already.

"How did I become this?" The Gatekeeper fingered a large crystal hanging from a golden chain. He picked up a second necklace, made of rings of sugar candy, the kind you could buy at the Stop & Steal, smoothing it back down inside its velvet-lined case. "The Council of the Far Keep is very powerful. They have powerful magic at their disposal, stronger than anything I witnessed as a Keeper."

"You were a Keeper?" This thing used to be like my mom and Liv and Marian?

His dull green eyes stared back at me. "You might want to take a seat...." He paused. "I don't think you told me your name."

"Ethan." I'd told him twice now.

"It's nice to meet you, Ethan. My name is—was—Xavier. No one calls me that anymore, but you can if it makes things easier."

I knew what he was trying to say—if it made it easier to imagine him as a man instead of a monster.

"Okay. Thanks, Xavier." It sounded funny, even coming from me.

He tapped the case with his fingers, some kind of nervous habit. "And to answer your question, yes. I was a Keeper. One who made the mistake of questioning Angelus, the head—"

"I know who he is." I remembered the one named Angelus, the Keeper with the bald head. I also remembered the ruthless expression on his face when he had come after Marian.

"Then you know he's dangerous. And corrupt." Xavier watched me carefully.

I nodded. "He tried to hurt a friend of mine—two, actually. He brought one of them to the Far Keep to stand trial."

"Trial." He laughed, only there was nothing like a smile on his nothing like a face.

"It wasn't funny."

"Of course not. Angelus must have been making an example

of your friend," Xavier said. "I was never given a trial. He finds them dull compared to the punishment."

"What did you do?" I was afraid to ask, but I felt like I had to.

Xavier sighed. "I questioned the authority of the Council, the decisions they were making. I never should have done it," he said quietly. "But they were breaking our vows, the laws we swore to abide by. Taking things that were not theirs to Keep."

I tried to imagine Xavier in a Caster library somewhere like Marian, stacking books and recording the details of the Caster world. He had created his own version of a Caster library here, a place filled with magical objects—and a few unmagical ones.

"What kind of things, Xavier?"

He glanced around the cavernous room, panicked. "I don't think we should be talking about this. What if the Council finds out?"

"How would they?"

"They will. They always do. I don't know what more they could do to me, but they would think of something."

"We're in the center of a mountain." My second one today. "It's not like they can hear you."

He pulled the collar of the heavy wool robe away from his neck. "You would be surprised at what they can find out. Let me show you."

I wasn't sure what he meant as he moved past a heap of

broken bicycles to another glass cabinet. He opened the doors and took out a cobalt-blue sphere the size of a baseball.

"What is that thing?"

"A Third Eye." He held it in his palm carefully. "It allows you to see the past, a specific memory in time."

The color began to swirl inside the ball, churning like storm clouds. Until it cleared, and a picture came into view...

A young man was sitting behind a heavy wooden desk in a dimly lit study. His long robe appeared to be too big for him, much like the ornately carved chair he was sitting in. His hands were clasped together as he leaned heavily on his elbows. "What is it now, Xavier?" he asked impatiently.

Xavier ran his hands through his dark hair and over his face, his green eyes darting around the room. It was obvious that he was dreading the conversation. He twisted the cord of his own robe in his lap. "I'm sorry to bother you, sir. But certain events have come to my attention—atrocities that violate our vows and threaten the mission of the Keepers."

Angelus looked bored. "What atrocities are you referring to, Xavier? Has someone failed to file a report? Lost a crescent key to one of the Caster libraries?"

Xavier straightened. "We're not talking about lost keys, Angelus. Something is going on in the dungeons below the Keep. At night I hear the screams, blood-curdling screams you can't—"

Angelus waved off the comment. "People have nightmares. We can't all sleep as blissfully as you. Some of us run the Council."

Xavier pushed back from his chair and stood. "I've been down there, Angelus. I know what they are hiding. The question is, do you?"

Angelus whipped around, his eyes narrowing. "What is it you think you've seen?"

The rage in Xavier's eyes was impossible to ignore. "Keepers using Dark power—Casting—as if they are Dark Casters. Conducting experiments on the living. I've seen enough to know that you must take action."

Angelus turned his back on Xavier, facing the window that overlooked the vast mountains surrounding the Far Keep. "Those experiments, as you call them, are for their protection. There is a war, Xavier. Between Light and Dark Casters, and the Mortals are caught in the middle." He turned. "Do you want to watch them die? Are you prepared to take responsibility for that atrocity? Your acts have already cost you enough, wouldn't you agree?"

"For your protection," Xavier corrected. "That is what you meant, isn't it, Angelus? Mortals are caught in the middle of the war. Or have you become something beyond Mortal?"

Angelus shook his head. "It's clear we aren't going to agree on this matter." He started to speak the words of a Cast in low tones.

"What are you doing?" Xavier pointed at Angelus. "Casting? This is not right. We are the balance— we observe and Keep the records. Keepers do not cross the line into the world of magic and monsters!"

Angelus closed his eyes and continued the incantation.

Xavier's skin seared and blackened, as if it was burnt.

"What are you doing?" he cried.

The charcoal color spread like a rash, the skin tightening as it turned impossibly smooth. Xavier screamed, clawing at his own skin.

Angelus spoke the final word of the Cast and opened his eyes in time to watch Xavier's hair fall out in tufts.

He smiled at the sight of the man he was destroying. "It seems to me that you are crossing a line right now."

Xavier's limbs started to lengthen unnaturally, bones cracking and breaking. Angelus listened. "You should consider having a bit more sympathy for monsters."

Xavier dropped to his knees. "Please. Have mercy...."

Angelus stood over the Keeper, who was almost unrecognizable. "This is the Far Keep. Removed from the Mortal and Caster worlds. The vows are the words I speak, and the laws the ones I choose." He pushed Xavier's devastated body over with his boot.

"There is no mercy here."

—⁊

The images faded, replaced by the swirling blue haze. For a second, I didn't move. I felt like I had just witnessed a man's execution—and he was standing right next to me. What was left of him.

Xavier looked like a monster, but he was a good guy, trying to do the right thing. I shuddered, thinking about what could have happened to Marian if Macon and John hadn't gotten there in time.

If I hadn't made a deal with the Lilum.

At least I knew enough not to regret what I did. As bad as things were, they could have been worse. I knew that now.

"I'm sorry, Xavier." I didn't know what else to say.

He put the Third Eye back on the shelf. "That was a long time ago. But I thought you should know what they are capable of, since you are so anxious to get inside. If I were you, I would run the other way."

I leaned against the cold wall of the cavern. "I wish I could."

"Why do you want so badly to get in there?"

I was sure he couldn't think of one good reason. For me, one reason was all I needed.

"Someone added a page in *The Caster Chronicles*, and I ended up dead. If I can destroy it—"

Xavier reached his hands toward me as if he was going to grab me by the shoulders and shake some sense into me. But he drew them back before he touched me. "Do you have any idea what they'll do to you if you're caught? Look at me, Ethan. I'm one of the lucky ones."

"Lucky? You?" I shut my mouth before I accidentally made it worse. Was he nuts?

"They've done this to others, Mortals and Casters alike. It's Dark power." His hands were shaking. "Most of them have gone mad, left to wander the Tunnels or the Otherworld like animals."

It was exactly the way Link had described the creature that attacked him the night Obidias Trueblood died. But what Link had encountered wasn't an animal. It was a man, or something that had been a man once—driven crazy as his body was mutated and tortured.

I felt sick.

The walls of the Far Keep were hiding more than *The Caster Chronicles*.

"I don't have a choice. If I don't destroy the page, I can't get back home." I could almost see his mind spinning. "There has to be a Cast—something in *The Book of Stars* or one of your books that could help me."

Xavier whipped around, pointing a broken finger inches from my face. "I would never let *anyone* touch one of my books or use them to Cast! Have you learned nothing here?"

I backed up. "I'm sorry. I shouldn't have said that. I'll find another way, but I still have to get inside."

Everything about his demeanor had changed when I suggested using a Cast. "You still have nothing to offer. I can't show you the Gates unless you give me something in return."

"Are you serious?" But I could tell from his expression that he was. "What the hell do you want?"

"*The Book of Moons*," he said without hesitation. "You know where it is. That's my price."

"It's in the Mortal realm. And if you haven't noticed, I'm dead. And by the way, Abraham Ravenwood has it. He's not what you'd call a nice guy." I was beginning to think that getting past the Gates was going to be the hardest part of finding my way home, if it was even possible.

Xavier started moving toward the slit in the rock that led back to the outside. "I think we both know there are ways around that. If you want to get through the Gates, bring me *The Book of Moons*."

"Even if I could get it, why would I give you the most powerful book in the Caster world?" I practically shouted. "How do I know you won't use it to do something terrible?"

His unnaturally large eyes widened. "What could be more terrible than how I am standing before you now? Is there something worse than watching your body betray you? Feeling your bones break as you move? Do you think I can risk the trade the Book might choose to make?"

He was right. You couldn't get something from *The Book of Moons* without giving something in return. We'd all learned that, the hard way. The other Ethan Wate. Genevieve. Macon and Amma and Lena and me. The Book made the choice.

"You could change your mind. People get desperate." I couldn't believe I was lecturing a desperate man about desperation.

Xavier turned to face me, his body already partially hidden in shadow. "Because I know what it is capable of—what it could do in the hands of men like Angelus—I would never speak a word from that book. And I would be sure it never left this room, so no one else could either."

He was telling the truth.

Xavier was terrified of magic, Light or Dark.

It had destroyed him in the worst possible way. He didn't want to Cast or wield supernatural power. If anything, he wanted to protect himself and others from that kind of power. If there was anywhere *The Book of Moons* would be safe, it was here—safer than in the *Lunae Libri* or some other far-away Caster library. Safer than hidden in the depths of Ravenwood or buried in Genevieve's grave. No one would ever find it here.

That was when I decided I was going to give it to him.

There was only one problem.

I had to figure out how to get it away from Abraham Ravenwood first.

I looked at Xavier.

"How many powerful objects would you say you've got in this room, Xavier?"

"It doesn't matter. I told you—they're not to be used."

I smiled. "What if I were to tell you I could get you *The Book of Moons*, but I'd need your help? Your help, and the help of a few of your treasures?"

He made a strange expression, twisting his uneven mouth from one side to the other. I really, really hoped it was a smile.

⊰ CHAPTER 18 ⊱

Shadows

How I get there isn't as important as getting there." I said it for the fifth time.

"To this Land of the Stars and Stripes?" he asked.

"Yeah. Well, kinda. The office anyway. On Main."

He nodded. "Ah, the Mainlands. Is that past the Swamp of the Coolers?"

"The swamp coolers? Yeah. More or less." I sighed.

I tried to explain my plan to Xavier. I wasn't sure when he had been in the Mortal world last, but whenever it was, it was way before swamp coolers and newspapers. Which was kind of funny, given how much he liked lunch boxes, vinyl records, and sweets.

I picked up another ancient book, opening it to a cloud of dust and possibility—and uncertainty. I was frustrated, and sitting on the floor surrounded by Caster Scrolls in the middle of this strange creature's cave made me feel as if I was back working in the Gatlin County Library on the first day of my summer break.

I tried to think. There had to be something we could do. "What about Traveling? Can Waywards use Casts that pertain to an Incubus?"

Xavier shook his head. "I don't think so."

I leaned back against a stack of books. I was close to giving up. Once again, if Link was here, he'd lecture me about being the Aquaman of the Caster world.

"A dead Aquaman," I said to myself.

"Excuse me?"

"Nothing," I muttered.

"A dead man?" he asked.

"You don't have to rub it in."

"No, that's it. You don't need Casts that work for a Mortal. You're not a Mortal anymore. You need Casts that work for a Sheer." He flipped page after page. "An *Umbra* Cast. Sending a shadow from one world to the next. That's you, the shadow. It should work."

I thought about it. Could it be that simple?

I stared at my hand, at the flesh and bones of it.

It only looks like flesh and bones. You're not really here, not like that. You don't have a body.

What was the big difference between a Sheer and a shadow?

"I need to be able to touch something, though. It won't work unless I can get the message to Lena, and I'll need to be able to move some papers around."

He cocked his head, twisting his face into a grimace. I hoped it was his thinking face.

"Do you need to touch something?"

"That's what I just said."

He shook his head. "No, it's not. You said you need to move something. That's different."

"Does it matter?"

"Entirely." He flipped a few more pages. "A *Veritas* Cast should allow the truth to appear. As long as you're looking for the truth."

"That'll work?"

I hoped he was right.

Minutes later, any doubts I had about Xavier were gone.

I was here. I hadn't flown across the Great River, or the Great Barrier, or any other supernatural seam. I hadn't turned on the crow-vision. I was here, on Main, staring into the office of *The Stars and Stripes*.

At least, my shadow was.

I felt like Peter Pan in reverse. Like Wendy had unstitched my shadow from me instead of sewing it back to my feet.

I moved through the wall and into the darkness of the

room, only I was even darker. I had no body, but it didn't matter. I lifted my hand—the shadow of my hand—and thought the words Xavier had taught me.

I watched as the words on the page rearranged themselves. I had no time for riddles. No time for games, hidden messages.

My words were simple.

Five across.

Read, in Spanish.

L. I. B. R. O.

Two down.

Belonging to.

O. F.

Five across.

Lunae.

M. O. O. N. S.

I lowered my hand and disappeared.

My last message, all I had left to say. Lena had figured out how to send me the river rock charm, and she would know how to send the Book to me. I hoped. If not, maybe Macon would.

If Abraham still had it, and Lena could get it away from him.

There were only about a thousand other ifs in between. I tried not to think about them, and all the people they involved. Or the danger that always surrounded *The Book of Moons.*

I couldn't afford to think like that. I'd come this far, right? She would find it, and I would find her.

It was the only Order of Things I cared about now.

BOOK TWO

Lena

⊰ CHAPTER 19 ⊱

Mortal Problems

Sometimes Link could be a real idiot.

"*Libro* what? *Book of Moons*? What does that mean?" Link looked from me to *The Stars and Stripes*, scratching his head. You would have thought I was bringing up the subject for the first time.

"Three words. It's a book, Link. I'm sure you've heard of it." It was only the book that had destroyed our lives, and the lives of all the Casters in my family before me on our sixteenth birthdays.

"That's not what I meant." He looked hurt.

I knew what Link meant.

But I didn't know why Ethan was asking for *The Book of*

Moons any more than Link did. So I just kept staring at the newspaper in the middle of the kitchen.

Amma was behind me, and she didn't say a word. She'd been that way for a while now—since Ethan. The silence was as wrong as everything else. It was strange to not hear her banging around in her kitchen. Even stranger that we were sitting around Ethan's kitchen table trying to figure out the message he'd left in today's crossword puzzle. I wondered if he could see us or knew we were here.

surrounded by strangers who love me
(un)strangers made strange
by pain

I felt my fingers twitch, looking for the pen that wasn't there. I fought the poetry off. It was a new habit. It hurt too much to write now. Three days after Ethan left, the word NO appeared, inked in black Sharpie on my left hand. WORDS appeared on my right.

I hadn't written a word since, not on paper. Not in my notebook. Not even on my walls. It seemed like forever since I had.

How long had Ethan been gone? Weeks? Months? It was all one long blur, as if time had stopped when he left.

Everything had stopped.

Link stared up at me from where he was sitting on the kitchen floor. When he unfolded his new quarter-Incubus body like that, he took up most of the kitchen. There were arms and legs everywhere, like a praying mantis, only with muscles.

Liv studied her own copy of the puzzle from the table—clipped and taped into her trusty red notebook, covered in her neatly penciled analysis—while John leaned over her shoulder. The way they moved together, you would think it hurt them *not* to touch.

Unlike Casters and Mortals.

A human and a hybrid Incubus. They don't know how good they have it. Nothing catches fire when they kiss.

I sighed, resisting the urge to Cast a *Discordia* on them. We were all here. You would have thought nothing had changed. Only one person was missing.

Which made everything different.

I folded up the morning paper, sinking into the chair next to Liv. "*Book of Moons.* That's all it says. I don't know why I keep reading it. If I read this thing any more times, I'm going to burn a hole in it with my eyes."

"You can do that?" Link looked interested.

I wriggled my fingers in front of him. "Maybe I can burn more than just paper. So don't tempt me."

Liv smiled at me sympathetically. As if the situation called for anything like a smile. "Well then, I suppose we have to think. Those are three rather specific words. So it seems the messages are changing." She sounded precise and logical, like a British version of Marian, as she always did.

"And?" Link sounded irritated, like he always did lately.

"So what's going on...over there?" *Where Ethan is.* Liv didn't say it. Nobody wanted to. Liv pulled the three crossword puzzles out of her notebook. "At first, it seems like he just wants you to know he is..."

"Alive? Hate to break it to you—" Link said, but John kicked him under the table. Amma dropped a pan behind me, sending it clattering toward where Link sat on the floor. "Oww. You know what I meant."

"Around," John corrected him, looking from Amma to me. I nodded, feeling Amma's hands slip down to rest on my shoulders.

I touched her hand with mine; her fingers curled tightly around it. Neither one of us wanted to let go. Especially now that it was possible Ethan wasn't gone forever. It had been weeks since Ethan had started sending me messages through *The Stars and Stripes.* It didn't matter what they said. They all said the same thing to me.

I'm here.

I'm still here.

You're not alone.

I wished there was a way I could say it to him.

I squeezed Amma's fingers harder. I tried to talk to her about it right after I found the first message, but she just muttered something about a fair trade and how it was her mess to sort out. How it was what she aimed to do, sooner or later.

But she didn't doubt me. Neither did my uncle, not anymore. In fact, Uncle Macon and Amma were the only ones who really believed me. They understood what I was going through, because they had gone through it themselves. I didn't know if Uncle Macon would ever get over losing Lila. And Amma seemed to be having as hard a time without Ethan as I was. They had seen the proof, too. Uncle Macon was there when I saw Ethan's crossword for the first time. And Amma had all but seen Ethan standing in the kitchen of Wate's Landing.

I said it out loud again to everyone, for the tenth time. "Of course he's around. I told you, he's going somewhere. He's got some kind of plan. He's not just sitting there, waiting in a grave full of dirt. He's trying to get back to us. I'm sure of it."

"How sure?" Link asked. "You're not sure, Lena. Nothin's sure, except death an' taxes. And when they said it, I think they were talkin' more about stayin' dead, not comin' back again."

I didn't know why Link was having so much trouble believing that Ethan was still there, that he could come home again. Wasn't Link the one who was part Incubus? He knew as well as anyone that strange things happened around here all the time. Why was it so hard for him to believe that this particular strange thing could be happening?

Maybe losing Ethan was harder on Link than it was for the rest of them. Maybe he couldn't let himself risk losing his best friend all over again, even if it was only the idea of him. No one knew what Link was going through.

Except me.

While Link and Liv returned to arguing about whether or not Ethan was actually gone, I felt myself slipping into the fog of nagging doubts that I worked so hard to push out of my mind.

They just kept coming.

What if this whole thing really was my imagination, like Reece and Gramma kept saying? What if they were right, and it was just too hard for me to accept my life without him? And it wasn't just them—Uncle Macon wouldn't try anything to bring him back either.

And if it was real—if Ethan could hear me—what would I say?

Come home.

I'm waiting.

I love you.

Nothing he didn't already know.

Why bother?

I refused to write, but the words were hard to even think now.

words same as always
same as nothing
when nothing is the same

There was no point in saying it to myself.

John kicked Link again, and I tried to focus on the present. The kitchen and the conversation. All the things I could do for Ethan, rather than all the things I felt about him.

"Let's say, for the sake of argument, that Ethan is— around." Liv looked at Link, who kept quiet this time. "Like I said, it seemed he spent all his energy trying to convince us of that a few weeks ago."

"Right around the time you measured the energy spiking at Ravenwood," John reminded her. Liv nodded, flipping pages in her notebook.

"Or maybe Reece was just usin' the microwave," Link muttered.

"Which was the same time Ethan moved the button at his grave," I said obstinately.

"Or maybe it was just windy." Link sighed.

"Something was definitely going on." John moved his foot closer to Link, the threat of another good kick shutting Link up for a while. I thought about slapping a *Silentium* Cast on him, but it didn't seem right. Plus, knowing Link, it would take more than magic to shut him up.

Liv went back to examining the papers in front of her. "But then, quite soon, his messages began to change. It's like he figured something out. What he needed to do."

"To come home," I said.

"Lena, I know you want to think that's what's happenin'." Amma's voice was bleak. "And I felt my boy here, same as you. But we don't know which end is up. There are no easy answers, not when it comes to gettin' someone in or outta the Otherworld. Believe me, if there was an easy way, I would've already done it."

She sounded so haggard and tired. I knew she had been working on getting Ethan home as hard as I had. And I'd tried everything at first—everything and everyone. The problem was trying to get Light Casters to talk about raising the dead. And I didn't have quite the access to the Dark Casters that I used to. Uncle Macon had come for me the moment I'd set foot in Exile. I suspected he made some kind of deal with the bartender, a shifty-looking Blood Incubus who looked like he'd do anything if he was thirsty enough.

"But we don't know that's not it," I said, looking at Liv.

"True. The logical assumption would be that wherever Ethan was, he would be trying to get back." Liv carefully erased a small mark in the margin. "To where you are." She didn't look at me, but I knew what she meant. Liv and Ethan had a history of their own, and even though Liv had found something better for her with John, she was always very careful of how she spoke about Ethan, especially to me.

She tapped the pencil. "First the river rock. Now *The Book of Moons*. He must need them for something."

John pulled the last puzzle toward him. "If he needs *The Book of Moons*, it's a good sign. It has to be."

"A mighty powerful book, on this side or the other. A book like that would be worth bargaining for." Amma rubbed my shoulders as she spoke, and I felt a shiver go down my spine.

John looked at both of us. "Bargaining for what? Why?"

Amma said nothing. I suspected she knew more than she

was saying, which was usually the case. Plus, she hadn't even mentioned the Greats in weeks, which was unlike her. Especially now that Ethan was in their care, technically speaking. But I had no idea what Amma was up to any more than I knew what Ethan was planning.

I finally answered for both of us, because there was only one possible answer. "I don't know. It's not like I can ask him."

"Why not? Can't you Cast something?" John looked frustrated.

"It doesn't work like that." I wished it did.

"Some kind of Reveal Cast?"

"There's nothing to Cast it on."

"His grave?" John looked at Liv, but she shook her head. No one had an answer, because none of us had ever even contemplated anything like this before. A Cast on someone who wasn't even on this plane of existence? Short of raising the dead—which Genevieve had done to start this whole mess in the first place, and I had done again, more than a hundred years later—what could anyone do?

I shook my head. "What does it matter? Ethan wants it, and we have to get it to him. That's the important thing."

Amma chimed in. "Besides, only one kind a bargain my boy would be makin' over there. Only one thing he wants bad enough. And that would be to get himself back home again, sure as the sunrise."

"Amma's right." I looked at them. "We have to get him the Book."

Link sat up. "Are you sure, Lena? Are you absolutely death-and-taxes sure it's Ethan who's even sendin' us these messages? What if it's Sarafine? Or even Colonel Sanders?" He shuddered.

I knew who Link meant. Abraham, in his rumpled white suit and his string tie. Satan himself, at least as far as Gatlin County was concerned.

That really would be the worst-case scenario.

"It's not Sarafine. I'd know."

"Would you really know if it was her?" Link rubbed his hair, which was sticking out in a thousand different directions. "How?"

Through the window, I watched as Mr. Wate's Volvo pulled into the driveway. I knew the conversation was over, even before I felt Amma's hands stiffen on my shoulders. "I just would."

Wouldn't I?

I stared at the stupid crossword puzzle as if it could give me some kind of answer, when all it could tell me was that I knew nothing at all.

The front door opened as the back door banged shut. John and Liv must have disappeared out the back. I braced for the inevitable.

"Afternoon, kids. You waitin' for Ethan to get home?" Mr. Wate looked at Amma hopefully. Link scrambled to his feet, but I looked away. I couldn't bear to answer.

More than anything. More than you know.

"Yes, sir. Waitin's hardly the word. Bored outta my thick skull without Ethan around." Link tried to smile, but even he looked like he was about to cry.

"Cheer up, Wesley. I miss him as much as you do." Mr. Wate reached for Link's spiked hair, rubbing it with one hand. Then he opened the pantry and looked inside. "You hear anything from our boy today, Amma?"

"Afraid not, Mitchell."

Mr. Wate stopped short, frozen in place with a box of cereal in his hand. "I've half a mind to drive down to Savannah myself. It makes no sense, keeping a boy out of school this long. Something's not right." His face clouded over.

I focused my eyes on the tall, gaunt figure of Mitchell Wate, just as I had so often since Ethan died. Once he was fixed in my sight, I slowly began reciting the words of the *Oblivio* Cast that Gramma had taught me to repeat every time I saw Ethan's dad.

He stared at me, curious. My eyes didn't even flicker. Only my lips began to move, and I whispered the words as they formed in my mind.

"Oblivio, Oblivio, Non Abest.
Oblivion, Oblivion, He Is Not Gone."

A bubble expanded inside my chest the moment I formed the Cast, pushing past me toward Ethan's father, reaching right across the room and wrapping itself around him. The room seemed to stretch and contract, and I thought for a moment the bubble was about to pop.

Then I felt the air snap around us, and suddenly it was over, and the air was just air, and everything seemed normal again.

As normal as things could be.

Mr. Wate's eyes brightened and glazed over. He shrugged, smiling at me, sticking one hand back inside the cereal box. "Ah well, what are you going to do? He's a good kid. But if Ethan doesn't get his tail home from Caroline's soon, he's going to be mighty behind when he gets back. At this rate, he'll be doing homework all the way through spring break. You tell him that for me, will you?"

"Yes, sir. I'll tell him." I smiled, wiping at my eye before anything like a tear could fall. "I'll tell him the next time I talk to him."

That's when Amma almost threw the pan of pork chops down on the burner. Link shook his head.

I turned and fled. I tried not to think, but the words followed me, like a curse, like a hex.

oblivion eyes on a cereal box,
the warm blinds of a father
lost and last to know
lost and last to love
last boy lost

you can't see
even a bubble
once it's
popped

I fought off the words.
But you couldn't unpop a bubble.
Even I knew that.

⊰ CHAPTER 20 ⊱

A Deal with the Devil

This is freakin' nuts. We don't even have the stupid *Book a Moons*. You sure *The Stars and Sucks* didn't say anythin' else?"

Link was sitting on the floor again, with only his feet sticking out from under the table—this time the one in Macon's study. We'd made no progress, but here we were again. New table. Same people. Same problems.

Only the presence of my Uncle Macon, half-hidden in the flickering shadows of the fireplace, changed the conversation. That, and the fact that we'd left Amma back at Wate's Landing to keep an eye on Ethan's father.

"I can't believe I'm actually saying this, but maybe Link's right. Even if we all agreed—even if we knew we had no choice but to get Ethan *The Book of Moons*—it still wouldn't matter. We don't know where it is, and we don't know how to get it to him." Liv said what we all were thinking.

I said nothing, twisting my charm necklace between my fingers.

It was Macon who finally answered. "Yes. Well. These things are difficulties, not impossibilities."

Link sat up. "The whole death thing, yeah, I'd say that's pretty difficult, sir. I mean, no offense, Mr. Ravenwood."

"Finding *The Book of Moons* is not out of the question, Mr. Lincoln. I'm sure I don't need to remind you where we last saw it and who last had it."

"Abraham." We all knew who he was talking about, but it was Liv who said it. "He had it with him at the Seventeenth Moon, in the cave. And he used it to bring up the Vexes, right before—"

"The Eighteenth Moon," John said quietly. None of us ever wanted to talk about the night at the water tower.

All of which just set Link off more. "Oh well. That's easy. Find the Book. How about we just find our way over to whatever backwoods swamp hole Colonel Sanders has been livin' in for the last two hundred years, and ask him real nice if he wouldn't mind handin' over his creepy book? So our dead friend can use it for who knows what, over in who knows where."

I flicked my wrist at Link, annoyed. A spark flew from the fire grating, singeing his leg.

He jerked away. "Cut it out!"

"Uncle Macon's right. It's not impossible," I said.

Liv played with the rubber band holding her red notebook closed—an anxious habit that meant she was thinking. "And this time Sarafine's dead. He won't have her backing him up."

Uncle Macon shook his head. "He never needed her, I'm afraid. Not really. You can't rely on him being any weaker now than he ever was. Don't underestimate Abraham."

Liv looked somber. "What about Hunting and his pack?"

Macon stared into the fire. I watched the flames grow taller, deepening into purple and red and orange. I couldn't tell if my uncle really believed me or not. I didn't know if he thought for a minute there was a way to bring Ethan back.

I didn't care what he thought, as long as he was willing to help me.

He looked at me as if he knew what I was thinking. "Hunting, though stupid, is a powerful Incubus. But Abraham alone is a formidable threat. If fear is going to stop us, we should concede failure right now."

Link huffed from the floor behind him.

Macon looked at him over his shoulder. "That is, if you're frightened."

"Who said anything about that?" Link was indignant. "I just like a better set a odds when I throw myself into a snake pit."

"It's me." John sat up and announced it, as if he'd just figured out the answer to all our problems.

"What?" Liv pulled away from him.

220

"I'm the one thing Abraham wants. And the only thing he can't have."

"Don't be stupid." Link groaned. "You sound like his girlfriend."

"I'm not stupid. I'm right. I thought I was the One Who Is Two, and I thought it was up to me to do…what Ethan did. But that wasn't about me. This is."

"Shut up," Link snapped.

Macon's face twisted into a frown, his green eyes darkening. I knew that expression too well.

Liv nodded. "I agree. Do as your brilliant Incubus brother says. Shut up."

John put his arm gently around her, as if he was speaking only to Liv. But I was hanging on his every word, because everything he was saying was starting to make sense. "I can't. Not this time. I'm not going to sit around and let Ethan take all the punches. For once, I'm going to get what's coming to me. Or *who*."

"And that is?" Liv wouldn't look at him.

"Abraham. If you tell him you'll make a trade, he'll come for me. He'll swap me for *The Book of Moons*." John looked at Macon, who nodded.

Link looked skeptical. "How do you know?"

John smiled weakly. "He'll come. Trust me."

Macon sighed, finally turning from the fireplace toward us. "John, I appreciate your honor and your courage. You're a fine young man, even if you have your own demons. We all do. But you should take some time to make certain this is a trade you're willing to make. It's a last course of action, nothing more."

"I'm willing." John stood up, like he was ready to enlist now.

"John!" Liv was furious.

Macon waved him into his seat. "Think it over. If Abraham does take you, it's not likely we will be able to bring you home, not anytime soon. And as much as I want to bring Ethan back—" Uncle Macon glanced over at me before continuing. "I'm not certain trading one life for another is worth the risk Abraham poses, for any of us."

Liv stepped in front of John, as if she wanted to protect him from everyone else in the room and everything else in the world. "He doesn't need time to think about it. It's a terrible plan. Absolutely horrid. The worst plan we've ever come up with. The worst plan in the history of plans." Liv was pale and shaking, but when she saw me watching her, she stopped talking.

She knew what I was thinking.

It didn't involve John jumping off the Summerville water tower. It wasn't the worst plan. I closed my eyes.

falling not flying
one lost muddy shoe
like the lost worlds
between me and you

"I'll do it," John said. "I don't like it any more than the rest of you, but this is the way it has to be."

It all sounded too familiar. I opened my eyes to see Liv, stricken. As the tears began to run down Liv's face, I felt like I was going to throw up.

"No." I heard myself say the word before I realized I was saying it. "My uncle's right. I'm not putting you through that, John. Any of you." I saw the color seep into Liv's cheeks, and she sank into the chair next to him. "It's a last-ditch effort. A last chance."

"Unless you've got another one, Lena, I think the land of last chances is right about where we are." John looked serious. He had made up his mind, and I loved him for it.

But I shook my head. "I do. What about Link's idea?"

"Link's—what?" Liv looked confused.

"My what?" Link scratched his head.

"We find our way to whatever backwoods swamp hole Abraham has been living in for the last two hundred years."

"And we ask him real nice to give us the Book?" Link looked hopeful. John looked like he thought I was having a stroke.

"No. We steal it, real nice."

Macon looked interested. "That presumes we can even find my grandfather's home. The nasty brand of Dark power he wields demands a lifestyle of secrecy, I'm afraid. Tracking Abraham down won't be easy. He keeps to the Underground."

I looked steadily back at him. "Well, as the smartest

person I know once said, these things are difficulties, not impossibilities."

My uncle smiled at me. John shook his head. "Don't look at me. I don't know where the guy lives; I was just a kid. I remember rooms without windows."

"Perfect," Link snapped. "There can't be many of those around."

Liv dropped her hand onto John's shoulder.

John shrugged. "Sorry. My childhood is one big dark cloud. I've done my best to block the whole thing out."

My uncle nodded, rising to his feet. "Very well. Then I suggest you start not with the smartest people but perhaps the oldest people. They might have a clue or two as to where you can find Abraham Ravenwood."

"The oldest people? You mean the Sisters? Do you think they remember Abraham?" My stomach tensed. It wasn't exactly scary, but it was hard to understand half the things they said—when they weren't talking crazy.

"If they can't, they're likely to invent something equally plausible. They are the closest thing my exponentially-great-grandfather has to contemporaries. Even if they're hardly what one would call contemporary."

Liv nodded. "It's worth a try."

I stood up.

"Just a conversation, Lena," Uncle Macon cautioned. "Don't get any ideas. You're not to set out on any kind of reconnaissance mission of your own. Am I perfectly clear?"

"Crystal," I said, because there was no talking to him about anything that seemed dangerous. He'd been like this since Ethan—

Since Ethan.

"I'll go with you for backup," Link said, pulling himself up from the floor of the study. Link, who couldn't add two-digit numbers, always sensed when my uncle and I were about to start fighting.

He grinned. "I can translate."

By now, I felt like I knew the Sisters as well as my own family. Though they were eccentric, to put it mildly, they were also the finest example of living history Gatlin had to offer.

That's what the people around here called it.

When Link and I walked up the steps of Wate's Landing, you could hear Gatlin's living history fighting with each other all the way through the screen door, true to form.

"You don't throw away perfectly good cut-ler-ee. That's a cryin' shame."

"Mercy Lynne. They're plastic spoons. Means you're supposed ta throw 'em away." Thelma was consoling her, patient as always. She should be sainted. Amma was the first one to say it every time Thelma broke up one of the Sisters' arguments.

"Just because *some people* think they're the queen a England doesn't give 'em a crown," Aunt Mercy responded.

Link stood next to me on the porch and tried not to laugh. I knocked on the door, but nobody seemed to notice.

"Now, what on earth is that supposed ta mean?" Aunt Grace interrupted. "Who's *some people*? Angelina Witherspoon an' all them partly nekkid stars—"

"Grace Ann! You don't speak like that, not in this house."

It didn't even slow Aunt Grace down. "—from those smutty magazines you're always askin' Thelma ta get from the market?"

"Now, girls..." Thelma started.

I knocked again, more loudly this time, but it was impossible to hear over the chaos.

Aunt Mercy was shouting. "It *means* you wash the good spoons same as you wash the bad spoons. Then you put 'em all back in the spoon drawer. Everyone knows that. Even the queen a England."

"Don't listen ta her, Thelma. She washes the garbage when you and Amma aren't lookin'."

Aunt Mercy sniffed. "What if I do? You don't want the neighbors talkin'. We're respectable, churchgoin' people. We don't smell like sinners, and there's no reason for the cans out front ta smell any different."

"Exceptin' they're full a garbage." Aunt Grace snorted.

I knocked on the screen door one more time. Link took over, banging once—and the door practically gave out, one hinge swinging down toward the porch.

"Whoops. Sorry about that." He shrugged awkwardly.

Amma appeared at the door, looking grateful for the distraction. "You ladies have some visitors." She pushed the screen open wide. The Sisters glanced up from their respective afghans, looking friendly and polite, like they hadn't been screaming bloody murder a second earlier.

I sat on the edge of a hard wooden chair, not making myself too comfortable. Link stood even less comfortably next to me.

"I reckon we do. Afternoon, Wesley. And who's there with y'all?" Aunt Mercy squinted, and Aunt Grace elbowed her.

"It's that girlfriend a Ethan's. That pretty Ravenwood gal. The one who always has her nose in a book, like Lila Jane."

"That's right. You know me, Aunt Mercy. I'm Ethan's girlfriend, ma'am." It was the same thing I said every time I came over.

Aunt Mercy harrumphed. "Well, what if it is? What're ya doin' around here now that Ethan's gone and passed on ta one world or another?"

Amma froze in the kitchen doorway. "Come again?"

Thelma didn't look up from her needlepoint.

"You heard me, Miss Amma," Aunt Mercy said.

"Wh-what?" I stammered.

"What are you talking about?" Link could barely speak.

"You know about Ethan? How?" I leaned forward in my chair.

"You think we don't catch a thing or two 'bout what's goin' on around here? Wasn't born yesterday, and we're smarter than y'all think. We know plenty 'bout the Casters, same as we do weather patterns and dress patterns and traffic patterns...." Aunt Grace wadded up her handkerchief, her voice trailing off.

"And the peach stand seasons." Aunt Mercy looked proud.

"A storm cloud's a storm cloud. This one's been workin' its way through the sky for a long time now. Near 'bout all our lives." Aunt Grace nodded at her sister.

"Seems to me any right-minded person would try to keep outta a storm like that," Amma bristled, tucking the edge of the blanket around Aunt Grace's legs.

"We didn't know you knew," I said.

"Lord have mercy, you're as bad as Prudence Jane. She thought we didn't have a clue between us 'bout her traipsin' all over underneath the County and back. Like we didn't know our daddy picked her ta keep the map. Like we didn't tell him ourselves ta pick Prudence Jane. Always thought she was the one with the steadiest hand outta all three a us." Aunt Mercy laughed.

"Sweet Redeemer, Mercy Lynne, you know our daddy woulda picked me 'fore he picked you. I only told him ta ask you on account a I didn't like my hair all curled up, the way it got in the Underground. Looked like a porkypine with a bad permanent, I swear." Aunt Grace shook her head.

Mercy sniffed. "You do swear, Grace Ann, and I'm the only one who knows it."

"You take that back." Aunt Grace pointed a bony finger at her sister.

"I will not."

"Please, ma'am. Ma'ams." What was the plural of *ma'am*? "We need your help. We're looking for Abraham Ravenwood. He has something of ours, something important." I looked from one Sister to the other.

"We need it ta—" Link corrected himself. "To bring Ethan home, lickety-split." If you hung around the Sisters long enough, you started talking like them.

I rolled my eyes.

"What're you fussin' 'bout?" Aunt Grace waved her handkerchief.

Aunt Mercy sniffed again. "Sounds like more Caster nonsense ta me."

Amma raised an eyebrow. "Why don't you catch us all up? Seein' as how we all love nonsense the way we do."

Link and I looked at each other. It was going to be a long night.

Caster nonsense or not, once Amma dragged out the Sisters' scrapbooks, wheels began turning and mouths started moving. At first Amma couldn't bear to hear the mention of Abraham Ravenwood's name, but Link kept talking.

And talking, and talking.

Still, Amma didn't stop him, which seemed like half a victory. Though talking to the Sisters themselves didn't seem anything like the other half of one.

Within the hour, Abraham Ravenwood was denounced as

the Devil, a cheat, a scoundrel, a no-goodnik, and a thief. He'd kept their daddy's daddy's daddy from the southeast corner of his old apple orchard, which was rightfully his, and his daddy's daddy from a seat on the county board, which also was rightfully his.

And on top of all that, they were more than certain that he danced with the Devil up at Ravenwood Plantation on more than one occasion, before it burned during the Civil War.

When I attempted to clarify, they didn't want to get more specific than that.

"That's what I said. He up and danced with the Devil. He made a deal. Don't like talkin' 'bout or thinkin' 'bout him neither." Aunt Mercy shook her head so violently, I thought her dentures were going to come unglued.

"Let's say you did think about him, though. Where would you picture him?" Link tried again, just as we had all night.

Finally, it was Aunt Grace who found the missing piece to the scrambled crossword puzzle the Sisters considered conversation.

"Why, at his place, a course. Anybody with a lick a sense knows that."

"Where's his place, Aunt Grace? Ma'am?" I put my hand on Link's arm, hopeful. It was the first clear sentence we'd gotten out of her in what felt like hours.

"The dark side a the moon, I reckon. Where all the Devils and Demons live when they're not burnin' down below."

My heart sank. I was never going to get anywhere with these two.

"Great. The dark side a the moon. So Abraham Raven-wood is alive and well in a Pink Floyd album." Link was getting as crabby as I was.

"That's what Grace Ann said. The dark side a the moon." Aunt Mercy looked annoyed. "Don't know why you two act like that's such a conundy-rum."

"Where, exactly, is the dark side of the moon, Aunt Mercy?" Amma sat down next to Ethan's great-aunt, taking the old woman's hands in her lap. "You know. Come on now."

Aunt Mercy smiled at Amma. " 'Course I do." She glared at Aunt Grace. " 'Cause Daddy picked me 'fore Grace. I know all sorts a things."

"Then, where is it?" Amma asked.

Grace snorted, pulling the photo album off the coffee table in front of them. "Young people. Actin' like they know everythin'. Actin' like we're one step from the home just 'cause we got a year or two on you." She leafed through the pages madly, as if she was looking for one thing in particular—

Which, apparently, she was.

Because there, on the last page, under a faded pressed camellia and a stretch of pale pink ribbon, was the ripped-off top of a book of matches. It was from some kind of bar or club.

"I'll be danged," Link marveled, earning himself a swat on the head from Aunt Mercy.

There it was, marked with a silvery moon.

231

The Dark Side o' the Moon was a place.

A place where I might be able to find Abraham Ravenwood and, I hoped, *The Book of Moons*. If the Sisters were not completely out of their minds, which was a possibility that could never be discounted.

Amma took one look at the matches and left the room. I remembered the story of Amma's visit to the bokor and knew better than to press her further.

Instead, I looked at Aunt Grace. "Do you mind?"

Aunt Grace nodded, and I pulled the antique shred of matchbook from the album page. Most of the paint was scratched off the embossed moon, but you could still see the writing. We were going to New Orleans.

—☽

You would have thought Link had solved the Rubik's Cube. The moment we got into the Beater, he started blasting some song from Pink Floyd's *Dark Side of the Moon* and shouting excitedly over the music.

When we slowed at the corner, I turned down the volume and cut him off. "Drop me off at Ravenwood, will you? I need to get something before I leave for New Orleans."

"Hold on. I'm comin' with you. I promised Ethan I'd keep my eye on you, and I keep my promises."

"I'm not taking you. I'm taking John."

"John? That's the somethin' you're gettin' from home?" His eyes narrowed. "No way."

"I wasn't asking your permission. Just so you know."

"Why? What's he got that I haven't?"

"Experience. He knows about Abraham, and he's the strongest hybrid Incubus in Gatlin County, as far as we know."

"We're the same, Lena." Link's feathers were getting ruffled.

"You're more Mortal than John is. That's what I like about you, Link. But it also makes you weaker."

"Who are you callin' weak?" Link flexed his muscles. To be fair, he did nearly split his T-shirt in half. He was like the Incredible Hulk of Stonewall Jackson High.

"I'm sorry. You're not weak. You're just three-quarters human. And that's a little too human for this trip."

"Whatever. Suit yourself. See if you even get ten feet through the Tunnels without me. You'll be back here, beggin' for my help, before I can say..." His face went blank. A classic Link moment. Sometimes the words just seemed to float away from him before they could make it all the way from his brain to his mouth. He finally gave up with a shrug. "Somethin'. Somethin' real dangerous."

I patted his shoulder. "Bye, Link."

Link frowned, hitting the gas pedal, and we ripped down

the street. Not the usual kind of rip for an Incubus, but then again, he was three-quarters rocker. Just the way I liked him—my favorite Linkubus.

I didn't say that, but I'm pretty sure he knew.

I changed every light green for him, all the way down Route 9. The Beater never had it so good.

⊰ CHAPTER 21 ⊱

Dark Side of the Moon

Saying we were going to New Orleans to find an old bar—and an even older Incubus—was one thing. Actually finding him was something different. What stood between those two things was talking my Uncle Macon into letting me go.

I tried my uncle at the dinner table, well after Kitchen had served up his favorite dinner, before the plates had disappeared from the endlessly long table.

Kitchen, who was never as accommodating as you'd think a Caster kitchen might be, seemed to know it was important and did everything I asked and more. When I walked downstairs, I found flickering candelabras and the scent of jasmine in the air. With a flutter of my fingers, orchids and tiger lilies bloomed across the length of the table. I fluttered them again, and my viola appeared in the corner of the room.

I stared at it, and it began to play Paganini. A favorite of my uncle's.

Perfect.

I looked down at my grubby jeans and Ethan's faded sweatshirt. I closed my eyes as my hair began to weave itself into a thick French braid. When I opened them again, I was dressed for dinner.

A simple black cocktail dress, the one Uncle Macon bought me last summer in Rome. I touched my neck, and the silver crescent moon necklace he gave me for the winter formal appeared at the base of my throat.

Ready.

"Uncle M? Dinnertime—" I called out into the hall, but he was already there next to me, appearing as swiftly as if he was still an Incubus and could rip through space and time whenever he wanted. Old habits died hard.

"Beautiful, Lena. I find the shoes an especially nice touch." I looked down and noticed my raggedy black Converse still on my feet. So much for dressing for dinner.

I shrugged and followed him to the table.

Fillet of sea bass with baby fennel. Warm lobster tail. Scallops carpaccio. Grilled peaches soaked in port. I had no appetite, especially not for food you could only find at a five-star restaurant on the Champs-Élysées in Paris—where Uncle

Macon took me at every opportunity—but he ate happily for the better part of an hour.

One thing about former Incubuses: They really appreciate Mortal food.

"What is it?" my uncle finally said, over a forkful of lobster.

"What's what?" I put down my fork.

"This." He gestured at the spread of silver platters between us, pulling the shiny dome off one overflowing with steaming, spicy oysters. "And this." He looked pointedly at my viola, still playing softly. "Paganini, of course. Am I really that predictable?"

I avoided his eyes. "It's called dinner. You eat it. Which you seem to have no problem doing, by the way." I grabbed a ridiculous flagon of ice water—where Kitchen found some of our tableware, I'd never know—before he could say anything else.

"This is not dinner. This is, as Mark Antony would say, a tantalizing table of treason. Or perhaps treachery." He swallowed another bite of lobster. "Or perhaps both, if Mark Antony were a fan of alliteration."

"No treason." I smiled. He smiled back, waiting. My uncle was many things—a snob, for one—but he wasn't a fool. "Just a simple request."

He set down his wineglass, heavy on the linen tablecloth. I waved a finger, and the glass filled itself.

Insurance, I thought.

"Absolutely not," said Uncle Macon.

"I haven't asked you anything."

"Whatever it is, no. The wine proves it. The last straw. The final pheasant feather on the proverbial fluffy feather bed."

"So you're saying Mark Antony isn't the only fan of alliteration?" I asked.

"Out with it. Now."

I pulled the matchbook cover out of my pocket and pushed it across the table so he could see it.

"Abraham?"

I nodded.

"And this is in New Orleans?"

I nodded again. He handed me back the matchbook, dabbing at his mouth with his linen napkin. "No." He returned to the wine.

"No? You were the one who agreed with me. You were the one who said we could find him ourselves."

"I did. And I will find him while you remain locked safely in your room, like the nice little girl you should be. You're not going to New Orleans alone."

"*New Orleans* is the problem?" I was stunned. "Not your ancient-but-deadly Incubus ancestor who tried to kill us on more than one occasion?"

"That and New Orleans. Your grandmother wouldn't hear of it, even if I said yes."

"She wouldn't hear of it? Or she *shouldn't* hear of it?"

He lifted an eyebrow. "I beg your pardon?"

"What about if she just doesn't hear of it? That way it's not an issue." I put my arms around my uncle. As angry as he made me, and as annoying as it was to have him pay off the Underground bartenders and ground me from various dangerous pursuits, I loved him, and I loved that he loved me as much as he did.

"How about no?"

"How about she'll be with Aunt Del and everyone in Barbados until next week, so why is this even a problem?"

"How about still no?"

At that point, I gave up. It was hard to stay angry at Uncle Macon. Impossible, even. Knowing how I felt about him was the only way I understood how hard it was for Ethan to live apart from his own mother.

Lila Evers Wate. How many times had her path crossed mine?

we love what we love and who
we love who we love and why
we love why we love and find
a falling shoelace knotted and strung
between the fingers of strangers

I didn't want to think about it, but I hoped it was true. I hoped wherever Ethan was, he was with her now.

At least give him that.

John and I left first thing in the morning. We needed to leave early, since we were taking the long way—the Tunnels, rather than Traveling, though if I'd let him, John could have easily gotten us there in the blink of an eye.

I didn't care. I wouldn't let him. I didn't want to be reminded of the other times I'd let John carry me—all the way to Sarafine.

So we did it my way. I Cast a *Resonantia* on my viola and set it to practice in the corner while I was gone. It would wear off eventually, but it might give me enough time.

I didn't tell my uncle I was going. I just went. Uncle Macon still slept most of the day, old habits being what they were. I figured I had at least six good hours before he noticed my absence. By which I mean, before he flipped out and came after me.

One thing I'd realized in the last year was that there were some things no one could give you permission to do. All the same, it didn't mean you couldn't or shouldn't do them— particularly when it came to the big things, like saving the world, or journeying to a supernatural seam between realities, or bringing your boyfriend back from the dead.

Sometimes you had to take matters into your own hands. Parents—or uncles who are the closest thing you have to them—aren't equipped to deal with that. Because no self-respecting parent in this world or any other is going to step aside and say, "Sure, risk your life. The world is at stake here."

How would they possibly say it?

Be back by dinner. Hope you don't die.

They couldn't do it. You couldn't blame them. But it didn't mean that you shouldn't go.

I had to go, no matter what Uncle Macon said. That's what I told myself, anyway, as John and I headed into the Tunnels far beneath Ravenwood. Where, in the darkness, it could have been any time of day or year—any century, anywhere in the world.

The Tunnels weren't the scary part.

Even spending time alone with John—something I hadn't done since he'd tricked me and dragged me into going to the Great Barrier for my Seventeenth Moon—wasn't the problem.

The truth was, Uncle Macon was right.

I was more afraid of the Doorwell that stood before me and of what I would find on the other side. The ancient Doorwell that brought light flooding down onto the stone steps of the Caster Tunnel where I waited now. The one marked NEW ORLEANS. The place where Amma had basically made a pact with the Darkest magic in the universe.

I shivered.

John looked at me, his head tilted. "Why are you stopping here?"

"No reason."

"You scared, Lena?"

"No. Why would I be scared? It's just a city." I tried to put all thoughts of black magic bokors and voodoo out of my mind. Just because Ethan had followed Amma into bad times there didn't mean I was going to encounter the same Darkness. At least not the same bokor.

Did it?

"If you think New Orleans is just a city, then you've got another thing coming." John's voice was low, and I could barely see his face in the darkness of the Tunnels. He sounded as spooked as I felt.

"What are you talking about?"

"The most powerful Caster city in the country—the greatest convergence of Dark and Light power in modern times. A place where anything can happen, at any hour of the day."

"At a hundred-year-old bar for two-hundred-year-old Supernaturals?" How frightening could it be? At least that's what I tried to tell myself.

He shrugged. "Might as well start there. Knowing Abraham, it won't be as easy to find him as we think."

We started up the stairs and into the bright sunlight that would take us to the Dark Side o' the Moon.

The street—a row of shabby bars, sandwiched between more shabby bars—was deserted, which made sense, considering it was still so early in the day. It looked like all the other streets we'd seen since the Doorwell brought us up into the infamous French Quarter of New Orleans. The ornately wrought iron railings swept across every balcony and along every building, even curving around the street corners. In the stark morning light, the faded colors of the painted plaster were sun-bleached and peeling. The road was lined with trash, trash piled upon more trash—the only remaining evidence of the night before.

"I'd hate to see how it looks around here the morning after Mardi Gras," I said, looking for a way to pick through the mountain of garbage standing between me and the sidewalk. "Remind me never to go to a bar."

"I don't know. We had some good times back at Exile. You and me and Rid, causing trouble on the dance floor." John smiled and I blushed, remembering.

arms around me
dancing, hurried
Ethan's face
pale and worried

I shook my head, letting the words fall away. "An underground hole for derelict Supernaturals isn't what I was talking about."

"Ah, come on. We weren't exactly derelicts. Well, you weren't. Rid and me, we probably qualified." He pushed me toward the doorway playfully.

I shoved him back, a little less playfully. "Stop it. That was a million years ago. Maybe two million. I don't want to think about it."

"Come on, Lena. I'm happy. You're—"

I shot him a look, and he cut himself off. "You will be happy again, I promise. That's why we're here, isn't it?"

I looked at him, standing there next to me in the middle of a run-down side street in the French Quarter far too early in the morning, helping me look for the not-quite-a-man John hated more than anyone in the universe. He had more of a reason to hate Abraham Ravenwood than I did. And he wasn't saying a word about what I was making him do.

Who would've thought John would end up being one of the best guys I'd ever met? And who would've thought John would end up volunteering to risk his life to bring back the love of mine?

I smiled at him, though I felt like crying. "John?"

"Yeah?" He wasn't paying attention. He was looking up at the bar signs, probably wondering how he was going to get up the nerve to go inside any of them. They all looked like serial killer hangouts.

"I'm sorry."

"Huh?" Now he was listening. Confused, but listening.

"About this. That it has to involve you. And if you don't want it to—I mean, if we don't find the Book—"

"We'll find it."

"I'm just saying, I won't blame you if you don't want to go through with it. Abraham and everything." I couldn't bear to do it to him. Not him and not Liv—no matter how much had gone down between us. No matter how much she had believed she loved Ethan.

Before.

"We'll find the Book. Come on. Quit talking crazy." John kicked a clearing in the trash heap, and we made our way past the empty beer bottles, past the soggy napkins, and up to the sidewalk.

By the time we made it halfway down the block, we were looking through the open doorways to see if anyone was inside. To my surprise, there were people hiding in the woodwork—literally. Slumping inside the darkened doorways. Sweeping the trash from deserted, shadowy alleys. Even silhouetted on a few of the empty balconies.

The French Quarter wasn't that different from the Caster world, I realized. Or from Gatlin County. There was a world within a world, all hidden in plain sight.

You just had to know where to look.

"There." I pointed.

The Dark Side o' the Moon

A carved wooden sign bearing the words swung back and forth, dangling by two ancient chains. It squeaked as it moved in the wind.

Even though there was no wind.

I squinted in the bright morning light, trying to see into the shadows of the open doorway.

This Dark Side was no different from the other nearly deserted bars in the neighborhood. Even from the street, I could hear voices echoing through the heavy door.

"People are in there this early?" John made a face.

"Maybe it's not early. Maybe it's late if you're them." I locked eyes with a scowling man who was leaning against the doorframe and trying to light a cigarette. He muttered to himself and looked away.

"Yeah. Way too late."

John shook his head. "You sure this is the right place?"

For the fifth time, I handed him the book of matches. He held up the cover, comparing it to the logo on the sign. They were identical. Even the crescent moon carved into the wooden sign was an exact duplicate of the one printed on the matchbook in John's hand.

"And I was so hoping the answer would be no." He handed the matchbook back to me.

"You wish," I said, kicking a stray piece of wet napkin off my black Chucks.

He winked at me. "Ladies first."

◄ CHAPTER 22 ►

Bird in a Gilded Cage

It took a while for my eyes to adjust to the dim light, and even longer for the rest of me to adjust to the stench. It smelled like must and rust and old beer—old everything. Through the shadows, I could see rows of small round tables and a high brass bar, almost as tall as I was. Bottles were stacked on shelves all the way to a high ceiling—so high the long brass chandeliers seemed to dangle down from nowhere.

Dust covered every surface and every bottle. It even swirled in the air, in the few places where beams of light poked through shuttered windows.

John elbowed me. "Isn't there some kind of Cast that can keep our noses from working? Like a *Stinkus Lessus* Cast?"

"No, but I can think of a few *Shutus Upus* Casts that might be applicable right about now."

"Temper, Caster Girl. You're supposed to be Light. You know, one of the good guys."

"I broke the mold, remember? On my Seventeenth Moon, when I was Claimed Light and Dark?" I shot him a serious look. "Don't forget. I've got my Dark side."

"I'm scared." He grinned.

"You should be. Very."

I pointed to a mirrored sign on the paneling, right behind him. A silhouette of a woman was painted next to a row of words. " 'Lips that touch liquor shall not touch ours.' " I shook my head. "Clearly not the slogan of the Jackson cheer squad."

"What?" John looked up.

"I bet this place used to be a speakeasy. A hidden bar during Prohibition. New Orleans was probably full of them." I looked around the room. "That means there has to be another room, right? A room behind this room."

John nodded. "Of course. Abraham would never hang out where anyone could walk into his hideout, no matter where it is. It was one thing all our homes had in common." He looked around. "But I don't remember a place like this."

"Maybe it was before your time, and he came back here because it was somewhere no one currently alive could find him."

"Maybe. Still, something feels off about this place."

Then I heard a familiar voice.

No. A familiar laugh, sweet and sinister. There was nothing else like it in the world.

Ridley? Is that you?

I Kelted, but she didn't answer. Maybe she didn't hear, or it had been too long since we had connected in any kind of meaningful way. I didn't know, but I had to try.

I ran up the wooden staircase at the back of the bar. John was just steps behind me. As soon as I got to the room at the top, I started banging on the wall where I thought her voice had come from, high above stacks of crates and cases of bottles. The storage-room wall was hollow, and there was clearly something behind it.

Ridley!

I needed a better look. I pushed a tall stack of crates out of the way. I closed my eyes and let myself rise high into the air, until I floated parallel with the window. I opened my eyes, hovering for a second. What I saw was so surprising it knocked me right to the floor.

I could have sworn I saw my cousin, and a whole lot of makeup, and what looked like a flash of gold. Rid wasn't in danger. She was probably lying around in there, painting her nails. Sucking on a lollipop, having the time of her life.

Either that, or I was hallucinating.

I'm going to kill her.

"I swear, Rid. If you're really this crazy, if you've really gone this Dark, I'm going to jam those lollipops of yours down your throat, one ball of sugar at a time."

"What?"

I felt John's arms behind me, pulling me back to the floor.

I pointed to the wall. "It's my cousin. She's on the other side of this wall." I knocked on the wall above the nearest row of crates.

"No. No, no, no—" He started backing away, like even the mention of my cousin had him wanting to make a break for it.

I felt myself turning red. She was my cousin, and I wanted to kill her. Still, she was *my* cousin, and *I* was the one who wanted to kill her. It was a family matter. Not something John needed to worry about. "Look, John, I have to get her."

"Have you lost your mind?"

"Probably."

"If she's hanging with Abraham, she's not going anywhere. And we don't want him to find us until we figure out how to get the Book."

"I don't think he's there," I said.

"You don't *think*, or you don't *know*?"

"If he was there, wouldn't you sense something? I thought you two were connected somehow. Wasn't that how he brainwashed you or whatever?"

John looked nervous, and I felt guilty for saying it. "I don't know. It's possible." He stared up at the high window. "Okay. You get in there and see what Ridley's problem is. I'll keep an eye out for Abraham outside and make sure he doesn't come back while you're inside."

"Thanks, John."

"But don't be an idiot. If she's gone too Dark, she's too Dark. You can't change Ridley. That's one thing we've all learned the hard way."

"I know." I probably knew it better than anyone, except maybe Link. But deep down, I also knew better than anyone how much my cousin was like everyone else. How badly she wanted to fit in and be loved and have friends and be happy—just like the rest of us.

How Dark can a person like that really be?

Hadn't the New Order shown us that the price had been paid—Ethan made sure he paid it—and that things weren't as simple as we all thought they were?

Didn't I Claim myself for Dark and Light?

"You're sure you'll be all right in there?"

Is it really any different for anyone else? Even Ridley? Especially *Ridley?*

John poked me in the side. "Earth to Lena. Just make some kind of noise so I know you heard me, before I throw you to that lion in there."

I tried to focus. "Go. I'm fine."

"Five minutes. That's all you have," he said.

"Got it. I'll only need four."

He disappeared, and I was alone to deal with my cousin. Dark or Light. Good or evil. Or maybe just somewhere in between.

I needed a better look. I grabbed a cask of wine, pulling it over to the space beneath the window that was cut into the

251

wall. I climbed up and the cask wobbled, threatening to topple, but I managed to balance myself.

I still couldn't see.

Oh, come on.

I closed my eyes and twisted my hands into the air next to me, pushing myself up toward the ceiling. The light in the room began to flicker.

That's it.

I wasn't much for flying, but this was more like levitating. I rose, wobbling, until my Chucks were hovering a few inches above the cask.

Just a little farther. I needed one good look to let me know if my cousin was forever lost, if she had joined the Darkest Incubus alive and would never come home to me again.

One last look.

I pulled myself up, barely level with the small window.

That's when I saw the bars swerving down from the ceiling, all the way around Ridley in every direction. It was some kind of gold prison. A literal gilded cage.

I couldn't believe it. Ridley wasn't lounging on a chaise in the lap of luxury in Abraham's place. She was trapped.

She turned, and our eyes locked. Rid leaped to her feet, rattling the bars in front of her. For a second, she looked kind of like a damaged Tinkerbell, with a lot of black mascara running down her face, and even more smeared red lipstick.

She'd been crying, or worse. Her arms looked bruised,

especially around the wrists. They were marked by some kind of ropes or chains. Shackles, maybe.

The room around her clearly belonged to Abraham—at least that's what I thought, considering it looked like a mad scientist's dorm room, with a lone bed next to a crammed bookshelf. A tall wooden table was covered with technical equipment. The place could have belonged to a chemist. Even stranger, the two sides of the window didn't seem to correlate exactly, in terms of physical space. Looking through the speakeasy window was like looking through a dirty telescope, and I couldn't tell exactly where the other end lay. It could have been anywhere in the Mortal universe, knowing Abraham.

But that didn't matter. It was Ridley. It was a terrible thing to see anyone like that, but for my careless, carefree cousin, it seemed especially cruel.

I felt my hair begin to twist in the familiar Caster breeze.

"Aurae Aspirent
Ubi tueor, ibi adeo.
Let the wind blow
Where I see I go."

I began to twist into nothingness. I felt the world give way beneath me, and when I tried to reach my feet out to touch solid ground, I realized I was now standing next to Ridley.

On the outside of the golden cage.

"Cuz! What are you doing here?" she called out to me, reaching her long pink fingernails through a space in the bars.

"I guess I could say the same to you, Rid. Are you okay?" I approached the bars carefully. I loved my cousin, but I couldn't forget everything that had happened. She chose Dark and left us—Link, me, all of us. It was impossible to know whose side she was on.

Ever.

"Think it's a little obvious, don't you?" she snapped. "I've been better." She rattled the bars. "Much."

Ridley sat back down on her heels and began to cry, like we were both little kids again and someone had hurt her feelings on the playground. Which didn't happen often, and if it did, it was usually me doing the crying.

Rid was always the strong one.

Maybe that's why her tears got to me now.

I slid down to the floor across from her, taking her hand through the cage bars. "I'm sorry, Rid. I was so angry with you for not coming back when Ethan—now that Ethan—"

She didn't look at me. "I know. I heard. I feel terrible. That's when everything happened. Abraham was furious, and I only made things worse when I made the mistake of trying to leave. I just wanted to go home. But he was so angry that he threw me in here." She shook her head as if she wanted to shake off the memory.

"I mean it, Rid. I should have known that you would've come unless something stopped you."

"Whatever. More water under another watery bridge." She wiped her eyes, smearing her mascara even more. "Let's blow this place before Abraham comes back, or you'll be stuck in here with me for the next two hundred years."

"Where did he go?"

"I don't know. Usually he spends all day in his creepy lab of creatures. But there's no way to know how long he'll be gone."

"Then we'd better get on with it." I looked around the room. "Rid, have you seen Abraham with *The Book of Moons*? Is it here?"

She shook her head. "Are you kidding? I wouldn't come within ten miles of that thing, not after the way it royally screws anyone who touches it."

"But have you seen it?"

"No way. Not here. If Abraham still has it, he's not dumb enough to keep it on him. He's evil, but he's not stupid."

My heart sank.

Ridley rattled the bars again. "Hurry up! I'm really stuck. Protection Casts, from what I can tell. I'm going crazy in here...."

Then I heard a terrible crash, and a pile of equipment crates next to me toppled to the ground. Broken glass and broken wood flew everywhere—like I had upset Abraham's project for the science fair. Some sort of glowing green goop was splattered in my hair.

Whoops.

Uncle Macon was trying to untangle himself from John Breed, who had one foot caught in the remnants of a wooden crate.

"Where are we?" Uncle M stared at the cage in disbelief. "What kind of twisted place is this?"

"Uncle M?" Ridley looked as relieved as she was confused. "Were you Traveling?"

"I found him out front," John said. "He wouldn't let me go. When I tried to come back, he just sort of came along for the ride." John must have seen my face, because he got defensive. "Hey, don't look at me. I wasn't exactly planning on picking up hitchhikers."

Uncle Macon glared at John, who glared right back at him.

"Lena Duchannes!" My uncle looked angrier than I'd ever seen him. Green goop was dripping from his otherwise impeccable suit. He glanced from Ridley to me, then pointed at both of us. "You two. Come out of there this instant."

I grabbed Ridley's hand and muttered the *Aurae Aspirent* while Uncle Macon tapped his foot impatiently. A second later, my cousin and I reappeared on the outside of the cage.

"Uncle Macon," I began.

He held up his gloved hand. "Don't. Not a word." His eyes flashed, and I knew better than to keep talking. "Now. Let's focus on what we came here to do, while we still have time to do it. The Book."

John had already started pulling open boxes, scanning the shelves for *The Book of Moons*. Uncle Macon and I joined him, looking until we had searched every possible hiding place. Ridley sat sullenly on a crate, not making things easier—but not making them more difficult either. Which I took as a good sign.

From what I could see, Abraham Ravenwood appeared to be the Caster answer to Dr. Frankenstein. I couldn't recognize much beyond the occasional burner or beaker, and I had taken chemistry. And at the rate John and Uncle Macon were trashing the room, it was going to look like our search was conducted by Frankenstein's monster.

"It's not here," John said, finally giving up.

"Then neither are we." Uncle Macon straightened in his overcoat. "Home, John. Now."

Traveling was one thing. The speed at which John managed to get us home—without so much as another word from Uncle Macon—was another. I found myself out of Abraham's hideaway and back in my room before Ridley could wipe off her smeared, raccoon-y mascara.

The viola was still playing Paganini's Caprice no. 24 when I got there.

⊰ CHAPTER 23 ⊱

Dar-ee Keen

The next day it was raining, and the Dar-ee Keen was leaking as if it was finally giving up. More depressing, Uncle Macon hadn't even bothered to ground me. Apparently, the situation was hopeless enough without locking me in my room. Which was pretty hopeless.

Rain fell everywhere at the Dar-ee Keen, on the inside and out. Water dripped from the square, buzzing light fixtures. It crept down the wall like a slow stain of tears beneath the crookedly mounted Employee of the Month photograph—from the look of it, a member of the Stonewall Jackson cheer squad, of course, though they all were starting to look the same.

No one worth crying over. Not anymore.

I scanned the nearly empty diner, waiting for Link to show up. Nobody was out on a day like today, not even the flies. I couldn't blame them.

"Seriously, could you cut it out? I'm sick of the rain, Lena. And I smell like a wet dog." Link appeared out of nowhere, sliding into the opposite side of the booth. He looked like a wet dog.

"That smell has nothing to do with the rain, my friend." I smiled. Unlike John, Link was apparently human enough that the natural elements still affected him. He assumed normal Link posture, leaning back in the corner of the booth and doing his best impression of someone physically capable of falling asleep.

"It's not me," I said.

"Right. Because it's been nothin' but sunshine and kitty cats out there since December."

Thunder rumbled in the sky. Link rolled his eyes.

I frowned. "I guess you must have heard. We found Abraham's place. The Book wasn't there. At least we couldn't find it."

"Figures. Now what?" He sighed.

"Plan B. We don't really have a choice."

John.

I couldn't say it. I curled my hand into a fist on the seat next to me.

Thunder rumbled again.

Was it me? I didn't know if I was doing it or if the weather outside was doing something to me. I had lost track of myself weeks ago. I stared at the rain dripping into the red plastic bucket in the center of the room.

red plastic rain
her tears stain

I tried to shake myself out of it, but I couldn't stop looking at the bucket. The water dripped down from the ceiling rhythmically. Like a heartbeat or a poem. A list of names of the dead.

First Macon.
Then Ethan.
No.
My father.
Then Macon.
My mother.
Then Ethan.
Now John.

How many people had I lost?

How many more would I lose? Would I lose John, too? Would Liv ever forgive me? Did it even matter anymore?

I watched the raindrops bead on the greasy table in front of me. Link and I sat together in silence, in front of wadded-up waxy paper, crushed ice in plastic glasses. A cold, soggy meal nobody was even thinking of eating. If he wasn't trapped at his own dinner table, Link didn't even pretend to move the food around anymore.

Link nudged me. "Hey. Come on, Lena. John knows what he's doing. He's a big boy. We're gonna get the Book and get Ethan back, no matter how crazy your plan is."

"I'm not crazy." I didn't know who I was saying it to, Link or myself.

"I didn't say you were."

"You say it every time you have the chance."

"You don't think I want him back?" Link said. "You don't think it sucks to shoot hoops without him watchin' to tell me how bad I suck or how big my head is gettin'? I drive around Gatlin in the Beater, blastin' the tunes we used to play, and there's no reason to play them anymore."

"I get that it's rough, Link. You know I get it, more than anyone."

His eyes welled up, and he dropped his head, staring down at the greasy table between us. "I don't even feel like singin'. The guys in the band, they're talkin' about breakin' up. The Holy Rollers could end up as a bowlin' team." He looked like he was going to be sick. "At this rate, I'm gonna have nowhere to go but college, or somewhere even worse."

"Link. Don't say that." It was true. If Link went to college—even Summerville Community College—it would mean the end of the world had finally arrived, no matter how many times Ethan tried to save us all.

Had tried.

"Maybe I'm just not as brave as you are, Lena."

"Sure you are. You've survived all those years in your house with your mom, haven't you?" I tried to smile, but Link was beyond cheering up.

It was like talking to myself.

"Maybe I just gotta give up when the odds are as bad as they are now."

"What are you talking about? The odds are always this bad," I said.

"I'm the guy who gets bit. I'm the guy who gets the F and then even fails summer school."

"That wasn't your fault, Link. You were helping Ethan rescue me."

"Face it. The only girl I ever loved chose Darkness over me."

"Rid loved you. You know that. And about Ridley…" I had almost forgotten why I'd brought him here. He still didn't know. "Seriously. You don't understand. Rid—"

"I don't want to talk about her. It wasn't meant to be. Nothin's ever gone my way before. I shoulda known it wouldn't work out."

Link stopped talking because the bell over the door rang in the distance, and time stopped—in a flurry of bright pink flapper feathers and purple tin beads. Not to mention eyeliner and lip liner and anything else that could possibly be lined or shined or painted any of the colors of the cosmetic rainbow.

Ridley.

I barely thought the word before I flew halfway up out of my seat and toward her for a hug.

I knew she was coming—I was the one who'd found her at Abraham's—but it was a different thing to see her making her way safe and sound through the plastic tables of the Dar-ee Keen. I almost knocked her off her three-inch platforms. Nobody walked in heels like my cousin.

Cuz.

She Kelted it as she buried her face in my shoulder, and all I could smell was hair spray and bath gel and sugar. Glitter swirled in the air around us, knocked loose from whatever sparkly goop she'd smeared all over her body.

Dark or Light, somehow it never mattered between us. Not when it really counted. We were still family, and we were together again.

It's strange to be here without Short Straw. I'm sorry, Cuz.

I know, Rid.

Here at the Dar-ee Keen, it was all hitting home, like she finally understood what happened.

What I'd lost.

"You okay, kid?" She pulled back, looking me in the eyes.

I shook my head as my eyes started to blur. "No."

"Somebody mind fillin' me in on what's goin' on here?" Link looked like he was about to pass out, or throw up, or both.

"I was trying to tell you. We found Ridley, stuck in one of Abraham's cages."

"You know it. Like a peacock, Hot Rod." She didn't look right at Link, and I wondered if it was because she didn't want to or because she didn't dare. "A really hot one."

I would never understand what went on between the two of them. I didn't think anyone could—not even them.

"Hey, Rid." Link was pale, even for a quarter Incubus. He looked like someone had just punched him in the face.

She blew him a kiss across the table. "Looking good, Hot Rod."

He was stammering. "You look…you're lookin'…I mean, you know."

"I know." Ridley winked and turned back to me. "Let's get out of here. It's been too long. I can't do this anymore."

"Do what?" Link managed not to stammer, though his face was now as red as the plastic bucket beneath the leaking ceiling.

Ridley sighed, sticking her lollipop to one side of her mouth. "Hello? I'm a Siren, Shrinky Dink. A bad girl. I need to be back among my own."

"Abraham, eh? That old goat?" Ridley shook her head.

I nodded. "That's the plan." For what it was worth, if it was worth anything.

The air was dark, and the ceiling lights of Exile only seemed to make it darker, instead of adding to the light. I didn't blame Ridley for wanting to bring us here. It was the first place she always wanted to go when she was Dark.

But if you weren't Dark, it wasn't the most relaxing place in the world. You spent half the night making sure not to accidentally look anyone in the eye or smile in the wrong direction.

"And you think getting Short Straw *The Book of Moons* is going to help him un-kick the can?"

Link growled from the next seat. He insisted on coming with us for safekeeping, but I could tell he hated it here even more than I did.

"Watch it, Rid. Ethan hasn't kicked the can. He's just—bent it outta shape a little."

I smiled. I guess Link could tell me Ethan was gone all he wanted, but it wasn't the same when someone else said it.

And it meant Ridley wasn't one of us anymore, at least not for Link. She really had left him, and she really was Dark.

She was an outsider.

Link seemed to sense it, too. "I need to use the bathroom." He hesitated, unwilling to leave my side. Everyone seemed to have their own brand of bodyguard at a club like Exile. My bodyguard happened to be a quarter Incubus with a heart of gold.

Ridley waited until he was out of earshot. "Your plan sucks."

"The plan doesn't suck."

"Abraham's not going to trade John Breed for *The Book of Moons*. John isn't worth anything to him now that the Order of Things has been set right. It's too late."

"You don't know that."

"You're forgetting I've spent more time than I wanted to with Abraham in the past few months. He's been keeping himself busy. He spends every day in that Frankenstein lab of his, trying to figure out what went wrong with John Breed. He's gone back to the mad science drawing board."

"That means he'll want John back, so he'll trade us the Book. Which is exactly what we want."

Ridley sighed. "Are you listening to yourself? He's not a good guy. You don't want to hand John over to him. When Abraham's not gluing wings onto bats, he's been having secret meetings with some creepy bald guy."

"Can you be more specific? That doesn't narrow it down."

Rid shrugged. "I don't know. Angel? Angelo? Something church-y like that."

I felt sick. My glass turned to ice in my hand. I could feel the frozen particles collecting at the tips of my fingers.

"Angelus?"

She popped a chip into her mouth from the black bowl on the bar. "That's it. They're teaming up for some supersecret takedown. I never heard the details. But this guy definitely hates Mortals as much as Abraham does."

What would a member of the Council of the Far Keep be doing with a Blood Incubus like Abraham Ravenwood? After what Angelus tried to do to Marian, I knew he was a monster, but I thought he was some kind of righteous lunatic. Not someone who would conspire with Abraham.

Still, it wasn't the first time Abraham and the Far Keep seemed to have their agendas aligned. Uncle Macon had brought it up before, right after Marian's trial.

I shook my head at the thought. "We have to tell Marian. After we get that book. So unless you have a better idea, we're meeting Abraham to make the trade." I drained what was left of my frozen soda water, knocking the glass back down to the bar.

It shattered in my hand.

The room quieted around me, and I could feel the eyes— nonhuman eyes, some gold and others black as the Tunnels themselves—staring back at me. I ducked my head from view.

The bartender made a face, and I glanced at the door from the corner of my eye—half-expecting to see my Uncle Macon standing there. The bartender was staring. "Those are some eyes you've got."

Rid shot me a look. "Hers? One of them didn't take," she said casually. "You know how it goes." We waited in our seats, nervous and tense. You didn't want to attract too much attention at Exile, not when you only had one gold eye to show for it.

The bartender studied me for another moment, then nodded and checked his watch. "Yeah. I know how it goes." This time he glanced at the door. He'd probably already made the call to my uncle.

That rat.

"You're going to need all the help you can get, Cuz."

"What are you saying, Rid?"

"I'm saying it looks like I'm going to have to rescue you fools again." She flicked a piece of broken glass off the counter.

"Rescue us how?"

"You leave that to me. Turns out I'm not just another pretty face. Well, I'm that, too." She smiled, but she couldn't quite pull it off. "All this *and* another pretty face."

Even her smart mouth seemed halfhearted to me now. I wondered if Ethan's disappearance was getting to her as much as the rest of us.

My instincts were still right about one thing.

Uncle Macon showed up at the door like clockwork, and I was back home in my bedroom before I could ask her.

CHAPTER 24

The Hand That Rocks
the Cradle

Ridley was waiting for us behind the farthest row of crypts, which, judging by the number of abandoned beer bottles in the bushes, was also a Gatlin County hot spot.

I couldn't imagine hanging out here willingly. His Garden of Perpetual Peace still had Abraham's fingerprints all over it. Nothing seemed to have changed since he had called up the Vexes only weeks before the Eighteenth Moon. Warning signs and yellow caution tape created a labyrinth between the broken mausoleums, uprooted trees, and cracked gravestones in the new section of the cemetery. Now that the Order of Things was repaired, the grass wasn't burning up anymore, and the lubbers were gone. But the other scars were still there if you knew where to look for them.

True to Gatlin form, the worst of the damage had already been hidden under the layers of fresh dirt Ridley was standing on now. The caskets had been reburied and the tombs sealed. I wasn't surprised. It wasn't like the good citizens of Gatlin to keep the skeletons out of the closet for long.

Rid unwrapped a cherry lollipop and waved it around dramatically. "I sold it to him. Hook, line, and stinker." She smiled at Link. "That's you, Shrinky Dink."

"You know what they say. Takes one to know one," Link shot back.

"You know I smell like frosting on a cupcake. Why don't you come on over here, and I'll show you just how sweet I can be?" She wriggled her long pink nails like claws.

Link walked over to John, who was leaning against a weeping angel that was split right down the middle. "Just callin' it like I see it, Babe. And I can smell you just fine from here."

Link was throwing Ridley more than just quarter-Incubus swagger today. Now that he'd wrapped his head around the fact that she was back, it was like he lived to trade insults with her.

Ridley turned back to me, annoyed that she hadn't gotten a bigger rise out of him. "All it took was a little trip back to N'awlins, and I had Abraham eating out of my hand."

That was hard to imagine, and John definitely wasn't buying it. "You expect us to believe you Charmed Abraham with a few Ridley pops? You and what chain of candy stores?"

Ridley pouted. "Of course not. I had to sell it. So I thought, who would be stupid enough to do whatever I say and play right into my hands?" She blew Link a kiss. "Our little Din-kubus, of course."

Link's jaw tightened. "She's full of crap."

"All I had to do was tell Abraham that I used Link and his feelings for me to infiltrate your stupid little circle and figure out your even stupider little plan. Then I complained about him keeping me caged like his prize pet. Of course, I said I couldn't blame him. Who wouldn't want me around full-time?"

"Is that a question? Because I'd be happy to answer," Link snapped.

"He wasn't mad that you broke out of your fancy bird-cage?" John asked.

Ridley's voice edged up a little. "Abraham knew I wouldn't stay in there if I could find a way out. I'm a Siren; it's not in my nature to be confined. I told him I used my Power of Persuasion on his pathetic Incubus errand boy and convinced him to let me out. It didn't end well. Abraham just got a bigger cage for him."

"What else did you say?" I wanted to know if there was really a chance we were getting the Book. I twisted my charm necklace around my finger, trying not to think about the memories slipping around it.

"I broke it down for him and said I'd rather bet on him than you guys." She gave Link a sweet smile. "You know how I like a winning team. Naturally, Abraham believed every word. Why wouldn't he? It's so utterly believable."

Link looked like he wanted to throw her across the graveyard.

"And Abraham will be there? Today?" John still didn't trust her.

"He'll be there. In the flesh. Of course, I'm using the term loosely." She shuddered. "Very loosely."

"He agreed to trade me for *The Book of Moons*?" John asked.

Ridley sighed, leaning against the crypt wall. "Well, technically, I believe it went something like, 'They're stupid enough to believe you'll trade John for the Book, but of course you won't.' And then there might have been some laughing. And some drunken Casting. It's all a haze."

Link folded his arms across his chest. "The thing is, Rid, how do we know you're not saying the same thing to him? You're Dark as they come. How can we know"—he stepped protectively in front of me—"whose side you're really on?"

"She's my cousin, Link." Even as I said it, I wasn't really sure of the answer. Ridley was a Dark Caster again. The last time she offered to help me, it was a trap, and she led me right to my mother and my Seventeenth Moon.

But I knew she loved me. As much as a Dark Caster could love anyone. And as much as Rid could love anyone other than herself.

Ridley leaned closer to Link. "Good question, Shrinky Dink. Too bad I have no intention of answering it."

"One of these days, I guess I'll figure out that one for myself." Link frowned, and I smiled.

"Let me give you a little clue," Rid purred. "Today's not the day."

Then in a swirl of cotton candy body glitter, the Siren he loved to hate was gone.

It was just starting to get dark when we left Liv and Uncle Macon in the study, poring over every Caster book they could find about Sheers and Ravenwood history, respectively. Liv was convinced that Ethan was trying to contact us, and she was determined to find a way to communicate with him. Every time I went down there, she was taking notes or adjusting the crazy gadget she used to measure supernatural frequencies. I think she was desperate to find a solution that didn't involve trading John for *The Book of Moons*.

I didn't blame her.

Uncle Macon was, too, even if he wouldn't admit it. He was scouring every journal and scrap of paper he could find for references to other places where Abraham could have hidden the Book.

That's why I couldn't tell them what we were doing. We already knew how Liv felt about the idea of trading John for the Book. And Uncle Macon wasn't going to trust Ridley. Instead, I told them I wanted to visit Ethan's grave, and John volunteered to go with me.

Link was waiting for John and me back at the cemetery.

The sky was dark now, and I could barely make out where a crow circled high in the air above us, shrieking, as we made our way toward the oldest part of His Garden of Perpetual Peace.

I shivered. That crow had to be some sort of omen. But there was no way of knowing which kind. Either things were going to go well, and I would end the day with *The Book of Moons* and a chance at getting Ethan back, or I'd fail and lose John in the process.

John Breed wasn't the love of my life, but he was the love of someone's life. And John and I had spent more than a few dark months together, when he and Rid seemed like the only people I could talk to. But John wasn't the same guy he was back then. He had changed, and he didn't deserve to go back to a life with Abraham. I wouldn't have wished that on anyone.

What had I become?

bargaining with a life
that isn't mine
isn't a bargain
misery
doesn't
come
cheap

John wouldn't look at me. Even Link kept his eyes fixed on the path ahead of us. I felt like they were disappointed in me for being so selfish.

I was disappointed in myself.

It is what it is, and I am what I am. I'm no better than Ridley. I only want what I want.

Either way, it didn't stop my feet from walking.

I tried not to think about it as I followed Link and John through the trees. While most of His Garden of Perpetual Peace was in the process of being restored to its pre–Vex attack state, the same wasn't true of the older part of the graveyard. I hadn't seen it since the night the earth cracked open, covering these hills with decomposing corpses and severed bones. Though the bodies were gone, the ground was still overturned, huge sinkholes replacing the graves that had surrounded generations of Wates since before the Civil War. Even if Ethan wasn't here.

Thank God.

"This blows." Link trudged up the hill with his garden shears in hand. "But don't worry. I got your back. He's not going to take you off to creepy-old-guy-land. Not without a fight. Not with these babies."

John shoved Link to the side. "Put those things away, rookie. You won't be able to get close enough to Hunting to clip the grass around his feet. And if Abraham sees them, he'll use them to slit your throat without even touching them."

Link shoved John back, and I ducked to avoid being knocked down the hill, as collateral damage. "Yeah, well, they helped me out on the way to that guy Obidias' place when

I took out that chicken-fried bat guy. Just don't get me killed, Caster Boy."

"Hold up a second." John, now serious, stopped walking and turned to both of us. "Abraham is no joke. You have no idea what he's capable of—I'm not sure anyone does. Stay out of the way and let me handle him. You're backup, in case Hunting or your girlfriend gives us trouble."

"Rid's on our side, remember?" I reminded him.

"At least she's supposed to be. And she's not my girlfriend." Link clenched his jaw.

"In my experience, the only side Ridley's ever on is her own." John stepped over a broken statue of a praying angel, her hands cracked at the wrists. All the broken angels around here were starting to feel like a bad omen.

Link looked annoyed, but he didn't say anything. He didn't seem to like it when anyone but him criticized Ridley. I wondered if things could ever really be over between them.

He and John navigated around the broken caskets and tree limbs, reaching an enormous sinkhole just beyond the old Honeycutt crypt. I did my best to keep up, but they were Incubuses, so there was nothing I could do, short of Casting an Incubus-cloning spell.

But soon it didn't matter, because we had nowhere left to go.

Abraham was waiting for us.

Either we had walked right into his trap or he had walked right into ours. It was almost time to find out.

Abraham Ravenwood was standing on the far side of the sink-hole. Wearing a long black coat and stovepipe hat and leaning against a splintered tree, he looked bored, as if this was an annoying errand.

The Book of Moons was tucked under his arm.

I breathed a sigh of relief. "He brought it," I said quietly.

"We don't have it yet," Link said under his breath.

Wearing a black turtleneck and a leather jacket, Hunting stood behind his great-great-great-grandfather. He was blow-ing smoke rings at Ridley. She coughed, waving the smoke away from her red dress, and gave her uncle a dirty look.

There was something disturbing about seeing her dressed in red, standing a few feet away from two Blood Incubuses. I hoped John was wrong and Ridley really was on our side—for Link's sake as much as my own.

We both loved her. And you couldn't control who you loved, even if you wanted to. That had been Genevieve's problem with Ethan Carter Wate. It had been Uncle Macon's problem with Lila, Link's with Ridley. Probably even Ridley's with Link.

Love was how all these knots started to unravel in the first place.

"You brought it," I called across to Abraham.

"And you've brought him." Abraham's eyes narrowed at the sight of John. "There's my boy. I've been so worried."

John tensed. "I'm not your boy. And you've never cared about me, so you can stop pretending."

"That's not true." Abraham acted hurt. "I've put a great deal of energy into you."

"Too much, if you ask me," Hunting said.

"No one did," Abraham snapped.

Hunting clenched his jaw and flicked his cigarette into the grass. He didn't look pleased. Which meant he would probably take that anger out on someone who didn't deserve it and didn't expect it. We were all plausible candidates.

John looked disgusted. "You mean treating me like a slave and using me to do your dirty work? Thanks, but I'm not interested in the kind of energy you put into things."

Abraham stepped forward, his black string tie blowing in the breeze. "I don't care what interests you. You serve a purpose, and when you stop serving it, you won't be useful to me anymore. I think we both know how I feel about things that aren't of any use to me." He smirked. "I watched Sarafine burn to death, and the only thing that bothered me was the ash on my jacket."

He was telling the truth. I had watched my mother burn, too. Not that I thought of Sarafine that way. But hearing Abraham talk about her like that made me feel something, even if I didn't know what.

Sympathy? Compassion?

Do I feel sorry for the woman who tried to kill me? Is that possible?

John had told me that Abraham hated Casters as much as

Mortals. I hadn't believed him until that moment. Abraham Ravenwood was cold, calculating, and evil. He really was the Devil, or the closest thing I'd ever met.

I watched as John raised his head high and called to Abraham. "Just give my friends the Book, and I'll leave with you. That was the deal."

Abraham laughed, the Book still safely tucked under his arm. "The terms have changed. I think I'll keep it after all." He nodded at Link. "And your new friend."

Ridley stopped sucking on her lollipop. "You don't want him. He's worthless—trust me." She was lying.

Abraham knew it, too. A vicious smile spread across his face. "As you wish. Then we can feed him to Hunting's dogs. When we get home."

There was a time when Link would've backed up, scared out of his mind. But that was before John bit him and his life changed. Before Ethan died and everything changed.

I watched Link standing next to John now. He wasn't going anywhere, even if he was afraid. That Link was long gone.

John tried to step in front of him, but Link held out his arm. "I can defend myself."

"Don't be stupid," John snapped. "You're only a quarter Incubus. That makes you half as strong as me, without the Caster blood."

"Boys." Abraham snapped his fingers. "This is all very moving, but it's time to get going. I have things to do and people to kill."

John squared his shoulders. "I'm not going anywhere with you unless you give them the Book. I've come into contact with some powerful Casters lately. I make my own choices now."

John collected powers the way Abraham collected victims. Ridley's Power of Persuasion, even some of my abilities as a Natural. Not to mention the ones he absorbed from all the other Casters who unknowingly touched him. Abraham had to be wondering whose power John had tapped into.

Still, I started to panic. Why hadn't we taken John back down into the Tunnels to collect a few more? Who was I to think we could take on Abraham?

Hunting glanced at Abraham, and a flash of recognition passed between them—a secret they shared.

"Is that so?" Abraham dropped *The Book of Moons* at his feet. "Then why don't you come over here and take it?"

John had to know it was some kind of trick, but he started walking anyway.

I wished Liv were here to see how brave he was. Then again, I was glad she wasn't. Because I could barely stand to watch him take another step closer to the ancient Incubus, and I wasn't the girl who loved him.

Abraham held out his hand and flicked his wrist, like he was turning a doorknob.

With that one motion, everything changed. Instantly, John grabbed his head like someone had just cracked it open from the inside, and dropped to his knees.

Abraham kept his arm in front of him, closing his fist slowly, and John jerked violently, screaming in pain.

"What the hell?" Link grabbed John's arm and yanked him to his feet.

John could barely stand. He swayed, trying to regain his balance.

Hunting laughed. Ridley was still standing next to him, and I could see the lollipop shaking in her hand.

I tried to think of a Cast, anything that would stop Abraham, even for a second.

Abraham stepped closer, gathering up the bottom of his coat to keep it from dragging in the mud. "Did you think I would create something as powerful as you if I couldn't control it?"

John froze, his green eyes fearful. He squinted hard, trying to fight the pain. "What are you talking about?"

"I think we both know," Abraham said. "I made you, boy. Found the right combination—the parentage I needed—and created a new breed of Incubus."

John staggered back, stunned. "That's a lie. You found me when I was a kid."

Abraham smiled. "That depends on your interpretation of the word *found*."

"What are you saying?" John's face was ashen.

"We took you. I did engineer you, after all." Abraham dug around in his jacket pocket and removed a cigar. "Your parents had a few happy years together. It's more than most of us get."

"What happened to my parents?" John gritted his teeth. I could almost see the rage.

Abraham turned to Hunting, who lit the cigar with a silver lighter. "Answer the boy, Hunting."

Hunting flipped the top of the lighter closed. He shrugged. "It was a long time ago, kid. They were juicy. And chewy. But I can't remember the details."

John lurched forward and ripped through the darkness.

One second he was there. The next, he was gone, sliding away in a ripple of air. He reappeared just inches in front of Abraham and wrapped his hand around the old Incubus' throat. "I'm going to kill you, you sick son of a bitch."

The tendons in John's arm tightened, but his grip didn't.

The muscles in his hand were tensing, his fingers obviously trying to close, but they wouldn't. John grabbed his wrist with his other hand, trying to brace it.

Abraham laughed. "You can't hurt me. I'm the architect of the design. Think I would build a weapon like you without a kill switch?"

Ridley stepped back, watching as John's hand loosened against his will, his fingers opening as he tried to force them closed again with his other hand. It was impossible.

I couldn't bear to watch. Abraham seemed more in control of John now than he had on the night of the Seventeenth Moon. Worse, John's awareness didn't seem to change the fact that he couldn't control his body. Abraham was pulling the strings.

"You're a monster," John hissed, still holding his wrist inches from Abraham's throat.

"Flattery won't get you anywhere. You've caused me lots of problems, boy. You owe me." Abraham smiled. "And I plan to take it out of your flesh."

He twitched his hands again, and John rose off the ground further, clutching his own neck with his hands, strangling himself.

Abraham was trying to do more than make a point. "You have outlived your usefulness. All that work for nothing."

John's eyes rolled back in his head, and his body went limp.

"Don't you need him?" Ridley shouted. "You said he was the ultimate weapon."

"Unfortunately, he's *defective*," Abraham answered.

I noticed something move in my peripheral vision a moment before I heard his voice.

"One could say the same thing about you, Grandfather." Uncle Macon stepped out from behind one of the crypts, his green eyes glowing in the darkness. "Put the boy down."

Abraham laughed, though his expression was anything but amused. "Defective? That's a compliment, coming from the little Incubus who wanted to be a Caster."

Abraham's grip on John loosened just enough for John to get some air. The Blood Incubus was focusing his anger on Uncle Macon now.

283

"I never wanted to be a Caster, but I'm glad to accept any fate that unburdens me from the Darkness you brought upon this family." Uncle Macon pointed a hand at John, and a wave of energy flashed across the graveyard, the blast hitting John squarely.

John yanked his hands away from his neck as his body dropped to the ground.

Hunting started toward his brother, but Abraham stopped him, clapping dramatically. "Nicely done. That's quite a party trick, son. Maybe next time you can light my cigar." Abraham's features settled in his familiar sneer. "Enough games. Let's finish this."

Hunting didn't hesitate.

He ripped through the darkness as Uncle Macon focused his green eyes on the black sky. Hunting materialized in front of his brother just as the sky exploded into a blanket of pure light.

Sunlight.

Uncle Macon had done it once before, in the parking lot of Jackson High, but this time the light was even more intense— and focused. That light coming from him had been Caster green. This time it was something stronger and more natural, as if the light came from the sky itself.

Hunting's body jerked. He reached out and grabbed his brother's shirt, taking them both to the ground.

But the killing light only intensified.

Abraham's skin went pale, the color of white ash. The light

seemed to weaken him, but not nearly as quickly as it was draining Hunting.

Even as Hunting desperately tried to stay alive, Abraham only seemed interested in trying to kill us. The old Blood Incubus was too strong, and he reached out for Uncle Macon. I knew better than to underestimate him. Even wounded, he wouldn't give up until he destroyed us all.

An overwhelming sense of panic surged inside me. I concentrated every thought, every cell on Abraham. The earth around him bucked, tearing itself from the ground like a rug being pulled out from under him. Abraham staggered and then turned his attention to me.

He closed his hand around the air in front of him, and an invisible force tightened around my throat. I felt my feet rise off the ground, my Chucks kicking below me.

"Lena!" John shouted. He closed his eyes, concentrating on Abraham, but whatever he was planning, he wasn't fast enough.

I couldn't breathe.

"I don't think so." Abraham twisted his free hand, bringing John to his knees in seconds.

Link charged Abraham, but another simple flick of the Blood Incubus' wrist sent him flying. Link's back hit the jagged stone crypt with a loud crack.

I struggled to stay conscious. Hunting was below me, his hands around Uncle Macon's neck. But he didn't seem to have enough strength left to hurt his brother. The color slowly drained from Hunting's skin, turning his body hauntingly transparent.

I gasped for breath, transfixed, as Hunting's hands slid from Uncle M's neck and he started writhing in pain.

"Macon! Stop!" he pleaded.

Uncle Macon focused his energy on his brother. The light held steady as the darkness leached out of Hunting's body and into the overturned earth.

Hunting seized, and sucked in his last breath. Then his body shuddered and froze.

"I'm sorry, brother. You left me no choice." Macon stared down at what was left before Hunting's corpse disintegrated, as if he had never existed at all.

"One down," he said grimly.

Abraham shielded his eyes, trying to determine if Hunting was really gone. The color was beginning to seep out of Abraham's skin now, but it had only made it as far as his wrists. He would kill me long before the sunlight took him out. I had to do something before we all ended up dead.

I closed my eyes, trying to push past the pain. My mind was slipping into numbness.

Thunder rumbled overhead.

"A storm? Is that all you've got, my dear?" Abraham said. "Such a waste. Just like your mother."

Anger and guilt churned inside me. Sarafine was a monster, but she was a monster Abraham had helped create. Abraham had used her weaknesses to lure her into Darkness. And I had watched her die. Maybe we were both monsters.

Maybe we all are.

"I'm nothing like my mother!" Sarafine's fate was decided for her, and she wasn't strong enough to fight it. I was.

Lightning tore across the sky and struck a tree behind Abraham. Flames raced down the trunk.

Abraham took off his hat and shook it with one hand, careful to keep the hand tethered to my throat tightly clenched. "I always say it's not a party until something catches fire."

My uncle rose to his feet, his black hair messy and his green eyes glowing even brighter than before. "I would have to agree."

The light in the sky intensified, blazing like a spotlight on Abraham. As we watched, the beam exploded in a blinding flash of white—forming two horizontal beams of pure energy.

Abraham swayed, shielding his eyes. His iron grip retracted, and my body fell to the rotting soil.

Time seemed to stop.

We all stared at the white beams spreading across the sky.

Except one of us.

Link ripped before anyone else had a chance to react—dematerializing in a split second, like he was a pro. I couldn't believe it. The only times he'd ever ripped in front of me, he practically flattened me like a pancake.

Not this time.

A crack in space opened up for him, only inches in front of Abraham Ravenwood.

Link yanked the garden shears out of the waistband of his jeans, raising them above his head. He plunged them into Abraham's heart before the old Incubus even realized what had happened.

Abraham's black eyes widened and he stared at Link, struggling to stay alive as a circle of red seeped slowly out around the blades.

Link leaned in close. "All that engineerin' wasn't for nothin', Mr. Ravenwood. I'm the best a both worlds. A hybrid Incubus with his own onboard navigation."

Abraham coughed desperately, his eyes fixed on the mostly Mortal boy who had taken him down. Finally, his body slid to the ground, the stolen science lab shears protruding from his chest.

Link stood over the body of the Blood Incubus who had hunted us for so long. The one person generations of Casters hadn't been able to touch.

Link grinned at John and nodded. "Screw all that Incubus crap. That's how you do it Mortal-style."

⊰ CHAPTER 25 ⊱

Death's Door

Link stood over Abraham's body, watching as it started to disintegrate into tiny particles of nothing.

Ridley stepped up beside him, looping her arm through his. "Grab the scissors, Hot Rod. They might come in handy if I need to cut myself out of a cage sometime."

Link pulled the shears from what was left of the Blood Incubus. "I would like to take this opportunity to thank the Jackson High Biology Department. Stay in school, kids." He shoved the shears back into his jeans.

John walked over and slapped Link on the shoulder. "Thanks for saving my ass. Mortal-style."

"You know it. I got some mad skills." Link grinned.

Uncle Macon brushed off his trousers. "I don't think any-one can argue with that assessment, Mr. Lincoln. Well played. Your timing was impeccable."

"How did you know we were here?" I asked. Had Amma seen something and given us away?

"Mr. Breed was kind enough to leave a note."

I turned to John, who was kicking at the dirt with his boot. "You told him what we were doing? What about our plans? What about the part where we agreed not to tell my uncle anything?"

"I didn't. The note was for Liv," he answered sheepishly. "I couldn't just disappear without saying good-bye."

Link shook his head. "Seriously, dude? Another note? Why didn't you just leave a map?"

This was the second time John's guilty conscience and one of his notes had led Liv—or, in this case, my uncle—to him.

"You should all be grateful for Mr. Breed's sentimental inclinations," Uncle M said. "Or I'm afraid this evening could have resulted in a very unfortunate outcome."

Link elbowed John. "You're still a sap."

I stopped listening.

Why couldn't Liv keep her mouth shut?

Another voice entered my mind.

I hardly think blaming Liv for your mistakes is necessary.

I was almost too stunned to speak. My uncle had never Kelted with me before. It was a power he could only have acquired after his transition into a Caster.

"How?"

"You know my abilities are constantly evolving. This one is unpredictable, I'm afraid." He shrugged innocently.

I tried not to think. It didn't seem to stop him from scolding me.

Really? You thought you could take on Abraham alone, in a graveyard?

"But how did you know where we were?" John asked. "I didn't put that in the note."

Oh my God....

"Uncle M? Can you read minds?"

"Hardly." My uncle snapped his fingers, and Boo lumbered up the hill. Knowing my uncle, it was practically a confession.

I felt my hair lift from my shoulders as a gentle wind whipped around me. I tried to calm down. "You were *spying* on me? I thought we made a deal about that."

"*That* was before you and your friends decided you were equipped to take on Abraham Ravenwood on your own." His voice rose. "Have you learned nothing?"

The Book of Moons lay in the dirt, the moon embossed on its black leather cover facing the sky.

Link bent down to pick it up.

"I wouldn't do that, Hot Rod," Ridley said. "You don't have that much Incubus in you." She picked up the Book and touched her lollipop to his lips almost like a kiss. "Wouldn't want those pretty hands to get burned."

"Thanks, Babe."

"Don't call me—"

Link grabbed the lollipop out of her hand. "Yeah, yeah. I know."

I watched the way they looked at each other. Any idiot could see they were in love, even if they were the only two idiots who couldn't.

My chest ached, and I thought about Ethan.

the missing piece
my breath
my heart
my memory
me
the other half
the missing half

Stop.

I didn't want to write poems in my mind, especially if my uncle could hear them. I needed to send a completely different kind of message. "Rid, give it to me."

She nodded and handed me *The Book of Moons*.

The Book that nearly killed Ethan and then Uncle Macon. The Book that took more than it ever gave. Part of me wanted to set it on fire and see if it would burn, though I doubted something as mundane as fire could destroy it.

It still would have been worth a try if it prevented even one person from using the Book to hurt someone else—or themselves. But Ethan needed it, and I trusted him. Whatever he was doing, I believed he wouldn't use it to hurt anyone. And I wasn't sure he could hurt himself now.

"We have to take it to Lila's grave."

Uncle Macon studied me for a long moment, an unfamiliar mixture of sadness and worry warring in his eyes. "All right."

I recognized his tone. He was indulging me.

I started walking toward Lila Wate's grave, next to the empty plot where the good folks of Gatlin believed my uncle was buried.

Ridley sighed dramatically. "Great. More time in the creepy graveyard."

Link slung his arm over her shoulders casually. "Don't worry, Babe. I'll protect you."

Ridley looked at him suspiciously. "Protect me? You do realize I'm a Dark Caster again?"

"I like to think you're kinda on the gray side. Either way, I'll give you a pass today. I did just kill the Galactus of Incubuses."

Rid flipped her blond and pink hair. "Whatever that means."

I stopped listening and wove my way through the cemetery, *The Book of Moons* pressed against my chest. I felt the heat radiating from it, as if the worn leather cover might burn me, too.

I knelt in front of Ethan's mother's grave. This was the spot where I'd left the black stone from my necklace for him. It seemed to work then; I could only hope it would work again. *The Book of Moons* had to be a whole lot more important than a rock.

My uncle stared at the headstone, transfixed. I wondered how long he would love her. Forever, that was my best guess.

For whatever reason, this place was a doorway I couldn't find my way through. The important thing was that Ethan could open it somehow.

He had to.

I put the Book on the grave, touching it for what I hoped would be the last time.

I don't know why you need it, Ethan. But here it is. Please come home.

I waited as if it might disappear right in front of me.

Nothing happened.

"Maybe we should leave it alone," Link suggested. "Ethan probably needs privacy or somethin' to do his ghost tricks."

"He's not a ghost," I snapped.

Link held up his hands. "Sorry. His Sheer tricks."

He didn't realize that the word didn't matter. It was the image the word called up in my mind. A pale, lifeless Ethan. Dead. The way I found him the night of my Sixteenth Moon, after Sarafine stabbed him. Panic pressed against my lungs like two hands squeezing the breath out of me. I couldn't stand to think about it.

"Let's leave it and see what happens," John said.

"Absolutely not." Uncle Macon was done indulging me. "I'm sorry, Lena—"

"What if it was Lila?"

His face clouded over at the mention of her name. The question hung in the air, but we both knew the answer.

If the woman he loved needed him, he would do anything to help—from this side of the grave or any other.

I knew that, too.

He studied me for a long moment. Then he sighed, nodding. "All right. You can try. But if it doesn't work—"

"Yeah, yeah. We can't just ditch the most powerful book in the Caster and Mortal worlds on some grave and walk away." Ridley was still perched on the headstone, smacking her gum. "What if someone finds it?"

"I'm afraid Ridley's right." Uncle Macon sighed. "I'll wait here."

"I don't think it will work if you're here, sir. You're a scary kinda person, too," Link said as respectfully as possible. "Sir."

"We are not leaving *The Book of Moons* unattended, Mr. Lincoln."

An idea took hold slowly, stretching out until it was perfectly formed. "Maybe we don't need someone to stay with the Book, but *something*."

"Huh?" Link scratched his head.

I bent down. "Boo, come here, boy."

Boo Radley stood up and shook his black fur, which was as thick as a wolf's.

I dug my fingers behind his ears. "That's my good boy."

"Not a bad idea." Rid put two fingers in her mouth and whistled.

"You really think one dog can fight off the Blood Pack if they show up?" Link asked.

Uncle Macon crossed his arms. "Boo Radley is hardly a common dog."

"Even a Caster dog can use a little help," Rid said.

A branch cracked, and something leaped from the bushes.

"Holy crap!" Link yanked the garden shears out of his waistband just as Bade's paws hit the ground.

Leah Ravenwood's enormous mountain cat growled.

Uncle M smiled. "My sister's cat. An excellent idea. She does provide a certain level of intimidation that Boo lacks."

Boo barked, offended.

"Here, kitty kitty...." Ridley reached out her hand, and Bade stalked over.

Link stared at her. "You're a total psycho."

Bade growled at Link again, and Rid laughed. "You're just mad because Bade doesn't like you, Hot Stuff."

John took a step back. "Yeah, well, I'm not petting her either."

"So we leave the Book for a little while and see what happens." I hugged Boo. "You stay here." The Caster dog sat down in front of the grave like a guard dog, and Bade came over and stretched out in front of him lazily.

I stood up, but I was having trouble forcing myself to walk away.

What if something happened to it? The Book might be Ethan's only chance to get back to me. Could I risk it?

John noticed I wasn't moving, and pointed to the rise a few yards beyond the grave. "We can hang out on the other side in case they need some backup. Okay?"

Ridley hopped off the headstone, her platforms smacking against the border of the plot. In the South, that had to be the equivalent of something like seven years of bad luck. Maybe more in Gatlin.

She draped her arm over my shoulders and waved a lollipop in front of me. "Come on. I'll tell you all about my adventures in shackles."

Link jogged up next to us. "Did you say shackles? Those are like handcuffs, right?" He seemed a little too excited about hearing the details.

"Mr. Lincoln!" Uncle M looked like he wanted to strangle him.

Link stopped in his tracks. "Uh, sorry, sir. It was just a joke. You know..."

I let Ridley drag me down the other side of the hill while Link tried to talk his way out of trouble with Uncle Macon. John trudged behind us, his boots as heavy as any Mortal's footsteps.

If I closed my eyes, I could pretend they were Ethan's.

But it was getting harder and harder to pretend. I was Kelting to him before I even realized it, the same three words over and over.

Please come home.

I wondered if he could hear me. If he was already on his way.

———————⌇⌇⌇

I counted the minutes, wondering how long we should wait before checking on the Book. Even Link and Ridley's banter couldn't distract me, which was saying a lot.

"I think all this quarter-Incubus stuff is going to your head," Ridley said.

Link flexed. "Or maybe it's taking out the baddest badass around."

Ridley rolled her eyes. "Please."

"Do you two ever stop?" John asked.

They both whipped around to look at him. "Stop what?" they asked at the same time.

I was about to tell John not to bother, when I saw a streak of black in the sky.

The crow. The same one that had watched us when we went to meet Abraham. Maybe it was following us.

Maybe it knew something.

It dipped and circled the area above Ethan's grave.

"It's the crow." I took off back up the hill.

John ripped and appeared at my side. "What are you talking about?"

Link and the others caught up to us. "Where's the fire?"

I pointed at the bird. "I think that crow has been following us."

Uncle Macon studied the bird. "Interesting."

Ridley smacked her gum. "What?"

"A Seer like Amarie would tell you that many believe crows can cross between the world of the living and the world of the dead."

We made it over the rise. Bade and Boo were staring up at the sleek black bird.

"So what? Even if it could fly from world to world, you really think that little bird could carry *The Book a Moons?*" Link asked.

I didn't know. But the crow was connected to Ethan somehow. I was sure of it.

"Why is it circling like that?" John asked.

Ridley strolled up behind us. "It's probably scared of the giant cat."

For once, she might be right.

"Bade and Boo, go home," I called. The big cat's ears perked up at the sound of her name.

Boo hesitated and looked up at Uncle Macon.

He nodded to the dog. "Go on."

Boo cocked his head. Then he turned and lumbered through the tall grass. Bade yawned, baring her huge white teeth, and followed, her tail swishing like a lion's from one of the nature shows Link was always watching on the Discovery

Channel. He blamed it on his mom, but in the last couple of months, I'd noticed him watching it by himself more than a few times.

The crow circled again and swooped toward us, landing on the headstone. Its beady black eyes seemed to be staring right at me.

"How come it's checkin' you out like that?" Link asked.

I stared back at the black bird.

Please. Take the Book or make it disappear. Whatever you have to do to get it to Ethan.

Uncle Macon looked at me from the other side of the headstone.

He can't hear you, Lena. You can't Kelt with a bird, I'm afraid.

I glared at my uncle. At this point, I would try anything.

How do you know?

The crow hopped down, its talons touching the thick leather cover for a split second before it squawked and pulled its legs up again quickly.

"I think the Book burned it," John said. "Poor guy."

I knew he was right. I felt the tears welling in my eyes. If the crow couldn't touch the Book, how would we get it to Ethan? I'd left the black stone Ethan had asked for, the one from my charm necklace, right here on the grave. I didn't know what had happened to it after that.

"Maybe the bird has nothing to do with it, and he's just a messenger or something," John offered.

I sniffled, swiping at my face. "Then what's the message?"

John squeezed my shoulder. "Don't worry."

"How are we going to get the Book to Ethan? He needs it, or he can't—" I couldn't finish. I couldn't stand to even think it.

We had risked our lives to track down Abraham Ravenwood, and we had found a way to kill him—at least Link had. *The Book of Moons* was right here at my feet, and there was no way to get it to Ethan.

"We'll figure it out, Cuz." Ridley picked up the Book, the back cover dragging across the stone. "Someone must have the answer."

John smiled at me. "Someone does. Especially when it comes to that book. Come on—let's go ask her."

A flutter of hope filled my chest. "Are you thinking what I'm thinking?"

He nodded. "It is Presidents' Day, which was still a bank holiday the last time I checked."

Ridley pulled on the bottom of her miniskirt, which didn't move an inch. "Who's thinking what, and where are we going?"

I grabbed her arm, tugging her down the hill. "Your favorite place, Rid. The library."

"It's not that bad," she said, inspecting her purple nail polish. "Except for all those books."

I didn't respond.

There was only one book that mattered right now, and my whole world—and Ethan's future—depended on it.

⊰ CHAPTER 26 ⊱

Quantum Physics

From just inside the hidden grating that led into the *Lunae Libri*, I could see all the way down to the bottom of the stairs. Marian sat behind the circular reception desk, exactly where I knew she would be. Liv was pacing at the far end of the room, where the stacks began.

As we came down into the *Lunae Libri*, Liv's neck snapped up. She bolted across the room the moment she saw John.

But he was faster. John ripped, materializing in Liv's path and gathering her up in his arms. My heart broke a little as I watched the relief spread across her face. I tried not to feel envious.

"You're all right!" Liv threw her arms around John's neck.

She pulled back, her expression changing. "What were you thinking? How many times are you going to sneak off to do something completely insane?" Liv turned her scowl on Link and me. "And how many times are you going to let him?"

Link raised his hands in surrender. "Hey, we weren't even there the last time."

John leaned his forehead against hers. "He's right. I'm the one you should be angry with."

A tear rolled down her cheek. "I don't know what I would have done—"

"I'm okay."

Link puffed his chest out. "Thanks to me."

"It's true," John said. "My protégée saved our asses."

Link raised an eyebrow. "That better mean somethin' good."

Uncle Macon cleared his throat and adjusted a cuff of his crisp white shirt. "It does indeed, Mr. Lincoln. It does indeed."

Arms crossed, Marian stepped out from behind the desk. "Would someone like to tell me exactly what happened tonight?" She stared at my uncle expectantly. "Liv and I have been worried sick."

He glared at me. "As you can imagine, their little showdown with my brother and Abraham did not go according to plan. And Mr. Breed almost met an untimely end."

"But Uncle M saved the day." Ridley didn't even try to hide her sarcasm. "He gave Hunting a sunburn where the sun don't shine. Now let's get on with the part where you give us a big lecture and we all get grounded."

Marian turned to my uncle. "Is she implying—?"

Uncle Macon nodded. "Hunting is no longer with us."

"Abraham's dead, too," John added.

Marian stared at Uncle Macon as if he had just parted the Red Sea. "You killed Abraham Ravenwood?"

Link cleared his throat loudly, grinning. "No, ma'am. I did."

For a moment Marian was speechless. "I think I need to sit down," she said, her knees beginning to buckle. John rushed behind the desk to get her a chair.

Marian pressed her fingers against her temples. "You're telling me that Hunting and Abraham are dead?"

"That would be correct," Uncle Macon said.

Marian shook her head. "Anything else?"

"Just this, Aunt Marian." Ethan's nickname for her just slipped out before I realized it. I dropped *The Book of Moons* on the polished wood tabletop next to her.

Liv inhaled sharply. "Oh my God."

I stared down at the worn black leather, embossed with a crescent moon, and the weight of the moment closed in on me. My hands shook, and my legs felt like they were about to give out, too.

"I can't believe it." Marian inspected the book suspiciously, as if I were returning a late library book into her system. She would never be anything less than 100 percent librarian.

"It's the real deal." Ridley leaned against one of the marble columns.

Marian stood up in front of her desk as if trying to position herself between Ridley and the most dangerous book in the Mortal and Caster worlds. "Ridley, I don't think you belong in here."

Ridley pushed her sunglasses up on her head, yellow cat eyes blinking back at Marian. "I know, I know. I'm a Dark Caster, and I don't belong in the good guys' secret clubhouse, right?" She rolled her eyes. "I am so over this."

"The *Lunae Libri* is open to all Casters, Light and Dark," Marian answered. "What I meant is that I'm not sure you belong with us."

"It's okay, Marian. Rid helped us get the Book," I explained.

Ridley blew a bubble and waited for it to pop, the sound echoing loudly off the walls. "Helped you? If by *help*, you mean set Abraham up for you so you could get *The Book of Moons* and kill him, then, yeah, I guess I helped."

Marian stared at her, speechless. Without a word, she walked over and held up a trash can in front of Ridley's mouth. "Not in my library. Spit it out now."

Ridley sighed. "You know it's not just gum, right?"

Marian didn't move.

Ridley spit.

Marian dropped the can. "What I don't understand is why you would risk your lives for that dreadful book. I appreciate the fact it is no longer in the hands of Blood Incubuses, but—"

"Ethan needs it," I blurted out. "He found a way to contact me, and he needs *The Book of Moons*. He's trying to get back here."

305

"Have you gotten another message?" Marian asked.

I nodded. "In the latest *Stars and Stripes*." I took a deep breath. "I need you to trust me." I looked into her eyes. "And I need your help."

Marian studied me for a long moment. I don't know what she was thinking, or debating, or even deciding. All I know is, she didn't say a word.

I don't think she could.

Then she nodded, pulling her chair a bit closer to me. "Tell me everything."

So I started talking. We took turns filling in the blanks— Link and John all but acting out our encounter with Abraham, and Rid and Uncle Macon helping me explain our plan to trade John for *The Book of Moons*. Liv looked on unhappily, as if she could hardly bear to hear it.

Marian didn't say a word until we finished, though it was easy to read her expressions, which ranged from shock and horror to sympathy and despair.

"Is that everything?" She looked at me, exhausted by our story.

"It gets worse." I looked at Ridley.

"You mean aside from the fact that Link dissected Abraham with the giant scissors?" Rid made a face.

"No, Rid. Tell her about Abraham's plans. Tell her what you heard about Angelus," I said.

Uncle Macon's head snapped up at the sound of the Keeper's name. "What is Lena talking about, Ridley?"

"Angelus and Abraham were up to something, but I don't know the details." She shrugged.

"Tell us exactly what you know."

Ridley twisted a lock of pink hair around her finger nervously. "This Angelus guy is a nutcase. He hates Mortals, and he thinks the Dark Casters and the Far Keep should be in control of the Mortal world, or something like that."

"Why?" Marian was thinking out loud. Her fists were clenched so tightly that her knuckles were white. Marian's own trouble with the Far Keep was all too fresh in her memory.

Rid shrugged. "Ah, maybe because he's *Special K-razy?*"

Marian looked over at my uncle, a silent conversation passing between them. "We can't let Angelus gain a foothold here. He's far too dangerous."

Uncle M nodded. "I agree. We need—"

I cut him off before he could finish. "All I know is first we need to get *The Book of Moons* to Ethan. There's still a chance we can get him back."

"Do you really think so?" Marian said the words quietly, almost under her breath. Though I couldn't be certain, it seemed like only I could hear them. Still, I knew Marian believed in the impossibilities of the Caster world—she'd seen them firsthand—and she loved Ethan as much as I did. He was like a son to her.

We both wanted to believe.

I nodded. "I do. I have to."

She rose from her chair and came back around the desk, poised as ever.

"Then it's settled. We'll get Ethan *The Book of Moons*, one way or another." I smiled at her, but she was already lost in thought, looking around the library as if it held the answers to all our problems.

Which, sometimes, it did.

"There has to be a way, right?" John asked. "Maybe in one of these scrolls or one of these old books—"

Ridley unscrewed the top of her nail polish bottle, wrinkling her nose. "Goody. Old books."

"Try to have a bit more respect, Ridley. A *book* is the reason the children in the Duchannes family suffered for generations." Marian was referring to our curse.

Rid crossed her arms, pouting. "Whatever."

Marian swiped the bottle out of her hand. "Another thing I don't allow in my library." It clattered to the bottom of the trash can.

Ridley glared, but she didn't say a word.

"Dr. Ashcroft, have you ever delivered a book to the Otherworld?" Liv asked.

Marian shook her head. "I can't say that I have."

"Maybe Carlton Eaton could just run it on over." Link looked hopeful. "You could wrap it up in one a those brown paper packages, like you do for my mom's books. And, you know, circulate it or somethin'."

Marian sighed. "I'm afraid not, Wesley." Even Carlton Eaton, who had his nose in every letter in town in both the Mortal and Caster worlds, couldn't make a delivery like that.

Frustrated, Liv flipped through her little red notebook. "There has to be a way. What were the odds you could get the Book from Abraham at all? And now that we have it, we're just going to give up?" She pulled the pencil from behind her ear, scribbling and mumbling to herself. "The laws of quantum physics must allow for this sort of eventuality...."

I didn't know anything about the laws of quantum physics, but I knew one thing. "The stone from my charm necklace disappeared when I left it for Ethan. Why would the Book be any different?"

I know you took it, Ethan. Why couldn't you take the Book, too?

I realized Uncle Macon could probably hear me, and I tried to stop.

It was no use. I couldn't stop Kelting any more than I could stop the words that strung themselves together, waiting for me to write them down somewhere.

*laws of physics
laws of love
of time and space
and the (in)between place
(in)between you and me
and where we are
lost and looking
looking and lost*

"Maybe the Book's too heavy," Link offered. "That little black rock wasn't any bigger than a quarter."

"I'm not sure that's the reason, Wesley. Though anything is possible," Marian said.

"Or impossible." Ridley pushed her sunglasses back into place and stuck out her red tongue.

"So why can't it make the jump?" John asked.

Marian glanced at Liv's notes, considering the question. *"The Book of Moons* is a powerful supernatural object. No one really understands the scope of its power. Not the Keepers or the Casters."

"And if the origin of its magic is in the Caster world, it could be deeply rooted here," Liv said. "The way a tree is rooted to a particular spot."

"Are you saying the Book doesn't want to cross over?" John asked.

Liv tucked the pencil behind her ear. "I'm saying maybe it can't."

"Or shouldn't." Uncle Macon's tone grew more serious.

Ridley slid to the floor and stretched out her long legs. "This is so messed up. I risked my life, and now we're stuck with that thing. Maybe we need to hit the Tunnels and see if any of the other bad guys know the answer. You know—Team Dark."

Liv crossed her arms over her EDISON DIDN'T INVENT THE LIGHTBULB T-shirt. "You want to take *The Book of Moons* to a Dark Caster bar?"

"You have a better idea?" Rid asked.

"I think I do." Marian slipped her red wool jacket on.

Liv scrambled after her. "Where are you going?"

"To see someone who knows a great deal about not just that book but a world that defies the physics of both the Caster and Mortal worlds. Someone who just may have the answers we need."

My uncle nodded. "An excellent idea."

There was only one person who fit that description.

Someone who loved Ethan as much as I did. Someone who would do anything for him, even rip a hole in the universe.

⊰ CHAPTER 27 ⊱

The Cracks in Everything

$\mathbf{N}$ow, don't you tell me you're thinkin' a settin' foot on my front walkway, you hear?" Amma refused to let Ridley anywhere near Wate's Landing. She said so in about fifteen different ways in the first conversation we unsuccessfully tried to have with her.

"Mmmm-nnnnnnn. No Dark Casters are comin' into this house while I'm here on this sweet earth. Or after I leave it. No, sir. No, ma'am. No how."

She agreed to meet us at Greenbrier instead.

Uncle Macon hung back. "It's better this way. Amarie and I haven't seen each other since the night…it happened," he explained. "I'm not sure this is the right moment."

"So what you're saying is that you're scared of her, too?" Ridley eyed him with new interest. "Imagine that."

"I'll be at Ravenwood if you need me," he said, giving Ridley a withering stare.

"Imagine that." I smiled.

The rest of us waited inside the crumbling wall of the old graveyard. I resisted the urge to wander over to Ethan's plot, though I felt the familiar pull, the longing to be with him there. I believed, with all my heart, that there was a way to get Ethan back, and I wasn't going to stop trying until I found it.

Amma was hopeful, too, but I had seen the fear and doubt in her eyes. She had already lost him twice. Every time I took her another crossword puzzle, she was desperate to get him back.

I think Amma wasn't about to let herself believe in anything she could stand to lose again.

With the Book, though, we were one step closer.

Ridley was leaning against a tree, a safe distance from the hole in the stone wall. I knew she was just as afraid of Amma as Uncle Macon was, even if she wouldn't admit it.

"Don't say anything to her when she gets here," Link warned Ridley. "You know how she gets about that book."

Ridley rolled her eyes. "I thought Abraham was a pain. Amma's even worse."

I saw a black orthopedic lace-up step through the opening.

"Worse than what?" Amma demanded. "Worse than your manners?" She looked Ridley up and down. "Or your taste in clothes?"

She was wearing a yellow dress, all sunlight and sweetness, which didn't match her expression. Her grayish-black hair was twisted into a neat bun, and she was carrying a patterned quilting bag. I'd been around long enough to know there weren't any quilting supplies inside.

"Or a stitch worse than the girl who gets pulled outta Hell only to walk back into the fire on her own?" Amma watched Ridley carefully.

Ridley didn't take off her sunglasses, but I could see the shame anyway. I knew her too well. There was something about Amma that made you feel completely awful if you disappointed her—even if you were a Siren with no ties to her.

"That's not what happened," Ridley said quietly.

Amma dropped her bag on the ground. "Isn't it, then? I have it on good authority that you had a chance to be on the right side a wrong for once, and you gave it up. Did I miss somethin' in the fine print?"

Ridley shifted nervously. "It's not that simple."

Amma sniffed. "You go on tellin' yourself that if it helps you sleep at night, but don't try to sell it to me, because I'm not buyin' it." Amma pointed to the lollipop in Ridley's hand. "And all that sugar will rot those teeth right outta your head, Caster or no Caster."

Link laughed nervously.

Amma focused her eagle eye on him. "What're you laughin' about, Wesley Lincoln? You're knee deep in more trouble than the day I caught you in my basement when you were nine years old."

Link's face reddened. "It sorta finds me, ma'am."

"You know you go lookin' for it, sure as the sun shines the same on the saints as it does on the sinners." She glanced at each of us. "So what is it this time? And it better not have anythin' to do with destroyin' the balance a the universe."

"All saints, ma'am. No sinners." Link backed away an inch or two, looking at me for help.

"Spit it out. I've got Aunt Mercy and Aunt Grace at the house, and I can't leave them alone with Thelma for too long, or the three a them will order everything that comes on the shoppin' channel." Amma rarely called Ethan's great-aunts "the Sisters" anymore, now that one of them was gone.

But now it was Marian who walked over and took Amma's arm reassuringly. "It's about *The Book of Moons*."

"*We have it*," I blurted out.

Liv stepped aside, revealing *The Book of Moons* lying on the ground behind her. Amma's eyes widened. "Do I wanna know how you got it?"

Link jumped in. "Nope. I mean no, ma'am, you sure don't."

"The fact remains we have it now," Marian said.

"But we can't get it to Ethan—" I heard the desperation in my voice.

Amma shook her head and approached the Book, circling it like she didn't want to get too close. " 'Course you can't.

315

This book is too powerful for one world. If you want to send it from the world a the livin' to the world a the dead, we'll need the power a both worlds to send it."

I wasn't sure what she meant, but I only cared about one thing. "Will you help us?"

"Not my help you need. You need help on the receivin' end."

Liv inched closer to Amma. "We left the Book for Ethan, but he didn't take it."

She sniffed. "Hmm. Ethan's not strong enough to carry that kinda weight across. He probably doesn't even know how."

"But there is someone strong enough," Marian coaxed. "Perhaps more than one someone." She was talking about the Greats.

The question was, would Amma call them?

I bit my lip.

Please say yes.

"Figured if you were callin', you were lookin' to test out just how far crazy will go." Amma opened the quilting bag and took out a shot glass and a bottle of Wild Turkey. "So I came prepared." She poured a shot and pointed to me. "You're gonna have to help, though. We need the power a both worlds, don't forget."

I nodded. "I'll do whatever I need to."

Amma nodded in the direction of Ravenwood. "You can start by gatherin' up the rest a your kin. You don't have the kinda power we need on your own."

"Rid is here, and John can help, too. He's half Caster."

Amma shook her head. "If you want that book to cross, you're gonna have to go get the rest a them."

"They're in Barbados."

"Actually, they returned a few hours ago," Marian said. "Reece stopped by the library earlier tonight. She said your grandmother wasn't fond of the humidity."

I tried not to smile. What my grandmother wasn't fond of was missing all the action, and Reece wasn't much better. With every Caster power in my extended family, I was certain they knew something was going on.

"I could ask them. But they might be tired from all the travel." I was worried enough that Uncle M was going to change his mind about all this. Adding the rest of my family into the mix fell somewhere between risky and idiotic.

Amma crossed her arms, as determined as I'd ever seen her. "What I know is that this book isn't going anywhere without them."

There was no use arguing with her. I had watched Ethan try to talk her down when her mind was made up, and he rarely succeeded. And Amma loved him more than anyone in the world. I didn't stand a chance.

Ridley nodded at me. "I'll go with you for backup."

"Your mom will freak if you just show up. I'm going to have to tell her you're back. And I should probably tell them that you've—" I hesitated. It wasn't going to be easy for anyone in my family to deal with the fact that Ridley ran back to Sarafine for her Dark Caster powers. "Changed."

Link looked away.

That wasn't the worst of it. "It's going to be hard enough to explain to Gramma why I have the Book."

Rid slung her arm over my shoulder. "Don't you know that the best way to distract someone from bad news is to give them some worse news?" She smiled, leading me toward Ravenwood. "News doesn't get much worse than me."

Link shook his head. "No kidding."

Ridley spun around and pushed her sunglasses up. "Zip it, Shrinky Dink. Or I'll make you want to rip into your mother's room and tell her you're becoming a Methodist."

"Your powers don't work on me anymore, Babe."

Ridley blew him a sticky pink kiss. "Try me."

CHAPTER 28

Caster Catfight

I opened the front door, and the air inside the house seemed to move. No—it was moving. Hundreds of butterflies fluttered through the air while others rested on the delicate antique furniture Uncle Macon had spent years collecting.

Butterflies.

What was I doing to Ravenwood?

A tiny green butterfly with streaks of gold across its wings landed on the bottom of the banister.

"Macon?" Gramma's voice called from the second floor. "Is that you?"

"No, Gramma. It's me. Lena."

She swept down the stairs in a high-neck white blouse, her

hair gathered neatly in a bun and her lace-up boots peeking out from under her long skirt. Against the perfectly restored flying staircase, she looked like a Southern belle right out of an old movie.

She glanced at the butterflies flitting around the room and gave me a hug. "I'm so glad to see you're in a good mood."

Gramma knew Ravenwood's interior constantly changed to mirror my moods. To her, a room full of butterflies meant happiness. But for me, it meant something entirely different— something I had been clinging to tightly.

Hope, borne on green and gold wings. Dark and Light, like I had become the night of my Claiming.

I touched the wire Christmas tree star on my charm necklace. I had to focus. Everything had come down to this. Ethan was out there somewhere, and there was a chance we could bring him home. I just had to convince my family to lend their powers to us.

"Gramma, I need your help with something."

"Of course, sweetheart."

She wouldn't be saying that if she knew what I was about to tell her. "What if I told you I found *The Book of Moons*?"

Gramma froze. "Why would you ask me something like that, Lena? Do you know where it is?"

I nodded.

She gathered her skirt, rushing toward the stairs. "We have to tell Macon. The sooner we get that book back to the *Lunae Libri*, the better."

"We can't."

Gramma turned around slowly, her eyes looking right through me. "Start explaining, young lady. And you can start by telling me how you found *The Book of Moons*."

Ridley stepped out from behind a marble column. "I helped her."

For one long moment, I held my breath, until it became clear Ravenwood wasn't about to fall to the ground.

"How did you get in here?" Gramma's voice was as controlled as Ridley's, maybe more. She'd been around a long time, and it would take more than my Dark-again cousin to throw her.

"Lena let me in."

There was a flicker of disappointment in my grandmother's eyes. "I see you're wearing your sunglasses again."

"It was kind of a self-preservation thing." Ridley bit her lip nervously. "The world's a dangerous place."

It was something my grandmother said to us all the time when we were kids—particularly to Ridley. I remembered something else she said, something that might delay the confession of the Abraham story long enough for me to get the Book to Ethan.

"Gramma, do you remember the deal you made with Ridley the first time she went to a party?"

She looked at me blankly. "I'm not sure I do."

"You told her not to get in a car with anyone who had been drinking."

"Certainly good advice, but I'm not sure how it relates to this situation."

"You told Rid that if she called and said her ride was drinking, you would send someone to pick her up, no questions asked." I saw a hint of recognition pass across her face. "You said she wouldn't get in trouble, no matter where she was or what she did."

Ridley leaned against the column awkwardly. "Yeah. It was like a Get Out of Jail Free card. I definitely needed one of those recently."

"Is this conversation going to explain why you two are in possession of the most dangerous book in the Caster or Mortal world?" Gramma looked skeptically from my cousin to me.

"I'm calling to tell you my ride has been drinking," I blurted out.

"Pardon me?"

"I need you to trust me and do something without asking any questions. Something for Ethan."

"Lena, Ethan is—"

I held up my hand. "Don't say it. We both know people can communicate from the other side. Ethan sent me a message. And I need your help."

"She's telling the truth. At least she thinks she is, for what it's worth." Reece was standing in the darkened doorway to the dining room. I hadn't even seen her, but she had obviously seen me. It only took a Sybil one look at your face to read it,

322

and Reece was among the best. Finally, it was working to my advantage.

"Even if you are telling the truth, you are asking for more than just a little faith. And no matter how much I love you, I can't help you use—"

"We aren't trying to use *The Book of Moons*." I wondered if she would believe me. "We're trying to send it to Ethan."

The room was silent, and I waited for her to say something. "What would lead you to believe that's possible?"

I explained the messages Ethan had been leaving in the crosswords, but I left out the part about how we actually got our hands on *The Book of Moons*, invoking the "my ride is drunk" clause. I wouldn't get away with it forever. Eventually, Gramma would insist on an explanation. But I didn't need forever—just tonight. After we sent the Book to Ethan, Gramma could interrogate me all she wanted.

Besides, Uncle M already had first dibs on the grounding.

She listened carefully, sipping from a black porcelain tea cup that appeared in her hand, compliments of Kitchen. She didn't offer a single word, and she didn't look away from me as I spoke.

Finally, the cup found its way back into the saucer, and I knew she had made a decision. My grandmother drew a deep breath. "If Ethan needs our assistance, we have no choice but to give it to him. After what he sacrificed for us all, it's the least we can do."

"Gramma!" Reece threw up her hands. "Listen to yourself!"

"How can she, when you're yelling?" Ridley snapped.

Reece ignored her. "You're really going to send the most powerful book in the Caster universe into the Otherworld, with no way of knowing who'll be on the other end?"

Rid shrugged. "At least you won't be there."

Reece looked like she wanted to stab Ridley with garden shears of her own.

"Ethan will be there," I argued.

Gramma hesitated, a new thought shaking her resolve. "It's not as if we are shipping a package, Lena. What if the Book doesn't end up where we intend?"

Reece looked satisfied. Ridley looked like now she was the one thinking about garden shears.

"Amma's going to call the Greats."

Gramma finished her tea, and the cup vanished. "Well, if Amarie is involved, I'm sure she has a plan. I'll get my coat."

"Wait." I looked over at Reece. "We need everyone to come. Amma says we won't have enough power unless we do this together."

Reece looked at Uncle Macon, who had sidled into the room at the first sign of the Caster family fighting. "Are you going to let her do this?"

He chose his words carefully. "On the one hand, I think this is a very bad idea."

"There." Reece smiled.

"What?" Losing my uncle's support was the one thing I had been afraid of when Amma sent me for reinforcements.

"Let him finish, girls." Gramma raised her voice.

"But," Uncle M continued, "we owe Ethan a debt we will never be able to properly repay. I watched him give his life for us, and I don't take that lightly."

I exhaled. *Thank goodness.*

"Uncle Macon—" Reece started.

He silenced her with a gesture. "This isn't up for discussion. If it weren't for Ethan, you could be powerless right now—or worse. The Order was broken, and we were only beginning to see the effects. Things were headed in a very grave direction indeed. I promise you that."

"I don't know why we're still talking about it, then." Gramma gathered her skirt and ascended the stairs. "I'll get Del, Barclay, and Ryan."

Ridley swallowed hard at the sound of her mother's name. Aunt Del was always heartsick when Ridley disappeared, and she had no idea her daughter was back. Or that she had returned as a Dark Caster.

I remembered how happy Aunt Del looked when Ridley lost her powers last summer. Being a Mortal was better than being Dark, especially in this family.

Reece turned to face her sister. "You shouldn't be here. Haven't you put everyone through enough pain?"

Ridley stiffened. "I thought you deserved a little more, Sis. Wouldn't want to leave you hanging. I mean, seeing how you've always been there for me." She said it sarcastically, but I could hear the pain. Ridley only pretended she didn't have a heart.

I heard voices, and Aunt Del appeared at the top of the staircase. Uncle Barclay's arm was wrapped tightly around her. I wasn't sure if she'd overheard us or if Gramma told her about Ridley. But I could tell by the way Aunt Del was wringing her hands that she already knew the truth.

Uncle Barclay led her down the stairs, his tall frame looming over her. His salt-and-pepper hair was combed neatly, and for once he looked like he belonged in the same era as the rest of us. Ryan trailed behind them, her long blond hair swinging in a ponytail.

When Ryan and Ridley were standing in the same room, it was impossible to ignore how much they resembled each other. In the last six months, Ryan had come to look more like a teenager than a little girl, even though she was only twelve.

Aunt Del smiled at Rid weakly. "I'm glad you're all right. I was so worried."

Ridley bit her lip and teetered on her stacked heels. "I'm sorry, you know. I couldn't exactly call."

"Abraham had Rid locked up." I blurted it out before I could stop myself. Ridley was guilty of lots of things, but it was hard to watch them judge her for something that was out of her control.

Aunt Del's face crumpled—everyone's did, except for

Reece's. She positioned herself protectively between her mother and her Dark sister.

"Is that true?" Uncle Barclay sounded genuinely concerned.

Ridley twisted a pink strand between her fingers nervously. "Yeah. He was a real prince." She Kelted to me desperately. *Don't tell them, Cuz. Not now.* "I'm fine," Ridley went on, waving off her father's concern. "Let's worry about Ethan. No one wants to hear about me and the Big Bad Wolf."

Ryan stepped closer to Ridley tentatively. "I do," she said quietly.

Rid didn't respond. Instead, she held out her empty hand.

I waited for a mouse or a lollipop to appear in her palm, some cheap trick to distract her sister from what she was now. But her hand stayed empty.

Ryan smiled and reached out her own hand, closing it around Ridley's.

I heard Aunt Del's breath catch, or maybe it was mine.

"If Lena trusts you, so do I," Ryan said. She looked at Reece. "Sisters should trust each other."

Reece didn't move, but I didn't need to be a Sybil to read her face.

Tiny cracks were already forming in the tough exterior Reece worked so hard to maintain. They were hard to see, but they were there. The beginning of something—tears, forgiveness, regret—I couldn't be sure.

It reminded me of something Marian told Ethan before everything happened. It was one of her famous quotes, by a guy named Leonard Cohen: "There is a crack in everything. That's how the light gets in."

That's what I thought of when I saw Reece's face.

The light was finally getting in.

"Lena, are you all right?" Uncle Barclay glanced at the ceiling. The crystal chandelier was swinging dangerously above us.

I took a deep breath, and it stopped immediately. *Get control of yourself.*

"I'm fine," I lied.

I composed the words in my head, even if I wouldn't let my pen write them.

> *bent*
> *like the branches of a tree*
> *broken*
> *like the pieces of my heart*
> *cracked*
> *like the seventeenth moon*
> *shattered*
> *like the glass in the window*
> *the day we met*

I closed my eyes, trying to silence the words that wouldn't stop coming.

No.

I ignored them, forcing them out of my mind. I wasn't Kelting them to Uncle Macon, and I wasn't writing a word until Ethan came back.

Not a single word.

"Amarie is expecting us. We should go." Uncle Macon slipped on his black cashmere coat. "She is not a woman who appreciates being kept waiting."

Boo lumbered behind him, his thick fur blending seamlessly into the darkness of the room.

Ridley opened the door, fleeing as fast as she could. She unwrapped a red lollipop before she even made it down the steps of the veranda. She hesitated for a second near the flower bed before pocketing the wrapper.

Maybe people could change—even the ones who made the wrong choices, if they tried hard enough to make them right. I wasn't sure, but I hoped so. I had made enough bad choices myself in the last year.

I walked toward the only one that had been right.

The only one that mattered.

Ethan.

I'm coming.

◄ CHAPTER 29 ►

The Hands of the Dead

It's about time." Her arms crossed impatiently, Amma was staring at the opening in the old stone wall when we stepped through.

Uncle Macon was right; she didn't like to be kept waiting.

Marian gently put her hand on Amma's shoulder. "I'm sure it was difficult to round everyone up."

Amma sniffed, ignoring the excuse. "There's difficult, and then there's difficult."

John and Liv were sitting on the ground next to each other, Liv's head resting casually on John's shoulder. Uncle Barclay stepped through after me and helped Aunt Del navigate the broken pieces of the wall. She blinked hard, staring at a spot not far from Genevieve's grave. She swayed, and Uncle Barclay steadied her.

The layers of time were obviously peeling themselves back, the way they did only for Aunt Del.

I wondered what she saw. So much had happened at Greenbrier. Ethan Carter Wate's death, the first time Genevieve used *The Book of Moons* to bring him back, the day Ethan and I found her locket and had the vision, and the night Aunt Del used her powers to show us those pieces of Genevieve's past in this very spot.

But everything had changed since then. The day Ethan and I were trying to figure out how to repair the Order and I accidentally burned the grass beneath us.

When I watched my mother burn to death.

Can Aunt Del see all of it? Can she see that?

An unexpected feeling of shame washed over me, and I secretly hoped she couldn't.

Amma nodded at Gramma. "Emmaline. You're lookin' well."

Gramma smiled. "As are you, Amarie."

Uncle Macon was the last one to enter the lost garden. He lingered near the wall, an uncharacteristic and almost imperceptible unease about him.

Amma locked eyes with him, as if they were having a conversation that only they could hear.

The tension was impossible to ignore. I hadn't seen them together since the night we lost Ethan. And both of them claimed everything was *fine*.

But now that they were standing only feet apart, it was clear nothing was fine. Actually, Amma looked like she wanted to tear my uncle's head off.

"Amarie," he said slowly, bowing his head respectfully.

"I'm surprised you showed up. Aren't you worried some a my wickedness might stain those fancy shoes a yours?" she said. "Wouldn't want that. Not when your party shoes cost such a pretty penny."

What is she talking about?

Amma was a saint—at least that's how I'd always thought of her.

Gramma and Aunt Del exchanged glances, looking equally confused. Marian turned away. She knew something, but she wasn't saying.

"Grief makes people desperate," Uncle M responded. "If anyone understands that, I do."

Amma turned her back on him, facing the whiskey and shot glass lying on the ground next to *The Book of Moons*. "I'm not sure you understand anything that doesn't suit your purpose, Melchizedek. If I didn't think we'd need your help, I would send you packin' straight back to your house."

"That's hardly fair. I was trying to protect you—" Uncle Macon stopped when he noticed we were all staring. All of us except Marian and John, who were doing everything they could not to look at Amma or my uncle. That pretty much meant looking at the mud on the ground or *The Book of Moons*, neither of which was going to make anyone any less uncomfortable.

Amma spun back around to face Uncle Macon. "Next time, try protectin' me a little less and my boy a little more. If there is a next time."

Did she blame Uncle Macon for not doing a better job of protecting Ethan when he was alive? It didn't make any sense....

"Why are you two fighting like this?" I demanded. "You're acting like Reece and Ridley."

"Hey," said Reece. Rid just shrugged.

I shot Amma and my uncle a look. "I thought we were here to help Ethan."

Amma sniffed, and my uncle looked unhappy, but neither of them said a word.

Marian finally spoke up. "I think we're all worried. It would probably be best if we put everything else aside and focused on the issue at hand. Amma, what is it you need us to do?"

Amma didn't take her eyes off my uncle. "Need the Casters to form a circle around me. Mortals can spread out between 'em. We need the power a this world to hand that evil thing off to the ones who can take it the rest a the way."

"The Greats, right?" I hoped so.

She nodded. "If they answer."

If they answered? Was there a chance they wouldn't?

Amma pointed to the ground at my feet. "Lena, I need you to bring me the Book."

I lifted the dusty leather volume and felt the power pulsing through it like a heartbeat.

"The Book's not gonna want to go," Amma explained. "It wants to stay here, where it can cause trouble. Like your cousin there." Ridley rolled her eyes, but Amma only looked at me. "I'll call the Greats, but you need to keep a hand on it till they take it."

What was it going to do? Fly away?

"Everyone else, make that circle. Hold hands nice and tight."

After Ridley and Link bickered about holding hands, and Reece refused to hold hands with Ridley or John, they finally completed the circle.

Amma glanced over at me. "The Greats haven't been exactly happy with me. They may not come. And if they do, I can't promise they'll take the Book."

I couldn't imagine the Greats being upset with Amma. They were her family, and they had come to our rescue more than once.

We just needed them to do it one more time.

"I need the Casters to concentrate everything you got inside the circle." Amma bent down and filled the shot glass with Wild Turkey. She drank the shot and then refilled it for Uncle Abner. "I don't care what happens—you send the power my way."

"What if you get hurt?" Liv asked, concerned.

Amma stared back at Liv, her expression twisted and broken. "Can't get any more hurt than I am already. You just hold on."

Uncle Macon stepped forward, dropping Aunt Del's hand. "Would it help if I assisted you?" he asked Amma.

She pointed a shaky finger at him. "You get outta my circle. You can do your part from there."

I felt a surge of heat from the Book, as if its anger flared to meet Amma's.

Uncle Macon stepped back and joined hands with everyone else. "One day you will forgive me, Amarie."

Her dark eyes narrowed to meet his green ones. "Not today."

Amma closed her eyes, and my hair began to curl involuntarily as she spoke the words only she could.

"Blood a my blood,
and roots a my soul,
I'm in need a your intercession."

The wind began to whip around me within the circle, and lightning cracked overhead. I felt the heat of the Book joining with the heat of my hands, the heat I could command—to burn and destroy.

Amma didn't stop, as if she was talking to the sky.

"I call you to carry what I cannot.
To see what I cannot.
To do what I cannot."

A green glow surged from Uncle Macon's hands and spread around the circle from one hand to the next. Gramma closed her eyes, as if she was trying to channel Macon's power. John noticed and closed his eyes, too, and the light intensified.

Lightning tore across the sky, but the universe didn't open up, and the Greats didn't appear.

Where are you? I pleaded silently.

Amma tried again.

"This is the crossroads I can't cross.
Only you can take this book to my boy.
Deliver it to your world from ours."

I concentrated harder, ignoring the heat of the Book in my hands. I heard a branch break, then another. I opened my eyes, and a burst of flames sprang up outside the circle. It caught like someone had lit the wick on a stick of dynamite, tearing through the grass and creating another circle outside the first.

The Wake of Fire—the uncontrollable flames that ignited sometimes against my will. The garden was burning again because of me. How many times could this earth char before the damage was irreparable?

Amma squeezed her eyes tighter. This time she spoke the words plainly. They weren't a chant but a plea. "I know you don't wanna come for me. So come for Ethan. He's waitin' on you, and you're as much his family as you are mine. Do the right thing. One last time. Uncle Abner. Aunt Delilah. Aunt Ivy. Grandmamma Sulla. Twyla. Please."

The sky opened up, and rain poured down from the heavens. But the fire still raged, and the Caster light still glowed.

I saw something small and black circling above us.

The crow.

Ethan's crow.

Amma opened her eyes and saw it, too. "That's right, Uncle Abner. Don't punish Ethan for my mistakes. I know you been lookin' after him over there, the same way you've always looked after us down here. He needs this book. Maybe you know why, even if I don't."

The crow circled closer and closer, and the faces began to appear in the dark sky, one by one—their features carving themselves out of the universe above us.

Uncle Abner appeared first, his lined face creased by time.

The crow landed on his shoulder like a tiny mouse at the feet of a giant.

Sulla the Prophet was next, regal braids cascading over her shoulder. Strands of tangled beads rested against her chest as if they weighed nothing. Or were worth the weight.

The Book of Moons bucked in my hands, as if trying to pull free. But I knew it wasn't the Greats reaching for it.

The Book was resisting.

I tightened my grip as Aunt Delilah and Aunt Ivy appeared simultaneously, holding hands and looking down like they were evaluating the scene. Our intentions or our abilities—it was impossible to know.

But they were judging us nonetheless. I could feel it, and

the Book could, too. It tried to pull free again, singeing the skin on my palms.

"Don't let go!" Amma warned.

"I won't," I called over the wind. "Aunt Twyla, where are you?"

Aunt Twyla's dark eyes appeared before her gentle face and arms laden with bracelets. Before her braided hair knotted with charms, or the rows of earrings that marched down her ears.

"Ethan needs this!" I shouted over the wind and the rain and the fire.

The Greats stared down at us, but they didn't react.

The Book of Moons did.

I felt the pulse beating within it, the power and rage spreading through my body like poison.

Don't let go.

Images flashed in front of my eyes.

Genevieve holding the Book, speaking the words that would bring Ethan Carter Wate back for a split second—and curse our family for generations.

Amma and me speaking the same words, standing over Ethan Lawson Wate—our Ethan.

His eyes opening and Uncle Macon's closing.

Abraham standing over the Book as the fire threatened Ravenwood in the distance, his brother's voice begging him to stop, right before he killed Jonah.

I could see it all.

All the people this book had touched and hurt.

The people I knew and the ones I didn't recognize.

I could feel it pulling away from me again, and I screamed louder this time.

Amma grabbed the Book, her hands over mine. Where parts of her skin were touching the leather, I could feel her skin burning.

Tears formed in her eyes, but she didn't let go.

"Help us," I screamed into the sky.

It wasn't the sky that answered.

Genevieve Duchannes materialized in the darkness, her hazy form close enough to touch.

Give it to me.

Amma could see her; it was obvious from her haunted expression. But I was the only one who could hear her Kelting.

Her long red hair blew in the wind, in a way that seemed both impossible and right at the same time.

I'll take it. It doesn't belong in this world. It never did.

I wanted to hand her the Book—to send it to Ethan and to stop Amma's hands from burning.

But Genevieve was a Dark Caster. I only had to look at her yellow eyes to remember.

Amma was trembling.

Genevieve reached out her hand. What if I made the wrong choice? Ethan would never get the Book, and I would never see him again....

How do I know I can trust you?

Genevieve's heartbroken eyes stared back at me.

You'll only know if you do.

The Greats looked down at us, and there was no way to know if they were going to help. Amma's Mortal hands were burning alongside my Caster ones, and *The Book of Moons* was no closer to Ethan than when it was in Abraham Raven-wood's hands, not long ago.

Sometimes there's only one choice.

Sometimes you just have to jump.

Or let go...

Take it, Genevieve.

I pulled my hands away, and Amma's moved with mine. The Book jerked free as if it sensed its only chance at escape. It lurched toward the outer circle, where John and Link were holding hands.

The glowing green light was still in place, and John concentrated his gaze on the Book. "I don't think so."

It hit the light and ricocheted back into the center of the circle and Genevieve's waiting hands. She closed her hazy palms around it, and the Book seemed to shudder.

Not this time.

I held my breath, listening to Amma cry.

Genevieve pressed the Book against her chest and dematerialized.

My heart dropped. "Amma! She took it!" I couldn't think or feel or breathe. I had made the wrong choice. I would never see Ethan again. My knees gave out, and I felt myself falling.

I heard a rip, and an arm caught me around the waist.

"Lena, look." It was Link.

I blinked back the tears and looked at him, his free hand pointing at the sky.

Genevieve was there in the darkness, her red hair trailing behind her. She held *The Book of Moons* out to Sulla, who took it from her hands.

Genevieve smiled at me.

You can trust me. I'm sorry. I'm so sorry.

She disappeared, leaving the Greats looming in the sky behind her like giants.

Amma held her burnt hands to her chest and stared up at her family from another world. The world where Ethan was trapped. Tears ran down her cheeks as the green glow died around us.

"You take that book to my boy, ya hear?"

Uncle Abner tipped his hat to her. "Be expectin' a pie now, Amma. One a those lemon meringues will do me just fine."

Amma choked back a final sob as her legs gave out from under her.

I dropped with her, breaking her fall. I watched as the rain drowned out the fire and the Greats disappeared. I had no way of knowing what was going to happen next. There was only one thing I knew for sure.

Ethan had a chance now.

The rest was up to him.

BOOK THREE

Ethan

⚜ CHAPTER 30 ⚜

Lost Time

L. Are you there? Can you hear me? I'm waiting. I know you'll find the Book soon.

You wouldn't believe this place. I feel like I'm living in a ten-thousand-year-old temple, or maybe a fortress. You wouldn't believe this guy either. My friend Xavier. At least I think he's my friend. He's like a ten-thousand-year-old monk. Or maybe some kind of ancient temple wombat.

Do you know what waiting feels like in a world where no time passes? Minutes feel like centuries—eternities—only worse, because you can't even tell which is which.

I find myself counting things. Compulsively. It's the only way I know how to mark the time.

Sixty-two plastic buttons. Eleven broken strands of between fourteen and thirty-six pearls each. One hundred and nine old baseball cards. Nine AA batteries. Twelve thousand seven hundred and fifty-four dollars and three cents in coins, from six countries. Or maybe just six centuries.

More or less.

I didn't know how to count the doubloons.

This morning I counted grains of rice falling through the split seam of a stuffed frog. I don't know where Xavier finds this stuff. I made it to nine hundred ninety-nine, and then I lost my place and had to start over again.

That was how I spent today.

Like I said, a person could go crazy trying to pass the time in a place with no time. When you find The Book of Moons, *L, I'll know. I'll be out of here the second I can. I keep my stuff ready to go, by the mouth of the cave. Aunt Prue's map. An empty flask of whiskey and a tobacco tin.*

Don't ask.

Can you believe, after everything, that the Book is still coming between us? I know you're going to find it. One day. You will.

And I'll be waiting.

I'm not sure if thinking about Lena makes the time pass faster or slower. But it doesn't matter. I couldn't stop thinking about her if I tried. Which I have—playing chess with these creepy figures Xavier collects. Helping him catalog everything from bottle caps and marbles to ancient Caster volumes. Today it's stones. Xavier must have hundreds of them, ranging from raw diamonds as big as strawberries to chunks of quartz and plain old rocks.

"It's important to keep careful records of everything I have." Xavier added three hunks of coal to the list.

I stared at the rocks in front of me. Gravel, Amma would say. Just the right shade of gray for Dean Wilks' driveway. I wondered what Amma was doing right now. And my mom. The two women who raised me were in two totally different worlds, and I couldn't see either of them.

I held up a handful of dusty driveway gravel. "Why do you collect these, anyway? They're just rocks."

Xavier looked shocked. "Stones have power. They absorb people's feelings and their fears. Even their memories."

I didn't need anyone else's fears. I had enough of my own.

I reached into my pocket and took out the black stone. I rubbed the smooth surface between my fingers. This one was Sulla's. It was shaped like a thick teardrop, while Lena's was rounder.

"Here." I held it out to Xavier. "You can add it to your collection."

I was pretty sure I wouldn't need it to cross the river again. I would either find my way back home or I would never leave here. Somehow I knew that, even if I didn't know anything else.

Xavier stared at the stone for a long minute. "You keep it, dead man. Those aren't—"

After that, I couldn't make out what he was saying. My vision started to blur, Xavier's leathery black skin and the stone in my palm shifting until they started to bleed together into a single dark shadow.

Sulla sat at an old wicker table, an oil lamp illuminating the small room. A spread was laid out in front of her, the Cards of Providence lined up in two neat rows, each stamped with a black sparrow in the corner—Sulla's mark. A tall man sat across from her, his smooth head gleaming in the light.

"The Bleeding Blade. Blind Man's Rage. Liar's Promise. The Stolen Heart." She frowned and shook her head. "Can tell you, none a this is good. What you're chasin', you ain't never gonna find. And it'll be worse if you do."

The man ran his huge hands over his scalp nervously. "What's that supposed to mean, Sulla? Stop talking in circles."

"It means they're never gonna give you what you want, Angelus. The Far Keep doesn't need a spread to know you've been breakin' their rules all along."

Angelus pushed away from the table violently. "I don't need them to give me what I want. I have other Keepers behind me. Keepers who want to be more than scribes. Why should we be forced to record history when we can be the ones who make it!"

"Can't change the cards—that's all I know."

Angelus stared at the beautiful woman with the golden skin and delicate braids. "Words can change things, Seer. You just have to put them in the right book."

Something caught Sulla's eye, and she was distracted for a moment. Her granddaughter crouched behind the door, listening. On any other night, Sulla wouldn't have minded. Amarie was seventeen, older than Sulla was when she learned to read cards. Sulla didn't want the girl to see this man. There was something evil inside him. She didn't need the cards to see that much.

Angelus started to stand, his huge hands clenched into fists.

Sulla tapped a card at the top of the spread, with a pair of golden gates inked across the face. "This one here's a wild card."

The man hesitated. "What does it mean?"

"Means sometimes we make our own fate. Things the cards can't see. Depends on which side a the gate you choose."

Angelus picked up the card, crumpling it in his hand. "I've stood outside the gates long enough."

The door slammed, and Amarie stepped out from her hiding place. "Who was that, Grandmamma?"

The older woman picked up the crumpled card, smoothing it with her hands. "He's a Keeper from up north. A man who wants more than any man should have."

"What does he want?"

Sulla's eyes met Amarie's, and for a second she was not sure if she would answer the girl. "To tamper with fate. Change the cards."

"But you can't change the cards."

Sulla looked away, remembering what she'd seen in the cards the day Amarie was born. "Sometimes you can. But there's always a price."

When I opened my eyes, Xavier was standing above me, his features twisted in concern. "What did you see, dead man?"

The black stone was warm in my hand. I squeezed it tighter, as if it could somehow bring me closer to Amma. To the memories locked within its shiny black surface. "How many times has Angelus changed *The Caster Chronicles*, Xavier?"

The Gatekeeper looked away, wringing his long fingers nervously.

"Xavier, answer me."

Our eyes met, and I saw the pain in his. "Too many times."

"Why is he doing it?" What did Angelus have to gain?

"Some men want to be more than Mortal. Angelus is one of those men."

"Are you saying he wanted to be a Caster?"

Xavier nodded slowly. "He wanted to change fate. To find a way to defy supernatural law and mix Mortal and Caster blood."

Genetic engineering. "So he wanted Mortals to have powers like Casters?"

Xavier ran his abnormally long hand over his bald head. "There is no reason to have power if you are left with no one to torment and control."

It didn't make sense. It was too late for Angelus. Was he, like Abraham Ravenwood, trying to create some kind of hybrid child? "Was he experimenting on children?"

Xavier turned away, and for a long moment he was silent. "He experimented on himself using Dark Casters."

A chill ran up my spine, and I couldn't swallow. I couldn't imagine what the Keeper must have done to them. I was trying to find the right words to ask, but Xavier told me before I had a chance.

"Angelus tested their blood, tissue—I don't know what else. And he injected a serum made from their blood into his own. It didn't give him the power he wanted. But he kept trying. Each injection made him paler and more desperate."

"That sounds horrible."

He turned his deformed face back toward mine. "That was not the horrible part, dead man. That would come later."

I didn't want to ask, but I couldn't stop myself. "What happened?"

"Eventually, he found a Caster whose blood gave him a mutated version of his own power. She was Light and beautiful and kind. And I…" He hesitated.

"Did you love her?"

His features looked more human than ever before. "I did. And Angelus destroyed her."

"I'm so sorry, Xavier."

He nodded. "She was a powerful Telepath before she went mad from Angelus' experiments."

A mind reader. Suddenly I understood.

"Are you saying Angelus can read minds?"

"Only Mortal ones."

Only Mortal ones. Like mine and Liv's and Marian's.

I needed to find my page in *The Caster Chronicles* and get back home.

"Don't look so sad, dead man."

I watched the hands on Xavier's clocks turn in different directions, marking the passage of time that didn't exist here. I didn't want to tell him that I wasn't sad.

I was afraid.

I kept my eyes on those clocks, but I still couldn't keep track of the time. Sometimes it got so bad that I started to forget what I was waiting for in the first place. Too much time will do that to you. Blur the edges between your memories and your imagination until everything feels like something you saw in a movie instead of your life.

I was beginning to give up on ever seeing *The Book of Moons* again. Which meant giving up on a whole lot more than some old Caster book.

It meant giving up on Gatlin, the good and the bad of it. Giving up on Amma and my dad and Aunt Marian. Link and Liv and John. Jackson High and the Dar-ee Keen and Wate's Landing and Route 9. The place where I first realized Lena was the girl from my dreams.

Giving up on the Book meant giving up on her.

I couldn't do that.

I wouldn't.

After what had to be a few days or a few weeks—it was impossible to know—Xavier realized I was losing more than time.

He was sitting on the dirt floor inside the cave, cataloging what looked like thousands of keys. "What did she look like?"

"Who?" I asked.

"The girl."

I watched him sort the keys by size, then shape. I wondered where they came from, whose doors they opened, as I searched for the right words. "She was...alive."

"Was she beautiful?"

Was she? It was getting harder to remember.

"Yeah. I think so."

Xavier stopped sorting the keys, watching me. "What did she look like, the girl?"

How could I tell him everything was swirling in my mind, blending together in a way that made it impossible to picture her clearly?

"Ethan? Did you hear me? You have to tell me. Otherwise you will forget. That's what happens if you spend too much time here. You'll lose everything that made you who you were. This place takes it from you."

I turned away before I answered. "I'm not sure. It's all a blur."

"Was her hair gold?" Xavier loved gold.

"No," I said. I was pretty sure, though I couldn't remember why. I stared at the wall in front of me, trying to picture her face. Then a single thought came to me, and I opened my eyes. "There were curls. Lots and lots of curls."

"The girl?"

"Yes." I looked at the rocky outcroppings at the top of the cave. "Lena."

"Her name is Lena?"

I nodded as tears began to stream down my face. I was so relieved I could still remember her name.

Hurry, Lena. I don't have much time left.

———

By the time I saw the crow again, I had forgotten. My memories were like dreams, except I never slept. I watched Xavier. I counted buttons and cataloged coins. I stared at the sky.

That's what I was trying to do now, but the stupid bird kept shrieking and flapping its enormous wings.

"Go away."

He shrieked even louder.

I rolled onto my side and swatted at him. That's when I saw the Book lying in the dirt in front of me.

"Xavier," I said, my voice unsteady. "Come here."

"What is it, dead man?" I heard him call from the cave.

"*The Book of Moons.*" I picked it up, and it was warm in my hands. But my hands didn't burn. I remembered thinking they should.

As I held the Book, my memories came flooding back to me. Just as this book had brought me back from the dead once before, so now was it bringing my life back to me again. I could picture every detail. The places I'd been. The things I'd done. The people I loved.

I could see Lena's delicate face. Her green and gold eyes and the crescent-shaped birthmark on her cheek. I remembered lemons and rosemary and hurricane-force winds and sponta-neous combustion. Everything that made Lena the girl I loved.

I was whole again.

And I knew I had to leave this place before it claimed me forever.

I picked up the Book in both hands and carried it into the cave. It was time to make a trade.

———

With every step, the Book was heavy in my hands. It didn't slow me down, though. Nothing could, not now.

Not until there were no more steps to take.

The Gates of the Far Keep rose before me, straight and tall. Now I understood why Xavier was so obsessed with gold. The Gates were a filthy blackish brown, but underneath I could see the gold fighting through. They rose in forbidding spires. They didn't seem to lead anywhere a person would want to go.

"They look so evil."

Xavier followed my eyes to the tips of the spires. "They are what they are. Power is neither good nor evil."

"Maybe that's true, but this place is evil."

"Ethan. You are a strong Mortal. You have more life in you than any dead man I've met." Somehow, that wasn't a comfort. "I cannot open the Gates if you do not truly wish to go." The words sounded ominous.

"I have to go. I have to get back to Lena, and Amma, and

Link. And my dad, and Marian, and Liv, and everybody." I saw their faces, every one of them. I felt surrounded by them, by their spirits, and by mine. I remembered what it was to live among them, my friends.

I remembered what it was to live.

"Lena. The girl with the golden curls?" Xavier sounded curious.

There was no point trying to explain, not to him. I just nodded—it seemed easier.

"And you love her?" He looked even more curious about that.

"Yes." There was no doubt. "I love her beyond the universe and back. I love her from this world to the next."

He blinked, expressionless. "Well. That's very serious."

I almost felt like smiling. "Yeah. I tried to tell you. It's like that."

He stared at me for a long moment, finally nodding. "All right. Follow me." Then he disappeared up the dusty pathway in front of me.

I followed him as the path twisted into an impossibly rocky staircase. We climbed until we reached a narrow cliff that dropped away into what seemed like oblivion. When I tried to look over the edge of the rock, all I could see were clouds and darkness.

In front of me were the imposing black Gates. I couldn't see anything beyond them. But I could hear terrible sounds—chains rattling, voices wailing and crying.

"It sounds like Hell."

He shook his head. "Not Hell. Only the Far Keep."

Xavier moved in front of me, blocking my path to the Gates. "Are you sure you want to do this, dead man?"

I nodded, keeping my eyes on his disfigured face.

"Human boy. The one called Ethan. My friend." His eyes went pale and glassy, as if he was going into some kind of trance.

"What is it, Xavier?" I was impatient, but more than that I was terrified. And the longer we stood outside listening to the terrible sounds of whatever was going on inside, the worse it seemed to get. I was afraid of losing my nerve—of giving up and turning back—of wasting everything Lena had gone through to get *The Book of Moons* to me.

He ignored me. "You propose a trade, dead man? What do you offer me if I open the Gates? How do you propose to pay your way for entrance into the Far Keep?"

I just stood there.

He opened one eye, hissing at me. "The Book. Give me the Book."

I gave it to him, but I couldn't move my hands away. It was like the Book and I were one thing, yet somehow connected to Xavier as well.

"What the—"

"I accept this offering, and in return I open the Gates of the Far Keep." Xavier's body went limp, and he collapsed in a heap around the Book.

"Are you okay, Xavier?"

"Shh." The sound coming from the heap of robes was the only thing that told me he was still alive.

I heard another sound, like rocks falling or cars crashing, but really it was just the enormous Gates opening. It seemed like they hadn't been opened in a thousand years. I watched the black walls give way to the world inside.

As a rush of relief and exhaustion and adrenaline made my heart race, one thought kept running through my mind.

It has to be over soon.

This had to be the hardest part. I paid the Ferryman. I crossed the river. I got the Book. I made the trade.

I made it to the Far Keep. I'm almost home. I'm coming, L.

I could picture her face. Imagined seeing her and holding her in my arms again.

It wouldn't be long.

At least that's what I thought as I walked through the Gates.

⊰ CHAPTER 31 ⊱

Keepers of Secrets

I don't remember what I saw when I walked into the Far Keep. What I remember are the feelings. The pure terror. The way my eyes couldn't find anything—not one familiar thing— to rest on. Nothing they could understand. I was prepared in no way, by any world I'd ever encountered, for the one I was encountering now.

This place was cold and evil, like Sauron's tower in *The Lord of the Rings*. I had that same feeling of being watched, the feeling that some sort of universal eye could see what I was seeing, could sense the innermost terrors of my heart and exploit them.

As I stepped away from the Gates, tall walls loomed on

either side of me. They extended toward an overlook, where I could see the greater part of a city. It was as if I was looking into a valley from a high mountaintop. Beneath me, the city extended toward the horizon in a great recess of structures. As I looked more closely, I realized it didn't resemble a regular city.

It was a labyrinth, a massive, interlocking puzzle of paths carved from cut hedges. It threaded through the whole of the city between me and the golden building that rose steeply toward the horizon ahead.

The building I needed to reach.

"Have you come here to face the labyrinth? Are you here for the games?" I heard a voice behind me, and I turned to see an unnaturally pale man, like the Keepers who had appeared in the Gatlin Library before Marian's trial. He had the opaque eyes and prismatic glasses I had come to associate with the Far Keep.

Over his thin frame hung a black robe like the ones the Council members had worn when they sentenced Marian—or whatever they had planned to do, before Macon, John, and Liv stopped them.

Those were the bravest people I knew. I couldn't let them down now.

Not Lena. Not any of them.

"I'm here for the library," I answered. "Can you show me the way?"

"That's what I said. The games?" He pointed to a braid of

gold rope around his shoulder. "I'm an officer. I'm here to make sure all who enter the Keep find their way."

"Huh?"

"You want to gain entrance to the Great Keep. Is that your desire?"

"That's right."

"Then you're here for the games." The pale man pointed at the overgrown green maze below us. "If you survive the labyrinth, you'll end up there." He moved his finger until he was pointing at the gold towers. "The Great Keep."

I didn't want to find my way through a labyrinth. Everything about the Otherworld felt like one gigantic maze, and all I wanted to do was find my way out.

"I don't think you understand. Isn't there some kind of door? A place where I can walk inside without having to play any games?" I didn't have time for this. I needed to find *The Caster Chronicles* and get out. Get home.

Come on.

He slapped his hand against my arm, and I struggled to stay standing. The man was incredibly strong—Link and John strong. "It would be too easy if you could walk into the Great Keep. What would be the point of that?"

I tried to hide my frustration. "I don't know? How about to get inside?"

He frowned. "Where have you come from?"

"The Otherworld."

"Dead man, listen well. The Great Keep is not like the

Otherworld. The Great Keep has many names. To the Norse it is Valhalla, Hall of the Lords. To the Greeks it is Olympus. There are as many names as there are men who would speak them."

"Okay. I'm down with all that. I just want to find my way inside this one library. If I could just find someone to talk to—"

"There is but one way into the Great Keep," he said. "The Warrior's Way."

I sighed. "So there's no other way? Like, a doorway? Maybe even a Warrior's Doorway?"

He shook his head. "There are no doors to the Great Keep."

Of course there weren't.

"Yeah? What about a stairway?" I asked. The pale man shook his head again. "Or maybe an alley?"

He was finished with this conversation. "There is only one way in, an honorable death. And there is only one way out."

"You mean I can be more dead than this?"

He smiled politely.

I tried again. "What's that, exactly? An honorable death?"

"You face the labyrinth. It does what it will with you. You accept your fate."

"And? What's the one way out?"

He shrugged. "No one leaves unless we choose to let them leave."

Great.

"Thanks, I guess." What else was there to say?

"Good luck, dead man. May you fight in peace."

I nodded. "Yeah, sure. I hope so."

The strange Keeper, if that's what he was, went back to guarding his post.

I stared down at the massive labyrinth, wondering once again what I'd gotten myself into and how I could possibly get myself out.

They shouldn't call death passing on. They should call it leveling up.

Because the game only got harder once I lost. And I was more than a little worried it had only just begun.

I couldn't put it off any longer. The only way to get through this whole labyrinth thing, like most other crappy things, was to just get through it.

I would have to find a path the hard way.

The Warrior's Way, or whatever.

And fight in peace? What was that about?

My guard was up as I stumbled my way down a staircase cut out of rock. I moved deeper into the valley below, and the stairs widened into layers of steep cliffs, where green moss grew between the rocks, and ivy clung to the walls. When I reached the base of the walled stairwell, I found myself in an immense garden.

Not just a garden like the ones folks in Gatlin grew their

tomatoes in, out behind their swamp coolers. A garden in the sense of the Garden of Eden—and not Gardens of Eden, the florist over on Main Street.

It looked like a dream. Because the colors were all wrong—they were too bright, and there were too many of them. As I moved closer, I realized where I was.

The labyrinth.

Rows of hedges tangled with so many flowering bushes that they made the gardens of Ravenwood look small and shabby in comparison.

The farther I walked, the less it seemed like walking and the more it felt like bushwhacking. I pulled branches out of my face and kicked my way through the waist-high brambles and brush. Root hog or die. That's what Amma would have said. Keep trying.

It reminded me of the time I tried to walk home from Wader's Creek when I was nine. I had been poking around in Amma's craft room, which wasn't a craft room at all. It was the room where she stored the supplies for her charms. She gave me a piece and a half of her mind, and I told her I was walking home. "I can find my own way"—that's what I told her. But I didn't find my way, or any way. Instead, I wandered deeper and deeper into the swamplands, spooked by the sound of gators' tails thrashing in the water.

I didn't know Amma was following me, until I dropped to my knees and started to cry. She stepped out into the moonlight, hands on her hips. "Guess you shoulda dropped some bread crumbs if you were plannin' to run off." She didn't say anything else, just held out her hand.

"I would've found my way back," I'd said.

She nodded. "I don't doubt it for a minute, Ethan Wate."

But now, yanking dirt and thorns out of my face, I didn't have Amma to come find me. This was something I had to do on my own.

Like plowing the Lilum's field and bringing the water back to Gatlin.

Or taking a dive off the Summerville water tower.

It didn't take long for me to figure out that I was pretty much in the same boat I'd been in that day in the swamp when I was nine. I was walking down the same pathways over and over, unless some other guy was wearing the same size Converse as me. I might as well be lost on the way home from Wader's Creek.

I tried to think.

A maze is just a big puzzle.

I was going about this wrong. I needed to mark the pathways I had already taken. I needed some of Amma's bread crumbs.

I stripped the nearest bush of its leaves, stuffing them in my pockets. I reached out my right hand until it touched the wall of bushes, and I started walking. I kept my right hand on the wall of the maze and used my left to drop the waxy leaves every few feet.

It was like a giant corn maze. Keep the same hand on the

stalks until you dead-end. Then switch hands and go the other way. Anyone who's ever been stuck in a corn maze can tell you that.

I followed the path to the right until it dead-ended. Then I switched hands and bread crumbs. This time I reached out with my left hand, and I used stones instead of leaves.

After what felt like hours of winding my way through this particular puzzle, hitting one dead end after another and stepping over the same rocks and leaves I had used to mark my tracks, I finally reached the very center of the maze, the place where all pathways came to an end. Only the center wasn't an exit. It was a pit, with what looked like enormous mud walls. As thick rolls of white fog spread toward me, I was forced to confront the truth.

The labyrinth wasn't a labyrinth at all.

It was a dead end.

Beyond the fog and dirt, there was nothing but the impenetrable brush.

Keep moving. Keep your bearings.

I walked forward, kicking waves in the dense mist that clung to the ground around me. Just as I made some progress, my foot hit something long and hard. Maybe a stick or a pipe.

I tried to navigate more carefully, but the fog made it hard to see. It was like looking through glasses smeared with Vaseline.

As I moved closer to the center, the white mist began to clear, and I tripped again.

This time I could see what was in the way.

It wasn't a pipe or a stick.

It was a human bone.

Long and thin, it must have been a leg bone, or maybe an arm.

"Holy crap." I yanked on it, and it pulled free, sending a human skull rolling toward my feet. The dirt around me was piled high with bones, as long and bare as the one I was holding in my hand.

I let the bone drop and backed away, stumbling over what I thought was a rock. But it was another skull. The faster I ran, the more I tripped, twisting my ankle in the loops of an old hip bone, catching my Chucks on a piece of spine.

Am I dreaming?

On top of that, I had an overpowering sense of déjà vu. The feeling that I was running toward a place I'd been before. Which didn't make sense, because I had no experience with pits or bones or wandering around being dead, until now.

Still.

It felt like I'd been here, like I'd always been here, and I couldn't get far enough away. Like every path I'd ever taken was here in this maze.

No way out but through it.

I had to keep moving. I had to face this place, this pit full of bones. Wherever it was leading me. Or to who.

Then a dark shadow emerged, and I knew I wasn't alone.

Across the clearing, there was a person sitting on what looked like a box, perched on a gruesome hill of human remains. No—it was a chair. I could see the back rising higher than the rest, the arms jutting wider.

It was a throne.

The figure laughed with impossible confidence as the fog parted to reveal the corpse-ridden waste of the uneven battleground. It didn't matter to the person on the throne.

To her.

Because as the fog rolled back to reveal the center of the pit, I knew immediately who was sitting tall on a hideous throne of bones. Back made of broken backs. Arms made of broken arms. Feet made of broken feet.

The Queen of the Dead and the Damned.

Laughing so hard her black curls slithered through the air, like the snakes on Obidias' hand. My worst nightmare.

Sarafine Duchannes.

CHAPTER 32

Throne of Bones

Her dark cloak flapped in the wind like a shadow. The mist swirled around her black-buckled boots, disappearing into the darkness, as if she could draw it to her. Maybe she could. After all, she was a Cataclyst—the most powerful Caster in two universes.

Or the second most powerful.

Sarafine pushed back her cloak, letting it fall off her shoulders, around her long black curls. My skin went cold.

"Karma's a bitch, wouldn't you say, Mortal Boy?" she called across the pit, her voice confident and strong. Full of energy and evil.

She stretched luxuriously, clasping the arms of the chair in her own bony claws.

"I wouldn't say anything, Sarafine. Not to you." I tried to keep my voice even. I hadn't wanted to see her in one lifetime, let alone two.

Sarafine beckoned with one curving finger. "Is that why you're hiding? Or are you still afraid of me?"

I took a step closer. "I'm not afraid of you."

She cocked her head. "I don't know that I blame you. After all, I did kill you. A knife to the chest, in warm Mortal blood."

"Hard to remember back that far. I guess you weren't that memorable." I folded my arms stubbornly. Trying to hold my ground.

It was no use.

She rolled a ball of mist toward me, and it wrapped around me, closing the gap between us. I felt myself moving forward, powerless, as if she was dragging me by a leash.

So she still had her powers even here.

Good to know.

I stumbled over the ridge of an inhuman skeleton, something twice as big as me, with twice as many arms and legs. I swallowed. More powerful creatures than a guy from Gatlin County had met their fates here. I hoped she wasn't the reason why.

"What are you doing here, Sarafine?" I tried not to sound as intimidated as I was. I dug my feet into the dirt.

Sarafine leaned back in her throne of bones, examining the nails on one of her claws. "Me? Lately I've spent most of my time being dead, like you. Oh, wait—you were there. You watched when my daughter let me burn to death. A real charmer, that one. Teenagers. What are you going to do?"

Sarafine had no right to mention Lena. She'd surrendered that right when she walked away from a burning house with her baby daughter inside. When she tried to kill Lena like she'd killed Lena's father. And me.

I wanted to throw myself at her, but every instinct I had left told me to stay back. "You're nothing, Sarafine. You're a ghost."

She smiled when I said the word "ghost," biting the tip of one of her long black nails. "Something we have in common now."

"We don't have anything in common." I could feel my hands clenching into fists. "You make me sick. Why don't you get out of my sight?"

I didn't know what I was saying. I wasn't in any position to be ordering her around. I didn't have a weapon. No possible means of attack. No way past her.

My mind raced, but I couldn't find an advantage—and you couldn't let Sarafine get the upper hand.

Kill or be killed, that was her style. Even when it seemed like we should have moved past something as Mortal as death.

Her mouth curled into a snarl. *"Your sight?"*

She laughed, a cold sound that rippled down my spine. "Maybe your girlfriend should have thought about that before she killed me. She's the reason I'm here. If it weren't for that ungrateful little witch, I would still be in the Mortal world. Instead of stuck in the dark, battling the ghosts of lost and pathetic Mortal boys."

She was close enough now that I could see her face. She didn't look too good, even for Sarafine. Her dress was ragged and black, the bodice charred into tattered pieces. Her face was smudged with soot, and her hair smelled like smoke.

Sarafine turned toward me, her eyes glowing and white— milky with an opaque light I had never seen before.

"Sarafine?"

I took a step back—just as she struck me with a bolt of electricity, the smell of burnt flesh traveling faster than her body possibly could.

I heard a psychotic scream. Saw her face, contorted into an inhuman death mask. Sharp teeth seemed to match the dagger she held in her hand—only inches from my throat.

I winced, pulling back from the blade, but I knew it was too late. I wasn't going to make it.

Lena!

Sarafine stopped short, as if smashed backward by an invisible current. Her arms stretched toward me, her blade shaking with anger.

Something was wrong with her.

I heard the sound of chains as she fell, stumbling back toward her throne. She dropped the blade, and her long skirt kicked open, and I saw the manacles around her ankles. The chains holding her to the ground and pinning her to the throne.

She wasn't the Queen of the Underworld. She was an angry dog trapped in a kennel. Sarafine screamed, beating her fists against the bones. I moved to the side, but she didn't even look at me.

Now I understood.

I picked up a bone and tossed it at her. She didn't react until it hit the throne, falling harmlessly into the pile of debris at her feet.

She spit at me, shaking with rage. "Fool!"

But I knew the truth.

Her white eyes saw nothing.

Her pupils were fixed.

She was blind.

Maybe it was from the fire that had killed her in the Mortal world. It all came flooding back to me—the terrible end of her terrible life. She was as damaged here as she was when she burned to death. But that wasn't all. Something else had happened. Even the fire couldn't explain the chains.

"What happened to your eyes?" I watched her recoil when I said it. Sarafine wasn't one to show weakness. She was better at finding and exploiting it.

"My new look. Old blind woman, like the Fates or the Furies. What do you think?" Her lips curved over her teeth, into a growl.

It was impossible to feel sorry for Sarafine, so I didn't. Still, she seemed bitter and broken.

"The leash is a nice touch," I said.

She laughed, but it was more like the hiss of an animal. She had become something that didn't resemble a Dark Caster, not anymore. She was a creature, maybe even more of one than Xavier or the River Master. She was losing it—whatever part of our world she'd known.

I tried again. "What happened to your sight? Was it the fire?"

Her white eyes burned as she answered. "The Far Keep wanted to have their fun with me. Angelus is a sadistic pig. He thought they would even the odds by forcing me to battle without being able to see my opponents. He wanted me to know how it would feel to be powerless." She sighed, picking at a bone. "Not that it's slowed me down yet."

I didn't think it had.

I looked at the circus of bones surrounding her, the bloodstains in the dirt at her feet. "Who cares? Why fight? You're dead. I'm dead. What do we even have left to fight about? Tell this Angelus guy to go jump off a—"

"Water tower?" She laughed.

But I had a point, if you thought about it. It was starting to feel like those old *Terminator* movies between us. If I killed her now, I could imagine her skeleton dragging itself across this pit with glowing red eyes until it could kill me a thousand more times.

She stopped laughing. "Why are you here? Think about it, Ethan." She lifted her hand, and I felt my throat beginning to close. I gasped for air.

I tried to back away, but it was pointless. Even with her dog chain, she still had enough power to make my not-quite-a-life miserable.

"I'm trying to get into the Great Keep." I choked. I tried to inhale, but I couldn't get a real breath.

Am I even breathing, or am I only imagining it?

Like she said herself, she'd already killed me once. What was left?

"I just want to take my page. You think I want to be stuck here forever, wandering through a maze of bones?"

"You'll never get past Angelus. He'd die before he'd let you near *The Caster Chronicles*." She smiled, twisting her fingers, and I gasped again. Now it felt like she had a hand around my lungs.

"Then I'll kill him." I grabbed at my neck with both hands. My face felt like it was on fire.

"The Keepers already know you're here. They sent an officer to lead you into the labyrinth. They didn't want to miss out on the fun." Sarafine twisted around at the mention of the Keepers, as if she was looking over her shoulder, which we both knew she wasn't. An old habit, I guess.

"I still have to try. It's the only way I can get home."

"To my daughter?" Sarafine rattled her chains, looking disgusted. "You never give up, do you?"

"No."

"It's like a sickness." She rose from her throne, crouching on her heels like an evil, overgrown little girl, dropping the hand that was choking me. I collapsed onto a heap of bones. "You really think you can hurt Angelus?"

"I can do anything if it will get me back to Lena." I looked straight into her sightless eyes. "Like I said, I'll kill him. At least part of him is Mortal. I can do it."

I don't know why I said it that way. I guess I wanted her to know, in case there was any small part of her that still cared about Lena. Any part of her that needed to hear I really would do anything under the sun to find a way back to her daughter.

Which I would.

For a second, Sarafine didn't move. "You actually believe that, don't you? It's charming, really. Shame you have to die again, Mortal Boy. You certainly amuse me."

Light flooded into the pit, as if we really were two gladiators competing for our lives.

"I don't want to fight. Not with you, Sarafine."

She smiled darkly. "You really don't know how this works, do you? The loser faces Eternal Darkness. It's simple enough." She sounded almost bored.

"There's something Darker than this?"

"Much."

"Please. I just need to get back to Lena. Your daughter. I want to make her happy. I know that doesn't mean anything to you, and I know you've never wanted to make anyone happy but yourself, but it's the only thing I want."

"I want something, too." She twisted the fog around her in her hands until it wasn't fog at all but something glowing and alive—a ball of fire. She stared right at me, even though I knew she couldn't see. "Kill Angelus."

Sarafine started to Cast, but I couldn't hear what she was saying. Fire shot from the base of her throne, spreading in all directions. It moved closer and closer, turning from orange to blue and purple flames as it ignited bone after bone.

I backed away from her.

Something was wrong. The fire was growing, spreading faster than I could run. She wasn't trying to stop the flames. *She was the one making them grow.*

"What are you doing?" I shouted. "Are you crazy?"

She was in the very center of the flames. "It's a battle to the death. Absolute destruction. Only one of us can survive. And as much as I hate you, I hate Angelus more." Sarafine raised her arms over her head, and the fire grew, as if she was pulling the flames up with her.

"Make him pay."

Her cloak caught fire, and her hair started burning.

"You can't just give up!" I shouted, but I didn't know if she could hear me. I couldn't see her anymore.

I hurled myself into the fire without thinking, falling toward her through the flames. I wasn't sure I could stop, even if I wanted to. But I didn't want to.

It was Sarafine or me.

Lena or Eternal Darkness.

It didn't matter. I wasn't going to sit there and watch anyone die chained like a dog. Not even Sarafine.

It wasn't about her. It was about me.

I reached for the manacles around her ankles, beating on

the iron with a bone at the base of her throne. "We have to get out of here."

The fire had completely surrounded me, when I heard the screaming. The sound tore across the barren dirt, rising into the air over the pit. It sounded like a wild animal dying. For a second, I thought I saw the distant golden spires of the Great Keep flicker at the sound of her voice through the flames.

Sarafine's burning body arched back, writhing in pain, and started to crumble into tiny pieces of burnt skin and bone. There was nothing I could do as the flames consumed her. I wanted to close my eyes or turn away. But it seemed like someone should bear witness to her last moments. Maybe I just didn't want her to die alone.

After a few minutes that felt more like hours, I watched as the last bits of the Darkest Caster in two worlds blew into cold white ash.

It was too late to get out.

I felt the fire crawl up my arms.

I was next.

I tried to picture Lena one last time, but I couldn't even think. The pain was unbearable. I knew I was going to pass out. This was it.

I closed my eyes. . . .

When I opened them again, the pit was gone, and I was standing in front of a quiet doorway in a still hallway, in a building that looked like a castle.

There was no pain.

No Sarafine.

No fire.

Exhausted, I wiped the ash out of my eyes and sank into a ball at the foot of the wooden doors. It was over. There were no bones beneath my feet, only marble tiles.

I tried to focus on the doors. They were so familiar.

I'd seen all of this before. It was even more familiar than the feeling I had when I saw Sarafine coming toward me.

Sarafine.

Where is she now? Where is her soul?

I didn't want to think about it, and I closed my eyes and let the tears fall. Crying for her felt impossible. She was an evil monster. No one ever felt sorry for her.

So that couldn't be it.

At least that's what I told myself, until I stopped shaking and stood up again.

The pathways of my life had doubled back on me, as if the universe was forcing me to choose them all over again. I was standing in front of the unmistakable doorway to all other doorways, to all other places and times.

I didn't know if I had the strength to go any farther, and I knew I didn't have the courage to give up. I reached out and touched the carved wood of the ancient Caster doorway.

The *Temporis Porta.*

⊰ CHAPTER 33 ⊱

The Wayward's Way

I took a deep breath and tried to let the power of the *Temporis Porta* flow into me. I needed to feel something other than shock. But they felt like two regular wooden doors, even if they were about a thousand years old and framed with Niadic script, an even older lost language.

I pressed my fingers against the wood. It felt like Sarafine's blood was on my hands in this world, as my blood had been on hers in the last. It didn't matter if I had tried to stop her.

She had sacrificed herself so I would have a chance to make it to the Great Keep, even if hate was her only motivation. Sarafine had still given me a shot at getting back home to the people I loved.

I had to keep going. Like the officer at the Gates said, there was only one way into the one place I needed to go—the Way of the Warrior. Maybe this was how it felt.

Awful.

I tried not to think about the other thing. The fact that Sarafine's soul was trapped in Eternal Darkness. It was hard to imagine.

I took a step back from the broad wooden doors of the *Temporis Porta*. It was identical to the doorway I found in the Caster Tunnels beneath Gatlin. The one that took me to the Far Keep for the first time. Rowan wood, carved into Caster circles.

I placed my palms against the rough exterior of the paneling.

Just like always, they gave way beneath me. I was the Wayward, and they were the Way. These doors would open for me in this world as they had in the other. They would show their pathway to me.

I pushed harder.

The doors swung open, and I stepped inside.

There were so many things I didn't realize when I was alive. So many things I took for granted. My life didn't seem precious when I had one.

But here, I'd fought through a mountain of bones, crossed a river, tunneled through a mountain, begged and bargained and bartered from one world to another, to get myself this close to these doors and this room.

Now I just had to find the library.

One page in one book.

One page in The Caster Chronicles, *and I can go home.*

The nearness of it swirled in the air around me. I had experienced this feeling only once before, at the Great Barrier— another seam between worlds. Then, just like now, I had felt the power crackling in the air, too, the magic. I was in a place where great things could happen and did happen.

There were some rooms that could change the world.

Worlds.

This was one of them, with its heavy drapes and dusty portraits and dark wood and rowan doors. A place where all things were judged and punished.

Sarafine had promised that Angelus would come for me— that he had practically led me here himself. There was no use trying to hide. He was probably the reason I was sentenced to die in the first place.

If there was a way around him, a way to get to the library and *The Caster Chronicles,* I hadn't figured it out yet. I just hoped it would come to me, the way so many ideas had in the past when my future was at stake.

The only question was, would he come first?

I decided to take my chances and try to find the library before Angelus found me. It would have been a good plan if it had actually worked out. I had barely crossed the room when I saw them.

The Council Keepers—the man with the hourglass, the albino woman, and Angelus—appeared in front of me.

Their robes fell around them, pooling at their feet, and they barely moved. I couldn't even tell if they were breathing.

"Puer Mortalis. Is qui, unus, duplex est. Is qui mundo, qui fuit, finem attulit." When one spoke, all their mouths moved like they were the same person, or at least governed by the same brain. I had almost forgotten.

I didn't say anything, and I didn't move.

They looked at one another and spoke again. "Mortal Boy. The One Who Is Two. He Who Endeth the World That Was."

"When you say it that way, it sounds kind of creepy." It wasn't Latin, but it was the best I could come up with. They didn't respond.

I heard the murmuring of foreign voices around me and turned to see the room suddenly crowded with unfamiliar people. I looked for the telltale tattoos and gold eyes of the Dark Casters, but I was too disoriented to register anything beyond the three robed figures who stood in front of me.

"Child of Lila Evers Wate, deceased Keeper of Gatlin." The choral voices filled the great hall like some kind of trumpet. It reminded me of Beginning Band with Miss Spider back at Jackson High, only less off-key.

"In the flesh." I shrugged. "Or not."

"You have taken the labyrinth and defeated the Cataclyst. Many have tried. Only you have been—" There was a hitch, a pause, like the Keepers didn't know what to say. I took a breath, half expecting them to say something like *extermi nated*. "Victorious."

It was almost like they couldn't bring themselves to say the word.

"Not really. She kind of defeated herself." I scowled at Angelus, who was standing in the center. I wanted him to look at me. I wanted him to know that I knew what he'd done to Sarafine. How he'd chained the Caster, like a dog, to a throne of bones. What kind of sick game was that?

But Angelus didn't flinch.

I took a step closer. "Or I guess you defeated her, Angelus. At least, that's what Sarafine said. That you enjoyed torturing her." I looked around the room. "Is that what Keepers do around here? Because it's not what Keepers do where I come from. Back home they're good people, who care about things like right and wrong and good and evil and all that. Like my mom."

I looked at the crowd behind me. "Seems like you guys are pretty messed up."

The three spoke again, in unison. "That is not our concern. *Victori spolia sunt.* To the victor go the spoils. The debt has been paid."

"About that—" If this was my way back to Gatlin, I wanted to know.

Angelus raised his hand, silencing me. "In return, you have gained entry to this Keep, the Warrior's Way. You are to be commended."

The crowd fell silent, which didn't exactly make me feel all that commended. More than anything, it felt like I was about to be sentenced. Or maybe that was how I was used to things going down in here.

I looked around. "It doesn't really sound like you mean it."

The crowd began to whisper again. The three Council Keepers stared at me. At least I think they did. It was impossible to see their eyes behind the strangely cut prism glasses, with the twisting strands of gold, silver, and copper holding them in place.

I tried again. "In terms of spoils, I was thinking more about going home to Gatlin. Wasn't that the deal? One of us goes to Eternal Darkness, and one of us gets to leave?"

The crowd burst into chaos.

Angelus stepped forward. "Enough!" The room fell silent again. This time he spoke alone. The other Keepers looked at me but said nothing. "The bargain was for the Cataclyst alone. We have made no such pact with a Mortal. Never would we return a Mortal to existence."

I remembered Amma's past, revealed through the black stone I still had in my pocket. Sulla had warned her that Angelus hated Mortals. He was never going to let me walk away. "What if the Mortal was never meant to be here?"

Angelus' eyes widened.

"I want my page back."

This time the crowd gasped.

"What is written in the *Chronicles* is law. The pages cannot be removed," Angelus hissed.

"But you can rewrite them however you want?" I couldn't hide the rage in my voice. He had taken everything from me. How many other lives had he destroyed?

And why? Because he couldn't be a Caster?

"You were the One Who Is Two. Your fate was to be punished. You should not have brought the Lilum into matters that were not hers to resolve."

"Wait. What does Lilian English—I mean, the Lilum—have to do with any of this?" My English teacher, whose body had been inhabited by the most powerful creature in the Demon world, had been the one who showed me what I had to do to fix the Order of Things.

Was that why he was punishing me? Did I get in the way of whatever he was planning with Abraham? Destroying the Mortal race? Using Casters as lab rats?

I always believed that when Lena and Amma brought me back from the dead with *The Book of Moons,* they had set something in motion that couldn't be undone. It started the unraveling that ripped the hole in the universe, which was the reason I had to right it at the water tower.

What if I had it backward?

What if the thing that was supposed to happen *was* the unraveling?

What if fixing it was the crime?

It was all so clear now. Like everything had been lost in darkness, and then the sun came out. Some moments are like that. But now I knew the truth.

I was supposed to fail.

The world as we knew it was supposed to end.

The Mortals weren't the point. They were the problem.

The Lilum wasn't supposed to help me, and I wasn't supposed to jump.

She was supposed to condemn me, and I was supposed to give up. Angelus had bet on the wrong team.

A sound echoed through the hall as the great doors on the far side pushed open, revealing a small figure standing between them. Talk about betting on the wrong team—I wouldn't have made this bet, not in a thousand lifetimes.

It was more unexpected than Angelus or any of the Keepers.

He smiled broadly; at least I think it was a smile. It was hard to tell with Xavier.

"He-hello." Xavier glanced around the intimidating room, clearing his throat. He tried again. "Hello, friend."

It was so quiet, you could've heard one of his precious buttons drop.

The only thing that wasn't quiet was Angelus. "How dare you show your defiled face here again, Xavier. If there is anything of Xavier left, beast."

Xavier's leathery wings shrugged.

Angelus only looked angrier. "Why have you involved yourself in this? Your fate is not intertwined with the Wayward. You are serving your sentence. You don't need to take a dead Mortal's battles on as your own."

"It is too late for that, Angelus," he said.

"Why?"

"Because he paid his way, and I accepted the price. Because"—Xavier slowed his words, as if he was letting them fall into place in his mind—"he is my friend, and I have no other."

"He's not your friend," Angelus hissed. "You're too brainless to have a friend. Brainless and heartless. All you care about are your worthless trinkets, your lost baubles." Angelus sounded frustrated. I wondered why he cared what Xavier thought or did.

What is Xavier to him?

There had to be a story there. But I didn't want to know about anything that involved Angelus and his minions, or the crimes they must have committed. The Far Keep was the closest thing I'd ever found to Hell in real life—at least in my real afterlife.

"What you know of me," said Xavier slowly, "is nothing." His twisted face was even more expressionless than usual. "Less than I know of myself."

"You are a fool," Angelus answered. "That I know."

"I am a friend. I have in my possession two thousand assorted buttons, eight hundred keys, and only one friend. Perhaps it is not something you can understand. I have not often been one before." He looked proud of himself. "I will be one now."

I was proud of him, too.

Angelus scoffed. "You will sacrifice your soul for a friend?"

"Is a friend different from a soul, Angelus?" The Council Keeper said nothing. Xavier cocked his head again. "Would you know if it were?"

Angelus didn't respond, but he didn't need to. We all knew the answer.

"What are you doing here, then? *Mortali Comes.*" Angelus took a step toward Xavier, and Xavier took a step back. "Friend of the Mortal," Angelus snarled.

I resisted the urge to insert myself between them, hoping that Xavier, for both our sakes, didn't try to run away.

"You seek to destroy the Mortal, do you not?" Xavier swallowed.

"I do," Angelus answered.

"You seek to end the Mortal race." It wasn't a question.

"Of course. Like any infestation, the ultimate goal is annihilation."

Even though I was expecting it, Angelus' answer caught me off guard. "You—what?"

Xavier looked at me like he was trying to shut me down. "It is no secret. The Mortals are an irritant to the supernatural races. This is not a new concept."

"I wish it was." I knew Abraham wanted to wipe out the Mortal race. If Angelus was working with him, their goals were aligned.

"You seek entertainment?" Xavier watched Angelus.

Angelus looked at Xavier's leathery wings, disgusted. "I seek solutions."

"To the Mortal condition?"

Angelus smiled, dark and joyless. "As I said. The Mortal infestation."

I felt sick, but Xavier only sighed. "As you wish to call it. I propose a challenge."

"A what?" I didn't like the sound of it.

"A challenge."

Angelus looked suspicious. "The Mortal defeated the Dark Queen and won. That was the only challenge he will face today."

I was annoyed. "I told you. I didn't kill Sarafine. She defeated herself."

"Semantics," Angelus said.

Xavier silenced us both. "So you are unwilling to face the Mortal in a challenge?"

There was an uproar in the crowd, and Angelus looked like he wanted to tear Xavier's wings off. "Silence!"

The chatter stopped immediately.

"I do not fear any Mortal!"

"Then this is my proposition." Xavier tried to keep his voice steady, but he was obviously terrified. "The Mortal will face you in the Great Keep and attempt to regain his page. You will attempt to stop him. If he succeeds, you will allow him to do with it as he likes. If you stop him from reaching his page, he will allow you to do with it as you like."

"What?" Xavier was suggesting that I face off against Angelus. My odds were not good in this scenario.

Angelus was aware that all eyes were on him as the crowd

and the other Council Keepers waited for his response. "Interesting."

I wanted to bolt out of the room. "Not interesting. I don't even know what you're talking about."

Angelus leaned toward me, his eyes sparking. "Let me explain it to you. A lifetime of servitude or the simple destruction of your soul. It doesn't really matter to me. I'll decide on a whim, as I like. When I like."

"I'm not sure about this." It sounded like a lose-lose proposition to me.

Xavier let one hand fall on my shoulder. "You don't have a choice. It's the only chance you have to get home to the girl with the curls." He turned to Angelus, holding out his hand. "Is it a deal?"

Angelus stared at Xavier's hand as if it was infected. "I accept."

CHAPTER 34

The Caster Chronicles

Angelus swept out of the room, the other Keepers right behind him.

I let out the breath I was holding. "Where are they going?"

"They have to give you a chance, or they will be perceived as unjust."

"Perceived as unjust?" Was he serious? "Are you saying no one's caught on to that before?"

"The Council is feared. No one questions them," Xavier said. "But they are also proud. Especially Angelus. He wishes his followers to believe he is giving you a chance."

"But he's not?"

"That depends on you now." Xavier turned to me with

something resembling a sad expression on what was left of his human face. "I can't help you. Not beyond this, my friend."

"What are you talking about?"

"I'm not going back there. I can't," he said. "Not to the Chamber of the Chronicles."

Of course. The room that housed the book. It had to be close.

I looked at the row of doors beyond us, bordering one side of the room. I wondered which one led to the end of my journey—or to the death of my soul.

"You can't go back there? And I can? Don't chicken out on me now." I lowered my voice. "You just took on Angelus. You made a deal with the Devil. You're my hero."

"I am no hero. As I said, I am your friend."

Xavier couldn't do it. Who could blame the guy? The Chamber of the Chronicles must have been some kind of house of horrors for him. And he had put himself in enough danger already.

"Thanks, Xavier. You're a great friend. One of the best." I smiled at him. The look he gave me in return was sobering.

"This is your journey, dead man. Yours alone. I can go no farther." He put his arm on my shoulder, pressing heavily.

"Why do I have to do everything alone?" As soon as I said it, I knew it wasn't true.

The Greats had sent me on my way.

Aunt Prue made sure I got a second chance.

Obidias told me everything I needed to know.

My mom gave me the strength to do it.

Amma watched for me, and believed it when she found me.

Lena sent me *The Book of Moons*, against all odds and all the way from the other side of the universe. Aunt Marian and Macon, Link and John and Liv—they were there for Lena when I couldn't be.

Even the River Master and Xavier had helped me move forward, when all along it would have been so much easier to give up and go back.

I had never been alone. Not for a minute.

I may have been a Wayward, but my way was full of people who loved me. They were the only way I knew.

I could do this.

I had to.

"I understand," I said. "Thanks, Xavier. For everything."

He nodded. "I will meet you again, Ethan. I will see you when next you cross the river."

"I hope it's not for a long time."

"I hope this as well, my friend. For you more than me." His eyes seemed to twinkle for a second. "But I will keep busy collecting and counting until you return."

I didn't say anything as he slipped through the shadows and back into the world where nothing ever happened and the days became the same as nights.

I hoped he would remember me.

I was pretty sure he wouldn't.

One by one, I touched the row of doors in front of me with my hand. Some felt as cold as ice. Some felt like nothing, like plain wood. There was only one that pulsed beneath my fingertips.

Only one burned at my touch.

I knew it was the right door, before I saw the telltale Caster circles carved into the rowan wood, just like the *Temporis Porta*.

This was the doorway to the heart of the Great Keep. The one place any son of Lila Jane Evers Wate would instinctively find his way, whether or not he was a Wayward.

The library.

Pushing my way through the massive doors directly across from the *Temporis Porta*, I knew it was time to face the most dangerous part of my journey.

Angelus would be waiting.

The doors were just the beginning. The moment I stepped into the inner chamber, I found myself standing in an almost entirely reflective room. If it was supposed to be a library, it was the strangest one I'd ever seen.

The crumbling stones beneath my feet, the stubbled cave walls, the ceiling and floor that grew into stalactites and sta-lagmites as the room circled back upon itself—they all seemed to be made of some kind of transparent gemstone, cut into a thousand impossible facets that reflected the light in every direction. It looked like I was standing in one of the eleven jewelry boxes in Xavier's collection.

Except less claustrophobic. A small opening in the ceiling let in enough natural light to catch the whole room in a dizzying glow. The effect reminded me of the tidal cave where we'd first met Abraham Ravenwood, on the night of Lena's Seventeenth Moon. In the center of this room, there was a pond of water the size of a swimming pool. The body of milky white water churned as if there was a fire beneath it. It was the color of Sarafine's sightless opaque eyes, before she died....

I shuddered. I couldn't think about her, not now. I had to focus on surviving Angelus. Defeating him. I took a deep breath and tried to get my bearings. What was I dealing with?

My eyes fixed on the bubbling white liquid. In the center of the pool, a small stretch of earth rose above the water, like a tiny island.

In the center of the island was a pedestal.

On the pedestal was a book, surrounded by candles that flickered with strange green and gold flames.

The book.

I didn't need someone to tell me which book it was, or what it was doing here. The reason there was an entire library devoted to only one book, and with a moat around it.

I knew exactly why it was here, and why I was.

It was the only part of this whole journey I understood. The only thing that was perfectly clear from the moment Obidias Trueblood told me the truth about what had happened to me. It was *The Caster Chronicles*, and I was here to destroy my page. The one that killed me. And I had to do it before Angelus could stop me.

After all I'd learned about being a Wayward and finding my way—this was where it led. There was no way left to go, no more path to find.

I was at the end.

And all I wanted was to go back.

But first I had to get to that island—to the pedestal and *The Caster Chronicles*. I had to do what I'd come here to do.

A shout from across the room startled me. "Mortal Boy. If you leave now, I will leave you your soul. How's that for a challenge?" Angelus appeared on the other side of the pool. I wondered how he got over there, and I wished there were as many ways to leave this room as there were to enter it.

Or at least, as many ways home.

"My soul? No, you won't." I stood at the edge of the pool and chucked a rock into the bubbling water, watching it disappear. I wasn't stupid. He would never let me go. I would end up like Xavier or Sarafine. Black wings or white eyes—it didn't make a difference. In the end, we were all bound in his chains, whether you could see them or not.

Angelus smiled. "No? I suppose that's true." He gestured with his hand, and at least a dozen rocks rose into the air around him. They fired themselves at me, one after another, hitting with uncanny accuracy. I flung my arms across my face as a rock sailed past.

"Very mature. What are you going to do now? Tie me up and stick me in your old boneyard? Blind and chained like an animal?"

"Don't flatter yourself. I don't want a Mortal pet." He twisted his finger, and the water began to spin into a kind of whirlpool. "I'll just destroy you. It's easier for all of us. Though not much of a challenge."

"Why did you torture Sarafine? She wasn't a Mortal. Why bother?" I shouted.

I had to know. It felt like our fates were tied together somehow—mine, Sarafine's, Xavier's, and those of all the other Mortals and Casters Angelus had destroyed.

What were we to him?

"Sarafine? Was that her name? I had almost forgotten." Angelus laughed. "Do you expect me to concern myself with every Dark Caster who ends up here?"

The water churned violently now. I knelt and touched it with one hand. It was freezing cold and sort of slimy. I didn't want to swim through it, but I couldn't tell if there was another way across.

I looked up at Angelus. I didn't know how this whole challenge thing was going to take shape, but I thought it was better to keep him talking until I figured it out. "Do you blind every Dark Caster and make them fight to the death?"

I looked back at the water. It rippled where I had touched it, turning clear and calm.

Angelus folded his arms, smiling.

I kept my hand in the water as the transparent current spread across the pool, though my hand was going numb. Now I could see what was really beneath the milky surface.

Corpses. Just like the ones in the river.

Floating upward, their green hair and blue lips looked like masks on their bloated dead bodies.

Like me, I thought. *That's what I look like, right now. Somewhere—where I still had a body.*

I heard Angelus laughing. But I could barely hear, barely think. I wanted to vomit.

I backed away from the water. I knew he was trying to frighten me, and I resolved not to look at it again.

Keep your mind on Lena. Get to the page, and you can go home.

Angelus watched me, laughing harder. He called to me as if I was a child. "Don't be afraid. Your final death doesn't have to happen like this. Sarafine failed to achieve the tasks entrusted to her."

"So you do know her name." I cracked a smile.

He glared. "I know she failed me."

"You and Abraham?"

Angelus stiffened. "Congratulations. I see you've been digging around in matters that are none of your concern. Which means you're no smarter than the first Ethan Wate who visited the Great Keep. And no more likely to see the Duchannes Caster you love than he was."

My whole body went numb.

Of course. Ethan Carter Wate had been here. Genevieve told me.

I didn't want to ask, but I had to. "What did you do to him?"

"What do you think?" A sadistic smile spread across Angelus' face. "He tried to take something that did not belong to him."

"His page?"

With every question, the Keeper looked more satisfied. I could tell he was enjoying this. "No. Genevieve's—the Duchannes girl he loved. He wanted to lift the curse she brought upon herself and the Duchannes children who would come after her. Instead, he lost his foolish soul."

Angelus looked down into the churning water. He nodded, and a single corpse rose to the surface. Empty eyes that looked too much like my own stared back at me.

"Look familiar, Mortal?"

I knew that face. I would've known it anywhere.

It was mine. Or actually, his.

Ethan Carter Wate was still wearing the Confederate uniform he died in.

My heart dropped. Genevieve would never see him again, not in this world or any other. He had died twice, like me. But he would never get back home. Never hold Genevieve in his arms, even in the Otherworld. He had tried to save the girl he loved, and Sarafine and Ridley and Lena and all the other Casters who would come after her in the Duchannes family.

He'd failed.

It didn't make a guy feel better. Not about standing where I stood. And not about leaving a Caster girl behind, the way we both had.

"You will fail as well." The words echoed across the cavern.

Which meant Angelus was reading my mind. At this point, it was the least surprising thing happening in the room.

I knew what I had to do.

I emptied my mind the best I could, picturing the old baseball diamond where Link and I used to play T-ball. I watched Link throw a bum pitch in the ninth inning as I stood on home plate punching my glove. I tried to picture the batter. Who was it? Earl Petty, chewing gum, since the coach had outlawed chaw?

I struggled to keep my mind on the game while my eyes did something else.

Come on, Earl. Knock it out of the park.

I glanced at the pedestal, then at the corpses floating at my feet. More bodies continued to rise, bumping into one another like sardines packed in a can. It wouldn't be long until they were so close that I wouldn't even be able to see the water.

If I waited, maybe I could use them as stepping stones....

Stop! Think about the game!

But it was too late.

"I wouldn't try it." Angelus watched me from the other side of the pool. "No Mortal can survive that water. You need the bridge to cross, and as you can see, it's been removed. A security precaution."

He held his hand in front of him, twisting the air into a current I could feel all the way across the water.

I had to brace myself to stay on my feet.

"You will not retrieve your page. You will die the same dishonorable death as your namesake. The death all Mortals deserve."

"Why me, and why him? Why any of us? What did we ever do to you, Angelus?" I shouted at him over the wind.

"You are inferior, born without the gifts of Supernaturals. Forcing us to stay in hiding while your cities and schools fill with children who will grow to do nothing more than occupy space. You've turned our world into our prison." The air picked up, and he twisted his hand further. "It's absurd. Like building a city for rodents."

I waited, picturing that stupid baseball game—Earl swinging, the crack of the bat—until the words formed, and I spoke them. "But you were born a Mortal. What does that make you?"

His eyes widened, his face a mask of pure rage. "What did you say?"

"You heard me." I turned my mind to the vision I'd seen, forcing myself to remember the faces, the words. Xavier, when he was just a Caster. Angelus, when he was just a man.

The wind increased, and I stumbled, the edge of my sneaker splashing at the edge of the pool of bodies. I braced myself, willing my feet not to slip.

Angelus' face had turned even paler than before. "You know nothing! Look what you sacrificed—to save what? A town full of pathetic Mortals?"

I closed my eyes, letting the words find him.

I know you were born a Mortal. All those experiments can't change that. I know your secret.

His eyes widened, hate raging across his face. "I am not a Mortal! I never was, and I never will be!"

I know your secret.

The wind picked up, and rocks flew again through the air—harder this time. I tried to shield my face as they pelted my ribs, smashing against the wall behind me. A trail of blood ran down my cheek.

"I will tear you to shreds, Wayward!"

I screamed over the din. "You may have powers, Angelus, but deep down, you're still a Mortal, just like me."

You can't harness Dark forces like Sarafine and Abraham, or Travel like an Incubus. You can't cross that water any more than I can.

"I am not Mortal!" he screamed.

Nobody can.

"Liar!"

Prove it.

There was a second, one terrible second, when Angelus and I stared across the water at each other.

Then, without a word, Angelus flung himself into the air, lunging across the corpses in the pool—as if he couldn't contain himself a moment longer. That's how desperate he was to prove he was better than me.

Better than a Mortal.

Better than anyone else who ever tried to walk on water.

I had been right.

The rotting corpses were packed so tight that he ran right over their bodies until they started to move. Arms reached for him, the hundreds of bloated hands rising up out of the water. This was not like the river I had crossed to get here.

This river was alive.

An arm slithered over his neck, weighing him down.

"No!"

I shuddered as his voice echoed against the walls.

The corpses tore at his robe desperately, pulling him down into the abyss of loss and misery. The same souls he had tortured were drowning him.

His eyes locked on mine. "Help me!"

Why should I?

But there was nothing I could do, even if I'd wanted to. I knew those corpses would drown me. I was Mortal, just as Angelus was— at least part of him.

Nobody walks on water, not where I come from. Nobody except the guy in the picture frame in Sunday school class.

Too bad Angelus wasn't from Gatlin; he would've known that.

His hands clawed at the surface of the water until there was nothing left but a sea of bodies again. The stench of death was everywhere. It was suffocating, and I tried to cover my mouth, but the distinct odor of rot and decay was too strong.

I knew what I'd done. I wasn't innocent. Not in Sarafine's death, and not in this one either. He was reading my mind and

I had pushed him to this, even if his hate and pride had propelled him into the pool.

It was too late.

A rotted arm slid around his neck, and within seconds he disappeared under the sea of bodies. It was a death I wouldn't have wished on anyone.

Not even Angelus.

Maybe just him.

Within moments, the pool turned milky white again, though I knew what was lurking underneath.

I shrugged. "Wasn't much of a challenge after all."

I had to find the bridge, or something I could use to cross.

The splintering plank wasn't well hidden. I found it in an alcove only a few yards from where Angelus stood moments ago. The wood was dry and cracked, which wasn't reassuring, considering what I had just witnessed.

But the book was so close.

As I slid the plank over the surface of the water, I could practically feel Lena in my arms and hear Amma hollering at me. I couldn't think straight. All I knew was I had to get across that water and get back to them.

Please. Let me cross. All I want is to go home.

With that thought, I took a breath.

Then a step.

Then another.

I was five feet from the edge of the water now, maybe six.

Halfway across. There was no turning back now.

The bridge was surprisingly light, though it creaked and wobbled with my every step. Still, it had held up so far.

I took a deep breath.

Five more feet.

Four—

I heard a crash like a wave behind me. The water began to thrash. I felt a shooting pain in my leg as it gave way beneath me. The old board snapped like a broken toothpick.

Before I could scream, I lost my balance, falling into the deadly water. Only then there wasn't any water—or if there was, I wasn't in it.

I was in the arms of the rising dead.

Worse.

I was face to face with the other Ethan Wate. He was as much a skeleton as he was a man, but I recognized him now. I tried to pull away, but he grabbed me around the neck with a bony hand. Water poured out of his mouth, where his teeth should have been. I'd had nightmares less terrifying.

I turned my head to keep corpse drool from my face.

"Could a Mortal Cast an *Ambulans Mortus?*" Angelus pushed past the dead who crowded around me, pulling my arms and legs in every direction with such force I thought my limbs would rip right out of their sockets. "From under the water? To wake the dead?" He stood triumphantly on the land, in front of the book. Looking crazier than I'd thought even a crazy-looking Keeper could. "The challenge is over. Your soul is mine."

I didn't answer. I couldn't speak. Instead, I found myself staring into Ethan Wate's empty eyes.

"Now. Bring him to me."

At Angelus' command, the corpses rose from the stinking water, pulling me with them up onto the shore. The other Ethan tossed me onto the dirt like I was weightless.

As he did, a small black stone rolled out of my pocket.

Angelus didn't notice. He was too busy staring at the book. But I saw it clear enough.

The river's eye.

I had forgotten to pay the River Master.

Of course. You couldn't just expect to cross the water anytime you wanted. Not around here. Not without paying a price.

I picked up the rock.

Ethan Wate, the dead one, whipped his head toward me. The look he gave me—if that's what you'd call it, considering the guy barely had eyes—sent a shiver down my spine. I felt sorry for him. But I sure didn't want to be him.

Between the two of us, we owed each other that much.

"So long, Ethan," I said.

With my last remaining bit of strength, I hurled the rock into the water. I heard it hit, making only the tiniest sound.

You wouldn't have noticed it unless you were me.

Or one of the dead.

Because they disappeared a few seconds after the rock hit the water. About as quickly as it took a rock to sink all the way down to the bottom of a pool of bodies.

I fell back on the tiny stretch of dry land, exhausted. For a second, I was too scared to move.

Then I saw Angelus standing there, glued to the book, reading in the light of the flickering green and gold flames.

I knew what I had to do. And I didn't have long to do it.

I pulled myself to my feet.

There it was. It was open on the pedestal, right in front of me.

In front of Angelus, too.

THE CASTER CHRONICLES

I reached for the book, and it burned my fingers.

"Don't," Angelus growled, grabbing my wrist. His eyes were shining, as if the book had some strange hold on him. He didn't even look up from the page. I'm not sure he could.

Because it was his page.

I could almost read it from where I stood, a thousand rewritten words, one crossed out over the next. I could see the quill, ink-stained at the tip, almost twitching in his fingers next to the book.

So this was how he'd done it. How he'd forced the super-natural world to bend to his will. He controlled the story. Not just his, but all of ours.

Angelus had changed everything.

One person could do that.

And one person could change it back.

"Angelus?"

He didn't answer. Staring into the book, he looked more like a zombie than the corpses did.

So I didn't look. Instead, I closed my eyes and pulled on the page, as hard and as fast as I could.

"What are you doing?" Angelus sounded frantic, but I didn't open my eyes. "What have you done?"

My hands were burning. The page wanted to rip free from me, but I wouldn't let go. I only held on tighter. Nothing was going to stop me now.

It came off in my hands.

The ripping sound reminded me of an Incubus, and I half expected to see John Breed or Link appear next to me. I opened my eyes.

No such luck. Angelus reached for the page, shoving me in one direction while pulling my arm in another.

I grabbed a dripping candle from the pedestal stand and lit the bottom of the page on fire. It began to smoke and flame, and Angelus howled with rage.

"Leave it! You don't know what you're doing! You could destroy everything—" He threw himself at me, punching and kicking, almost ripping my shirt off. His nails raked my skin, again and again, but I didn't let go.

I didn't let go when I felt the flames sear their way down to my fingers.

I didn't let go when the ink-smeared page crumbled into ash.

I didn't let go until Angelus himself crumbled into nothing, as if he was made of parchment.

Finally, when the wind had blown every last trace of the Keeper and his page into oblivion, I found myself staring at my burnt, blackened hands.

"My turn."

Ducking my head, I flipped through the delicate pages of parchment. I could see dates and names at the top, penned by different hands. I wondered which ones Xavier had written. If Obidias had changed anyone else's page. I hoped he wasn't the one who changed Ethan Carter Wate's.

I thought of my namesake and shuddered, fighting to keep the bile down.

That could have been me.

Halfway through the book, I found our pages.

Ethan Carter's was right before mine, the two pages clearly written by different hands.

I skimmed Ethan Carter's page until I reached the part of the story I already knew. It read like a script of the vision I had witnessed with Lena, the story of the night he died and Genevieve used *The Book of Moons* to bring him back. The night that started it all.

I stared at the edge where the page met the binding. I almost tore it out, but I knew it wouldn't have made a difference. It was too late for the other Ethan.

I was the only one who still had a chance to change his fate.

Finally, I turned the page to find I was staring at Obidias' script.

Ethan Lawson Wate

I didn't read my page. I couldn't risk it. I could already feel the pull of the book on my eyes, powerful enough to Bind me to my page, forever.

I looked away. I already knew what happened in the end of this revision.

Now I was changing it.

I tore the page, the edges pulling away from the binding in a flash of electricity stronger and brighter than lightning. I heard what sounded like thunder in the sky above me, but I kept tearing.

This time, I kept the candles as far from the parchment as I could.

I pulled until the words came loose, disappearing like they had been written in invisible ink.

I looked down at the page again and it was blank.

I let it drop into the water around me, watching as it fell through the milky depths, vanishing into the endless shadow of the chasm.

My page was gone.

And in that second, I knew I was, too.

I stared at my Chucks beneath me

until they were gone

and I was gone
and it didn't matter anymore....

because

there

was

nothing

beneath

me

now

and

then

no

me

⊰ CHAPTER 35 ⊱

A Crack in the Universe

The toes of my Chucks hung over the white metal edge, a town sleeping hundreds of feet below me. The tiny houses and tiny cars looked like toys, and it was easy to imagine them dusted with glitter under the tree with the rest of my mother's Christmas town.

But they weren't toys.

I knew this view.

You don't forget the last thing you see before you die. Trust me.

I was standing on top of the Summerville water tower, veins of cracked white paint spreading out from under my sneakers. The curve of a black heart drawn in Sharpie caught my eye.

Was it possible? Could I really be home?

I didn't know until I saw her.

The fronts of her black orthopedic shoes were lined up perfectly with my Chucks.

Amma was wearing her black Sunday dress with the tiny violets scattered all over it, and a wide-brimmed black hat. Her white gloves gripped the handles of her patent-leather pocketbook.

Our eyes met for a split second, and she smiled—relief spreading across her features in a way that was impossible to describe. It was almost peaceful, a word that I would never use to describe Amma.

That's when I realized something was wrong. The kind of wrong you can't stop or change or fix.

I reached for her at the exact same moment she stepped off the edge, into the blue-black sky.

"Amma!" I reached for her, the way I used to reach for Lena in my dreams when she was the one falling. But I couldn't catch Amma.

And she didn't fall.

The sky split open like the universe was tearing, or like someone had finally picked that hole in it. Amma turned her face toward it, tears running down her cheeks even as she smiled at me.

The sky held her up, as though Amma was worthy of standing on it, until a hand reached out from the center of the tear and the blinking stars. It was a hand I recognized—the one that had offered me his crow so I could cross from one world to another.

Now Uncle Abner was offering that hand to Amma.

His face blurred in the darkness next to Sulla, Ivy, and Delilah. Amma's other family. Twyla's face smiled down at me, charms tied into her long braids. Amma's Caster family was waiting for her.

But I didn't care.

I couldn't lose her.

"Amma! Don't leave me!" I shouted.

Her lips didn't move, but I heard her voice, as sure as if she was standing next to me. *"I could never leave you, Ethan Wate. I'll always be watchin'. Make me proud."*

My heart felt like it was collapsing in on itself, shattering into pieces so small I might never find them. I dropped to my knees and looked up into the heavens, screaming louder than I ever thought possible. "Why?"

It was Amma who answered. She was farther away now, stepping into the sliver of sky that opened just for her. *"A woman's only as good as her word."* Another one of Amma's riddles.

The last one.

She touched her fingers to her lips and reached them out to me as the universe swallowed her up. Her words echoed across the sky, as if she had spoken them aloud.

"And everyone said I couldn't change the cards...."

The cards.

She was talking about the spread that predicted my death so many months ago. The spread she had bargained with the bokor to change. The one she swore she'd do anything to change.

She'd done it.

Defied the universe and fate and everything she believed in. For me.

Amma was trading her life for mine, protecting the Order by offering one life for another. That was the deal she had made with the bokor. I understood now.

I watched the sky knit itself back together one stitch at a time.

But it didn't look the same. I could still see the invisible seams where the world had torn itself in half to take her. And I would always know they were there, even if no one else could see them.

Like torn edges of my heart.

-≼ CHAPTER 36 ≽-

Translation

As I sat on the cold metal in the darkness, part of me wondered if I imagined the whole thing. I knew I didn't. I could still see those stitches in the sky, no matter how dark it was.

Still, I didn't move.

If I left, it would be real.

If I left, she would be gone.

I don't know how long I sat there trying to make sense of everything, but the sun came up, and I was still sitting in the same spot. No matter how many times I tried to work it out, I kept getting stuck.

I had this old Bible story in my head, playing over and over, like a bad song from the radio. I'm probably getting it wrong, but I remember it like this: There was this city of people who were so righteous, they got picked right up off the earth and taken to Heaven. Just like that.

They didn't even die.

They got to skip dying, the way you pass Go and head directly to Jail if you pull the wrong card in Monopoly.

Translated—that's the name for what happened to them. I remember because Link was in my Sunday school class, and he said *teleported*, then *transported*, and finally *transportated*.

We were supposed to act real jealous about it, like those people were so lucky to get plucked up and taken into the Lap o' the Lord.

Like it was a place or something.

I remember coming home and asking my mom about it, because that's how creeped out I was. I don't remember what she said, but I decided right then and there that the goal wasn't to be good. It was to be *just good enough*.

I didn't want to risk getting translated, or even teleported.

I wasn't looking to go live in the Lap o' the Lord. I was more excited about Little League.

But it seemed like that's what happened to Amma. She was lapped right up, transported, transportated—all of it.

Did the universe, or the Lord and his lap, or the Greats expect me to feel happy about it? I had just been through hell to get back to the regular world of Gatlin—back to Amma, and Lena, and Link, and Marian.

How long did we have together?

Was I supposed to be okay with that?

One minute she was there, and then it was over. Now the sky was the sky again, flat and blue and calm, as if it really was just painted plaster, like my bedroom ceiling. Even if someone I loved was trapped somewhere behind it.

That's how I felt now. Trapped on the wrong side of the sky.

Alone on the top of the Summerville water tower, looking out over the world I had known my entire life, a world of dirt roads and paved routes, of gas stations and grocery stores and strip malls. And everything was the same, and nothing was the same.

I wasn't the same.

I guess that's the thing about a hero's journey. You might not start out a hero, and you might not even come back that way. But you change, which is the same as everything changing. The journey changes you, whether or not you know it, and whether or not you want it to. I had changed.

I had come back from the dead, and Amma was gone, even if she was one of the Greats now.

You couldn't get more changed than that.

I heard a clanging on the ladder beneath me, and I knew who it was before I felt her curling around my heart. The warmth exploded across me, across the water tower, across Summerville. The sky was striped with gold and red, as if the sunrise was reversing itself, lighting up the sky all over again.

There was only one person who could do that to a sky or my heart.

Ethan, is that you?

I smiled even as my eyes turned wet and blurry.

It's me, L. I'm right here. Everything's going to be okay now.

I reached my hand down and wrapped it around hers, pulling her up onto the platform at the top of the water tower.

She slid into my arms, falling into sobs that beat against my chest. I don't know which one of us was crying harder. I'm not even sure we remembered to kiss. What we had went so much deeper than a kiss.

When we were together, she turned me completely inside out.

It didn't matter if we were dead or alive. We could never be kept apart. There were some things more powerful than worlds or universes. She was my world, as much as I was hers. What we had, we knew.

The poems are all wrong. It's a bang, a really big bang. Not a whimper.

And sometimes gold can stay.

Anybody who's ever been in love can tell you that.

⊰ CHAPTER 37 ⊱

What the Words Never Say

Amma Treadeau has been declared legally dead, following her disappearance from Wate's Landing, the home of Mitchell and Ethan Wate, on Cotton Bend, in Central Gatlin'—" I stopped reading out loud.

I was sitting at her kitchen table, where her One-Eyed Menace waited sadly in the mason jar on her counter, and it didn't seem possible that I was reading Amma's obituary. Not when I could still smell the Red Hots and the pencil lead.

"Keep readin'." Aunt Grace was leaning over my shoulder, trying to read the print that her bifocals were ten strengths too weak to read.

Aunt Mercy was sitting in her wheelchair, on the other side

of the table, next to my dad. "They best say somethin' about Amma's pie. Or the Good Lord as my witness, I'll go down there ta *The Stars 'n' Bars* and give them a piece a my mind." Aunt Mercy still thought our town newspaper was named after the Confederate flag.

"It's *The Stars and Stripes*," my father corrected gently. "And I'm sure they worked hard to assure Amma is remembered for all her talents."

"Hmm." Aunt Grace sniffed. "Folks 'round here don't know a lick about talent. Prudence Jane's singin' was looked over by the choir for years."

Aunt Mercy crossed her arms. "She had the voice of an angel if I ever heard one."

I was surprised Aunt Mercy could hear anything without her hearing aid. She was still carrying on when Lena began to Kelt with me.

Ethan? Are you okay?

I'm okay, L.

You don't sound okay.

I'm dealing.

Hold on. I'm coming.

Amma's face stared out at me from the newspaper, printed in black and white. Wearing her best Sunday dress, the one with the white collar. I wondered if someone had taken that photo at my mom's funeral or Aunt Prue's. It could've been Macon's.

There had been so many.

I laid the paper down on the scarred wood. I hated that obituary. Someone from the paper must have written it, not someone who knew Amma. They'd gotten everything wrong. I guess I had a new reason to hate *The Stars and Stripes* as much as Aunt Grace did.

I closed my eyes, listening to the Sisters fuss about everything from Amma's obituary to the fact that Thelma couldn't make grits the right way. I knew it was their way of paying their respects to the woman who had raised my dad and me. The woman who had made them pitcher after pitcher of sweet tea and made sure they didn't leave the house with their skirts hitched up in their pantyhose when they left for church.

After a while, I couldn't hear them at all. Just the quiet sound of Wate's Landing mourning, too. The floorboards creaked, but this time I knew it wasn't Amma in the next room. None of her pots were banging. No cleavers were attacking the cutting board. No warm food would be coming my way.

Not unless my dad and I taught ourselves how to cook.

There were no casseroles piled up on our porch either. Not this time. There wasn't a soul in Gatlin who would have dared bring their sorry excuse for a pot roast to mark Miss Amma Treadeau's passing. And if they did, we wouldn't have eaten it.

Not that anyone around here really believed she was gone. At least that's what they said. "She'll come back, Ethan. 'Member the way she just showed up without sayin' a word, the day you were born?" It was true. Amma had raised my father and moved out to Wader's Creek with her family. But as the story goes, the day my parents brought me home from the hospital, she showed up with her quilting bag and moved back in.

Now Amma was gone, and she wasn't coming back. More than anyone, I knew how that worked. I looked at the worn spot on the floorboards over by the stove, in front of the oven door.

I miss her, L.

I miss her, too.

I miss both of them.

I know.

I heard Thelma walk into the room, a hunk of tobacco tucked under her lip. "All right, girls. I think y'all have had enough excitement for one mornin'. Let's go on in the other room and see what we can win on *The Price Is Right*."

Thelma winked at me and wheeled Aunt Mercy out of the room. Aunt Grace was right behind them, with Harlon James at her feet. "I hope they're givin' away one a those iceboxes that makes water all on its own."

My dad reached for the newspaper and started reading where I left off. " 'Memorial services will be held at the Chapel at Wader's Creek.' " My mind flashed on Amma and Macon, standing face to face in the middle of the foggy swamp on the wrong side of midnight.

"Aw, hell, I tried to tell anyone who would listen. Amma doesn't want a service." He sighed.

"Nope."

"She's fussing around somewhere right now, saying, 'I don't see why you're wastin' good time mournin' me. Sure as my Sweet Redeemer, I'm not wastin' my time mournin' you.'"

I smiled. He cocked his head to the left, just like Amma did when she was on the rampage. "T. O. M. F. O. O. L. E. R. Y. Ten down. As in, this whole thing's nothin' but hodgepodge and nonsense, Mitchell Wate."

This time I laughed, because my dad was right. I could hear her saying it. She hated being the center of attention, especially when it involved the infamous Gatlin Funerary Pity Parade.

My dad read the next paragraph. "'Miss Amma Treadeau was born in Unincorporated Gatlin County, South Carolina, the sixth of seven children born to the late Treadeau family.'" The sixth of seven children? Had Amma ever mentioned her sisters and brothers? I only remembered her talking about the Greats.

He skimmed the length of the obituary. "'By some count, her career as a baker of local renown spanned at least five decades and as many county fairs.'" He shook his head again. "But no mention of her Carolina Gold? Good Lord, I hope Amma's not reading this from some cloud up on high. She'll be sending lightning bolts down, left and right."

She's not, I thought. *Amma doesn't care what they say about her now. Not the folks in Gatlin. She's sitting on a porch somewhere with the Greats.*

He kept going. "'Miss Amma leaves behind her extended family, a host of cousins, and a circle of close family friends.'"

He folded up the paper and tossed it back onto the table. "Where's the part where Miss Amma leaves behind two of the sorriest, hungriest, saddest boys ever to inhabit Wate's Landing?" He tapped his fingers restlessly on the wood tabletop between us.

I didn't know what to say at first. "Dad?"

"Yeah?"

"We're going to be okay, you know?"

It was true. That's what she'd been doing all this time, if you thought about it. Getting us ready for a time when she wouldn't be there to get us ready for all the times after that.

For now.

My dad must have understood, because he let his hand fall heavily on my shoulder. "Yes, sir. Don't I know it."

I didn't say anything else.

We sat there together, staring out the kitchen window. "Anything else would be downright disrespectful." His voice sounded wobbly, and I knew he was crying. "She raised us pretty well, Ethan."

"She sure did." I fought back the tears myself. Out of respect, I guess, like my dad said. This was how it had to be now.

This was real.

It hurt—it almost killed me—but it was real, the same way losing my mom was real. I had to accept it. Maybe this was the way the universe was meant to unravel, at least this part of it.

The right thing and the easy thing are never the same.

Amma had taught me that, better than anyone.

"Maybe she and Lila Jane are taking care of each other now. Maybe they're sitting together, talking over fried tomatoes and sweet tea." My dad laughed, even though he was crying.

He had no idea how close to the truth he was, and I didn't tell him.

"Cherries." That was all I said.

"What?" My dad looked at me funny.

"Mom likes cherries. Straight out of the colander, remember?" I turned my head his way. "But I'm not sure Aunt Prue is letting either one of them get a word in edgewise."

He nodded and stretched out his hand until it brushed against my arm. "Your mom doesn't care. She just wants to be left in peace with her books for a while, don't you think? At least until we get there?"

"At least," I said, though I couldn't look at him now. My heart was pulled so many different ways at once, I didn't know what I was feeling. Part of me wished I could tell him that I'd seen my mom. That she was okay.

We sat like that, not moving or talking, until I felt my heart start to pound.

L? Is that you?

Come out, Ethan. I'm waiting.

I heard the music before I saw the Beater roll into view through the windowpanes. I stood up and nodded at my dad. "I'm going up to Lena's for a while."

"You take all the time you need."

428

"Thanks, Dad."

As I turned to leave the kitchen, I caught one last sight of my dad, sitting alone at the table with the newspaper. I couldn't do it. I couldn't leave him like that.

I reached back for the paper.

I don't know why I took it. Maybe I just wanted to keep her with me a little while longer. Maybe I didn't want my dad to sit alone with all those feelings, wrapped in a stupid paper with a bad crossword puzzle and a worse obituary.

Then it came to me.

I pulled open Amma's drawer and grabbed a #2 pencil. I held it up to show my dad.

He grinned. "Started out sharp, and then she sharpened it."

"It's what she would have wanted. One last time."

He leaned back in his chair until he could reach the drawer and tossed me a box of Red Hots. "One last time."

I gave him a hug. "I love you, Dad."

Then I swept my hand across the length of the kitchen windows, sending salt spraying all over the kitchen floor.

"It's time to let the ghosts in."

———

I only made it halfway down the porch steps before Lena found me. She jumped up into my arms, circling her skinny legs around mine. She clung to me and I held on to her, like neither one of us was ever letting go.

There was electricity, plenty of electricity. But as her lips found mine, there was nothing but sweetness and peace. Kind of like coming home, when a home's still a shelter and not the storm itself.

Everything was different between us. There was nothing keeping us apart anymore. I didn't know if it was because of the New Order, or because I'd journeyed to the end of the Otherworld and back. Either way, I could hold Lena's hand without burning a hole in my palm.

Her touch was warm. Her fingers were soft. Her kiss was just a kiss now. A kiss that was every bit as big and every bit as small as a kiss can be.

It wasn't an electrical storm or a fire. Nothing exploded or burned or even short-circuited. Lena belonged to me, the same way I belonged to her. And now we could be together.

The Beater honked, and we broke off kissing.

"Any day now." Link stuck his head out the window. "I'm gettin' gray hairs sittin' here watchin' you kids."

I grinned at him, but I couldn't pull myself away from her. "I love you, Lena Duchannes. I always have, and I always will." The words were as true today as the first time I'd said them, on her Sixteenth Moon.

"And I love you, Ethan Wate. I've loved you since the first day we met. Or before." Lena looked straight in my eyes, smiling.

"Way before." I smiled back, deep into hers.

"But I have something to tell you." She leaned closer.

"Something you should probably know about the girl you love."

My stomach flipped a little. "What is it?"

"My name."

"You're not serious?" I knew Casters learned their real names after they were Claimed, but Lena was never willing to tell me hers, no matter how many times I asked. I figured it was hers to tell when she felt like the time was right. Which, I guess, was now.

"Do you still want to know?" She grinned because she already knew the answer.

I nodded.

"It's Josephine Duchannes. Josephine, daughter of Sarafine." The last word was a whisper, but I heard it, as if she had shouted it from the rooftops.

I squeezed her hand.

Her name. The last missing piece of her family puzzle, and the one thing you couldn't find on any family tree.

I hadn't told Lena about her mother yet. Part of me wanted to believe that Sarafine had given up her soul so I could be with Lena again—that her sacrifice was about more than just revenge. Someday I would tell Lena what her mother did for me. Lena deserved to know Sarafine wasn't all bad.

The Beater honked again.

"Come on, lovebirds. We gotta get to the Dar-ee Keen. Everyone's waitin'."

I grabbed Lena's other hand and pulled her down the front

lawn to the Beater. "We have to make a quick stop on the way."

"Is this gonna involve any Dark Casters? Do I need the shears?"

"We're just going to the library."

Link leaned his forehead against the steering wheel. "I haven't renewed my library card since I was ten. I think I'd have better odds with Dark Casters."

I stood in front of the car door and looked at Lena. The back door opened by itself, and we both climbed in.

"Aw, man. Now I'm your cabdriver? You Casters and Mortals have a really screwed-up way a showin' your appreciation to a guy." Link turned up the music, as if he didn't want to hear whatever I had to say.

"I appreciate you." I smacked his head from behind, good and hard. He didn't even seem to feel it. I was talking to Link, but I was looking at Lena. I couldn't stop looking at her. She was more beautiful than I remembered, more beautiful and more real.

I curled a strand of her hair through my fingers, and she leaned her cheek against my hand. We were together. It was hard to think or see or even talk about anything else. Then I felt bad for feeling so good when I was still carrying *The Stars and Stripes* in my back pocket.

"Wait. Check it out." Link paused. "That's exactly what I needed to finish my new lyrics. 'Candy girl. Hurts so sweet she'll make you want to hurl—' "

Lena put her head on my shoulder. "Did I mention that my cousin's back in town?"

"Of course she is." I smiled.

Link winked at me in the rearview mirror. I smacked him in the head again as the car pulled down the street.

"I think you're gonna be a rock star," I said.

"I gotta get back to workin' on my demo track, you know? 'Cause as soon as we graduate, I'm headin' straight to New York, the big time...."

Link was so full of crap, he could pass for a toilet. Just like the old days. Just like it was supposed to be.

It was all the proof I needed.

I was really home.

⊰ CHAPTER 38 ⊱

Eleven Across

You kids go on in," Link said, turning up the latest Holy Rollers demo. "I'm gonna wait here. I get enough a books at school."

Lena and I climbed out of the Beater and stood in front of the Gatlin County Library. The repairs were further along than I remembered. All the major construction was finished on the outside, and the fine ladies of the DAR had already started planting saplings near the door.

The inside of the building was less finished. Plastic sheets hung across one side, and I could see tools and sawhorses on the other. But Aunt Marian had already set up this particular area, which didn't surprise me at all. She would rather have half a library than no library, any day.

"Aunt Marian?" My voice echoed more than usual, and within seconds she appeared at the end of the aisle in her stocking feet. I could see the tears in her eyes as she rushed in for a hug.

"I still can't believe it." She hugged me tighter.

"Trust me, I know."

I heard the sound of dress shoes against the uncarpeted concrete.

"Mr. Wate, it is a pleasure to see you, son." Macon had a huge smile plastered across his face. It was the same one he seemed to have every time he saw me now, and it was starting to creep me out a little.

He gave Lena a squeeze and made his way over to me. I held out my hand to shake his, but he swung his arm around my neck instead.

"It's good to see you, too, sir. We kinda wanted to talk to you and Aunt Marian."

She raised an eyebrow. "Oh?"

Lena was twisting her charm necklace, waiting for me to explain. I guess she didn't want to break the news to her uncle that we could make out all we wanted now without putting my life in danger. So I did the honors. And as intrigued as Macon seemed, I was pretty sure he liked it better when kissing Lena posed the threat of electric shock.

Marian turned to Macon, at a loss. "Remarkable. What do you think it means?"

He was pacing in front of the stacks. "I'm not entirely sure."

435

"Whatever it is, do you think it will affect other Casters and Mortals?" Lena was hoping this was some kind of change in the Order of Things. Maybe a cosmic bonus, after everything I'd been through.

"That's doubtful, but we will certainly look into it." He glanced at Marian.

She nodded. "Of course."

Lena tried to hide her disappointment, but her uncle knew her too well. "Even if this isn't affecting other Casters and Mortals, it is affecting the two of you. Change has to start somewhere, even in the supernatural world."

I heard a creak, and the front door slammed. "Dr. Ashcroft?"

I looked at Lena. I would've known that voice anywhere. Apparently, Macon recognized it, too, because he ducked behind the stacks with Lena and me.

"Hello, Martha." Marian gave Mrs. Lincoln her friendliest librarian voice.

"Was that Wesley's car I saw out front? Is he in here?"

"I'm sorry. He's not."

Link was probably scrunched down on the floor of the Beater, hiding from his mother.

"Is there anything else I can do for you today?" Marian asked politely.

"What you can do," Mrs. Lincoln fussed, "is try to read this book a witchcraft and explain to me how we can allow our children to check this out a the public library."

I didn't have to look to know what series she was referring

to, but I just couldn't help myself. I poked my head around the corner to see Link's mom waving a copy of *Harry Potter and the Half-Blood Prince* in the air.

I couldn't stop myself from smiling. It was good to know some things in Gatlin would never change.

I didn't take *The Stars and Stripes* out during lunch. They say that when someone you love dies, you can't eat. But today I had a cheeseburger with extra pickles, a double order of fries, a raspberry Oreo shake, and a banana split with hot fudge, caramel, and extra whip.

I felt like I hadn't eaten in weeks. I guess I hadn't actually eaten anything in the Otherworld, and my body seemed to know it.

As Lena and I ate, Link and Ridley were joking around together, which sounded more like fighting to anyone who didn't know better.

Ridley shook her head. "Seriously? The Beater? Didn't we go over this on the way here?"

"I wasn't listenin'. I only pay attention to about ten percent a what you say." He glanced at her over his shoulder. "I'm ninety percent too busy lookin' at you sayin' it."

"Yeah, well, maybe I'm a hundred percent too busy looking the other way." She acted annoyed, but I knew Ridley better than that.

Link only grinned. "And they say you don't use math in real life."

Ridley unwrapped a red lollipop and made a show of it, like always. "If you think I'm going to New York with you in that rust bucket, you're crazier than I thought, Hot Rod."

Link nuzzled her neck, and Rid swatted him. "Come on, Babe. It was awesome last time. And this time we won't have to sleep in the Beater."

Lena raised an eyebrow at her cousin. "You slept in a car?"

Rid tossed her blond and pink hair. "I couldn't leave Shrinky Dink alone. It's not like he was a hybrid back then."

Link wiped his greasy hands on his Iron Maiden T-shirt. "You know you love me, Rid. Admit it."

Ridley pretended to scoot away from him, but she barely moved an inch. "I'm a Siren, in case you've forgotten. I don't *love* anything."

Link kissed her on the cheek. "Except me."

"You got room for two more?" John was balancing a tray of freezes and french fries in one hand, his other hand locked around Liv's.

Lena smiled at Liv and moved over. "Always."

There was a time when I couldn't get the two of them to stand in the same room. But that felt like a lifetime ago. Technically, for me, I guess it was.

Liv tucked herself under John's arm. She was wearing her periodic table shirt and her trademark blond braids. "I hope you don't think we're sharing those." She slid the paper boat full of chili fries in front of her.

"I would never get between you and your fries, Olivia." John leaned over and gave her a quick kiss.

"Smart boy." Liv looked happy—not make-the-best-of-it happy but the real kind of happy. And I was happy for both of them.

Charlotte Chase called out from behind the counter; looked like her summer job had turned into a year-round after-school job. "Anybody wanna slice a pecan pie? Fresh outta the oven?" She held up the sad-looking boxed pie. It wasn't fresh out of anybody's oven, not even Sara Lee's.

"No, thanks," Lena said.

Link was still staring at the pie. "Bet it's not good enough to be Amma's worst pecan pie." He missed Amma, too. I could tell. She had always been on him about one thing or another, but she loved Link. And he knew it. Amma let him get away with things I never could, which reminded me of something.

"Link, what did you do in my basement when you were nine years old?" To this day, Link had never told me what Amma had on him. I had always wanted to know, but it was the one secret I'd never been able to get out of him.

Link squirmed in his seat. "Come on, man. Some things are private."

Ridley looked at him suspiciously. "Is that when you got into the schnapps and puked everywhere?"

He shook his head. "Naw. That was someone else's basement." He shrugged. "Hey, there's a whole lotta basements around here."

We were all staring at him.

"Fine." He ran his hand over his spiky hair nervously. "She caught me..." He hesitated. "She caught me dressed up—"

"Dressed up?" I didn't even want to think about what that meant.

Link rubbed his face, embarrassed. "It was awful, dude. And if my mom ever found out, she'd kill you for sayin' it and me for doin' it."

"What were you wearing?" Lena asked. "A dress? High heels?"

He shook his head. His face was turning red with shame. "Worse."

Ridley whacked him on the arm, looking pretty nervous herself. "Spill. What the hell did you have on?"

Link hung his head. "A Union soldier's uniform. I stole it from Jimmy Weeks' garage."

I burst out laughing, and within seconds so did Link. No one else at the table understood the sin in a Southern boy— with a father who led the Confederate Cavalry in the Reenactment of the Battle of Honey Hill, and a mother who was a proud member of the Sisters of the Confederacy—trying on a Civil War uniform for the opposing side. You had to be from Gatlin.

It was one of those unspoken truths, like you don't make a

pie for the Wates because it won't be better than Amma's; you don't sit in front of Sissy Honeycutt in church because she talks the whole time right along with the preacher; and you don't choose the paint color for your house without consulting Mrs. Lincoln, not unless your name happens to be Lila Evers Wate.

Gatlin was like that.

It was family, all of it and all of them—the good parts and the bad.

Mrs. Asher even told Mrs. Snow to tell Mrs. Lincoln to tell Link to tell me that she was glad to have me home from Aunt Caroline's in one piece. I told Link to thank her, and I meant it. Maybe Mrs. Lincoln would even make me some of her famous brownies again one day.

If she did, I bet I would clean the plate.

———⟋○⟍———

When Link dropped us off, Lena and I headed straight for Greenbrier. It was our place, and no matter how many terrible things happened here, it would always be the place where we found the locket. Where I saw Lena move the clouds for the first time, even if I didn't realize it. Where we'd practically taught ourselves Latin, trying to translate from *The Book of Moons*.

The secret garden at Greenbrier held our secrets from the beginning. And in a way, we were beginning again.

Lena gave me a funny look when I finally unrolled the paper I had been carrying around all afternoon.

"What's that?" She closed her spiral notebook, the one she spent all her time writing in, like she couldn't get everything on the page fast enough.

"The crossword puzzle." We lay on our stomachs in the grass, curled up against each other in our old spot by the tree near the lemon groves, near the hearthstone. True to its name, Greenbrier was the greenest I'd ever seen it. Not a lubber or a bunch of dead brown grass in sight. Gatlin really was back to the best version of its old self.

We did this, L. We didn't know how powerful we were.

She leaned her head on my shoulder.

We do now.

I didn't know how long it would last, but I swore to myself that I wouldn't take it for granted ever again. Not one minute of what we had.

"I thought we could do it. You know, for Amma."

"The crossword?"

I nodded, and she laughed. "You know, I never even looked at those crossword puzzles? Not once. Not until you were gone and started using them to talk to me."

"Pretty clever, right?" I nudged her.

"Better than you trying to write songs. Though your puzzles weren't that great either." She smiled, biting her lower lip. I couldn't resist kissing it over and over and over, until she finally pulled away, laughing.

"Okay. They were much better." She touched her forehead to mine.

I smiled. "Admit it, L. You loved my crosswords."

"Are you kidding? Of course I did. You came back to me every time I looked at those stupid puzzles."

"I was desperate."

We unrolled the paper between us, and I got out the #2 pencil. I should have known what we'd see.

Amma had left me a message, like the ones I left for Lena.

Two across. As in, to be or not to.

B. E.

Four down. As in, the opposite of evil.

G. O. O. D.

Five down. As in, the victim of a sledding injury, from an Edith Wharton novel.

E. T. H. A. N.

Ten across. As in, an expression of joy.

H. A. L. L. E. L. U. J. A. H.

I crumpled up the paper and pulled Lena toward me.

Amma was home.

Amma was with me.

And Amma was gone.

I pretty much wept until the sun fell out of the sky and the meadow around me was as dark and as light as I felt.

CHAPTER 39

A Hymn for Amma

order is not orderly
no more than things are things
hallelujah
no sense to be made of water towers
or christmas towns
when you can't tell up from down
hallelujah
graves are always grave
from inside or out
and love breaks what can't be broken
hallelujah
one I loved I loved, one I loved I lost

now she is strong though she is gone
found and paid her way
she flew away
hallelujah
light the dark — sing the greats
a new day
hallelujah

⊰ EPILOGUE ⊱

After

That night, I lay in my ancient mahogany bed in my room, like generations of Wates before me. Books beneath me. Broken cell phone next to me. Old iPod hanging around my neck. Even my road map was back on the wall again. Lena had taped it up herself. It didn't matter how comfortable everything was. I couldn't sleep—that's how much thinking I had to do.

At least, remembering.

When I was little, my grandfather died. I loved my grandfather, for a thousand reasons I couldn't tell you, and a thousand stories I could barely remember.

After it happened, I hid out back, up in the tree that grew

halfway out of our fence, where the neighbors used to throw green peaches at my friends and me, and where we used to throw them at the neighbors.

I couldn't stop crying, no matter how hard I jammed my fists into my eyes. I guess I never realized people could die before.

First my dad came outside and tried to talk me down out of that stupid tree. Then my mom tried. Nothing they said could make me feel any better. I asked if my grandpa was in Heaven, like they said in Sunday school. My mom said she wasn't sure. It was the historian in her. She said no one really knew what happened when we died.

Maybe we became butterflies. Maybe we became people all over again. Maybe we just died and nothing happened.

I only cried harder. A historian isn't really what you're looking for in that kind of situation. That's when I told her I didn't want Poppi to die, but more than that, I didn't want her to die, and even more than that, I didn't want to die either. Then she broke down.

It was her dad.

I came down from the tree on my own afterward, and we cried together. She pulled me into her arms, right there on the back steps of Wate's Landing, and said I wouldn't die.

I wouldn't.

She promised.

I wasn't going to die, and neither would she.

After that, the only thing I remember was going inside and

eating three pieces of raspberry-cherry pie, the kind with the crisscross sugar crust. Someone had to die before Amma would make that pie.

Eventually, I grew up and grew older and stopped looking for my mom's lap every time I felt like crying. I even stopped going in that old tree. But it was years before I realized my mom had lied to me. It wasn't until she left me that I even remembered what she'd said.

I don't know what I'm trying to say. I don't know what any of this is really about.

Why we bother.

Why we're here.

Why we love.

I had a family, and they were everything to me, and I didn't even know it when I had them. I had a girl, and she was everything to me, and I knew it every second I had her.

I lost them all. Everything a guy could ever want.

I found my way home again, but don't be fooled. Nothing's the same as before. I'm not sure I'd want it to be.

Either way, I'm still one of the luckiest guys around.

I'm not a church kind of a person, not when it comes to praying. To be honest, for me it never gets much past hoping. But I know this, and I want to say it. And I really hope someone will listen.

There is a point. I don't know what it is, but everything I've had, and everything I've lost, and everything I felt—it meant something.

Maybe there isn't a meaning to life. Maybe there's only a meaning to living.

That's what I've learned. That's what I'm going to be doing from now on.

Living.

And loving, sappy as it sounds.

Lena Duchannes. Her name rhymes with rain.

I'm not falling anymore. That's what L says, and she's right.

I guess you could say I'm flying.

We both are.

And I'm pretty sure somewhere up there in the real blue sky and carpenter bee greatness, Amma's flying, too.

We all are, depending on how you look at it. Flying or falling, it's up to us.

Because the sky isn't really made of blue paint, and there aren't just two kinds of people in this world, the stupid and the stuck. We only think there are. Don't waste your time with either—with anything. It's not worth it.

You can ask my mom, if it's the right kind of starry night. The kind with two Caster moons and a Northern and a Southern Star.

At least I know I can.

I get up in the night and make my way across the creaking floorboards. They feel astonishingly real, and there isn't a moment I think I'm dreaming. In the kitchen, I take an armful of spotless glasses out of the cupboard that hangs over the counter.

One by one, I set them on the table in a row.

Empty except for moonlight.

The refrigerator light is so bright, it surprises me. On the bottom shelf, tucked behind a rotting head of unchopped cabbage, I find it.

Chocolate milk.

Just as I suspected.

I might not have wanted it anymore, and I might not have been here to drink it, but I knew there was no way Amma had stopped buying it.

I rip open the cardboard and fold out the spout—something I could do in my sleep, which is practically the state I'm in. I couldn't make Uncle Abner a pie if my life depended on it, and I don't even know where Amma keeps the recipe for Tunnel of Fudge.

But this I know.

One by one, I fill the glasses.

One for Aunt Prue, who saw everything without blinking.

One for Twyla, who gave up everything without hesitating.

One for my mom, who let me go not once but twice.

One for Amma, who took her place with the Greats so I could take mine in Gatlin again.

A glass of chocolate milk doesn't seem like enough, but it isn't really the milk, and we all know that—all of us here, anyway.

Because the moonlight shimmers in the empty wooden chairs around me, and I know, as always, that I am not alone.

I'm never alone.

I push the last glass through the patch of moonlight across the scarred kitchen table. The light flutters like the twinkling of a Sheer's eye.

"Drink up," I say, but it's not what I mean.

Especially not to Amma and my mom.

I love you, and I always will.

I need you, and I keep you with me.

The good and the bad, the sugar and the salt, the kicks and the kisses—what's come before and what will come after, you and me—

We are all mixed up in this together, under one warm piecrust.

Everything about me remembers everything about you.

Then I take a fifth glass down from the shelf, the last of our clean glasses. I fill it to the brim with milk, so close that I have to slurp the top to keep it from overflowing.

Lena laughs at the way I always fill my cup as full as it can go. I feel her smiling in her sleep.

I raise my glass to the moon and drink it myself.

Life has never tasted sweeter.

HERE ENDETH

THE
CASTER
CHRONICLES

Fabula Peracta Est.
Scripta Aeterna Manent.

A Seer's moons, a Siren's tears,
Nineteen Mortal, Wayward fears,
Incubus graves and Caster rivers,
The Final Page the End delivers.

Acknowledgments

We've loved every minute of this.
Every character, every chapter, every page.
More than anything, all we need to acknowledge now is
the one person who made it all happen—
YOU.
Our favorite Caster Reader(s).
Thank you. For everything. For all of it.
It's been a wild ride—
we hope you'll keep reading
and keep believing
in true love,
things hidden in plain sight,
the world between the cracks,
and, more than anything, yourself.
We know we will.

Love always—and we do mean that—

KAMI & MARGIE

Special thanks to:

OUR EDITOR—JULIE SCHEINA

OUR LATIN TRANSLATOR—DR. SARA LINDHEIM

OUR CREATIVE DIRECTOR—DAVE CAPLAN

OUR COPY EDITOR—BARBARA BAKOWSKI

OUR PUBLICITY MANAGER—JESSICA BROMBERG

OUR MARKETING MANAGER—LISA ICKOWICZ

AND THE ENTIRE BEAUTIFUL CREATURES NOVELS TEAM
AT LITTLE, BROWN BOOKS FOR YOUNG READERS!

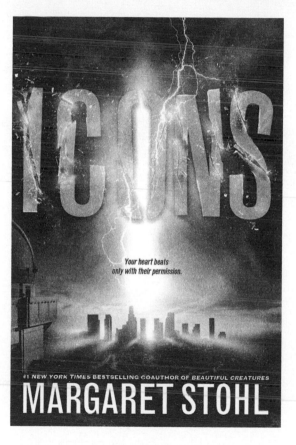

PROLOGUE
THE DAY

One tiny gray dot, no bigger than a freckle, marks the inside of the baby's chubby arm. It slips in and out of view as she cries, waving her yellow rubber duck back and forth.

Her mother holds her over the old ceramic bathtub. The little feet kick harder, twisting above the water. "You can complain all you want, Doloria, but you're still taking a bath. It will make you feel better."

She slides her daughter into the warm tub. The baby kicks again, splashing the blue patterned wallpaper above the tiles. The water surprises her, and she quiets.

"That's it. You can't feel sad in the water. There is no sadness there." She kisses Doloria's cheek. "I love you, *mi corazón*. I love you and your brothers today and tomorrow and every day until the day after heaven."

The baby stops crying. She does not cry as she is

scrubbed and sung to, pink and clean. She does not cry as she is kissed and swaddled in blankets. She does not cry as she is tickled and tucked into her crib.

The mother smiles, wiping a damp strand of hair from her child's warm forehead. "Dream well, Doloria. *Que sueñes con los angelitos.*" She reaches for the light, but the room floods with darkness before she can touch the switch. Across the hall, the radio is silenced midsentence, as if on cue. Over in the kitchen, the television fades to sudden black, to a dot the size of a pinprick, then to nothing.

The mother calls up the stairs. "The power's gone off again, *querido*! Check the fuse box." She turns back, tucking the blanket corner snugly beneath Doloria. "Don't worry. It's nothing your *papi* can't fix."

The baby sucks on her fist, five small fingers the size of tiny wriggling earthworms, as the walls start to shake and bits of plaster swirl in the air like fireworks, like confetti.

She blinks as the windows shatter and the ceiling fan hits the carpet and the shouting begins.

She yawns as her father rolls down the staircase like a funny rag doll that never stands up.

She closes her eyes as the falling birds patter against the roof like rain.

She starts to dream as her mother's heart stops beating.

I start to dream as my mother's heart stops beating.

HAPPY BIRTHDAY TO ME

"Dol? Are you okay?"

The memory fades at the sound of his voice.

Ro.

I feel him somewhere in my mind, the nameless place where I see everything, feel everyone. The spark that is Ro. I hold on to it, warm and close, like a mug of steamed milk or a lit candle.

And then I open my eyes and come back to him.

Always.

Ro's here with me. He's fine, and I'm fine.

I'm fine.

I think it, over and over, until I believe it. Until I remember what is real and what is not.

Slowly the physical world comes into focus. I'm standing on a dirt trail halfway up the side of a mountain—staring down at the Mission, where the goats and pigs in the field below are small as ants.

"All right?" Ro reaches toward me and touches my arm.

I nod. But I'm lying.

I've let the feelings—and the memories—overtake me again. I can't do that. Everyone at the Mission knows I have a gift for feeling things—strangers, friends, even Ramona Jamona the pig, when she's hungry—but it doesn't mean I have to let the feelings control me.

At least that's what the Padre keeps telling me.

I try to control myself, and usually I can. But I wish I didn't feel anything, sometimes. Especially not when everything is so overwhelming, so unbearably sad.

"Don't disappear on me, Dol. Not now." Ro locks his eyes on me and motions with his big tan hands. His brown-gold eyes flicker with fire and light under his dark tangle of hair. His face is all broad planes and rough angles—as solid as a brambled oak, softening only for me. He could climb halfway up the mountain again by now, or halfway down. Holding Ro back is like trying to stop an earthquake or a mud slide. Maybe a train.

But not now. Now he waits. Because he knows me, and he knows where I've gone.

Where I go.

I stare up at the sky, spattered with bursts of gray rain and orange light. It's hard to see past the wide-brimmed hat I stole off the hook behind the Padre's office door.

Still, the setting sun is in my eyes, pulsing from behind the clouds, bright and broken.

I remember what we are doing and why we are here.

My birthday. It's my seventeenth birthday tomorrow.

Ro has a present for me, but first we have to climb the hill. He wants to surprise me.

"Give me a clue, Ro." I pull myself up the hill after him, leaving a twisting trail of dried brush and dirt behind me.

"Nope."

I turn to look down the mountain again. I can't stop myself. I like how everything looks from up here.

Peaceful. Smaller. Like a painting, or one of the Padre's impossible puzzles, except there aren't any missing pieces. In the distance below, I can see the yellowing patch of field that belongs to our Mission, then the fringe of green trees, then the deep blue wash of the ocean.

Home.

The view is so serene, you almost wouldn't know about The Day. That's why I like it here. If you don't leave the Mission, you don't have to think about it. The Day and the Icons and the Lords. The way they control us.

How powerless we are.

This far up the Tracks, away from the cities, nothing ever changes. This land has always been wild.

A person can feel safe here.

Safer.

I raise my voice. "It'll be getting dark soon."

He's up the trail, once again. Then I hear a ripple through the brush, and the sound of rolling rock, and he lands behind me, nimble as a mountain goat.

Ro smiles. "I know, Dol."

I take his calloused hand and relax my fingers into his. Instantly, I am flooded with the feeling of Ro—physical contact always makes our connection that much stronger.

He is as warm as the sun behind me. As hot as I am cold. As rough as I am smooth. That's our balance, just one of the invisible threads that tie us together.

It's who we are.

My best-and-only friend and me.

He rummages in his pocket, then pushes something into my hands, suddenly shy. "All right, I'll hurry it up. Your first present."

I look down. A lone blue glass bead rolls between my fingers. A slender leather cord loops in a circle around it.

A necklace.

It's the blue of the sky, of my eyes, of the ocean.

"Ro," I breathe. "It's perfect."

"It reminded me of you. It's the water, see? So you can always keep it with you." His face reddens as he tries to explain, the words sticking in his mouth. "I know—how it makes you feel."

Peaceful. Permanent. Unbroken.

"Bigger helped me with the cord. It used to be part of a saddle." Ro has an eye for things like that, things other people overlook. Bigger, the Mission cook, is the same way, and the two of them are inseparable. Biggest, Bigger's wife, tries her best to keep both of them out of trouble.

"I love it." I thread my arm around his neck in a rough hug. Not so much an embrace as a cuff of arms, the clench of friends and family.

Ro looks embarrassed, all the same. "It's not your whole present. For that you have to climb a little farther."

"But it's not even my birthday yet."

"It's your birthday eve. I thought it was only fair to start tonight. Besides, this kind of present is best after sundown." Ro holds out his hand, a wicked look in his eyes.

"Come on. Just one little hint." I squint up at him and he grins.

"But it's a surprise."

"You're making me hike all this way through the brush."

He laughs. "Okay. It's the last thing you'd ever expect. The very last thing." He bounces up and down a bit where he stands, and I can tell he's practically ready to bolt up the mountain.

"What are you talking about?"

He shakes his head, holding out his hand again. "You'll see."

I take it. There's no getting Ro to talk when he doesn't want to. Besides, his hand in mine is a good thing.

I feel the beating of his heart, the pulse of his adrenaline.

Even now, when he's relaxed and hiking, and it's just the two of us. He is a coiled spring. He has no resting state, not really.

Not Ro.

A shadow crosses the hillside, and instinctively we dive for cover under the brush. The ship in the sky is sleek and silver, glinting ominously with the last reflective rays of the setting sun. I shiver, even though I'm not at all cold, and my face is half buried in Ro's warm shoulder.

I can't help it.

Ro murmurs into my ear as if he is talking to one of the Padre's puppies. It's more his tone than the words—that's how you speak to scared animals. "Don't be afraid, Dol. It's headed up the coast, probably to Goldengate. They never come this far inland, not here. They're not coming for us."

"You don't know that." The words sound grim in my mouth, but they're true.

"I do."

He slips his arm around me and we wait like that until the sky is clear.

Because he doesn't know. Not really.

People have hidden in these bushes for centuries, long before us. Long before there were ships in the skies.

First the Chumash lived here, then the Rancheros, then the Spanish missionaries, then the Californians, then the Americans, then the Grass. Which is me, at least since the Padre brought me back as a baby to La Purísima, our old Grass Mission, in the hills beyond the ocean.

These hills.

The Padre tells it like a story; he was on a crew searching for survivors in the silent city after The Day, only there were none. Whole city blocks were quiet as rain. Finally, he heard a tiny sound—so small, he thought he was imagining it—and there I was, crying purple-faced in my crib. He wrapped me in his coat and brought me home, just as he now brings us stray dogs.

It was also the Padre who taught me the history of these hills as we sat by the fire at night, along with the constellations of the stars and the phases of the moon. The names of the people who knew our land before we did.

Maybe it was supposed to be like this. Maybe this, the Occupation, the Embassies, all of it, maybe this is just another part of nature. Like the seasons of a year, or how a caterpillar turns into a cocoon. The water cycle. The tides.

Chumash Rancheros Spaniards Californians Americans Grass.

Sometimes I repeat the names of my people, all the people who have ever lived in my Mission. I say the names and I think, *I am them and they are me.*

I am the Misíon La Purísima de Concepción de la Santísima Virgen María, founded in Las Californias on the Day of the Feast of the Immaculate Conception of the

Blessed Virgin, on the Eighth Day of the Twelfth Month of the Year of Our Lord One Thousand Seven Hundred Eighty-Seven. Three hundred years ago.

Chumash Rancheros Spaniards Californians Americans Grass.

When I say the names they're not gone, not to me. Nobody died. Nothing ended. We're still here.

I'm still here.

That's all I want. To stay. And for Ro to stay, and the Padre. For us to stay safe, everyone here on the Mission.

But as I look back down the mountain I know that nothing stays, and the gold flush and fade of everything tells me that the sun is setting now.

No one can stop it from going. Not even me.

As my bare feet sank into the wet earth, I tried not to think about the dead bodies buried beneath me. I had passed this tiny graveyard a handful of times but never at night, and always outside the boundaries of its peeling iron gates.

I would've given anything to be standing outside them now.

In the moonlight, rows of weathered headstones exposed the neat stretch of lawn for what it truly was—the grassy lid of an enormous coffin.

A branch snapped, and I spun around.

"Elvis?" I searched for a trace of my cat's gray and white ringed tail.

Elvis never ran away, usually content to thread his way

between my ankles whenever I opened the door—until tonight. He had taken off so fast that I didn't even have time to grab my shoes, and I had chased him eight blocks until I ended up here.

Muffled voices drifted through the trees, and I froze.

On the other side of the gates, a girl wearing blue and gray Georgetown University sweats passed underneath the pale glow of the lamppost. Her friends caught up with her, laughing and stumbling down the sidewalk. They reached one of the academic buildings and disappeared inside.

It was easy to forget that the cemetery was in the middle of a college campus. As I walked deeper into the uneven rows, the lampposts vanished behind the trees, and the clouds plunged the graveyard in and out of shadow. I ignored the whispers in the back of my mind urging me to go home.

Something moved in my peripheral vision—a flash of white.

I scanned the stones, now completely bathed in black.

Come on, Elvis. Where are you?

Nothing scared me more than the dark. I liked to see what was coming, and darkness was a place where things could hide.

Think about something else.

The memory closed in before I could stop it....

My mother's face hovering above mine as I blinked

myself awake. The panic in her eyes as she pressed a finger over her lips, signaling me to be quiet. The cold floor against my feet as we made our way to her closet, where she pushed aside the dresses.

"Someone's in the house," she whispered, pulling a board away from the wall to reveal a small opening. "Stay here until I come back. Don't make a sound."

I squeezed inside as she worked the board back into place. I had never experienced absolute darkness before. I stared at a spot inches in front of me, where my palm rested on the board. But I couldn't see it.

I closed my eyes against the blackness. There were sounds—the stairs creaking, furniture scraping against the floor, muffled voices—and one thought replaying over and over in my mind.

What if she didn't come back?

Too terrified to see if I could get out from the inside, I kept my hand on the wood. I listened to my ragged breathing, convinced that whoever was in the house could hear it, too.

Eventually, the wood gave beneath my palm and a thin stream of light flooded the space. My mom reached for me, promising the intruders had fled. As she carried me out of her closet, I couldn't hear anything beyond the pounding of my heart, and I couldn't think about anything except the crushing weight of the dark.

I was only five when it happened, but I still remembered

every minute in the crawl space. It made the air around me now feel suffocating. Part of me wanted to go home, with or without my cat.

"Elvis, get out here!"

Something shifted between the chipped headstones in front of me.

"Elvis?"

A silhouette emerged from behind a stone cross.

I jumped, a tiny gasp escaping my lips. "Sorry." My voice wavered. "I'm looking for my cat."

The stranger didn't say a word.

Sounds intensified at a dizzying rate—branches breaking, leaves rustling, my pulse throbbing. I thought about the hundreds of unsolved crime shows I'd watched with my mom that began exactly like this—a girl standing alone somewhere she shouldn't be, staring at the guy who was about to attack her.

I stepped back, thick mud pushing up around my ankles like a hand rooting me to the spot.

Please don't hurt me.

The wind cut through the graveyard, lifting tangles of long hair off the stranger's shoulders and the thin fabric of a white dress from her legs.

Her legs.

Relief washed over me. "Have you seen a gray and white Siamese cat? I'm going to kill him when I find him."

Silence.

Her dress caught the moonlight, and I realized it wasn't a dress at all. She was wearing a nightgown. Who wandered around a cemetery in their nightgown?

Someone crazy.

Or someone sleepwalking.

You aren't supposed to wake a sleepwalker, but I couldn't leave her out here alone at night either.

"Hey? Can you hear me?"

The girl didn't move, gazing at me as if she could see my features in the darkness. An empty feeling unfolded in the pit of my stomach. I wanted to look at something else—anything but her unnerving stare.

My eyes drifted down to the base of the cross.

The girl's feet were as bare as mine, and it looked like they weren't touching the ground.

I blinked hard, unwilling to consider the other possibility. It had to be an effect of the moonlight and the shadows. I glanced at my own feet, caked in mud, and back to hers.

They were pale and spotless.

A flash of white fur darted in front of her and rushed toward me.

Elvis.

I grabbed him before he could get away. He hissed at me, clawing and twisting violently until I dropped him. My heart hammered in my chest as he darted across the grass and squeezed under the gate.

I looked back at the stone cross.

The girl was gone, the ground nothing but a smooth, untouched layer of mud.

Blood from the scratches trailed down my arm as I crossed the graveyard, trying to reason away the girl in the white nightgown.

Silently reminding myself that I didn't believe in ghosts.

When I stumbled back onto the well-lit sidewalk, there was no sign of Elvis. A guy with a backpack slung over his shoulder walked by and gave me a strange look when he noticed I was barefoot, and covered in mud up to my ankles. He probably thought I was a pledge.

My hands didn't stop shaking until I hit O Street, where the shadows of the campus ended and the lights of the DC traffic began. Tonight, even the tourists posing for pictures at the top of *The Exorcist* stairs were somehow reassuring.

The cemetery suddenly felt miles away, and I started second-guessing myself.

The girl in the graveyard hadn't been hazy or transparent like the ghosts in movies. She had looked like a regular girl.

Except she was floating.

Wasn't she?

Maybe the moonlight had only made it appear that way. And maybe the girl's feet weren't muddy because the ground where she'd been standing was dry. By the time I reached my block, lined with row houses crushed together like sardines, I convinced myself there were dozens of explanations.

Elvis lounged on our front steps, looking docile and bored. I considered leaving him outside to teach him a lesson, but I loved that stupid cat.

I still remembered the day my mom bought him for me. I came home from school crying because we'd made Father's Day gifts in class, and I was the only kid without a father. Mine had walked away when I was five and never looked back. My mom had wiped my tears and said, "I bet you're also the only kid in your class getting a kitten today."

Elvis had turned one of my worst days into one of my best.

I opened the door, and he darted inside. "You're lucky I let you in."

The house smelled like tomatoes and garlic, and my mom's voice drifted into the hallway. "I've got plans this weekend. Next weekend, too. I'm sorry, but I have to run. I think my daughter just came home. Kennedy?"

"Yeah, Mom."

"Were you at Elle's? I was about to call you."

I stepped into the doorway as she hung up the phone. "Not exactly."

She threw me a quick glance, and the wooden spoon slipped out of her hand and hit the floor, sending a spray of red sauce across the white tile. "What happened?"

"I'm fine. Elvis ran off, and it took forever to catch him."

Mom rushed over and examined the angry claw marks. "Elvis did this? He's never scratched anyone before."

"I guess he freaked out when I grabbed him."

Her gaze dropped to my mud-caked feet. "Where were you?"

I prepared for the standard lecture Mom issued whenever I went out at night: always carry your cell phone, don't walk alone, stay in well-lit areas, and her personal favorite—scream first and ask questions later. Tonight, I had violated them all.

"The old Jesuit cemetery?" My answer sounded more like a question—as in, exactly how upset was she going to be?

Mom stiffened and she drew in a sharp breath. "I'd never go into a graveyard at night," she responded automatically, as though it was something she'd said a thousand times before. Except it wasn't.

"Suddenly you're superstitious?"

She shook her head and looked away. "Of course not.

You don't have to be superstitious to know that secluded places are dangerous at night."

I waited for the lecture.

Instead, she handed me a wet towel. "Wipe off your feet and throw that away. I don't want dirt from a cemetery in my washing machine."

Mom rummaged through the junk drawer until she found a giant Band-Aid that looked like a leftover from my Big Wheel days.

"Who were you talking to on the phone?" I asked, hoping to change the subject.

"Just someone from work."

"Did that *someone* ask you out?"

She frowned, concentrating on my arm. "I'm not interested in dating. One broken heart is enough for me." She bit her lip. "I didn't mean—"

"I know what you meant." My mom had cried herself to sleep for what felt like months after my dad left. I still heard her sometimes.

After she bandaged my arm, I sat on the counter while she finished the marinara sauce. Watching her cook was comforting. It made the cemetery feel even farther away.

She dipped her finger in the pot and tasted the sauce before taking the pan off the stove.

"Mom, you forgot the red pepper flakes."

"Right." She shook her head and forced a laugh.

My mom could've held her own with Julia Child, and

marinara was her signature dish. She was more likely to forget her own name than the secret ingredient. I almost called her on it, but I felt guilty. Maybe she was imagining me in one of those unsolved crime shows.

I hopped down from the counter. "I'm going upstairs to draw."

She stared out the kitchen window, preoccupied. "Mmm...that's a good idea. It will probably make you feel better."

Actually, it wouldn't make me feel anything.

That was the point.

As long as my hand kept moving over the page, my problems disappeared, and I was somewhere or *someone* else for a little while. My drawings were fueled by a world only I could see—a boy carrying his nightmares in a sack as bits and pieces spilled out behind him, or a mouthless man banging away at the keys of a broken typewriter in the dark.

Like the piece I was working on now.

I stood in front of my easel and studied the girl perched on a rooftop, with one foot hanging tentatively over the edge. She stared at the ground below, her face twisted in fear. Delicate blue-black swallow wings stretched out from her dress. The fabric was torn where the wings had ripped through it, growing from her back like the branches of a tree.

I read somewhere that if a swallow builds a nest on your roof, it will bring you good luck. But if it abandons the nest, you'll have nothing but misfortune. Like so many things, the bird could be a blessing or a curse, a fact the girl bearing its wings knew too well.

I fell asleep thinking about her. Wondering what it would be like to have wings if you were too scared to fly.